About the author

Straddling two countries, Canada and England, Victoria Gates has grown up with a strong sense of culture and family. Her wanderlust is a strong influence in her life and writing, as she travels and experiences the world, finding inspiration with every new place. Currently residing outside Halifax, NS, Canada, when she is not working, you can find her reading or writing with the company of her dogs.

THE BETA'S BRIDE

Victoria Gates

THE BETA'S BRIDE

Vanguard Press

VANGUARD PAPERBACK

A CIP catalogue record for this title is
available from the British Library.

ISBN 978 1 784658 60 1

Vanguard Press is an imprint of
Pegasus Elliot MacKenzie Publishers Ltd.
www.pegasuspublishers.com

First Published in 2021

Vanguard Press
Sheraton House Castle Park
Cambridge England

Printed & Bound in Great Britain

Dedication

For Nan.
For your beautiful spirit,
your love and
unflinching belief in us.
Forever my happy place.
XOX

Acknowledgements

Amanda (Mom), Craig (Dad) and Jordan McMullin as well as my honorary brother, Alex Hudgins, thank you all for being my supporters, cheerleaders and believing in my crazy dream to become a writer. I love you all and I am so thankful for all of you every single day. Uncle Stuart MacLeod, thank you for being my main inspiration for Charlie. 'The Fun Uncle', kind and caring and always a good laugh, thank you for just being you.

Brenda Gates, to whom this book is dedicated. Nan, thank-you for the donation of the conservatory where the majority of this novel was conceptualized and written, you are one of my favourite people and mean the world to me. This book was also inspired by our many days out to Wales whenever I was in the UK. Helen McMullin, you supported my writing with enthusiasm, even when enthusiasm was definitely not warranted. You always asked for whatever I had been working on, always eager to hear all about it. I miss you and I hope you can see this and are proud.

Meaghan Salter, my best friend, so much of what I am and what I do would never have been a possibility without you. When I am stuck, you always encourage me to keep going, have always supported me and my dreams and I am thankful for you and who you are every day.

Hart Stoffman, my incredible eighth grade English teacher. You saw more in the thirteen-year-old girl, than the one who could barely string two thoughts together to form a sentence. You were the first teacher to work with me and help me build the foundation that I needed. The effort you put into me turned me into an avid reader with a passion for writing. Conrad MacNeil, you instilled in me a passion for vocabulary and an understanding of the capabilities of language. Your lesson on language being the most important invention, remains to be one of the most memorable and important lessons in all my years of learning. Thank you both, for your passion, encouragement, time and the effort that you spent teaching me. Without you I would never have been able to excel, consequently, this book would never have become a reality.

Finally, thank you to Mary Wollstonecraft, Mary Shelly, Jane Austen, Anne Bradstreet, Louisa May Alcott, Charlotte, Emily and Anne Bronte, and many others who paved the way for other women with a story to tell and the courage to pursue their dreams.

Chapter 1

The day the man walked into the large corner office, I knew that everything in my life was about to change. Now in his defense it is his office, and he is one of the top lawyers in Seattle. But it was something else, something I couldn't put my finger on. Mr. Thomas Sharpe was tall and lean, with dark hair and tanned skin. His eyes though were beautiful and light, a stark contrast to the darkness of his other features, teal blue like the clearest of oceans; they were startling to look at, yet I couldn't look away.

"Miss Davis, what can I help you with today?" the tall, intimidating man asked, sitting in a high-backed leather office chair at the other side of the desk watching me intently. I squirmed slightly under his beautiful gaze.

"Astrid," I corrected him, "and it's Doctor, actually."

"Really?" he said looking at me then down at his notes, his eyebrows pursed. "Okay, well, what can I help you with today? I assure you everything you say to me is completely confidential." *Yeah I know how client confidentiality works,* I thought, I am a doctor after all.

"I'm not really sure if you can help, but a friend of mine recommended you," I said.

"Well, why don't you tell me what it is and we'll see if I can."

"I want to sue my workplace." There it was, the words were out. No taking them back now.

"I am going to assume that it's a hospital or a doctor's office of some kind."

"Southeast Hospital," I clarified.

I heard his audible gulp before he said, "I'm going to need you to explain to me what happened." He leaned forward on his elbows.

"It's a mixture of things, but the reason is, I'm being sexually harassed by a superior and although I've reported it in the past. So far it's been disregarded, leading to more serious altercations. I keep going to HR, but they won't listen or take me seriously. He has them wrapped around his disgusting fingers."

"Am I to assume that you can't take it anymore which is why you came here?"

"Well, you see I can handle it, I have been through much worse. I just figured that doctors would be more evolved and now my career is starting to be affected. I'm being ostracized from surgery and other training opportunities that I should be receiving."

"And do you have any proof of these allegations?" he asked, coming around the desk to sit in the chair beside to me.

"Here," I said, handing him my phone after opening a file.

"All these?" he breathed, his shoulders slumped as he sat back astonished.

"Yes, and they're all dated with the other people involved labeled."

"Can I?" he asked. I nodded, looking down.

"Dr. Schneider, is he the man who has been harassing you?" I just nodded, as he clicked on an audio file.

"You really think you can report me?" Dr. Schneider's voice rang from the phone. "I have decades on you, little girl."

"Look, Dr. Schneider, you can't keep doing this."

"I can and I will if you ever want to become an actual doctor."

"Dr. Schneider, get your hands off me."

"Now you listen to me, if you want to practice medicine, these allegations are going to stop." Dr. Schneider growled, and the recording ended after what sounded like a door slamming.

"The next file is me reporting that incident to HR."

"Although I know I'll have to listen to all of these eventually, I am going to assume that as you're in my office looking for help, reporting it didn't work."

I nodded.

"Do they know about the recordings?"

Again, I just nodded.

"And the more serious altercation is that on here too?"

I reached over and hit the correct file. "I started recording every time he came into a room I was in," I explained. "The few times I have operated with him. I recorded the audio from the entire surgery, unfortunately, he's too smart to do anything in front of a roomful of doctors and nurses." Stealing a breath, I pressed play on the recording.

"Hey there, Welsh Pixie."

"What? How did you?" I remember feeling startled and scared, looking around me hoping no one heard him, but also mortified he knew about that.

"I have my ways, now do you really think someone like you should be practicing medicine?"

"Look Dr. Schneider, you don't understand. I'm on my own and had to put myself through school somehow."

"What do you think our co-workers will think? It could be our secret. No one needs to know you're a whore." Although you can't see it, he'd placed his hands on my waist and was trying to pull me towards him.

"No, get your hands off me," I said hastily.

"Come on Astrid, you were willing to compromise yourself for your career before, why not now? We can make you a better doctor with my mentorship," he said.

"I am not a prostitute, please stop."

"Just relax, you may enjoy—"

Mr. Sharpe turned off the recording. His face twisted in an image of disgust. "Did he?"

"No, I managed to ward him off."

"Did you go to HR?"

"What was the point?"

"Do they know about the recordings?"

"They were mentioned to them. I have that conversation recorded as well."

"And?"

"It was like they were ignoring it all together, you hear me say it clear as day."

"Okay, Astrid, I am going to take your case. I think it's going to be easy enough to prove; you have done an excellent job of procuring evidence for us and making sure that they know of the existence of said evidence."

"I can't afford to pay you," I admitted, embarrassed.

"When we win, we'll be paid through commission."

"Thank you, Mr. Sharpe."

"Don't thank me yet, there's still a lot of work to do. First though, you need to go to the police and file a report. It'll be the first step towards a trial, against both Dr. Schneider and the hospital. But I need to know, Welsh Pixie?" he looked at me questioningly.

"Well, you know medical school is expensive, right?" I said, and he just nodded watching me. "Well, I started dancing in clubs."

"And you're Welsh?"

"Yes, sir."

"When did you move here?"

"I was seventeen."

"And your family?"

"With a little luck they still don't know where I am."

"Are you prepared for the possibility of them learning where you are? You're suing a hospital, that's a pretty big deal."

"I have a life now, they don't mean anything. I'll deal with them if it happens." I put on a brave face, ignoring my own anxiety and fear, though I was unsure what scared me the most.

"And if your dancing becomes public knowledge?"

"I'll defend myself, and if they have any questions, I'll refer them to my lawyer."

"You know your stuff, Astrid."

"At one point I was undecided. I took pre-med and pre-law courses and sat both tests, before settling on medical school."

"I'm impressed," he nodded. "Do you have a backup of these files?"

"Yes, sir."

"Do you mind if I copy them here where they'll be safe and start having them transcribed."

"Go right ahead." I nodded and he went behind his desk, digging in a drawer pulling out a cord he plugged one end into my phone and the other into his computer.

After Mr. Sharpe copied over the files and assigned his assistant to find a third-party source to transcribe them, I went about going to the precinct. We were there for about four hours, as they forced me to explain to them how he'd harassed me for months and exactly what happened the other day. Then the officer and Mr. Sharpe shook my hand and promised to be in touch.

It was three days after I'd met Mr. Sharpe and I still hadn't heard anything back. I was starting to get anxious. Today was my first day back at work since the last incident with Dr. Schneider. I'd been grateful for the break to get my thoughts in order, and that there are always staff looking for more shifts.

I was sitting using one of the computers at the nurses' station, looking at some of the results for a recent patient. She'd come in for a simple hip replacement and had a bad reaction to the anesthetic; now here we were a week later and she was still in a coma.

Too warm I removed my white jacket. "Stripping down for me, babe? Did you decide to take me up on that offer?" Dr. Schneider whispered, leaning over the high wall of the desk.

"No, just too warm," I said, trying to put him off.

"A little bothered, are we?"

"Dr. Schneider, I will remind you we are in our place of work."

"Come on, baby, how about it?" he said pulling on my tied-back red hair.

"Ahem." I heard someone clear their throat just down the hall from us. Gina McCurdy, the head of Human Resources for the hospital, stood next to a few men in dark suits. "Gregor, I need you to come with us, please."

"Gina, I have patients… can't this wait?"

"No, Dr. Schneider, it can't," one of the well-dressed men answered.

"What did you do?" Dr. Schneider whispered hurriedly to me. I just looked down, the tone of his voice making my tummy do flops.

"Dr. Davis, I recommend that you go home and take the day off," Gina McCurdy said. Something in her tone told me it was not a suggestion. I stood up, nodded, grabbed my lab coat and turned down the hall.

I bought a pint of cookie dough ice-cream and a bottle of merlot on my way home, where I tucked into both and typed a quick email to Mr. Sharpe:

Dear Mr. Sharpe

I am not sure what just happened. I have just been sent home from work at the same time that Dr. Schneider was taken to a meeting with a number of men. Just before they arrived, he was once again harassing me. On this occasion, Gina McCurdy witnessed him grabbing my hair. I would like to meet with you to understand what is going to be happening next.

Thank you
Astrid Davis, MD
Southeast Hospital, Seattle, Washington

After hitting send I changed into my favorite leggings and old university sweater. *Better,* I thought, sitting down, picking up my kindle and opening my favorite comfort book: *Alice in Wonderland.* I was just getting into it when my phone dinged.

Dear Astrid,

I have heard from the hospital's lawyers. They're looking to set up a meeting with us tomorrow if possible. I have been informed you have the afternoon shift so it will be held in the morning. I have recommended it be held in my office at ten o'clock. I would, however, like to meet with you to discuss your options beforehand. Could we meet in my office around six? Email me with your response.

Tom Sharpe
Sharpe, Sharpe and Meadow, Ltd.

Looking at the clock, I groaned, so much for my book. I changed into my favorite jeans, put on a clean T-shirt and my jacket. *It's a clear night, I'll take my bike.* I smiled, grabbing my helmet from beside the door. At first the bike was all that I could afford, and let's face it, when the dancer shows up on a bike that every man in the bar is lusting over, it helps with tips. It wasn't long before the impracticalities of my sleek black motorbike in Seattle became evident to me. So, I saved up for my little blue bug, affectionately nicknamed Bluebell; but I couldn't give up my bike. The bug was a complete contrast to my bike, but they both had personality.

There was something about flying down those Seattle streets on the bike; you just can't beat the feeling, plus it's a lot quicker than fighting the congested streets in a full sized vehicle. I may be a little bit of an adrenaline junkie, but that wasn't going to change anytime soon. Overlapping scars behind my right shoulder, now camouflaged by overlapping symbols, mandalas and florals were evidence of that. A coordinating tattoo on my left thigh camouflaged another mess of scars from a separate non-adrenaline related incident. I parked my bike in front of the office and put my helmet in the compartment under the seat before locking it.

I headed up to the offices; the mirrored elevator left nothing to the imagination as I waited to get to the twenty-third floor. The light blue jeans, accentuated my slim hips and the jacket made my tiny frame look almost bulky, but it was protective in the event of an accident. I maybe an adrenaline junkie but I'm far from stupid. I unzipped it all the way down. The V-neck top accentuated my perky chest, showing a modest amount of what little cleavage I have. My stage-name, Welsh Pixie, was fairly accurate, small and delicate, almost pixie like, but with a real tough streak.

My hair was fiery and windblown from the ride, what part of it was free from my helmet that is. I was slightly flushed, and my lower lip was slightly swollen from chewing on it, which I often do when I am nervous or concentrating.

The ding of the elevator alerted me that I was at my floor and I went back to concentrating on the job at hand. As with how I organize most of my life, I separate everything into tasks that I can easily tick off, allowing myself as much control over it as possible.

It occurred to me that this wasn't something I have or could control, which is probably why I'd been chewing my lip so much, but now I could and I would. It was a matter of making it through the individual tasks.

Thomas Sharpe met me at the elevator. "Thank you, for coming, Astrid. I know it is short notice, but the hospital is moving quickly; they have friends in high places and want this over with, in order to minimize potential media exposure."

"Um… okay, thank you, Mr. Sharpe."

"Please call me Tom. I call you Astrid, there's no need to stand on formalities, I want you to think of me as a friend."

"Thank you, Tom."

"Follow me," he smiled. I followed him to a large room with a long table and chairs around it. "This is where we are going to be meeting tomorrow, so I want you to feel comfortable in here."

I walked in and noticed another man and a woman sitting there. The man looked startling like Tom, though slightly broader and with the more-expectedly dark eyes. The woman was tall, with high cheekbones, dark hair and a beautiful tan. She was lean and elegant and exuded confidence just sitting in her chair, beside the striking gentleman. *Why didn't I wear something nice and take the bug?* I look ridiculous compared to these beautiful well-bred people.

"This is my partner and brother Jared," Tom motioned to the beautiful man, "and his wife Contessa is our head of human resources," he smiled. "Before we go any further forward we need to fill out some paperwork."

"No problem," I smiled, finishing shaking the hands of the two new people helping me. I signed and filled out all the paperwork, with their witnessing.

"Tom has explained to us the specifications of the case," Contessa said, flashing a large white smile. Her teeth were slightly too big and pointy, making them noticeable. "I am sorry about what you have been through, I hope that everything goes well." Her eyes told me that she was sincere; I forced a smile as she took her leave.

"So, here's the thing," Jared said, "tomorrow is going to be about a show of force, on their side not ours. They know we hold all the cards, but they have an army of lawyers. They don't want to go to court. Any negative publicity for their hospital is not something an institution based on donors and investors wants.

"They're basically going to low ball us; they are hoping that there are things that you aren't going to want as public knowledge. They'll try to intimidate you."

"I have nothing to hide that you don't already know. I left Wales when I was young, made a few questionable choices to get by. I have a clean criminal record, and I was at the top of my class all through school and, still am."

"And how old are you, Miss Davis?" Jared asked

"Twenty-seven, and it's Doctor."

"And you're in your final year of residency — how?"

"I excelled a little quickly," I admitted.

"Well, that did not go well?" Jared said, standing in the doorway of Tom's office. Tom sat at his desk and I sat in one of the comfortable chairs on the other side of the office.

"You think?" Tom said, glaring at his brother.

"What do I do now?" I inquired.

"You fight," Tom said. "We knew this wasn't going to be a walk in the park."

"I was fired," I spat, eyeing him, looking for some sort of understanding or sympathy.

"Don't worry, they can't do that." Jared crossed his arms.

"I don't know if you noticed, Mr. Sharpe, but they didn't really seem to care," I pointed out, my tone heavy and venomous.

"But, did you see the look on their lawyers' faces? They were petrified; they know that what they did is illegal."

"That was the head of HR, the chief of surgery and the hospital CEO," I again pointed out.

"Just because they have fancy titles doesn't mean they're smart. They think, just because they have a well-known doctor as their defendant, they'll be victorious," Tom said. "Don't worry, they won't be," he winked at me.

"How am I supposed to get by without a job?" I said.

Tom nodded to Jared, who took his leave from the room pushing off from the door frame. Tom came around the desk and sat in front of me. "We're going to push for a quick trial, and now we can push undue hardship. You have some savings, right?"

"Yeah, but they aren't going to last very long."

"We'll do our best, but try and be cautious."

Leaving the office, I didn't even turn on the engine after getting into Bluebell, opting instead to stare at the dash and mentally scream at myself for letting myself get into another mess. I can't afford it, I can't crawl back to my family; can't go back to my old work. I prayed that Tom and Jared really would be able to pull this off — quickly.

Chapter 2

Six Months Later

It's been hard. Trying to get by every single day without work or income. I just sit with a book, tap water and my fish, Bubbles, who was once a fat fish but who's been on a small diet due to his mother's serious loss of income. The employment insurance has helped, but barely. Every week I met with Tom and Jared to discuss the case, which has become all hands-on deck since the press caught wind of it.

After each meeting Tom and I would go out for coffee and discuss how things were going. I'd complain that this wasn't part of his job, but he wouldn't hear of it, saying that his job is to watch out for his clients. Turns out Tom is a fantastic listener, though his brother tends to get on my nerves. Even after spending countless hours combing through my life and doing voir dire with him and the team, you'd think we'd get past that as I had so easily with Tom.

Tom was open, warm and easy to be around. It was like all he wanted was for everything to go well for the people around him; often bending over backwards to make it happen. Even in my few weeks spending short periods of time together I noticed it. Jared was very much the opposite; he exuded authority and wanted nothing more than obedience. Meanwhile, Contessa walked around in crazy high heels with perfect calves and her head held high, like she owned the place.

"Astrid, the court date is on Thursday. As you know both sides have elected for a trial without a jury."

"I understand that," I nodded.

"I have asked Tessa, she's a colleague of ours, to join us." He waved in another tall, dark-haired woman, whose hair was cut bluntly at her shoulders. This woman had large lips and piercing black eyes and walked with the same subtle elegance as Contessa.

"Hello, Dr. Davis, I'm Tessa, I'm pleased to meet you." She offered me her hand.

"Hi, thank you for helping," I said, taking her hand.

"My job is to ensure that you don't look like, ahem, you did in your previous employment in front of the judge." *Excuse me!* "As such, we recommend that you dress respectably to reflect your current career; we recommend a traditional-style suit, nothing too trendy, but something that is nice and new-ish. Nothing old, stained or torn."

"I know just the thing," I promised.

"Now, shoes. Ultra-high heels, sneakers and motorcycle boots are inappropriate."

"Seriously, is this necessary?" I looked to Tom, a man who I have been trusting since I strolled into his office all those weeks ago. But whose judgement since this woman had entered the room I was starting to question.

"Yes, as you're likely aware, they are going to be using your past against you. This is a sexual harassment case at its core, and we need to establish that it was not provoked or that he wasn't led on in any way," Tom explained.

"Why don't I just show up in my scrubs and lab coat, there will be no denying it then!"

"You still need to look respectful," Tessa said, in complete seriousness.

I cocked my head to one side and looked at her incredulously.

"Okay, Tessa, thank you for your help, I will take it from here."

"But I still have six…"

"No, I got this, don't worry about it," Tom insisted.

After she was gone I just looked at Tom with a questioning expression on my face.

"I am sorry about her," he said quietly, "she is basically a cousin. We had to hire her and she considers herself a fashionista so… we found something for her to do."

"How old is she?"

"Nineteen."

"Darling," I sneered. "A teenager is telling me how to dress appropriately for my court appearance."

"I'm sorry."

"It's okay, just do me a favor and find her any other job than insulting your clients. Pointing out my previous and current sartorial staples and why they're inappropriate for court with all the tact of a chainsaw might not be the best job for her… or anyone."

"You're right. Do you have any other questions before tomorrow?"

"Not really, do you have any for me?"

"No."

"Shall we go for that coffee now, Dr. Davis?"

"I'd be honoured, Mr. Sharpe," I said laughing.

"Now, Ms. Davis," the lawyer for the hospital said. Vaguely, I remember his name being Mr. Colin Dobson, but I wasn't sure. A short, middle-aged man with unpronounced features, greying hair and an extremely overpriced suit, he was entirely forgettable and probably regularly overlooked. But my guess is that he's good at what he does, otherwise the hospital would not have hired him.

"Doctor," I corrected.

"I'm sorry, what was that?" he said to me, removing his glasses and wiping them with a little cloth, clearly trying to portray a lack of caring.

"My name is: Doctor Astrid Davis."

"But it says here you are only twenty-seven. Most people don't truly become doctors until their thirties, isn't that correct?"

"I am a surgical resident in my final year," I clarified.

"Even then, that's very young."

"Look with all due respect, your honour and Mr. Dobson, let me make this easier for you. I acquired my GED when I was seventeen. I graduated at the top of my class in bio-chemistry and instrumental music a year early. I sat my MCAT and LSAT. I was accepted to a number of universities in both fields and decided on medicine. I was at the top of my class in medical school and I am one of the best surgical residents at Southwest."

"Objection. That is speculation," one of the men sitting at their desk rang out, this one significantly younger, but I hadn't cared enough to remember his name.

"I hold here documents with each of the surgical residents' stats and evaluations," Tom said, standing up as Jared passed them to him.

Judge Thorpe made a motion for her to be given the document. Tom handed it to the bailiff who handed it to her. She looked it over and declared, "It's not speculation, hubris, or an opinion when I am holding the proof in my hand," she said, slamming her hand down on the podium. Judge Thorpe, by all appearances, seemed like an amazing woman. Smart and a major feminist, her crow's feet showing the ware of years on her mocha skin.

"So, Dr. Davis, you did a lot in a few short years, that must have been a lot of work; you couldn't have had much time on your hands. Did your parents help you pay for your schooling?"

"No."

"So, you paid for your schooling?"

"Yes."

"And your housing, were you living with any family or friends at that time?"

"No."

"Then, you must have a lot of debt, and accusations against a prominent hospital could help you eliminate that."

"No."

"To which? Not needing money or not having debt?"

"Both."

"But your accounts say you're broke."

"Then you know I am not in debt," I spat at the stupid overly stuffed suit of Mr. Dobson. "I gave up my other jobs when I started working at the hospital, and at the beginning of this entire situation the hospital fired me because I dared to bring a lawsuit against them."

"And what did you do before you went to work at the hospital."

"I was a dancer," I answered with my head held high, confidently not defiantly.

"That wasn't all there was to it though, was it?"

"I danced in a club."

"A strip club," he clarified.

"Technically it was a bikini bar, I would never degrade myself that far."

"So you must've known how to seduce a man."

"No, I know how to dance."

24

"Did you ever dance for Dr. Schneider?"

"Not to my knowledge, but if he chose to go to one of the bars I frequented prior to our acquaintance, I wouldn't know."

"But he did know what you used to do."

"As the recording we listened to earlier clearly stated, yes, he knew about my previous employment."

"Was anyone else aware of this, as you say, employment?"

"Not to my knowledge, but I can't read other people's minds."

"And the behavior — you reported it — right?"

"If you remember from the recordings earlier, you can hear that on multiple occasions Gina McCurdy and the head of the hospital, Dr. Eli Young, brushed off my complaints." Why was he asking me these questions? Prior to my taking the stand Tom had presented all of this evidence.

"And did you ever send them anything in writing?"

"Yes, sir, on multiple occasions, but again no cigar," I coined a phrase.

"Can I ask what made you seek out representation?"

"I was tired and the entire situation was causing me stress. Every time I went into the ER, or doctor's lounge or to run labs, he was there. The nurses' station stopped being a refuge. Most importantly, I no longer felt safe at work."

He continued to question me in circles, asking me about my time working at the hospital, when things began, the first time I reported it, etcetera; it was starting to get on my nerves. But I let out a sigh of relief when he finished and failed to ask about my family.

Tom was much more forgiving; he was sorry for what I had been through. I knew, he knew I was just tired of the situation. I wanted to be done with the entire situation. He asked me about the incidents, especially the one that ended in the words "get your hands off me." And the one where I finally gave up, and after getting away I found a lawyer, filed a police report and distanced myself from my work place for a couple of days. He asked me about the trauma I suffered, requiring me to trade off shifts for a couple days and I was honest. He asked me about the undue hardship imposed upon me by the hospital since the

25

termination of my contract and the potential consequences it is going to have on my career having lost all those weeks of learning.

The police report was shown, and then there was the questioning of Gina McCurdy and Dr. Young, who both testified that following my complaint and the escalation of the matter they had laid off Dr. Schneider, which I found annoying, and I even noticed that Tom seemed angry when they first declared it.

"Mrs. McCurdy, can you explain to me, why did you wait for things to escalate before heeding the words of Dr. Astrid Davis?"

"This is not our first time dealing with a situation like this. In the past we have had allegations and the complainants have always said that they were being over dramatic, and then they would retract their statements after a period of time."

"So you decided after that, that they all would be?"

"Yes."

"But in this case the complainant was not being dramatic."

"That is correct."

"And what have you done with the other documents portraying these past allegations?"

"Once the case was closed and nothing transpired, they were discarded."

"But correct me if I am wrong, aren't all files regarding personnel supposed to be kept?"

"Yes."

"But you discarded them anyway?"

"Yes."

"Why?"

"Look, Dr. Schneider is a respected doctor and a talent. Allegations such as this could go against him, so we chose to give him the benefit of the doubt and discarded them."

"Who is we?"

"Dr. Schneider, Dr. Young and myself."

"Thank you, Mrs. McCurdy, that is everything," he nodded to her.

"I wish they hadn't gotten rid of those files. I would have loved to have those women's names," Tom whispered to me after taking his seat.

Shortly after they dismissed us, and the judge promised that as soon as she had a verdict, she would be in contact with us. "Come, it looks like you could use a drink," Tom said to me as we left the courtroom.

"You in, brother?" He turned to Jared.

"Nah, you two enjoy yourselves. Contessa and I have some paperwork to catch up on back at the office. Call me when the verdict comes in, I'll be here."

After Jared, who still gave me a weird vibe, was gone I turned to his gentler, calmer, less fear-inducing brother. "Why did he come? It seemed like you had everything under control?"

"I know, we are partners, but he is technically the head of the firm, and as this is a high profile case he thought he should be here, plus he was useful for picking up on things I didn't."

"I noticed that," I mentioned. "It seemed like you were better with the bigger picture while he concentrated on the smaller details, like the inflection in voices and wording."

"We make a good pair." He winked at me, then offered me his arm so that I could semi-gracefully get up on the barstool.

"Hard to believe we have been in court for two days," I sighed.

"Tell me about it," he said, leaning forward onto the bar. "However, I am not surprised; you did have almost a day's worth of evidence for us to listen to."

"Can't say I am not thorough," I chuckled. "Plus, it's their own fault. I gave them every opportunity to put it right and they ignored me. I had a feeling eventually it would come to this; they were just so stubborn and kept hoping it would go away on its own."

"What are you having?" the bartender said, suddenly showing up in front of us.

"Two whiskeys, neat," Tom said to the bartender, who nodded and started fishing for glasses.

"You remembered," I smiled at him.

"Of course I did. I do pay attention to some details," he smiled at me. "Make hers a double. She's earned it," he called over to the bartender, who smiled and continued pouring.

"Thanks," I smiled at him.

"It got tough in there," he said.

"I deviated." I half smiled at him, knowing that was the one thing that I had been told not to do, offer more information than was asked for.

"I know, but it was enjoyable watching you put them in their place."

"Tom," I said, appalled as the bartender came back handing us our drinks. "Thank you," I said to both of them.

"Any plans now that the trial is over?" Tom asked me.

"I don't know, I mean technically it isn't over. I don't know if I'm going to get my job back after all this."

"I'm pretty confident the hospital won't have a choice."

"I could try another hospital."

"Go back," he encouraged me, "it is the best hospital in the area, finish your education. I'm positive the outcome is going to come out in your favour. They're going to have to offer you your job back." He smiled, pushing back a stray strand of hair that had fallen in my face.

"Everyone is going to hate me," I said.

"No decisions have to be made tonight. Plus, if what Mrs. McCurdy said today is to be believed, I think you may be welcomed back as a hero."

"I'll see what happens and figure things out from there. This is the first time we don't have to talk about what is happening with the case. All we can do is wait at this point. Maybe we can talk about something other than this?" I asked shyly, rubbing my teeth along my lower lip.

"Sounds great," he smiled. "I know we've discussed your family being from Wales before, but I don't think I've ever mentioned that's where my family was originally from; my grandfather moved here almost a hundred years ago."

"Well, there you go, a connection." I took a sip of my drink shyly.

"What was it like growing up in Wales?"

"My childhood wasn't great but the country and surrounding areas are beautiful."

"And do you speak Welsh?"

"Of course I do."

"Okay, go…" he said, encouraging me to say something in the language.

"That is not what I intended," I said.

"Come on, say whatever comes to mind," he said, piercing me with his eyes, like two beautiful crystal-clear bodies of water.

"Mae gennych lugaid hardd." I said the first thing that came to mind.

"What does that mean?" he asked.

"That wasn't part of the agreement," I said, like a small child complaining about the rules of a game being unfair but smiling all the same.

"You had to know that I would ask, otherwise you could make up anything."

"Promise you won't laugh at me," I made him swear, taking another sip of my drink for courage.

"Scouts honour," he promised, but something gave me the feeling he was never a boy scout.

"I said, 'you have beautiful eyes.'" I felt my cheeks grow hot.

"Nid mor hardd â chi." He smiled at me, gently stroking his fingers along my temple.

"You knew exactly what I said," I accused shocked.

"I wanted to see whether you'd lie to me or not."

"Well I am glad I passed the test."

"Did I say that right?"

"Honestly."

"Of course, I wouldn't have asked if I couldn't take the truth."

"Okay, then no, you said 'not as beautiful as your,' as in possessive singular. I had two eyes last time I checked. So it is, 'Nid mor brydferth â'ch un ch.'"

"Good to know. I'll have to remember that," he mused.

"You do that." I winked. "You have spent the last few months combing through the last few years of my life. I think it is only fair that I have my turn to comb through yours."

"What do you want to know?" he said.

"I don't know. Maybe I should have prepared something before asking," I mused, and he smiled at me raising his eyebrows as if to say 'you think?' "Did you always want to be a lawyer?" I decided would be a safe place to start.

"Sort of, it's the family business, my father and uncle were lawyers. My grandfather founded the firm. My family has been running it ever since. I feel like being a lawyer is in my blood, it's what I was meant to do, but if I had chosen another path my family would have supported it, without hesitation."

"If you had chosen another path, what would it have been?"

"I really don't know; I've never really thought about it. I've always been good at bringing things to a bigger picture, making the little things less huge. I might've made a good psychologist."

"I've never been good at things like that," I admitted.

"It was my major in college."

"So is the law firm entirely family run?"

"Yes and no. Most of the family work for it, but there are plenty of other staff as well."

"Okay, so you grew up around here?"

"Yeah, believe it, or not, I roamed these streets. My family owns a few places, the place in the city, and a collection of cottages about twenty minutes outside of town in the woods."

"That must be gorgeous, that's the one thing I miss about Wales."

"What's that?"

"Being in the woods, all the green and the lack of cement."

"So you're not a city girl?"

"Far from it, but it was the best place for me to go to find new opportunities."

"What were you running from?"

I didn't answer, just shook my head.

"Another time then," he said gently, and I pursed my lips. "How's Bubbles fairing?" It was an immature topic but it got us out of whatever was making me uncomfortable.

"Better than I am, we're both in need of a treat when all this is over. So, tell me about your family."

We hadn't heard anything from the judge before Tom informed me that it was now too late and I wouldn't be hearing anything now. But it was an eye-opening evening. I learned that his brother, though only two years older, had all the weight of the world thrust upon his shoulder. He described it as a patriarchal family; since he took over the law firm, Jared was considered the head of the family. His wife was a well-approved choice with strong family ties, well loved by everyone, and smart. Now she runs HR at the firm. All I could think of was that darker tanned woman with legs for days and every bit the picture of perfection.

Their father is a director for all intents and purposes. He is wise and someone that everyone looks up to. I liked the idea of that, my father should have been that way but he died and my mother remarried. I wasn't a fan of my new stepfather; he had a tendency to talk a lot, boisterously and rudely, and require order.

Tom went to Harvard Law which he says was the hardest time of his life, having to be so far from everyone and everything he loves. The editor of the Harvard newspaper considered Tom one of the thirty under thirty to watch three years ago. All of which were big accomplishments but told me little about who he was. What told me who he was, was his listening, asking questions, noticing the slightest inference and change of expression. The gentle way that he would move my ever-straying hair out of my eyes, remembering my drink order, always making me feel like I am more than my past employment, my background — which he knew little of — and the victim — which I would never allow myself to be — again.

After our drink and conversation we decided it had been a long enough day; it was time to go home.

"Let me walk you home," Tom insisted.

"Really, it's only ten minutes away, I am more than capable."

"I am not doubting that, I am just saying that a beautiful woman such as yourself shouldn't be risking walking home alone in the dark."

"I have been doing it for years," I told him, but couldn't help but smile at the prospect.

"Well, today you're with someone who believes that chivalry is not dead, let me walk you."

"I appreciate your chivalry, good sir, I would be honoured to have you accompany me." I laughed lightheartedly, taking his offered arm.

The walk was pleasant, it was a calm, balmy night.

"You know it's not safe to be wandering the streets on your own," he told me. "Before we know it I could have you back in my office for another reason."

"Some people aren't safe in their own home," I interjected.

"Touché," he said. "But I hope you never have to experience that."

"Thank you, me too," I said, forcing memories down to where I have been burying them.

Tom left me on my front step promising that he would be calling me in the morning, hoping that once and for all we will have an end to this. I smiled at him and thought, how thankful I was for what he had done for me.

I laid awake that night, nervous about what was going to happen tomorrow or maybe the next day. Tired and feeling useless. I needed to start working again and moving forward. Maybe Tom could be part of that. So far, he had been the only man who connected with me. I made choices and decisions on my journey, but ultimately, I'd lost something along the way. Friendships. Cutting people off meant losing meaningful relationships.

"Hello?" I said groggily into the phone.

"Astrid are you up?"

"No, but I can be," I moaned. Realizing it was Tom and that I knew this could happen, I should have been prepared.

"I will be outside your place in an hour, get ready for a fire storm. The judge has made her decision and the media already knows and are anxiously awaiting the verdict."

"I'll be ready," I promised.

And I was; fifty-eight minutes later when he pulled up. I was dressed in a grey skirt suit, with a white blouse tied at the neck. My hair was pulled back, I carried a small black cross body bag, and wore shoes to match. Getting in the town car, I noticed that Jared was there as well. He sat facing us, with a smirk on his face watching my every move.

"You ready?" Jared asked me.

"As I will ever be." I took a deep breath as the car pulled up outside of the courthouse.

"Stay close," Tom whispered to me, opening the door.

"Dr. Davis, what are you hoping the outcome will be today?" one reporter said thrusting a microphone in my face. I looked at both my lawyers, who gently shook their heads indicating that I shouldn't say anything.

"Dr. Davis, what do you think about Dr. Schneider being hired at another hospital?" another vulture asked. *I think it is disgusting and his license should be revoked,* I thought but said nothing.

"Dr. Davis, what do you have to say about the rumors that this is a money grab?"

The questions were ridiculous, many of which were out of order. If that is what people think, they should have paid better attention to the trial. The evidence to the contrary was presented, but I said nothing. Jared, Tom and a couple police officers led me safely into the confines of the courthouse and I let out a sigh of relief.

"I find the hospital guilty of negligence, failure to follow proper harassment guidelines, slander, and false dismissal causing undue hardship to the plaintiff, Dr. Astrid Davis. The court orders the reinstatement of Dr. Davis and rewards her twenty million dollars in compensation. That will be all." The gavel slammed. I didn't hear another word that was said as I fell into my chair, staring at the spot where the judge had previously been sitting.

"We did it," Tom said, sitting down and turning my chair to face him.

"We did it," I repeated, throwing my arms around him and hugging him, then turning to Jared and back to Tom.

"I got my job back," I said elated.

Tom gave me a questioning look, and I heard Jared whisper. "Just give her a second," from behind me.

Tom watched my face. "You're going to go back to work then?" he asked.

"You bet your… Wait did she just say twenty million?"

"There it is," Jared said, as the penny dropped.

"She did," Tom said, as Jared leaned his hands down on the back of my chair, clearly curious as to how it was going to play out from here.

"What am I supposed to do with all that?"

"You could probably start with getting Bubbles some new fish food," Tom laughed, reiterating his joke from the previous night.

"What do we do now?"

"Well, we arrange a meeting hopefully for this afternoon with the hospital and their lawyers. They'll write you a big fat check and you go back to work," Tom said, watching me intently.

"Can we do it at your offices?"

"If that is what you want."

"Good, because in my medical opinion I am in shock, and I don't really want to go into the hospital like this."

"We should probably get her out of here," Jared encouraged Tom.

"You're right, you feel up to answering a few questions?"

"Yeah." I nodded, nervously.

The front of the court house was still as it was when I entered. "Dr. Davis, how do you feel?"

"I'm in shock," I admitted, "but I am excited to be able to get back to work, start working towards getting my life back on track and helping people."

"So, you are planning on going back to work then?"

"Oh, absolutely, I love what I do, being able to help and heal people."

"Do you have anything to say to those who may be dealing with a similar situation right now?"

"Absolutely. Stick to your guns — figuratively of course — but know that what they are doing is wrong. Don't let anyone tell you otherwise. If you have to, seek help from an outside source. Going to the law firm of Sharpe, Sharpe and Meadow for help was the best decision I could have made."

"Any plans on what to do with the settlement?"

"Yeah, I am going to go and buy my fish some food," I laughed, appropriating a phrase from Tom, getting into the car that Tom was holding open for me.

"That was perfect," Tom said.

"Our PR department is going to love what you just did," Jared agreed.

Two days later everything was settled, I was going back to work tomorrow. I'd received my check, and it was now hanging out in cyberspace growing interest and making me more money than I will ever have any idea what to do with. I had paid the law firm, who had agreed to wait until the money had finished being processed before depositing theirs.

I finished some paperwork releasing the firm and was going on my first official date with Tom. He was picking me up in fifteen minutes and nervous didn't even cover it. I chose a red bandage dress — who said redheads shouldn't wear red — a pair of black stilettos, a clutch, and the ruby ring that had been given to me by my grandmother before she passed away. My hair was falling in soft curls and my makeup was subtle but beautiful.

"You got this," I told my reflection. "Who cares if it is your first date in two years? He is smart, good looking and already knows one of the worst things of your past and accepts you. Plus, you're smart, he will see that." I pulled my dress down one last time making sure that it was securely covering my tattoo, before sitting down on a high bar stool to relax watching my fish swim around in his tank.

The date had gone wonderfully; we started the evening with drinks, moving on to an incredible dinner at one of the best restaurants in the city, ending with dancing. Finishing off an incredible evening of laughing, talking and getting to know one another with the perfect goodnight kiss on my front porch.

The man was genuine, was interesting, and didn't appear to get too lost. We told stories and I explained to him how I got the scar on the back of my shoulder. He'd noticed the tattoo and asked. Then wanted to know the symbolism behind it. Dinner was spent with him holding my right hand and spinning the ring nestled on my third finger.

"This new?" he'd wondered.

"No, it was my grandmother's; she gave it to me a long time ago," I said, thankful he didn't push for more.

Getting up this morning I was tired but so wired at the same time. I was going to work. I donned my best scrubs and pulled out the lab coat that had been hanging in the back of the closet, then got out my stethoscope that had been a gift from the girls I used to dance with at the club when I graduated. I put on my sneakers, and got my little blue bug, ready for what could be the hardest second first day of work, ever. My plan for the day had been to keep my head down and get through the day unnoticed. By now it had been all over the news about exactly what happened. The last thing I expected was what happened.

As I walked onto the main ward, many of the doctors, the nurses and even Gina McCurdy lined the halls. The applause was deafening. "What is going on?" I said, shocked. People started poking their heads out of the rooms to see what was happening.

"Thank you," was whispered in my ear by one of the doctors, a few years older than me; she had been a resident when I was interning.

I walked down the hall of women, as they thanked and congratulated me on my courage. I stopped in front of Gina McCurdy.

"I am sorry," she said to me. "He has a talent for blackmail, the things he learned and would use."

"All you had to do was tell someone."

"Our secrets, he knows more than a few of ours," said a nurse standing beside her.

"I can assure you, whatever your secrets, they weren't worse than some of mine."

"All the same, thank you."

"Okay, everyone get back to work." A new woman I didn't recognize came down the hall.

"Dr. Davis, I would like to speak to you for a moment if I may."

"Absolutely," I said.

I followed the new well-dressed woman with the long blonde hair to the administrative offices, into a room I knew all too well as being Gina McCurdy's office. However, a new nameplate on the door indicated it wasn't any longer.

"I'm Caryn Lane, I've taken over from Gina," she said sitting down.

"Oh, it's very nice to meet you," I said, reaching over her desk to shake her hand before taking my own seat.

"Everyone here is sorry about everything that has transpired over the last few months."

"Okay," I said, unsure.

"I want to make sure nothing like that ever happens again."

"I'm glad to hear it," I said.

36

"So, I want you to know that a lot is going to be changing around here. Every allegation is going to be investigated fully. We determined Gina failed to uphold her duty in this position."

"I'm glad to hear it, Mrs. Lane."

"No, Caryn, we are going to be friends, I hope."

"Thank you."

"Now go, and do what you are best at, and welcome back," she said, with a huge encouraging smile.

It turned out there were a number of women who had been in my position at one time or another. Many of them like me with Dr. Schneider, but he was an expert at getting away with it. Many expressed their stories to me, and I felt for them. They didn't have the past or hadn't built up the strength to fight back. It was eye opening.

Many of the doctors were helping me get back into the swing of things, getting me the best surgeries and best work; it was surely not to last, but I had missed my work and I was thankful.

"See, I told you they would welcome you back with open arms," Tom told me, smiling. "Though I wasn't exactly expecting that kind of reaction."

"And you think I was? I've spent months fighting them and now they're behind me, thanking me."

"To a woman full of courage," Tom toasted me, sipping his drink and watching me intently. He'd called me as I was leaving work and asked me to come out and celebrate my first day back. It occurred to me that two dates in a row might have been moving a little fast. But when I thought about how long the last six months had really been, it was actually slow. So I'd quickly changed when I got home and allowed him to pick me up again.

"Oh yes, the strength of having no shame left," I said, half appreciatively for the toast but half mocking.

"Strength is always beautiful." He ignored my shame comment.

"Thank you," I blushed.

"Are you happy to finally be back at work?" Tom wondered.

"Yeah, I really missed it, the patients and the other staff at the hospital. They've fired Gina and I can't really say that I am disappointed to see her go, along with Dr. Schneider. The new head of HR seems great and completely no nonsense, which is what that hospital needs."

"That's excellent and unsurprising; a lot of the restitution in the suit came from their not following certain labor laws. She should have known better."

After dinner Tom took me back to his apartment for a drink. His spacious penthouse apartment was located not far from where we work. The apartment was light and meticulously well-decorated; he clearly had taste. "Wow!" was all I was able to enunciate in response to the enormity of the place.

"Come on in, make yourself at home," he said, guiding me by the hand to the sofa, in front of a large glass wall. A patio door opened up to a large balcony, which I wasn't sure I'd ever get the courage to go out from this high up. The window must've overlooked the entire skyline.

"It's gorgeous," I remarked of the view of the Seattle skyline.

"If you like this, you'll have to see the family land one day. All green land, trees, ponds, lakes, streams, mountains and forests. It's all private, with a bunch of houses lined up together."

"Sounds amazing," I admitted. "I miss those types of views."

"Any view would pale in comparison to the one I have right here," he told me, his blue eyes melting into mine.

"Does that line usually work for you?" I asked him, but I can't lie, it did give me butterflies in the pit of my stomach. I felt a blush rise up to my cheeks.

"I don't know, I've never meant it before so I've never said it," he shrugged, a slight flush shone behind his short scruff. I thought about it for a second, who was I kidding? I didn't need to think about it, I reached up, cupped his cheek, his arm wrapped around my shoulder and leaned in. He pulled me towards him or maybe I pulled him towards me I'm not really sure. His lips touched mine, first gently then with a little more urgency. After a moment he slowed and pulled back, watching me.

"I'm sorry, is it too soon?" he asked too fast.

"Not at all, it's been months. I'm surprised it took you so long."

"I had to be professional until the trial was over," he smirked.

"We barely managed that in all honesty," I smirked.

He smiled, before his lips were back on mine, his tongue gently parting my lips.

His hand started searching my side, curling around my hip it moved to my thigh, before lifting me so I was sat on his lap, my knees on either side of his hips. His lips traveled down my neck and along my shoulder as he moved my shirt strap, exposing my bare shoulder; his other hand moved up my thigh, moving my skirt out of the way for his strong fingers. I fought the urge to hike it back down, I hadn't been embarrassed by my marred flesh since the tattoo, why now?

Chapter 3

We were sitting on the sofa, my legs carelessly thrown across his lap. It had been six months since the trial ended, but I kept pointedly ignoring the huge sum of money that was currently growing in my bank account. Tom and I had become just about inseparable. The only exceptions being when he had to go on family business, but I always stayed at his condo. So — we decided it was time for me to move in with him when my lease came up a month ago. It made me smile thinking about the decision we made for me to move in with him.

"Come on, it will be great, I have tons of space — you know that, and it isn't like we don't already spend every night or every other night together." It was true — of course — for months since the trial I had been to work, and spending time with Tom almost every weekday.

"Most weekends you disappear to your family home," I countered, but he had a point. My lease was up now, and Tom certainly wasn't very happy with where I was living. In his defence it is a high crime neighbourhood, but for those on a low income it worked.

"Yes, except then, but you'll be living here, and will be safer. I would be more comfortable with you here rather than where you're currently living."

"I was planning on leaving that place anyway."

"Great, leave it and stay here." He was magnanimous.

"But what if we don't work?"

"Then you'll move out, no biggie, but I personally don't think that you're going anywhere, unless there is something I should know."

"Of course not," I said quickly.

"Then come, stay here," he said, kissing first the side of my mouth before moving down to the hollow between the base of my neck and my collarbone.

"That's cheating," I whispered, leaning my head back, granting him better access.

"But it's working, and if you really didn't want to…"

"If I really didn't want to I wouldn't," I finished.

"Is that a yes?"

"Yes, I will move in with you," I said, capturing his mouth with mine.

The move was easy, almost everything I owned was junk, and I live alone other than Bubbles, the most important thing to transfer over to Tom's amazing skyrise apartment. A few of my things we decided to keep, but I had pretty much planned on replacing everything anyway so I was more than happy to only bring the things that belonged primarily to me and that were useful.

"You don't own a proper couch, but this is the sixth box of shoes I am dragging into the apartment," Tom said accusingly.

"They were an investment."

"How so?"

"Put the box down," I said, before bending over, opening the lid, and pulling out a pair of eight-inch gold platform heels. How much do you think I've made from these alone?" I asked, raising one eyebrow.

"Understood, the ridiculous quantity of shoes was an investment," he cajoled.

"Thank you."

"Where are you planning on putting all of them?"

"I found room in my tiny little apartment, I am sure in your enormous apartment that we can find somewhere," I said, leaning up on my tiptoes to kiss his cheek.

"We are building you a shoe rack," he told me.

"Good."

"I have a friend, though he works at the firm I think he may be able to help us out here."

"Good."

"These bar stools are great though."

"Thanks," I said.

"Where did you get them?" he asked, putting the box down outside of the bedroom and coming to help me push the red low-backed bar stools into place.

"Why haven't you bought bar stools for this before?" I replied, avoiding the question.

"I never thought they were necessary, but these are pretty cool."

"I'm glad you like them. I think they are a great contrast between the stark lightness of the apartment."

"I think they are perfect."

"Thank you," I said as he lifted me onto the bar stool.

"I like how it raises you up," he said, placing his hands on either side of the counter and leaning down ever so slightly. This effectively ended the moving and unpacking for the day.

"There's something I need to tell you," he said, pulling me out of my happy little reprieve of ignoring whatever I was supposed to be reading.

I lifted my head from my journal and looked at him. "What's up?"

He moved me too easily so that I was facing him and sat himself on the coffee table.

"Okay, this is serious." I sat the medical journal on the sofa, in a manner that would save my page for when I got back to it later.

"A lot of what I am going to say is going to seem really fast, but I feel like we're on the same page."

"Okay?"

"I know we say it all the time, but Astrid, I really do love you."

"Tom, you know I love you too." I moved to grab his hand.

He held up a hand halting me. "I spent so many years in a fog, looking for someone I felt could be a partner in my life. Then one day, this petite young woman was sitting in my office, and though she should have been broken she was strong. I knew that day that I needed to get to know you and protect…" I just stared at him.

"Thing is," he continued, "I think that what we have is special. It's built on trust, respect and strength. You were unrepentant, no matter what you were having to share. Then every week we went out after our meetings but calling it a meeting was inaccurate. You were always so upbeat, ready to take on the world, even when you had every reason to give up.

"When the trial finally ended, I was thrilled because that meant I could finally pursue what I really wanted: the beautiful, fair-skinned redhead with the cute accent and eyes like emeralds."

"And you got me."

"And I feel like we have developed enough for you to accept me for me."

"Haven't I already done that? There's nothing about you I don't love."

"Well, yes, but haven't you ever wondered why I have never taken you on family business."

"Yeah, because Jared and Contessa don't approve of me or my past."

"That's not the entire truth."

"Okay, please tell me you're not in some kind of cartel or mafia," I demanded. "I mean I'll probably accept it but it's a lot…"

"It's not that, and it's not that they don't like you or your past, it's that we live in a really close-knit community that tends to marry within their own kind. We have to get permission from the head of the family to mate outside of it." The words 'kind' and 'mate' suddenly stood out to me.

"And I am outside of it… this community?"

"Yes," he nodded. "But I finally convinced my brother that you are strong and that you can handle the secret, because you love me, and I don't think you'll leave me when you find out. Jared agrees."

"What does it matter what Jared thinks? I'm here. I'm in and I'm not going anywhere."

"Jared is the head of the family."

"Okay, because that is normal. He's the head of the firm, that doesn't mean he controls your personal life."

"For us it does."

"Is that why you made me go to dinner with him and Contessa last night?" I asked, curious.

"Yeah, it's what it took."

"You aren't part of some kind of commune, are you?"

"Not exactly."

"Okay, believe it or not, that wasn't really the answer I was hoping for," I said, looking at him very seriously.

"Just trust me," he said, getting up off the coffee table and lifting his shirt above his head and depositing it unceremoniously onto the floor; a moment later his pants, and boxer shorts joined them. Before I knew it the most beautiful man was standing in front of me, all muscles with thick shapely thighs and dark hair.

"Tom, we were having a serious conversation, what are you doing?" I asked my now naked boyfriend standing in front of me in a most peculiar manner, with a worried look on his face.

"Just keep an open mind. We consider ourselves part of a pack, a family who survives together. We're shifters." Seconds later there was a very large bald eagle with the most peculiar and beautiful blue eyes sitting on the coffee table.

I was dating a shifter? Of course, because that happens every day, right? Wrong! This was not happening.

"Tom," I stuttered, and the enormous bird nodded, before closing his eyes and turning back into a man. "You know a group of eagles is called a convocation, right?" was the first thing that came to mind. He smiled. Why did I say that? Seriously my boyfriend just shifted into an enormous bird and I go with that? A convocation.

"We don't only shift to eagles, we shift to wolves as well, I just figured, eagles are less scary."

"Can I see?"

"The wolf?"

"Yeah," I said, a silly grin spreading on my face. He squeezed his eyes shut and again shifted to another form, this time it was a burly wolf, again with the same peculiar eyes. "You're amazing," I said, reaching out, but he shifted back before I could reach him.

Quickly, he worked to get his jeans on, before sitting back on the table not worrying about the other clothes strewn on the floor forgotten.

"My boyfriend is a werewolf," I laughed.

"No, we're shifters, one of the other four sects outside of humans."

"Okay," I nodded.

"You're not afraid?"

"No."

"You're not worried I could hurt you?"

"I don't think you are capable of that. Plus, you haven't yet, right?"

"You don't want to run or feel unsafe?"

"Should I? Do you want me to?"

"No, I would never want that. But it would be a more normal reaction."

"So, what's the problem? You think that you being yourself in front of me is going to make me suddenly dislike you?"

"Well, yeah."

"Would it make you feel better if I started to run screaming through the streets?"

"No, but aren't you freaking?"

"Are you kidding? I was a girl who loved fairy tales, this is incredible."

"Well then I guess there is only one thing for me to do," he said, getting down on one knee, completing the fairy tale. Astrid Davis, I have laid my heart on the line for you, and I will do for you every day for the rest of my life. You are beautiful, strong, intelligent, and everything that I have ever wanted. I know it is quick, but would you do me the honour of becoming my wife?" He opened the small box that was dwarfed in his hands. Nestled in the gentle velvet was a huge diamond nestled in a golden setting surrounded by rubies.

"Wow," I said. "Yes," I said, putting my hand on his face and kneeling on the floor in front of him, kissing him quickly but deeply. We pulled back, stood up and he slid the ring expertly on my finger.

"It's so gorgeous." I smiled, moving it to make it glitter.

"Matches its wearer perfectly," he said, kissing me again before sitting us down again across from each other.

"I can't believe this."

"Feels right, doesn't it?"

"It does," I said, reaching over and placing my hand on his knee.

"Now, tell me what happened to your thigh," he demanded.

"What?" I looked at him incredulously. "Two minutes ago you informed me that you're a shifter, we got engaged and now you want to know about my thigh."

"Yeah, I can see the scars and burns under the tattoo. You might be able to fool humans who don't know what lies beneath that covering, but I can see it. It's been bothering me for a while."

"It's just something that happened when I was younger, don't worry about it." I gulped, hoping he'd accept the response.

"Don't know if you are accident or disaster prone." He shook his head. I don't think he believed me but I think he knew to drop the subject.

"I fell in love with a shifter and had to sue a hospital I worked for. Disaster, definitely disaster." I tried to joke. His eyes shone and his lips were suddenly on mine. There was no starting slow, or warning. They were intense and demanding as his tongue penetrated my lips and caressed my own. His hands traveled down to the hem of my own T-shirt and our kiss broke as he pulled it roughly over my head and threw it to join his own T-shirt and boxers on the floor beside us. Soon after my bra joined them, as my hand searched his hard chest and curled through his chest hair. His hands moved under my bottom, as he hoisted me off the sofa. Not breaking the hunger in our kiss, I wrapped my arms around his neck as he moved us to the bedroom.

"Stop worrying." Tom came up behind me, nibbling my neck as I stared in our full-length mirror, straightening out the green sundress I had chosen to wear. I paired it with a pair of wedges that might be a little too tall, but it was the best I had to go with the dress, and it wasn't like I would be awkwardly toddling on them.

Suddenly the ring felt like it weighed a hundred pounds. "That's easy for you to say." I looked at him. "You didn't wake up to the words 'I'm going to take you to meet my parents, today.'"

"Okay, I didn't say it like that."

"Well, you might as well have."

"They are going to love you."

"Outsider, remember."

"Today you just have to meet them. Have lunch, get to know them."

"I don't even know what it means to be a member of a pack."

"Most important thing that you can do if you are confused is look to me. I love you. I'm going to help you."

"And Jared, he is the Alpha."

"Correct."

"And Contessa?"

"She is a shifter as well and the head woman also known as the Alpha's Queen. When it comes to the shea, I am going to leave Contessa to all of that."

"And what is a shea?"

"So, it is very uncommon for a woman to be a shifter, only first borns who happen to be daughters become shifters, like my mother Leonora and obviously Contessa."

"But all sons are?"

"Exactly. Women who are born shifters but aren't a first-born daughter are shea. They're stronger, faster and heal quicker than mortal women."

"And I am a mortal woman?" I asked and he nodded. "So what are you? Just another member of the pack?"

"Not exactly, I am Jared's second in command, his Beta." He wrapped his arms around my shoulders.

"Should I be worried about going into a pack of shifters and shea as a mortal?"

"There are laws and hierarchical rules for both sides of the pack, but don't worry, as long as you're mine, you'll be protected. There are certain perks to being in charge." He held me tighter, kissing my forehead.

"Now come on, we can't be late," he said, pulling me towards the door. We took his car.

"Am I going to be underdressed for this place?" I asked him.

"You look fine, this is lunch, not dinner," he promised me. "Plus, that dress makes your ring pop and camouflages the tattoos." He kissed my hand.

"What's wrong with my tattoos?"

"My parents are conservative, they're not really fans."

"Your parents don't like tattoos? They're shifters but have an issue with a little ink?"

"Your tattoos cover things that made you self-conscious; they will see what lies beneath and understand, but maybe let's not lead with it though."

The valet opened the door for me and offered me his hand. I took it politely, stealing my breath Tom handed the keys to the valet who in turn handed him a ticket. Tom offered me his hand and I bit the bullet.

"Mom, Dad," Tom said, arriving at a table where they, Contessa and Jared were sitting. "This is my fiancée, Astrid."

"It's very nice to meet you," I offered, nodding politely.

"Oh, it is so great to finally meet you," Tom's mother said, coming around the table and giving me the hardest hug, I think I have ever experienced.

"Careful, Mother, she's mortal," Tom warned quietly after I squeaked.

"Oh, sorry, I am so used to, well, you know." She winked at me as her men shook their heads at her.

"It's okay, Mrs. Sharpe," I told her, smiling.

"Oh no. None of that nonsense, we are family now. I am Leonora, and that stuffy old man over there is Allain." Leonora winked at her husband.

"Thank you," I said.

"Now sit, sit," she said. "I want to know everything."

I looked at Tom, who smiled at me and pulled out my chair.

Leonora had to be hands down the most exuberant, lovely and kind woman I had ever met. She wanted to know everything and anything I would be willing to offer about myself. I shared about my , how beautiful the area around where I grew up in Wales was, and my career, including how much I've enjoyed where I worked and the people I work with since the trial. Even about allowing myself to open up and be friends with the people who'd come to me afterwards. I learned that Leonora had come from another pack when she was younger and married Allain. It was an arranged marriage, but one that they both wanted. Leonora has three brothers, one of whom joined her and never left the pack, and two more in other packs.

Allain was a man of few words, one of those people who you knew had prematurely grown old. Allain had stepped down as Alpha when Jared turned thirty, giving the sixty-year-old time to finally slow down. There was something calming about the man with graying hair and kind eyes that mirrored his youngest sons. He seemed to be quite comfortable allowing his wife to control the conversation.

"So this wedding," Contessa said.

"I haven't really talked to her about it," Tom said.

"Oh, well there's no time like the present," Leonora said.

"Mom, she's a mortal woman, she has family too," Tom said. I was surprised to hear him say it considering not once have I ever spoken to him about my family.

"We've worked around that before," Leonora said.

"Look, I'm estranged from my family, I will go with anything," I promised, grabbing Tom's hand.

"Well, in our family, we typically do a full moon ritual, led by the Alpha," Tom said. "The pack is there and we pronounce ourselves to the gods, each other, and in your case, to the pack itself."

"As long as by the end we are married, it's fine by me," I said.

"Fantastic," Contessa said. Her smile spanned from ear to ear showing her unbelievable teeth.

"We'll do it the full moon after next," Jared declared.

"Thank you, brother." Tom nodded.

"Bring her to Sanctuary this weekend. We'll introduce her to the pack," Jared said.

"She'll be ready."

"Our world is hard, but our world holds more wonders, magic and freedom than most," Leonora said.

"Thank you, I look forward to meeting your pack." I nodded.

"You're vegetarian," Allain asked, noticing my meal.

"I am, yes," I smiled.

"An interesting trait for the Beta's Bride," Jared said.

"Excuse me?" I asked, confused.

"It's a pack term, you're marrying the second in command, the Beta, making you the..." Leonora started.

"Beta's Bride, I get it," I finished.

"There are a couple of ladies, as well as myself, who are going to love getting going on your gown. When you come and meet them, we'll get started," Leonora said.

"Are there some stores nearby?"

"Oh, no, we'll make it. Rox is particularly talented."

It was a little overwhelming talking about my wedding with Tom's family. But I was glad to know that it wasn't going to be a huge affair, and people weren't going to think worse of me because my family wasn't going to be there.

I learned a little bit about the different members of my new family, one that seemed to laugh and joke. They were comfortable with each other in a way that I couldn't imagine being.

"Oh, is that the time?" Jared eventually said. "I'm sorry, guys, we've got to get going."

Contessa began standing up with her husband. Jared motioned to take out his wallet. "Don't worry, we got this." Tom smiled.

"It was great seeing you again," Contessa said.

"Welcome to the family," Jared said, bending down and giving me a conscientious hug. "Careful to keep this covered a little longer, little sister," he whispered, and replaced my dress strap kindly.

"Thank you." I smiled at him. He pulled back and his face became hard again.

With Contessa and Jared gone, Allain became a little more animated. "So, what was your family like?" he asked. Tom's face turned to mine as my own face dropped.

"Um," I began, pushing my hair back. "My father died when I was little and my mother was the kind who cared more about her new husband than her daughter. We've been estranged since I left Wales."

"Oh, I'm sorry. How long have you been in America?"

"It's okay, it's no loss for me. I have been here since I was seventeen."

"Oh."

"Yeah, but I like it here. I have created a life here, so it's good."

"And you two met when you were a client?"

"That is correct."

"Well, I'm glad it worked out."

I learned a little more about Allain and the traditions of the pack from him. I felt like I should have been writing things down as we went, but I figured I could just remember it; if not, once I was in the pack I'd learn through experience. I was told that as the second woman, I should watch Contessa. After eating I insisted on paying.

"You don't have to do that, my darling," Leonora said.

"It's nothing," I promised.

We paid, I promised that I was going to be there this weekend, hugged and left. "I think my family likes you," Tom told me in the car.

"I am glad to hear it." I smiled.

"I don't think Jared has actually hugged another pack member before."

"Hey, I'm not a pack member, remember?"

"Which makes it even more unlikely."

"He warned me about my tattoo," I said.

"Protective already, interesting."

"You might as well drop me off at work early," I said, "I have my stuff with me anyway."

"You'll be able to tell them about the engagement."

"I imagine that will be fun," I said sarcastically.

"Your friends will be happy to hear the good news."

"What one? The engagement or the part that they won't be attending the wedding."

"Well, I wouldn't lead with that. Go to HR, get the date off, and we'll start working on this together. Also, show them the ring, they'll forget."

"Not helpful, Tom."

"Maybe go see Caryn first."

"That's probably a good idea." I smiled. My friendship with Caryn had become cemented since her starting at the hospital. Between the two of us we'd even started a couple of movements against harassment and violence in the workplace. I wasn't a business person, but I was helping and voicing my experiences.

"I'll pick you up after work," he promised me.

"It will be early, I can walk." I felt him growl. "Or you can pick me up," I said quickly.

He kissed me quickly.

"I'll call you when I'm done."

"Good."

"I love you," I said, getting out of his car.

"I love you more, babe," he called back before driving off without giving me the chance to argue.

I took a deep breath looking up at the hospital in front of me, headed straight to Caryn's office, and knocked gently.

"Come in," she called.

"Hey, Caryn," I said, smiling at my friend and taking a seat in a chair without being offered.

"Hey, you're not here to report someone again, right?" she joked at my arriving unannounced.

"Not this time," I promised.

"Okay, you look like you are about to jump out of that seat, spill," she demanded, clasping her hands and leaning forward on the desk, reminding me very much of Tom the day we met.

"Well, I'm going to need some time off around June sixteenth."

"Why?"

"Well, I am getting married," I said, holding up my left hand.

"Oh my god," she screamed, jumping up and rounding the desk. I stood up and she hugged me. "Let me see," she said, backing away and grabbing my hand.

"Oh my god, it's gorgeous," she said.

"I know."

"I guess you're going to need a new lawyer," she joked.

"I guess so, but it's worth it. He's amazing, Caryn, and his family are so warm. I'm meeting the rest of them on Friday after shift."

"How do you feel?" She sat down next to me.

"Excited, nervous. I don't even know any more. He's amazing, his family is great. I'm over the moon."

"I am so happy for you. If you need anything, you let me know."

"I will."

"Now, you should probably get to work, we wouldn't want you to be late. I might have to tell you off."

"And we wouldn't want that," I joked back.

Work was fun. My fellow residents were over the moon for me, saying that with everything that had happened I deserved to have something work out. The nurses declared they were going to have to come up with a way to celebrate. My older patients kept grabbing my hand and giving me marriage advice, which was sweet and well meant so I couldn't help but smile. One particular little girl who needed a kidney transplant last week drew me the most adorable little card. I swear I went around the entire night with a constant grin on my face, but I couldn't help it. I was so happy, and every time someone I worked with saw me, they'd clap me on the shoulder.

"How was work?" Tom asked, picking me up.

"I think my face hurts, I've been smiling so much."

"I'm glad to know that I was the one who put that beautiful smile on that gorgeous face."

"Well, I would get used to that feeling if I was you." I smiled at him, looking deeply into the two pools that make up his eyes.

Chapter 4

"You're going to love Sanctuary," Tom said from the driver's seat, one hand on the steering wheel and the other firmly holding mine.

"What's it like? You haven't told me much about it."

"For us it is home, it's an area with tons of land to run and fly, it's all lakes and forest. The pavilion is like our main meeting place, it's also where the Alpha lives. A courtyard, the water shrine, two main houses and numerous little bungalows and cottages for all of the other families. My parents and I live in the main houses on either side of the pavilion."

"It sounds like a little village."

"It is."

"It's going to be so much better than the city."

"You are a conundrum, you know that, right?"

"How so?" I asked as he mindlessly played with my engagement ring watching the road.

"To meet you, everything about you screams city girl. The clothes, the shoes, your mannerisms, even the way you speak, but you regularly mention your dislike for the city."

"I don't like the noise, dirtiness or the greyness."

"Hmm…"

"Just drive." I laughed.

Tom was right, Sanctuary was beautiful. He parked the car on a small gravel slab, behind a sign marked Beta on one side of a gate leading to a path. The path was short and ended between two small bungalows. Looking around, there were numerous other bungalows all situated in a circle offset to almost create two circles both of which opened to create a clearing by the water.

"Woah," I breathed.

"Come on, we're this way," he said, shouldering our duffle bags. Tom hadn't needed to bring much, as his second home Sanctuary already had what he needed. As it was my first time, I'd filled the duffel bags that he now carried.

"We're the house on the left," he told me.

"At first I didn't really understand, but it became abundantly clear as a large building came into view, on either side of which sat two identical two-story houses, significantly bigger than the bungalows but nothing in comparison to what the bungalows and cottages surrounded.

"Huh," I said, not negatively, just at a loss for words

"There aren't keys or locks, we're all family here, plus we can track the scent of whoever was there."

"Interesting." I smiled.

"Come on in." He smiled, opening the door for me.

"Just like the apartment." I observed the décor as he guided me inside.

"Yeah, I really like the modern look, it makes me feel like I'm home wherever I am. But we can change it if you would like."

"Don't you dare," I swore. Tom and I had come early. He thought it would be better this way. This way I wouldn't be bombarded by the entire pack, the moment I arrived. I'd meet them this evening.

Tom urged that his family is a little eccentric, so I'm sure his recommendation was for the best, and for my own sake. My experience with family had never been great, and I wasn't sure what to expect or what I was getting into. Tom, however, seemed to have a lot of love and respect for them, so I'd force myself to be as open as he appeared to be.

"You planning on standing in the doorway all day?" he asked, wrapping his arms around me, holding my back tight against his front.

"Just taking it all in," I leaned my head against his chest.

"I'll take you hiking tomorrow if you'd like."

"Really?"

"Of course, there's a great place, it's about three miles each way, but it is absolutely gorgeous."

"I'd like that. I'll pack a picnic," I suggested enthusiastically.

"Sounds great."

"Good," I smiled. "It will be fun."

"That it will. Now come on, let me show you the rest of the house," he said, shutting the door gently. "It's bigger than the other houses on the property, but still, it isn't much. There are three bedrooms upstairs, a living room, dining room and kitchen and a couple bathrooms, but this is the extent of it."

"I like it." I smiled. "It still holds a cottage-y feel."

"It does? Even with the modern finishes?" he asked, like that was something he'd been trying to avoid.

"It's a matter of perspective."

"But you like it?"

"Consider my old apartment and ask me that again."

"Yeah, I take that back."

I smiled. "I particularly like the fireplace. I always loved fires."

"You're a little odd, aren't you?"

"I thought we'd already established that."

"Hmm," he murmured.

"Any way your secret is out, now you're stuck with me."

"Wouldn't have it any other way."

"So, what should I be expecting out of tonight."

"Are the nerves finally settling in? Worried about meeting a pack of shifters?"

"It's not the shifter part I am afraid of."

"What is it then?"

"If I told you I had a family of over fifty people and wanted you to meet them all at once, are you seriously telling me you wouldn't be nervous?"

"Okay, when you put it like that," he surrendered.

"Ah, there we go."

"Yeah, I can see how that could be considered nerve wrecking.

"Could be? Really?"

"Shh…" he said, his lips in my hair. "My family is great. The biggest hurdle was Jared and Contessa."

"But they were two, not fifty."

"Relax, okay?"

"Okay," I said, closing my eyes.

"If it makes you feel any better, I am really looking forward to tonight."

"I'm glad. But listen, don't get me wrong, I'm looking forward to meeting them. I'm just a little nervous."

"I know, but I also know there is no way they could possibly not love you."

"Not that you're biased or anything."

"I'll admit I may have a slightly blurred view of the matter, but I'm also positive they'll see how amazing you are and what made me fall in love with you in the first place."

Our night — well, afternoon — was simple. Just like being at home. We had dinner, talked, sat, and simply enjoyed each other's company. But afterwards it was a little different; we had family commitments, something that I hadn't had in a really long time.

"What do I wear?" I called down the stairs as the sun began to set.

"Seriously, Astrid?" Tom called up to me.

"Yes, seriously, what do you people typically wear to these things?"

"Astrid, we're all family, in the woods. It doesn't matter as long as you're wearing clothes, actually that doesn't really matter either."

"Do you want me to point out the problems with that statement?"

"No, don't bother, I get it. I'm coming up," he said, and I heard his steps coming up the stairs quickly. I sat on the bed clad solely in my bra and dark denim. My duffle lay open with the majority of its previous contents scattered across the bed around me.

"Okay, let's see what we have," he said, scanning the items after his eyes had finished lingering on myself. "Here," he said, handing me my black, long-sleeved cowl-necked sweater.

"Seriously?"

"Yes, this looks good on you, pair it with your jeans and timberlands and you're good to go."

"Okay," I said, jumping up and slipping on the sweater. "Good?"

"Perfect." He grabbed me, kissing me.

"You're going to make us late," I said, pushing on his chest... just enough to get his attention.

"We could miss it?"

"Really, after all this work was done to get me here for tonight, you really want to blow it off?"

"No. Fine, come on," he said, kissing me one more time before reaching for my hand and keeping it all the way down the stairs. "It's a nice night," Tom pointed out.

"It is." I smiled, as we walked out the front door. I took in the cool night air, damp with the night, but balmy.

I followed Tom's lead, continuously taking in the night and my surroundings as he led me to the area just outside of the pavilion and between the numerous little houses.

"Perfect," I heard Tom say, slightly under his breath.

"What's perfect?" I asked, grabbing onto his arm a little tighter.

"Charlie is here already."

"Your best friend from childhood."

"He still is my best friend."

"Good, I've been looking forward to meeting him."

"Hey, Charlie," Tom called.

"Tommy." He smiled.

"Charles," Tom growled in warning.

"And this must be the famous Astrid," Charlie said, ignoring Tom. "How are you, little lady?"

"Well, thank you," I said coughing, slightly taken off guard. "It's nice to meet you, Charlie." I smiled. Charlie was striking, though broader than Tom, he was shorter, and his hair was lighter, more of a chestnut. His face was angular in a way that would make any sane person wary of him.

"And you, little lady," he said, picking me up in a bone-breaking tight hug.

I was laughing uncontrollably by the time the gigantic man had finally put me down.

"Tom has told me a lot about you," I said to him.

"Well, that can't be good," Charlie said with a smirk, catching Tom's eye with a wink.

"Oh, I don't know so much, as far as I heard you are a brave, kind and hilarious friend, with respect for your gods, your friends and family. Also, not too bad with your hands, that shoe rack is perfect."

"Oh, now I have a lot to live up to, I pray I'm not a disappointment. And you're very welcome, I'm glad you like it."

"Nah, you couldn't be." I winked. "And thank you."

"Remember how I explained to you about the division of the packs?"

"Yeah," I said, remembering his mentioning the Alpha (Jared), Beta (him) and how there are five subpacks. The Alpha pack that Jared heads, Tom's Beta pack which he heads, then the subpacks, puppies and bitches.

"Well Charlie is my second in command," Tom pointed out to me.

"Which only makes me fourth overall," Charlie joked, which made me smile. He was infectious.

"I take it we are very hierarchical here," I said.

"Not really," Charlie said, ignoring Tom's obvious disagreement.

"Okay, why not?"

"We're really all about respect. The elders and the Alpha and sometimes Beta would like you to believe that we care about our position in terms of the hierarchy, but as long as you are respectful. When you earn the trust of those in the pack, it doesn't matter what your position is."

"Sounds like a brilliant place. The kind I've been looking for."

"Look, don't be ashamed but we all know what you've been through recently. Confidentiality is a thing, I know, but when everyone here is a member of the pack and firm, it stops being quite so confidential. We all know what came about in the trial, we live and work together as a family, you will find no judgement here."

"Thanks," I said, unsure of myself.

"You're fine," Tom said, kissing the top of my head.

By this time more and more people were starting to gather around the circle one at a time. They all walked over and stood in the perfect spot as though they had assigned positions and knew exactly where they were supposed to be.

"I have to go up on the dais with my brother, when you are my wife," he grinned at the prospect, "you will be up there with myself, Jared and Contessa. For now, stay here with Charlie until I motion for you, okay?"

"I understand," I said, slightly nervous about having to stay down here by myself with all these people I don't know watching me.

"Relax," he said, kissing my temple. "I love you."

"Okay, I love you too," I said, grateful for the encouragement.

"Take care of her, Charlie," Tom warned.

"She is going to be a maximum of twenty feet away from you… what do you think is going to happen?" Charlie asked incredulously.

"Not the point, watch out for her."

"Yes, sir." Charlie saluted much to Tom's chagrin.

"So, Tommy, huh?" I asked, after Tom walked away, wondering what the story was there.

"You can't hear, but he just growled so I think it would be better for both of our health if I didn't," Charlie said, putting an arm around me.

"I think you may be right."

"Do me a favour, okay?" Charlie said.

"I have known you for five minutes."

"All the same, Tom is complex. The pack is complex. So much more than you have ever realized is about to be opened to you. Don't worry or freak out, okay?"

"Charlie, when I found out about Tom, I wasn't scared. I was intrigued. It wasn't something I expected or could have imagined. But I know and trust him. I have never had much luck with humans, I figured he had to be better," I said, looking up at him on the short dais with his brother and sister-in-law. "I love him," I told Charlie, and oddly felt comfortable doing so.

"I can tell, and believe it or not, he does you. I never thought I would see the day. He never paid much mind to women or shifters, inside or outside of the pack."

"Why me?"

"I don't know."

Suddenly a howl went up around the circle, originating at the dais. I turned to see a great wolf standing between Contessa and Tom. As everyone turned and became silent the wolf turned back into a man. I quickly averted my eyes thinking it the right thing to do but no one else did. Nudity, not shameful… understood, I made a mental note.

"Many blessings," Jared said, replacing his trousers.

"Many blessings," everyone repeated, and I followed along.

"To the gods of the sky, we thank them for another day, another night and welcome them to our circle," Jared chanted, as everyone turned their faces upwards. "Tonight we give our thanks to the full moon."

Everyone suddenly ended up on their knees. Charlie carefully pulled me down with them.

"The Wolf and the Phoenix surround and guide us," Jared continued. "They give us life, our abilities, our humanity and our world. We thank them for the gifts. They are our creators. The Phoenix, our eagle, the giver and goddess of our sun. The mother of life, heat, and giver of day. The Wolf, our god of water, the tides, the moon and our great world."

"Thank you, great beasts of the sky," the congregation said. I think Charlie noticed that I was at a loss so he squeezed my arm to let me know that it was okay.

"With one life, one dedication and one self we allow our lives to be guided by the light of our gods. We answer to you and give ourselves willingly to your guidance."

Between then and the end of the ceremony I was required to drink out of a clear chalice after Jared, Contessa then Tom, before it was handed around the circle.

"Finally, on a night fought with fortune, we continue our circle with one more fortunate event," Jared announced, and I knew instinctively he was talking about me. "Our Beta has found himself a bride. A smart woman, she's a doctor at one of the most prestigious hospitals in the area." I felt everyone's eyes turn to me. I mean, I knew that I was a hot topic tonight. I knew that I was being watched by the pack, but this was different as every member of the pack turned to me, including Tom and Charlie — who placed another gentle hand on my lower back reassuringly. "Dr. Astrid Davis, though not a shea nor a bitch, will be an excellent addition to our pack and more importantly our family," Jared concluded.

Tom stepped forward. "Astrid has done me the honour of agreeing to be my wife. As such I hope all of you will do me the honour of welcoming this amazing woman," Tom said, motioning for me to join him. Charlie gave me a gentle nudge and I quickly mounted the steps towards my amazing man, taking his hand, holding it for support from my nerves.

Slowly every male and a number of female members began to strip, before shifting into their eagle form. They circled; I watched the sky as each of these magnificent shifters did their rounds. Their next move was to all shift into a wolf and landed directly where they were before. At this point, those who did not shift before fell to one knee, as those in their wolf form dropped so their muzzles were to the ground. The only two who remained standing were Contessa and Jared.

"They're showing us respect," Tom whispered in my ear.

"Why?" I said, confused, watching all these strong beings in submission to my fiancé and I.

"Because we head the pack, we lead them and work to keep them safe. It is respect. It's our duty to protect and make the hard decisions and theirs to follow," he explained, pulling me closer.

"Okay," I said, still confused but accepting.

"The shifters tend to go out on a run now, it will just be you and the majority of the women. Will you be okay?"

"I'll be fine. Go."

Tom and Jared joined the shifters, first in nudity then in their wolf form before running off.

"For our men, we remain a place of home and solitude as they go out, our protectors, our kin, our shifters, they will return to their women, their lives, and loves with the blessings of the beasts. The Circle has ended and the women remain, for our home is here though many women sometimes go with them," Contessa said, stepping to the center of the dais. Contessa stepped down and I followed her, unsure of exactly what I was supposed to do. But it didn't remain that way; it took no time at all for the women who remained to converge on me in the massive circle.

"It's amazing to meet you," a woman who looked a lot like Tom and Jared said. She was beautiful with long dark hair and teal eyes that perfectly magnified her high cheekbones, as though it was Tom staring back at me and not this gorgeous, tall woman. "My name is Lorelai. I'm Tom and Jared's older sister."

"Oh, hi! It's great to meet you," I said, as suddenly the woman's arms were around my shoulders.

"We're going to be great friends, I know it," she said, tossing her long hair behind her shoulder.

"I fervently hope so," I said, but something inside of me was wary. There was something about her that was dark, but I hoped I was wrong.

"I'm Laura," another woman said. She was pretty, with short mousey hair, a round face and curvy features. Her smile was radiant.

"It's nice to meet you," I smiled.

"My husband is Markus, he is a member of your fiancé's subpack."

"You'll have to introduce me to him some time over this weekend," I nodded.

"Oh, of course," she smiled. "Markus, Charlie and Tom all grew up together."

"To be fair most of the pack has grown up together," said a blonde, average sized woman, with eyes just slightly too far apart and a lower lip that made it look like she was pouting, but again, very pretty. "I'm Shiloh." She smiled.

"Hi." I smiled back.

"Come on, let's go inside, we can all have something to drink, then you can all interrogate her to your heart's content," Contessa said, turning to the pavilion.

Unquestioningly the entire group turned and moved inside. "I know how you feel." A woman came up beside me, taking my arm. I turned to the woman with the warm hand and comforting gesture. She was about my height, strawberry blonde, with big brown eyes and a crooked toothed grin. "I'm Lesley, I'm human too. I'm a nurse in a rehab center, halfway between here and the city."

"Really?"

"Yeah. I know it's a lot to take in at first. But you'll fall in so easily. Everyone is easy going and open, like a big family."

"It's oddly comforting to know that someone else understands."

"You're a doctor?" Lesley said.

"I am, I'm a surgical resident."

"Hmm…"

"So you work a lot?"

"I do, but I never minded working and earning my living."

"What about your family?" Shiloh asked, as I sat down on a long sofa in a light, soft, plush room with a bar at one end.

"My family? Well, we haven't spoken in a long time."

"You're from somewhere in England, correct?"

"Let me guess the accent gives me away?" I said.

"You think?" Lesley joked beside me.

"Would you like something to drink?" Contessa asked.

"Please, that would be great," I replied.

"Wine?"

"Please," I said and a glass of red wine was handed to me by another woman whose name I hadn't gotten yet. "Thank you," I said. "But to answer your question, I am Welsh."

"What's it like there?"

"A bit like it is here: it's beautiful, green and lush and full of trees and winding roads."

"You sound like you miss it," Laura said.

"I do and I don't."

"How have you been, Tessa?" I asked the young girl sitting across from me, she being the person who tried to explain to me how to dress appropriately before my court date.

"I'm good," she smiled nervously. "I am sorry if I came off a little strongly before."

"It's okay, I probably didn't give the best first impression either."

"Let's start fresh," Tessa suggested.

"Let's," I agreed.

"So what do you do for fun?" said a short, dark-brown-haired woman wearing a knee length jean shirt and with a nose slightly too large for her face.

"Not a lot, up until recently so much of my life was geared towards survival. And I am sorry I didn't get your name."

"Oh, sorry I'm Roxanne, but everyone just calls me Rox."

"Well, it's nice to meet you, Rox."

"I'm sorry to hear that you had a hard time."

"Don't, my life led me here."

"That's a really good way of looking at it."

"So, Tom said that the law firm is run by the family. How many of you work there?"

"Honestly, every member of the pack works there, except Lesley — who you know, is a nurse — and Francis, he's a cop with the Seattle police department. Then of course you," Lorelai explained. "But why would anyone want to do anything else? They know that we choose a position that interests us in the firm and we will have guaranteed employment."

"I guess that is fair," I said. "Being a lawyer was my other option when I was trying to decide what to do after my Bachelor's Degree, and if I had known that there would have been a definite place for me it might have swayed me. Then again, I love being a doctor and don't think I will ever regret my decision."

"I can respect that," Lesley said. "I love helping people, it is one of the most rewarding parts of my life."

The night wore on and I slowly learned more and more about the women around me. Those who would be my family. The ones who crowded around me most were the ones closer in age to myself. But the room was packed, filled with little girls who were playing in the corner and older women working on their knitting and gossiping about goodness knows what. I started to notice that a few women and kids were starting to make a move. I was about to attempt the same when Laura piped up.

"So, Leonora wants us to meet here tomorrow," she said to me.

"Okay," I said.

"There's a tradition in the family, all wedding dresses are handmade," Rox said.

"Yeah, Leonora mentioned something about that the other day when I met with them for lunch."

"Yes, well we would like to get started, so do you think you could come here around ten?" Rox said.

"I think I can be here for then," I smiled.

"Great, it will just be me and a few of us tomorrow," Rox promised me.

"Okay, no problem," I said. "For now though, I think I am going to head back, I could use a lie down."

"Still trying to take everything in?"

"Precisely."

I slowly got up and moved outside. It was still a gorgeous night, there was barely a cloud in the sky. It was perfectly still but for a few minor rustlings of some trees. The smell of the forest and the night air was intoxicating.

I stopped for a minute and just took in the night, raising my face to the soft light of the moon.

"It calls to you, doesn't it?" came a soft voice behind me. I jumped slightly from the unexpected visitor.

"Oh, Leonora," I said.

"I'm sorry I didn't mean to frighten you, child."

"It's all right, I just didn't expect anyone else to be out here."

"We're creatures of the night, someone is always out here," she informed me.

"I'll keep that in mind." I smiled.

"All the same, I saw you basking in it."

"Sorry."

"No, don't apologise, there is nothing wrong with that. It's just surprising, there is something about you. I just can't put my finger on it. But I have a good feeling."

"Oh…" I said, confused. "Well that is good I guess."

"Don't worry that pretty little head of yours, it's an astounding amount of respect for something so new it amazes me and thrills me."

"I've always loved the night, it's so calm and peaceful," I explained.

"If you could hear what I could, you would realize just how alive it really is."

"Maybe so, but when I was a child it was my sanctuary, my one time when I was truly alone."

"You were heading home, weren't you?"

"I was, but I got distracted." I smiled.

"It's never wrong to become distracted with centering yourself, especially now when you are being thrust into something so new and I'm sure absurd by your standards."

"It's okay."

"What did you think when Tom told you?"

"I thought I must be going crazy, then there was fear, apprehension, and the realization that it doesn't matter. I love the man, that should be the only thing that matters."

"It warms a mother's heart to hear that."

"He deserves it, you know."

"I do, he is a good, kind and gentle boy."

"He is," I said once again looking to the sky.

"Go, home," she encouraged me. "I'll see you tomorrow after all."

"I will, goodnight, Leonora."

"Goodnight, child."

"How was your night?" Tom said, sitting on the sofa reading some files he had brought with him as I opened the front door.

"Good, your family is great, but I have to say exhausting," I said, curling up beside him, placing my head on his chest and closing my eyes. "How was your run?"

"Freeing," he said.

"I wish I could feel what that is like," I said.

"I wish you could too."

"I ran into your mother on the way here."

"Really?"

"Yeah, I was sort of standing outside, enjoying the night and she found me."

"You really should have been born a shifter. What did she have to say?"

"Nothing much, just about our different perspectives of the night. I think it's calm and peaceful, she says it's noisy and alive."

"They are two true and reasonable perspectives, depending on how you are able to perceive it."

"Exactly."

"Should we go to bed."

"All of my clothes are still all over it," I moaned lazily.

"Then we are just going to have to clean them up now, aren't we?" he said, ever the realist.

Chapter 5

"We all know your history, you know?" A tall, thin, long-blonde-haired woman came up beside us. She was clearly a bit older than myself, I'd say mid-forties, but apparently wasn't capable of acting it and holding her tongue.

"Carmellia, we have spoken about this," Shiloh said, sitting beside me on the back patio of the pavilion. Tom, Jared and Lorelai were busy working inside. I thought I'd sit down and enjoy watching the pack move from place to place and the kids play between the houses. It was the kind of view anyone could get used to; behind them there was a large lake, and a number of mountains that created a picture-perfect backdrop. "This is my older sister Carmellia," Shiloh said to me. "She's a bitch in both forms of the word."

"I don't believe that," I said standing up. "But I do wish for us to get off on a better foot. My name is Astrid Davis. I have made questionable decisions in the past but I regret none of them. So how about I forget this little occurrence of slut shaming, and you try not to judge someone you just met and know nothing about," I smiled, taking her hand.

I noticed her bite her lips and turn on her heels before turning into the woods.

"See, now if that was me, she would go full shifter on me," Shiloh said.

"Oh please, she's probably just going to run off her frustrations now. Any idea why she has already decided that she hates me?" I asked her sister.

"It's probably not very sisterly of me to divulge."

"Come on, your secret's safe with me."

"Everyone always thought that her eldest daughter would be the one to marry Tom. They were friends growing up, truth be told they still are but he never really saw her that way. For a while we thought that he might be gay."

"Oh."

"Yeah. A large part of pack goals and dynamics revolve around preservation of the power in our bloodlines."

"Should I be worried about her?"

"Nah, I wouldn't be, she's all bark." She laughed at her little pun.

"And her daughter?"

"Oh, Naveah, nah, she's a sweetie. She was in Law school, but, took a few years off to discover the world. Joined up with a pack in Wales for a little bit. Rumour has it she may be in with a future Alpha back there."

"Really?"

"Oh, yeah."

"Wouldn't a patriarchal and hierarchical society like this one see that as an upgrade from being the Beta Bride?"

"Theoretically yes, but what momma doesn't want her babies at home."

"I guess you are right," I said, thinking about my mother and thinking that I'd be lucky if she was even thinking about me at all. Missing her estranged daughter? Was I even considered missing?

"Do you have any children, Shiloh?"

"I do, four of them."

"Really? Will I meet them?"

"Well, you'll meet the boys, Wilson and Toby, they are in school and come back regularly, especially for special rituals, but Polly and Amy have since married and joined other packs."

"Who's your husband?"

"Oh, Landry, I'll have to introduce you, he's great, he's been a private investigator for the firm for years, like me. He's smart, and sweet. I just know you'll love him."

"I look forward to it." I said, looking at my watch. "Wait, is that the time?"

"It's ten o'clock, why?"

"I'm supposed to meet up with Leonora and some of the ladies that are going to be helping to make my wedding dress." I smiled excitedly at my new found friend." "I am sorry I have to go."

"No worries, girl, have fun," Shiloh said, turning back to the water and the mountains.

"I'm sorry I am late," I said, showing up in the room where the others were already congregated with measuring tapes, paper, pencil and fabric swatches.

"No problem," Leonora smiled, "just come here so we can get your measurements and we can start coming up with some design ideas." She motioned to a small platform.

"We can't do it with you fully clothed like that," Rox said, a small laugh behind her tone.

"Come on, we need to get your measurements," Leonora said. She was holding up a tape measure, it was just me, her, Laura, Rox and Tessa in the women's room, and they were trying to get me to strip to my underwear to get the perfect measurements.

"Is it really necessary?"

"Depends, do you want to look frumpy on your wedding day?"

"I'm sorry, Leonora," I said, stripping down as instructed.

"What on earth happened?" she said, walking over and tentatively touched my thigh.

"Leonora?" Rox asked.

"They're tattoos," I explained unnecessarily.

"Not those she said. Underneath them."

"They're some old scars, just things that happened when I was a child," I promised. "I got the tattoos to mask them."

"I see that the artist did a good job, the lines really do conceal the scarring."

"What are you talking about?" Laura said.

"You probably can't see it, unless you look close. Under the tattoos on her shoulder and thigh are crisscrossing scars, the shoulder doesn't look too bad but the thigh however…" she ended her explanation there.

"You did a good job with them, I imagine they mean something."

"They do," I nodded.

"Do I get to know then?"

"Maybe another day," I promised.

"Whenever you're ready, child, no hurry."

"Thanks."

"You apologised before showing me, my sons told you my husband and I don't like them."

70

"They did," I nodded.

"I don't know what happened and I don't think that I care to, but don't be afraid to be yourself around us, okay, my darling?"

"I wish my mother had been more like you, Leonora."

"That is the nicest thing anyone has ever said to me." She hugged me. "From now on I'd love it if you thought of me as your mother."

"I'd like that."

"Now, let's make you a dress to knock my son's socks off, shall we?"

"I think we shall," I said, beaming.

The dress design was going to be gorgeous and the women had actually decided to use the tattoo designs as inspiration and pulled colours from my ring and the red flowers in my tattoo. They said that they had some idea that they knew I was going to love. They wanted to surprise me with them and I obliged. I allowed them carte blanche over the entire thing.

What they had been describing to me was so out of my depth, but I trusted them. I knew that above all Leonora wanted to impress her son, so I let her go, and she seemed generally happy to do so. The four of them captivated in what they were doing, I quickly made my escape and went for a walk down to the water this time.

Though, logically, walking alone surrounded by strangers who were also shifters should scare me. I wasn't nervous or uneasy, maybe because I knew that I had the power of Tom behind me if I needed him. Maybe it was because I knew that above all I was safe here, even if it did remind me of a place where I was never safe in.

I smiled at the water, sitting on a rock before taking off my shoes and dipping my feet in the cool water. It wasn't cold, but it was refreshing. Two kids came over, the oldest being no more than twelve.

"Hi, you're Astrid, right?" the oldest said. She was cute, she had medium brown hair, dirt on her face, and a tear in her blue floral shirt, and wore black cloth shorts.

"Yeah, I am," I said, pulling my feet out of the water to face them. "What are your names?"

"I'm Carly," the older girl said.

"And what about you?" I asked the younger girl, who was clearly her sister; she had the same face shape but had a toothless grin, missing her two front teeth.

"Marlee," she smiled.

"And how old are you, Marlee?"

"I am eight, ma'am."

"How about you call me Astrid, okay?" I said.

"Are you really marrying Tom?" Carly asked me again.

"I am." I nodded. "I am going to join the pack. What do you think about that?"

"Momma said that you're an outsider, and that you're going to dilute the bloodline."

"I promise you that though I am an outsider, I'm still strong." I winked at the little girls. "Do you like swimming?" I asked the girls, hoping to change the subject.

"Yeah."

"Is there a dock for you to play on?" I asked them.

"No."

"Really?"

"Yeah."

"Then how do you jump in and have the biggest splash competitions?" I asked, remembering the many better days back home with my brother.

"What?"

"You don't have biggest splash competitions?" I asked, feigning dumbfoundedness.

The little girls were gorgeous and curious, and made me promise to teach them how to dive one day, and have the biggest sand castle competition ever. Their minds were all over the place. Eventually we ended up playing twenty questions. Favourite color, favourite flower, favorite food, movie, song. They were everything that I should have been at their age.

"Carly and Marlee, what are you doing?" a very tall and unhappy looking man said, coming down the beach. He had a beard, dark hair and arms that looked twice the size of even Tom's, and I thought that he was a big man.

"We were making a new friend, Daddy."

"Girls, you know better than to talk to strangers," he said.

"I really hope that I don't come off as a stranger," I said, standing up but remaining very calm. "I thought that I was joining the pack."

"No, I'm sorry, you're right, nobody here is a stranger, but I am sorry if they have been bothering you."

"Oh, no, not at all, they're great, we were just getting to know each other." I smiled at the little girls who were now blushing ashamedly. "You have two amazing girls here," I complimented him, hoping to ease some of the tension.

"Thank you," he said, smiling. "I'm Francis by the way." He offered me his hand.

"Astrid," I said, taking it.

"I know," he said, "we don't get newcomers very often."

"Right, sorry."

"Don't worry about it." He smiled again and this time it reached his eyes and I could tell that he was a kind, good laugh sort like my father was.

"Look, I am sorry, but I came to get the girls for lunch, their mother will be pissed if they're not fed when she gets back."

"Hey, not a problem, it was great to meet you," I said.

"And you," he smiled, then waited a moment, when neither of them said anything he prompted them. "Girls, Dr. Davis said that it was nice to meet you, what do you say?"

"It was nice meeting you too, Astrid," they said together.

"Girls…" Francis started.

"Don't worry, we're on a first name basis, right, girls?"

Marlee and Carly smiled and nodded.

"Okay, as long as you're sure, we're sort of big on respect here."

"Oh I am."

"We'll see you around, Astrid," Francis said, before taking each of his daughters' hands and guiding them down the beach.

I hadn't realized that I was hungry either until Francis had reminded me. I began to wonder if Tom was home yet or if he was still working. I knew this morning that it was unlikely that our hike was going to happen, but still he can't work all day on a Saturday… right?

I walked back to the house along the outskirts of the clearing, lightly touching the trees as I went, though I was unsure why it was comforting and grounding. Something about the house was so charming, like it belonged in a fairy tale, and though it didn't feel like home, I hoped that it would soon. In all fairness, my life was upside down, and though I was fully capable of living on my own, I was living with him and technically reliant on him and it was not something that I wanted to feel.

"Something is bothering you," he said, as I walked in the front door.

"You always beat me home," I pointed out.

"You're a wanderer," he pointed out. "Now stop changing the subject."

"How did you know something was bothering me?" I asked, sitting down on the sofa but not touching him. I cocked my head to the side.

"I could smell it on you," he said monotonously.

"I don't like feeling dependent on you," I admitted, ignoring the comment that he could smell that there was something wrong.

"What do you mean?"

"You have two homes. I live with you in the apartment and here, I don't pay for either, you won't let me pay half the electricity bill, you won't let me pay for internet or anything else."

"Okay, well this place is paid for, as for the apartment, the mortgage is expensive…"

"But between the two of us."

"Fair, and I have given this some thought before."

"Okay… and…"

"I thought we could combine accounts eventually."

"I would be willing to do that, I want us to be equal."

"And we are."

"No, I'm your ward."

"Okay, I wouldn't go that far."

"Look, I am willing to put in my share, it's not like I can't afford it."

"Tomorrow I am getting your name put on the deed. And we'll get a joint account, any and all household bills will be put on that account and we will put an equal share into it every month, sound fair?"

"Can I ask you one thing?"

"What is it?"

"Can I pay half the cost of the apartment right now?"

"What?"

"Look I have twenty million sitting in the bank doing nothing. How much did the apartment cost?"

"One point eight million."

"How much is paid off?"

"Eight hundred thousand."

"Okay… can I pay off the last million?"

"No, you can pay off nine hundred thousand, I'll pay off the last one. We will transfer the deed into both our names and it will become our home."

"Really?"

"Yes."

"Can you do that?"

"Yes, do you feel better now?"

"I do."

"Good, thank you for being open with me. Now, why don't we get some lunch so that we can go over to Lorelai's. I promised that we would head over after you got back. She wants you to meet her husband and son, officially."

"William, right?"

"Yeah."

"Sounds good."

The weekend went by too fast and before I knew it I was daydreaming in the doctors' lounge. My nephew, wow, that was odd to say. The minute I walked into Lorelai's little cabin and met her husband, I was Auntie Astrid. Jeremiah was different — he's Francis's brother — I mentioned I had met him and his daughters on the beach and he became much more animated, clearly a proud uncle.

Jeremiah was a lot like his brother, though very to the point, respect oriented and into the whole pack dynamics. I found the way that he gave way to Tom and I quite odd. Tom and Jeremiah had a beer on the deck while I talked to Lorelai, I sat on the floor playing with the little boy. So much of the kid seemed to reflect his mother, with the dark almost black hair, the tanned almost olive skin and the long face, that it was almost a sin that he had gotten his father's eyes and, apparent, build. All the same he was an adorable little man with an infectious laugh and a headstrong little personality.

I also had a number of opportunities to meet many more members of the pack. Tom wanted me to have as many as possible, and although I was going to have a hard time keeping them straight for a while, it wasn't for Tom's lack of trying and encouragement.

Some members I was becoming fast friends with. Charlie was amazing, he was the first one to arrive to the bonfire that Tom had built on my second night in Sanctuary. He reminded me a lot of my brother. Always looking to crack a joke and make everyone feel as comfortable as possible. He chose the spot next to me, so I was sandwiched between him and Tom and from that moment on, that night became one laugh after another.

So many people came and went over the night. I found out who Francis was married to — Carmellia — which was a shock, I had found him so nice, though formal. Whereas she wanted nothing more than to make me feel inferior as a non-shifter, which I drastically hope will change. When Jeremiah, William and Lorelai arrived at the fire, they sat across from us, watching us, but my heart melted as William crawled into my lap and proceeded to fall asleep as one of his uncle's hands drew circles on my back and held his little hand.

"He likes you," Tom told me. "One thing about a three-year-old, they don't hide their feelings, if he wasn't comfortable he wouldn't be able to fall asleep here."

"He's beautiful," I said, kissing his soft forehead.

I finally met Landry that night, as well as Lesley and Laura's husbands around the fire. Shiloh had motioned me to her. At this point Jeremiah and Lorelai had decided that it was best to take William home to bed, so I wasn't hindered by a small child. Landry was exactly like his wife, extremely soft spoken, a bit shy, but understanding that not everyone can be born into the family. He was kind to me. Though they were clearly older than me, they didn't make me feel like a child or inferior.

I met so many husbands that night. Whereas the night before I had been grouped together with the women; instead of branching off men and women, it was a family and I welcomed the opportunity to meet more people. Lesley was married to a bald, pale man named Faelen; he was lanky but loud, in comparison to most of the pack. Markus, on the other hand, was Laura's husband; he was short, a stark contrast to the majority of the pack, but he was broad, with kind eyes. I liked him immediately, as I had Laura.

"Dr. Davis? You're needed in Room 4189," a nurse said, arriving in the lounge.

"Why wasn't I paged?" I demanded.

"It's not a code yet," Amanda said — I read her name badge. "We knew where you were, your post op is having a hard time breathing." Fortunately we were able to get the patient settled and restore her rhythm before any other complications could arise. Other than that and an emergency surgery on a police officer who was shot in the line of duty, my day was uneventful. Worried police officers are one of the worst for overprotectiveness and being bullies.

"How was your day, beautiful girl?" Tom said picking me up from the hospital.

"Good, long, but good. I saved a police officer today," I said.

"Really?"

"Yeah, and you will not believe who one of the officers in the waiting room was."

"Based on that, I am going to say that it was Francis."

"You're very smart."

"The police officer is going to be okay though?"

"Yeah. The bullet was lodged in his side, but it didn't hit any major organs."

"You have Wednesday off, right?" Tom asked, changing the subject.

"Yeah, why?"

"Mom called, she wants to go shopping for the wedding ceremony."

"Really?"

"Yeah, just you girls apparently."

"Okay, I guess. What do we need?"

"Honestly, I don't know, I want you and beyond that I don't care."

"Nice words, but seriously?"

"Yeah, you'll need a charm and a ring for me. I've never been into that but I have always wanted an amazing wife and to find the perfect woman."

"Stop sweet-talking, take us home," I blushed. "Hey, Tom," I asked, as we pulled away.

"Yeah?"

"Why didn't Lorelai go running with you the other night? She's the oldest right?"

"She is."

"So she's a shifter, oldest daughters get the gene."

"Usually?" he nodded.

"Usually," I echoed.

"Lor is kind of an anomaly."

"Kind of?"

"Lorelai can't shift."

"But she is the oldest."

"I know."

"And your mother can shift."

"She can."

"Damn."

"What?"

"Seriously?"

"Yeah, what?"

"In your family of five the only member of the family that can't shift should be able to."

"Yeah, but that isn't all that unusual."

"Tom?"

"It isn't. And the immediate family isn't all that matters. She has people, don't worry about her, okay?"

"If you're sure?"

"Oh, I am, she's fine."

"Okay," I said. The conversation ended, but I couldn't help but feel for the girl… first born into a family of shifters with every right to be one but not.

Chapter 6

"Good morning," Leonora said from my door on Wednesday morning. I was exhausted, I had been on call all night and had ended up in the hospital at one in the morning for emergency surgery. Tom had told me that I should cancel but I didn't feel right. The wedding was only a month away and I knew how excited and anxious she was. If I could help Leonora, I would. So two hours after arriving home and much too short a nap later, I was caffeinated and ready to go.

"Good morning, Leonora." I forced a smile.

"Are you ready?" she asked. Her eyebrows rose to the point that if they went any further they would probably jump off her face.

"Yep." I feigned excitement.

"Then come on, let's go and find you the perfect charm," Leonora said, grabbing my hand and dragging me from the apartment.

"I find all these traditions odd and confusing," I said to her as she led me to the elevator.

"But you embrace them in your stride," she said, putting one arm around me, "which is call we can expect of anyone."

"I love them," I smiled. "I like that your family has traditions."

"It's yours too now," she reminded me.

"That only makes it better."

"I promise you, with this budget we are going to find something absolutely beautiful," she said as we exited the building.

"Shouldn't Tom be here for this?" I asked.

"Nah, he has other things to do, plus I figured this might be a good opportunity for the four of us to truly get to know one another."

"Four of us?" I questioned, opening the passenger car door.

"Surprise," two very loud voices yelled from the back seat of the car.

"What?" I said shocked, looking behind me. Contessa and Lorelai sat back there with a silly look on their faces, both of them trying to supress uncharacteristic giggles.

"What are you doing here?" I demanded, taking in my future sisters-in-law.

"As I said, I thought that this would be a great chance for all of us to get to know each other, so I asked Lorelai and Contessa to join us, and they agreed. So here you have it, girls' day out."

I steeled myself for a moment. "This is going to be great," I smiled.

"So the plans for the day are shopping, then lunch and we will continue shopping," Leonora told me.

"That's not much of a plan Mom," Lorelai said from over my shoulder.

"Okay, how much detail do you want? Store by store? Object by object perhaps?" Leonora teased back.

"I don't know I was thinking more of an every fifteen minute timetable."

"We are kidding right?" I asked still not quite used to my new family and their sense of humour.

"Don't worry child, they're trying to wind me up not you."

"That's encouraging, so and what exactly do I need to get?" I asked more than a little unnerved by all the new traditions and requirements for mine and Tom's big day.

"We need a crystal bowl, your charm and a signet ring for his little finger. Once blessed it will shift with his finger," Lorelai said.

"And how do we get it blessed?"

"It's why we need to get it now. We have to send it to our High Council in Llangollen, Wales, where a caster will bless it with a shifter representative before sending it back. Then of course we need table linens, we already have enough picnic benches at Sanctuary, but it has been far too long since we have had a red wedding, so some fresh runners and napkins probably wouldn't go a miss," Contessa tacked on excitedly.

"What do you mean by charm?" I questioned.

"Basically it's a pendant for a necklace, but it is supposed to symbolize something for you and bring you luck in your marriage, so we call it a charm," Leonora explained.

"Seriously?"

Lorelai placed a hand on my shoulder. "It will take time, but you will get used to our little traditions eventually."

"Out of curiosity, are all the packs' traditions the same?"

"Oh, goodness, no," Lorelai said, I'd turned in my seat to look at my two future sisters behind me. "The religious stuff is the same, like the actual ceremony and our rituals, but the rest is sort of particular to individual packs. They're our traditions and the way that our family operates."

"Also, pack structure tends to differ depending on packs as well. We found a way that works for us, others have a way that works for them," Contessa added.

"I'm tired," I said, flopping down on the sofa and throwing my legs across Tom's lap.

"How did shopping with Mom go?"

"You mean shopping with your mom, sister and sister-in-law, right?"

"Really?" he said, mindlessly running his hands up and down my calves.

"Really, you didn't know I was going to be spending the day with all three Sharpe women?"

"How was I supposed to know that?"

"They didn't mention it?"

"What can I say? Nothing was said to me."

"Huh," I grunted.

"So how was it?"

"It was like shopping with three energizer bunnies."

"You were with a shea and two bitches, and it's not their fault that you ended up having to go into the hospital with an emergency surgery in the middle of the night."

"So, what, the shifter half of their DNA makes them more energetic?"

"No, they just don't get tired like you do."

"Are you kidding? I was exhausted at lunch." I laughed.

"Did you have a good time at least?"

"Of course, I did."

"You liked Lorelai then, I take it?"

"Oh yeah, she is a sweetheart."

"Yeah, but she's quiet, she tends to spend most of her time with Jeremiah and William."

"I really like her, she's kinder and gentler than Contessa is."

"Contessa is an acquired taste but I promise that you will get used to her — eventually. She also has a tendency to be a little bit more hesitant towards outsiders, particularly the non-shifter ones."

"Okay, if you say so."

"So, what did you accomplish today?"

"Shopping, lunch and then even more shopping."

"Get anything nice?"

"A bunch of stuff for the wedding."

"Anything I need to know about?"

"I got my charm, your ring, the crystal bowl and some linens."

"Flowers?"

"Not yet, but we are still in agreement about what we want right?"

"Red roses and baby's breath," Tom nodded.

"Good."

"I am still trying to find you a chain for your charm."

"I'm sure you will find something," I assured him.

"I want something thick and different that reflects you."

"I appreciate it, but I am sure that I will love whatever you choose" I grabbed his hand. "Let's face it, you did an incredible job with my ring."

"Why don't you take a nap before dinner?" Tom encouraged me, smiling and raising my hand to his lips to softly kiss the back of it.

"I think I will do that," I said, closing my eyes. I felt Tom grab the blanket from behind the sofa and place it over me, as I finally drifted off after much too long a day.

"Dr. Davis, I haven't checked on you for a while. How are things going?" Caryn came by where I was working in the Emergency Room nurses' station, counting the minutes until it was time to go home, which fortunately was soon.

"I'm doing well," I said.

"So… studying is going well?"

"Of course," I said, pushing a stray lock of hair that had fallen in my face.

"And I assume you are fielding a number of offers from other hospitals."

"I am. Of course all offers are dependent on me passing my boards next week; concentrating on that while I am also trying to plan a wedding and get to know my new family is a lot," I said.

"Well, this is for you," she said, handing me an envelope.

"Is this?"

"It is, again, as you said, it is conditional on your passing next week, but I think you will find it is a fair and generous offer."

"Thank you."

"I want you to know that this was a controversial offer after everything, but one thing was clear, you are a talent and would be an asset to the hospital."

"Thank you."

"Now go knock them dead." She winked at me.

"Thanks, Caryn, I really appreciate it." And I'm telling you my smile couldn't have dimmed if an asteroid had flattened the hospital.

Popping what I needed into my backpack, I hopped on my bike and made a beeline for home.

"Someone's happy," Tom said, as I bounded over to him on the sofa.

"I've just got some great news," I said jumping into his lap, kissing him.

"Okay, care to share?" he asked, clamping his hands down on my hips holding me steady.

"You know how we've been worried?"

"About you getting a job after residency, or about the wedding?"

"The first one."

"Did you get a job offer?"

"I did."

"Can I see?"

I pulled the envelope out of my backpack.

"You haven't opened it?"

"Nope."

"Are you going to?"

"Yep," I said, twisting off his lap beside him, smiling and opening it. I pulled out a thick stack of papers.

"So?"

"I think I need to have my lawyer look this over," I teased.

"Well, let me see and maybe I can get him to give it a once over."

I kissed him then moved sideways slinging my feet over his lap.

"Babe, look at this number. Two hundred and forty-eight thousand dollars."

"That's not the salary, right?"

"It is… the starting salary."

"For a first year attending?"

"I guess they see something in you?"

"But wouldn't they want rid of me after everything?"

"I thought so, and it would be the easiest way they could rid themselves of you, legally."

"You've thought this through?"

"When you were getting offers from hospitals you'd never considered and not the one that you work at."

"But I got one now."

"You do, which is great."

"I just have to pass my boards."

"Then you better get studying," he said, kissing my cheek, then my jaw.

"Well, that's not going to help," I complained.

"Anatomy," he tried.

"Tom," I warned.

"You've been at work all day and all you do is study; we should celebrate your good news."

"Tom… I leave for the board exam tomorrow." Tom won.

"I'm going to miss you."

"I'll miss you too, but don't worry I will be back in a couple of days, and with a little luck I will be a fully certified surgeon."

"Then we can get married?"

"I already agreed to that."

"I know, but I can't wait."

"Two days and I'll be back, two days after that I will be your wife."

"You'll have to pass first."

"Thanks for that."

"I know you will."

84

Chapter 7

Two days later, I was a little shocked when I wasn't met at the bus stop by Tom. "Shiloh, what's going on?"

"Nothing. Follow me."

"Yeah, that's ominous, what makes you think I am going to follow... where's Tom?"

"It doesn't matter."

"Well, this is kidnapping... I've had a really long few days and the only thing I want is to go to bed."

"He's hunting," Lorelai said, popping out from around a corner. In a short black dress.

"Very nice," I told her nodding. "Where are you going?"

"We're going dancing."

"No, we're not," I said, completely serious.

"Oh, we are." Contessa smiled, coming over dressed similarly.

I was pulled into the bus stop bathroom where Rox, Carmellia and Leonora waited. "Shi, watch the door."

"Guys, I really want to go home and go to bed."

"Too bad, this is your bachelorette party and we're damn well going to celebrate."

"Does Tom know you're kidnapping me?"

"He should by now, Charlie, Allain and Jared as well as a good number of the guys should have gotten their hands on him."

"There is no way I am going to get out of this, am I?"

"Absolutely not."

"Okay... what am I wearing?" I gave in.

"I stole this from your closet last night," Leonora said, smiling and handing me my red bandage dress. The same dress I wore on my first real date with Tom. The memory making me smile.

"This will do." I put it on, followed by a pair of red stilettos. Rox made up my hair and put on my makeup for me. Before I knew it, I was being whisked from the small bathroom out to the remainder of our female pack members.

"You ready?" Carmellia asked me, slipping a very glittery Bride to Be sash, and black veil over my head.

"I don't know, should I be?"

"Oh girl, you're in for a night," Contessa smiled. "Let's party, girls," she then screamed. I was led onto a party bus where I was handed a large glass of champagne.

"To the soon-to-be Mrs. Sharpe," Rox announced and there was screaming a lot of screaming. The night started off with the bus, taking me to goodness only knows where. When we stopped, we were outside a beautiful, little restaurant surrounded by trees covered in fairy lights.

"This one was my idea," Leonora said. "I figured you'd be hungry, plus you're going to need the energy."

"This looks great," I said slightly unsure.

"And very much to the chagrin of everyone else, it's completely vegan," Carmellia said.

"But it has amazing reviews so we thought we'd try to experience something new with an open mind," Shiloh said placing her arm around the shoulders of her sister, almost as if you say 'be nice,' without actually saying it.

"Open mind?"

"At least we all know why you're so skinny," Rox winked at me.

"I've always been slim," I admitted. "It comes with my lack of height."

"All right, come on, girl, this is just the beginning of the night, let's go."

Dinner was delicious and everyone agreed that although they do prefer their meat, there was nothing wrong with the vegan food, which made me happy to hear.

"Okay where to next?" I asked, finally getting into the evening.

"We are going to a cocktail bar then dancing."

"We read that there is a common cocktail in England called Pimm's — we found one."

After arriving at the cocktail bar, Leonora, Contessa and Shiloh all toasted to me, welcoming me to the family, which made me happier and even more excited about joining their family. When my phone vibrated, my stomach dropped. I stopped and picked it up.

"Astrid are you okay?" Leonora asked.

"Yeah, I just need to check this." I opened the email knowing there was either going to be a passed or failed notice.

"Astrid?" Contessa asked as I stared at the phone.

"Astrid, what does it say?"

"I passed," I said, finally smiling, a weight lifted from my shoulders, as I began laughing from relief and joy..

"You passed."

"I did, I'm an actual doctor."

"Congratulations, honey." Leonora hugged me. A fresh set of cheers rang out among our group.

"Tom… I can't wait to tell him."

"Tomorrow, tonight let's go celebrate."

I didn't get home until four in the morning and after two days of testing and a long night I just passed out. Leonora promised to come and pick me up in the afternoon after I'd slept. I was suddenly really thankful to have a family that would go through the trouble for me. But after a good morning's sleep and a couple large glasses of water I was feeling better.

"Tom," I screamed excitedly.

"Hey, baby girl," he said hugging me.

"How was your night?"

"Busy, long… good."

"Did you get your results?"

"I did," I smiled.

"Come on, I want to hear you say it. Am I marrying a fancy doctor tomorrow?"

"You are."

"You passed."

"I passed, I am now a fully fledged doctor," I smiled.

"Congratulations," Tom said, hugging and spinning me around.

"Oh careful," I laughed.

"Careful?"

"Your family are quite the party animals."

"Well, it sounds like you had a lot to celebrate."

"I did… now I only have one more thing I need to do," I leaned up kissing him.

"What's that?"

"Officially taking you off the market."

"That's my girl. No cold feet, do you understand?" he told me.

"Don't you worry there. They will be toasty warm tonight," I smiled biting my lower lip, looking at him.

"I love you, I'm so proud of you," his eyes like perfect blue lakes shone down at me, his arms firmly grasping behind my back, my own hands gripping behind his neck, gently curling a strand of his dark hair around my finger.

"I love you too, thank you."

"Tom, come on," Contessa said.

"Sorry, apparently they are determined to keep me busy until the moment of the ceremony," he rolled his eyes in his sister-in-law's direction.

"Tomorrow night," I frowned at the idea of not seeing him until then. Some pack traditions I certainly was not a fan of.

"I know, but it will just make being together that much sweeter." He kissed me.

"I love you."

"I love you too."

"Come on, you're with Lor, Rox and I," Leonora said, pulling me to mine and Tom's little house and for half a second I wondered where Tom was sleeping tonight but after that I didn't have time to do so again.

Chapter 8

"It's time," Leonora said, clapping her hands, her smile stretching from ear to ear.

"Time for what?" I asked, Rox had already had me in a low-backed chair for the past hour.

"To get you dressed, of course."

"You know I'm probably the only bride in history who hasn't seen her dress before the wedding day.

"Girl, we got you," Rox promised. I started getting dressed with their assistance. "So what do you think?" Rox asked me, taking a step back so I could get the full impact of my beautiful black wedding dress. The sweetheart neckline led to off-the-shoulder gothic sleeves. The bodice had cut outs in the sides with beautiful lace camouflaging the openings, covering the entire length. A low back and removable train accentuated my shoulder tattoos. The kerchief hem of the skirt was beautiful picking up at my left thigh. Red beading bordered the neckline and train systematically maneuvering its way around the bodice.

"It is absolutely gorgeous," I said, beaming and running my hands down the exquisite bodice. "You guys are incredibly talented."

"I'm glad you think so," Leonora said.

"Are you kidding me? It is one of the most beautiful things that I have ever seen," I said, hugging my soon to be mother-in -law gently. "You guys could make a killing making and selling dresses like these."

"We'd never thought of that," Rox said, but I could see the wheels turning.

"How many have you made before?"

"Quite a few actually," Leonora said. "Especially some of the retired female elders. They tend to spend the majority of their time in Sanctuary, so it gives them something to do."

"Do you have any of the past dresses?" I asked curious to see them.

"Of course we do, as a pack we have a tendency to keep everything."

"Okay, and how much do the materials cost?"

"Depending on the dress between four and five hundred dollars."

"Interesting, and how long?"

"Usually a couple of weeks."

"Interesting."

"Okay, come on," Contessa said. "It's your wedding day, stop over thinking these things and let's finish getting you ready."

Lorelai grabbed my hand and gently led me to the chair in front of the vanity. They wound my hair to the base of my neck and somehow managed to secure it in a single comb. By the time I was ready to go my eyes were large and dramatic, and a lip stain hugged my pout.

"Okay, it's time to go," Allain called from outside the door. Leonora opened the door. "You ladies need to get out there."

"Good luck," Leonora called to me as they scuttled out of the room.

"I know that your father can't be here, I was wondering if you would do me the honour of allowing me to deliver you to my son."

"I would be honoured," I said, taking his outstretched arm. Allain led me towards the circle through the wood, concealing the two of us, but I was fairly certain that if any of the shifters tried hard enough, they would be able to see us.

"Shall we begin?" I heard Jared call from afar. A collective howl went up around the pack. "I'll take that as a yes."

A lone fiddle began to play as Allain and I emerged from the woods. We headed for the mouth of the circle, directly across from which, was the most beautiful man standing on the banks of the lake, bare from the waist up, the contours of his muscular chest were accentuated by the differences in the light punctuated by the moon.

Slowly Allain and I crossed the center of the circle to the sound of the fiddle. The train of my dress dragged behind me and the red beading sparkled in the glow of the full moon overhead. "You look gorgeous," Tom mouthed to me as his father deposited me in front of the man who was going to be my husband in a few short moments.

"State your name for the gods," Jared said, as I watched Tom watch me intently.

"Astrid Alora Wren Davis." I smiled.

"And you." He turned to Tom.

"Thomas Neil Sharpe."

"Please kneel," he demanded, lifting his arms. We both knelt, gently sitting back on our heels. The crystal bowl sat between us.

"A token of your devotion to one another," Jared said, lifting the chain carrying my pendant and the signet ring that I had chosen for Tom. Jared placed them in the bowl as Tom reached across, grabbing both my hands creating a circle above the bowl.

"The grace of the gods reflected inside us." Jared poured a carafe of water into the crystal bowl.

The pack remained silent until the water stilled in the bowl magnifying the jewelry in its depths.

"The mighty Wolf watches us and bathes us in his power. We give these two souls to him to protect, may the Wolf grant them the wisdom to love and become something greater than themselves."

"Unto the mighty Wolf we give ourselves, our mind and body," Tom and I said together, watching each others eyes intently.

"The great Phoenix," Jared continued, "burns within us, giving us the drive to move forward with our ambition and passions."

"Unto the Phoenix we give our souls, blood and heart," Tom and I said together again.

"The Phoenix and the Wolf grant us our physical and spiritual bodies."

"By their grace we give ourselves to each other, mind, body and spirit."

"Tom, by the gods what vows do you bestow upon Astrid?"

Suddenly he was higher on his knees and raising me with him. "Before the great Phoenix and the mighty Wolf I promise to do everything in my power to ensure that you always feel safe, loved, honoured and protected. I will cherish you, for you are part of me now, I cannot deny you, any more than I could deny my right hand. You are mine, you are my future, you are my present, you are my forever. By the gods as they watch over us tonight, I declare I will be faithful, loyal, honest, your greatest confidant, your best friend, I will be yours."

"Astrid, before the gods what do you vow to Tom?"

"Before the great Phoenix and mighty Wolf I swear to remain yours, faithful and loyal. I vow to honour you, love you and cherish you. For I am yours, as I have been since the day that I stumbled into your office. Never in my life did I think I would deserve anyone as amazing as you, but here we are and I am looking at you, and thanking the gods that they found me worthy enough of your love. You are my everyday from now until eternity."

"By blood we grant each other ourselves, for eternity," we said once again together.

Jared handed Tom a long knife, I handed him my left hand, keeping his eyes on mine he sliced down my palm, I in turn took the knife and made an identical cut down his palm, before handing the knife back to Jared.

"By blood we become one through spirit, body and soul," we said, as we opened our hands above the crystal bowl, releasing our blood into the water, over our jewelry.

"Thomas," Jared motioned towards the bowl.

"I, Thomas Neil Sharpe do take you Astrid Alora Wren Davis as my wedded wife before the gods, on this night and for all nights to come." Tom reached into the bowl grabbing the beautiful diamond infinity charm that hung from a thick chain with an elaborate closure, leaving the signet behind in the water. He reached behind my neck and expertly fastened it before adjusting it, a bead of water rolled down my chest taking my breath away as I felt more than just the cool tickle from the water. It was like I could feel Tom's love touching my heart directly and it swelled choking me up slightly.

"Astrid," Jared continued motioning towards the bowl.

"I, Astrid Alora Wren Davis do take you Thomas Neil Sharpe as my wedded husband before the gods on this night and for all nights to come," I said, feeling a happy tear run down my cheek, reaching in to the bowl, picking up the signet ring and placing it on his little finger on his right hand.

"I, Jared Sharpe, Alpha of the Seattle pack, on this the sixth full moon of the year do name you husband and wife. Tom, you may kiss your bride." I was glad to know that some traditions don't change.

Hoisting me to my feet, Tom kissed me first slowly, then building, eventually culminating in a hungry, slightly too passionate kiss until the entire pack was either cheering or howling, and he let me go. Well my face, the rest of me he held tightly, I was more than happy to do the same, and never let him go either.

"I love you," I whispered to the man of my dreams.

"Not as much as I love you," he whispered to me kissing the tip of my nose.

Before we knew it we were being passed from pack member to pack member, being hugged and patted on the back as we went. Charlie, enthusiastically as ever, lifted me off the ground with the ferocity of his hug as Tom laughed beside us.

"Charlie." I laughed, trying to steady myself by placing my hands on his shoulders.

"Welcome to the pack," Charlie said, kissing my temple before putting me down.

"Thanks, Charlie," I said, feeling Tom's arm reclaiming and steadying me.

"Hey, little sister, let me see your hand," Lorelai said, taking over the now vacant spot Charlie left behind.

Dutifully I handed her my left hand, which was still oozing slowly. Quickly and methodically without saying a word she bandaged my palm and helped me into a pair of wrist length lace gloves.

"There we go." Lorelai smiled at me. "Can't have my new sister getting an infection." She smiled at me before hugging first me tightly, then her brother.

"Thanks, sis," Tom said to her.

"Yes, thank you, Lorelai."

"Anytime, we sisters have to look out for each other," she gave me an affectionate little hip bump, then grabbed my good hand and gave it a squeeze.

"That we do," I agreed.

"I'll be expecting a dance later, little brother." She winked before taking her momentary leave of us.

"Welcome to the family," Leonora said, hugging me.

"Thank you, Leonora."

"You picked a good one," Allain said, hugging his son. "I can see how happy you make each other."

"Thanks, Dad," he smiled.

Then we switched. "I'm so proud of you, son," Leonora told Tom.

"Welcome to the pack and the family," Allain said to me. "I understand all this is an adjustment, but you are doing great. I'm thrilled for the two of you."

Somehow, as we were greeted by our family and being congratulated, they managed to turn the area on the shore into a dance floor. A number or exquisitely red and black decorated tables housed more food than I have ever seen.

The table next to the one where Tom and I were to sit was adorned with a gorgeous white cake, decorated with red roses and black ribbon.

"Come," Tom said, offering me his hand, which I took gladly.

"My gorgeous bride," he said gently into my ear.

"My incredible husband," I said back.

"I'm the luckiest man in the world," he countered.

"I am the luckiest woman in the world," I repeated back, as we sat watching our family.

"Your dress is amazing."

"Thanks, your mother and the other ladies did a stunning job."

"That they did."

"So how do you feel?" Tom asked, gently moving me in a circle.

"Good, happy, like for once in my life things want to work out."

"I'm sorry you couldn't have invited anyone."

"It's okay." I smiled. I'd told everyone at the hospital it was immediate family only, very small and non-traditional, trying for a ceremony that was simple and reflected us and they accepted it.

"I love that they've all accepted you," he said. I'd spent the past hour dancing in large circles with any number of girls and women. Charlie is a character, break dancing, the worm, spinning whoever is closest to him.

"You'd be surprised how half a dozen drinks can loosen some women up. Did you know Lesley used to be an OR nurse?"

"I did actually."

"Why didn't you tell me?"

"I wasn't aware you wanted a briefing on the background of every member of the pack."

"Not a briefing, more of a short essay, bullet points really."

"You're a menace."

"There are worse things," I teased.

"Like?"

"Being married to a wolf." I winked.

"You little madam." He spun me around, dipping and kissing me.

"Mrs. Wolf?" I tried.

"Mrs. Sharpe," he teased, "you're playing with fire."

"Hmm… good." We danced most of the night with our family, before having to head home for sleep.

It was amazing the next day knowing that I was leaving our home as a married woman. I was the Beta's Bride, Mrs. Sharpe and Dr. Davis. "You're quiet," Tom said, wrapping his arm around my shoulder.

"I'm sorry," I said, sipping my tea, and enjoying Tom's gentle rocking of the porch swing.

"Penny for your thoughts." He stroked a hand down my hair.

"I'm happy." I smiled. "This may very well have been the best week of my life."

"I know it was mine." He kissed my temple. I tucked my head into the crook of his neck.

"I never thought this could be my life?"

"What?"

"Peaceful, look around. Marlee and Carly are down by the water. Francis and Carmellia are on the porch watching them. Down by the lake you can see wolves running along the shore. Charlie is already working on something; I never understand what he's working on but he is going something. Some of the older kids are studying at picnic benches. Everything is perfect and peaceful."

"I wish I could see everything through your eyes."

"Why don't you see it?"

"Without heartache and disappointment, you will never truly appreciate the subtlety of beauty," Tom said to me.

"I never appreciated it until I had reason to."

"Reason?"

"You make me want to see the beauty in everything." I smiled up at my new husband.

Chapter 9

"What I would like to do is propose something to you. Something that I think would be a good addition to the pack. I would be willing to make it a small business for other packs in the surrounding area." I took a deep breath realizing that I was babbling. "I would like to open a small medical clinic here at Sanctuary."

"Seriously?"

"Listen, I was talking to Tom, asking about what you guys do in terms of medical treatment, and he said that a few things are passed down. But for the most part, the majority of medical treatment is done here or at home so that you can avoid potential exposure. I was thinking of opening a facility, a clean, sterile environment. I am a doctor and surgeon, we could decrease the potential for exposure, no more having babies at home, no more self stitching, no more not getting X-rays and waiting for bones to heal on their own. Plus, I am also a biomedical chemist. I could run tests and create most medications and what we need right here at Sanctuary."

"Do you have a number for me?" Jared asked.

"Depending on how many forms of equipment we want to acquire, I am going to say less than twelve million, but I am willing to use my compensation from the suit," I added.

"We do have a resident nurse," Jared mused, clearly referring to Lesley. "Can I show you something?" He then asked me.

"Sure." I shrugged.

"This is an old book of medicine for shifters,." He handed me the book. "We don't have the means to…"

"I can make these," I said, flipping through.

"Really? Usually, these things are made by casters or well mainly mages and bought by the packs; the knowledge of how to do these things isn't something we have."

"I can do it."

"Look, if we do this, it's your baby, your project. I need you to take full responsibility for it."

"I understand."

"But you're not paying for it. The pack has been self-sufficient for years, we have the resources, money is not going to be a problem."

"Jared."

"I also want you to do something else with it."

"What is that?"

"Study us."

"What, do you mean you want me to study you?"

"I mean physiologically. I don't know of any information out there that looks at the differences in us and why we shift and what stresses it puts on the body. Mainly, I want you to see if you can figure out why Lorelai can't shift even though she should be able to... don't tell her though, I don't want her to get her hopes up before you're sure."

"Jared, are you serious?"

"Completely. There's a spot a few hundred feet behind the pavilion, it's all yours."

"Really?"

"Oh yes, this is something that the whole pack can get excited about."

"Thank you."

"I assume you have an idea of what you need it to look like and the size?"

"I do."

"Let's see," he said.

I handed him a sheet. "I am not an architect, but I do spend a decent amount of time around hospitals and figure this is what I am going to need. A couple rooms are storage, which can always be converted into something else if we need it. I have a couple diagnostic machine rooms, my lab, a ward, which I hope you won't have filled but it will have four beds, and a small operating theatre, which with a little help, I should be able to man just myself, Lesley and one or two others, the exception being complicated surgery, when I will do my best to encourage us going to the hospital I work at... I'm sorry... I am babbling."

97

"Hey, don't worry about it, I like everything that I see here. There's no convincing required."

"Really?"

"Yeah. Does Tom know about this little plan of yours?"

"Not really?"

"Define not really."

"Well, I didn't want him to force you into letting me do this, I only wanted to do this if it was truly going to be beneficial and not because I am someone's wife."

"Which is understandable, but my brother isn't going to like the idea that you went behind his back."

"Jared, I did not go behind Tom's back."

"And if he doesn't like the idea?"

"Jared, Tom and I are fine."

"Okay, well either way, we are going to need Tom and Charlie to begin working on this. Why don't you call Tom while I call Charlie?"

"Now?"

"I can't think of a better time, can you? I would like it built before the end of the month."

"Seriously?"

"Dial," was all Jared said, motioning with his chin.

"Hello?" Tom said, answering on the first ring.

"Hey, babe, can you come into Jared's office, please?"

"Astrid, what's going on? Why are you in Jared's office?"

"I'll explain when you get here. It's all good, just come okay."

"I'll be there in two." Click.

"He'll be here in a second," I said to Jared, who had just got off the phone as well.

"Charlie too."

"I hope they like the idea as well," I mused.

"I wouldn't worry."

"I'd ask you to tell me more, but I figure we should wait for them."

"That's fine," I smiled. I still felt awkward around my brother-in-law, which made the silence uncomfortable. I wish I was able to come up with something to ask him. So we sat in silence while I held the additional pages I had been working on in my lap.

"Hey, boss, you wanted to see me?" Charlie said stepping into the solid wood doorway. "Oh, hey there, little lady," he nodded taking me in.

"I wanted to talk to you and Tom about something Astrid has brought up to me. Take a seat until Tom gets here."

"Cool, boss," he said, taking the chair on my left, facing Jared on the other side of the desk.

"What is going on?" Tom demanded, alternating his gaze between, myself, his brother and best friend. He sat down in the seat beside me, in a much more formal manner than the person who came before him. But then, I don't think Charlie has formality in him. Tom's back was ramrod straight, like there was an invisible string on the ceiling holding him straight.

"Everything is fine," I assured my husband, placing an assuring hand on his arm.

"So this has nothing to do with Carmellia?" Tom demanded.

"Carmellia?" I repeated.

"Don't worry about it," Jared told me insistently and quickly shot his brother a warning glare.

"Okay, well if it isn't about that, what is it about?"

"Astrid, why don't you explain to them?"

"I have just presented Jared with the proposal to build a medical clinic here at Sanctuary. The idea is that I want to create a more medically approved and risk-free place for people of your particular peculiarities."

"She means shifters," Charlie said, stating the obvious, but for whose benefit I wasn't sure.

"Thank you, Charlie, I got that, actually," Tom said.

"I, of course understand that there are risks where shifters are involved. And there will likely be times that I am not going to be able to do everything alone. But I saw the need for something like this here, and I would like to fill it, because I am the only one who can. Think of it like my giving back to the pack."

"You want to create a medical clinic?" Tom said incredulously.

"I do."

"We would like you to run the building of the clinic," Jared said to Charlie.

"Well, that is to be expected," Charlie said, leaning back and throwing an arm over the back of my chair.

"Are you sure you want to take this on?" Tom said to me, leaning forward resting his elbows on his knees.

"I am, yes."

"You realize our pack alone is over fifty people."

"I do," I said to my husband.

"She is willing to aid other neighbouring packs," Jared explained.

"Jared. I love the idea, but the stress and constraint that it is going to put on Astrid." I could feel Tom's concern.

"It is going to benefit all of us though," I pointed out.

"All the same, do you really want to take this on?"

"I really do." I smiled. "The only thing I ask is, I know you have an open-door policy, but some of the chemicals and technologies could be potentially dangerous if people don't know what they are doing."

"You want a lock?"

"Just on a couple of rooms or cupboards."

"I think with some of the things that you are looking to include in the clinic that it is a reasonable request."

"Thank you."

"Okay, so do we have a location we are looking at for the clinic?" Charlie asked.

"The parcel of land a few hundred feet behind the pavilion."

"Really?"

"Yeah, it's big enough for anything she has planned, it's also quiet and private while still accessible." I was amazed that he had actually put that much thought into the entire situation already.

"If you're willing, Charlie, Astrid has a number of ideas and plans already written down and I would like this as close to finished as possible before the end of the month."

"Really?"

"Yes, I think with some help, it should be manageable."

"I don't see why not, I'll start talking to her and get the basics figured."

"Great, once you've done that come to me and let me know what you need and I'll start putting things into motion," Jared told Charlie.

100

"Absolutely, boss."

"Great. Does anyone have any other questions?"

I shook my head, as did Tom and Charlie. Tom stood up and I understood that was all of our cues to go.

"Should we start now?" Charlie asked me as the door was shut behind us.

"She'll catch up with you later," Tom told Charlie, "I would like a word with my wife."

"Good luck," Charlie told me but said nothing else as he ducked out of a side door.

"Tom," I said gently.

"No, home," was all he said. I was starting to feel nervous as we moved between the two buildings. I was thankful the buildings weren't further apart. But also kind of wished I wasn't the wife.

Tom opened the door for me. "Why didn't you tell me what you planned?" he asked, closing the door behind himself.

"It wasn't a conscious thing; I just didn't want you to pressure your brother into something that he didn't think was beneficial to the pack."

He watched me intently.

"Tom," I said.

"Is that really the reason why you didn't tell me, your husband and the Beta of the pack, of your idea to create a medical clinic at Sanctuary."

"Tom?"

"Didn't you think I would think it was a brilliant idea, but would be worried about the toll it could take on you?"

"Sit," I said, grabbing his hand and pulling him down to the sofa beside me. "I want to create a clinic, because I want to bring something to the pack that has given me something that I haven't had in a really long time and I feel with my skills this could be my contribution."

"Astrid, the different packs on the west coast contain over seven hundred pack members."

"So?"

"You want to be the sole woman responsible for seven hundred shifters?"

"I am not responsible for them."

"Medically you will be. Once there is word out there that you are looking to be a pack doctor. That you know about the packs and there isn't any fear of discovery."

"I want to do this."

"Why?"

"Tom, I have never had a family like this before. My mother was not someone that ever allowed me to feel at home. This Sanctuary is home."

"But you are still so new, we've been married two weeks, you're getting used to being a new attending. Also, you don't understand pack or inter-pack politics."

"Do you really think for one second that I think you would let me drown?"

"Well, no."

"And are you planning on letting me drown?"

"I haven't really decided yet."

"Thanks. Well I am pretty sure that Jared and Charlie won't. So, that's something at least."

"It's still a lot to take on."

"Yeah, well what about me makes you think I am afraid to take on a challenge? Look at me. I'm a human doctor, with a shifter husband and a family of shifters. I think I can handle it."

"I forget, because you are so little, and delicate, how strong you are underneath all of that. I want to protect you so much."

"And Tom, I love you for that, but I can handle things. I did before you. And the thing is just like before when I need help, I know where to get it. The difference is, this time instead of stumbling blindly into the office of a man I have never met, I know where I am going and I am going to find more than what I am looking for."

"Look, I know you are capable, and I never want to belittle you, your ideas, or your confidence. I just worry."

"I know."

"I'm still not in love with this idea."

"But?"

"But I support you. I respect what you are doing for the pack, and I will help you, when and if you need it."

"I knew you would. And Tom…"

"Yeah?"

"I am sorry I went behind your back."

"You didn't go behind my back really."

"I know, but you seem upset."

"Astrid, nothing you did was done with any malicious intent or to deceive me, so you have nothing to apologize for."

"I didn't mean to hurt and upset you though, I wanted you to be proud of me."

"Oh, you silly, silly girl," he said, pulling me down to the couch to him, then against him so I was nestled in his arms.

"What?" I asked, confused, wiggling one arm behind him and forcing myself tighter against him.

He pulled me quickly and effortlessly so I was straddling his lap and forced to look at him. "I will always be proud of you," he whispered, before kissing me, startlingly slow, then before becoming more like him, he bit my lower lip, causing me to gasp before retaking my mouth. Pulling away, he grabbed my hair forcing my head back, kissing up my jaw. "There is no one I could love more or be more proud of," he said gently in my ear.

That afternoon I met up with Charlie. Tom had work to do but was confident that Charlie and I would get everything all but sorted without him. "You know you work too much." I smiled, bending down and kissing my husband's temple before leaving.

"Says the woman who is literally bringing her work home with her."

"Oh, give it a rest, it's done, and it's not working. Can you say the same?"

"No, I cannot," he concurred, grabbing and kissing my hand before letting me go.

It didn't take long to find Charlie. He was already at the lot of land given to me, well, the clinic. "What are you thinking?"

"Ah, hey, little lady, I was just taking a look at the area."

"And how does it look?"

"Even enough. I'll rent a machine to move and level out what we need by next weekend we should have everything for the foundation prepared."

It'll be laid that quickly?"

"Look around us. Every building you see, everything from the dais to the fire pits, to the pavilion and everything in between was built and maintained over generations."

"Seriously?"

"Of course, we have some friends in neighbouring packs that do a lot of the well drilling, and septic work, the packs are pretty big on family business."

"Interesting."

"Astrid, we're not kidding when we say that we are largely self-sufficient, we've got most tasks down to a science. We'll have your clinic ready in no time."

"Okay, but you can't do everything by yourself."

"Oh, I'm not going to be doing it by myself. Some of the pups should be here soon. Their summer should be starting any time now."

"Seriously?"

"Oh yeah, Brady, Matteo, Toby, Colby and even some of the girls are always looking to earn a little extra cash."

"So there's a lot that I am going to have to purchase for this. What should I be expecting for a timeline?" I asked, sitting down in the middle of the grass where my clinic was going to stand.

"The ground work will be done in a week, the outer walls a few days after that."

"That quick?"

"It would be faster if we wouldn't have to wait for the foundation to dry," Charlie said, sitting down beside me.

"But how are you going to be able to do all this while you are working?"

"Oh, I've been tasked with this. Jared wants this done, I'll be paid, just for different work."

"I guess that is the benefit of your boss actually being family," I smiled.

"Yeah, or more difficult… we're literally on top of each other all the time as a pack, work, home, Sanctuary."

"I guess you have a point, I still can't imagine having a problem with that. What you have here is a family. Plus, there's so much room here, it's not like you can't get away. It was the same in Wales, when I had too much of my family, I just went to the woods, the pond, the backyard."

"You were meant to marry into a pack. It took Lesley much longer than you to get used to our ways, you were born for it, I can already tell." Charlie nudged my shoulder.

"Thanks." I giggled.

"Question, if everyone is going to be at work in the city, are you going to be here alone with all those pups?"

"Oh, yeah."

"Well, that seems like a lot. You versus all of those teenagers?"

"Oh, don't worry about me, little Beta, I can handle a few puppies." Charlie winked at me.

"I don't doubt that, from what I have observed Uncle Charlie is really big hit."

"What about you and Tom, huh? Am I going to get to be Uncle Charlie to any Beta pups anytime soon?"

"Charlie," I said, stunned. "Tom and I have been married for all of twenty minutes."

"So. We could really use some heirs."

"Charlie," I scoffed.

"Hey, he's my best friend. Just looking out for him."

"Well, unless you are planning on producing those heirs with him."

"Little Beta is getting snippy."

"Can you blame her?" I asked, cocking my head to one side.

"Well, I guess not. I feel like Tom may have a thing to say about your suggestion anyway."

"Possibly." I nodded, laughing, to which he loudly joined in.

Work had been difficult the first week that Charlie was working on my new clinic. A lot of emergencies came through the hospital with a brand-new load of interns. The fourth of July always brings out the crazies. So all in all it was a good time for the newbies. It was good getting back to what was quickly becoming one of my favorite places. The calm and peace were welcome. Everyone loved everyone, and for the most part got along. It made it a great place to unwind after the craziness of the city.

"I know you want to go to see how the clinic is coming, and I would put money on Charlie being there. Why don't we head there first?" Tom said, nonchalantly throwing an arm around my shoulders.

As we approached the area that housed an enormous cement slab there were more than a few people standing around staring at the spot. Charlie, Francis, Carmellia, Matteo, Colby, Brady, Corey, Tobias and Wilson.

"Hey, guys," Tom called, not bothering to remove his arm.

"Hey," a number of them called back.

"So what do you think?" Charlie asked as I went to stand next to him. Tom came with me.

"It's huge," I pointed out wide-eyed.

"It's to your specifications," he assured me.

"It's incredible," I smiled incredulously.

"We did make one small change to your plans though," Carmellia said from beside her husband; I was a little shocked to see her here at all. Mind you, I'd thought that at my bachelorette party, so I guess I shouldn't be too surprised.

"We wanted to give you a little something extra, so we added an area to the front," Charlie explained.

"What is it?" I asked confused, staring at the small but spacious area at the front of the left side of the rectangular building.

"An office."

"A what now?"

"A room designed to be your personal space, to work, research and anything else you need to do."

"An office?" I said again incredulously, but grinning, I hadn't really required the definition.

"Precisely."

"The work will be slightly more, but the cost won't be. The pack wanted to give you something, because we know you are doing this for us. It's something that could have benefitted us long before now, but we didn't have the capability to do it," Francis said.

"You're going to be the pack physician and we wanted to thank you," Colby tacked on.

"I'm speechless," I said.

"Well, that's a first," Tom said.

"Did you know about this?" I demanded, nudging my husband with my shoulder for the jab.

"Of course I did, Charlie asked me if you would be upset by the change after the pack discussed it."

"I really can't thank you enough."

"You will," Francis assured me.

"We want you to have everything you need and this office will give you more space," Jared assured me.

I just smiled at the amazing slab that was going to become something myself and the whole pack could be proud of.

Chapter 10

Tonight was a rare occasion where I was home before Tom. My shift work really did have its down side in comparison to Tom's regular hours as a lawyer. So for a change I had dinner in the oven before Tom got home. I didn't even turn when he came in. "Hey," I called, continuing the research I was doing on diagnostic machinery for the clinic.

He flopped down on the sofa and closed his eyes. "Well, that's not a good sign," I said putting down my computer.

"Nope." I got up and went to the kitchen. Two glasses and a bottle of French red and I was next to my husband again.

"Pack or work problems," I asked, curling up next to him but not quite touching him and handing him a glass.

"Thanks," he said, turning to look at me, my cheek cradled in my hand. "And both."

"Okay, what can you tell me?"

"Where do you want me to start?"

"Tom…" I gently placed a hand on his head. "What's going on?"

"Do you remember when I told you that there are more than just shifter sects?"

"Of course, there are the pyres, casters and mages as well."

"Exactly, and the most dangerous?"

"Pyres and shifters."

"To us."

"Pyres."

"Exactly.

"Wait are you telling me that there are vampyres in Seattle?"

"As far as we can tell it's only the one, but…"

"But nothing, isn't it considered dangerous to have two predatory species operating in the same city?" Tom turned to face me, raising an eyebrow. "What? I joined a shifter family, I've been reading."

"Reading what?"

"Books."

"Okay, not important," he shook his head.

"Tom, who knows?"

"For now, the two of us, Jared, Contessa and Francis, but sooner than later we are going to have to loop in my parents and the other shifters."

"Francis?"

"Yeah, he recognized some of the signs and looped in Jared, who looped in me. We were able to look like concerned lawyers in order to get a good look, but even then, we can't be certain."

"So we wait until the medical examiner finishes their report, that should give us a better idea, shouldn't it?"

"Francis is too low on the totem pole for access to it without special permission and unless its related to one of mine or the firm's cases we can't."

"You can't access it." I let out a deep breath, pursing my lips.

"And without access, we just have to wait for the next body."

"Oh my god." I said, not enjoying the sound of that.

"Exactly, but not only that. We don't want any of the pack having some sort of a run in with them. Peaceful pass through and send them along," he said like a mantra.

"Okay. Well, what's the worst thing that could happen?"

"A species war, having to bring in the shifter and high councils."

I took a large mouthful of wine. Yep, we definitely don't want that, I thought, nodding at my husband.

"Don't tell the pack or anyone, okay?"

"I won't, but what if I told you, I should be able to get us a copy of the medical examiner's report?"

"You can?" He sat up straight clearly intrigued

"I went to school with a girl who now works in the medical examiner's office; she might owe me a favour."… *or two*, I thought but refrained from mentioning.

"You did?"

"I did. Do you know the victim's name?"

"Sure, Francis said he was Samuel Keddy."

"Okay, leave it with me."

"Look, if you can do this, the sooner the better."

"I understand that, but I need to do this face to face."

"Okay."

"You trust me?"

"I do. Of course I do."

"Good. Anyway, I'm kind of liking feeling helpful. I want to do whatever I can for the pack. Come on, I'll work on it in the morning, for now dinner is going to be ready any second, get up." I kissed his forehead.

"You cooked."

"I did."

"Is it edible?"

"Possibly."

"I'll get the takeout menus out," he rolled his eyes and I smirked.

"Hey, Penelope," I called to her, her favourite chai latte outstretched towards her.

"Hey, Astrid, what's this for?" she took the drink appreciatively, but sceptically.

"I need a favour."

"What kind of favour?"

"I need the medical examiner's report for Samuel Keddy."

"I can do that, be here by twelve, okay?"

"That's it?"

"Yeah."

"Okay, done, thanks," I said, nodding before going to my respective side of the hospital.

My morning was much less 007 after that. I rounded on all my recent patients, checked everything, made sure everyone was stable and made my way to the OR for an appendectomy. I was meeting Penelope and thinking it was a damn good thing my husband is a lawyer.

"Thank you for getting this for me," I said, sliding the files into my folio.

"Really, don't mention it, you never ask for favours even when you should."

"Penny, I've always come out of situations, on the other side."

"Then tell me something — what is this?" she said, tapping the charm around my neck.

"Penelope don't…" I warned carefully.

Then her eyes widened a fraction. "A shifter? Really…?"

"Thanks again." I ran off, putting some finality behind my voice.

"Hey?" I said to too many sets of eyes in my living room.

"Did you get the report?" Jared asked.

"Really, Tom, I told you I might be able to get it. Not that I definitely would."

"Astrid."

"Here." I handed the file to them.

"How did you get it?"

"I have friends and resources too. A decade alone in this city with my history, you meet people."

"Okay, fair enough." He raised his hands in surrender. "The pack owes you a debt of gratitude."

"Anything for the pack. However, just in case you lawyer folk were wondering, this is a felony."

"Oh please, we'd have you off or out of the country in ten minutes." Tom winked at me and I rolled my eyes.

"Sometimes it's like I married into the Mafia."

"Nah, just a family," Contessa said.

I sat down on the sofa beside Tom, who was busy looking over the papers I'd given them, then without even looking up he handed me a glass of club soda — oh, the joys of being on call. "You've got yours well trained." She winked at me.

"Nah, we're about at the same level, we're hyper aware of each other."

"That's a good omen in a mate," Contessa smiled.

"Thank you." I nodded. "You two doing okay over there, don't need any help?"

"No, we've read plenty in the past," Jared promised.

"We hunt tonight," Tom said, suddenly.

"You're right," Jared agreed. "Do you want to wait here?" he then proceeded to ask his wife.

"Well, how many are you planning on having flying over the city this evening?"

"Just us."

"No, I'm coming, I have to keep you boys in check," Contessa declared. Jared opened the balcony door.

"I'll meet you out there," Tom told them as they disappeared. "What did you get from that?" He looked at me.

"There's a vampyre here."

"Yes, there is. They could just been passing through, but if they're not, we need to find them and explain to them that this is pack territory and advise them to leave. Most do."

"Okay."

"They're just like us, reasonable, but if provoked..."

"I understand. Go."

"I love you." He kissed my forehead.

"I love you too." I smiled.

After my own look through the file I had brought home, I returned to what I had been today's reading, a new book: *Mage and Shifters, The Apothecary Guide*, which was so far proving to be an interesting and informative read, giving me lots of information on the differences in shifters and the effects a number of treatments and herbs can have on their bodies. I was just writing down something I would like to try when my pager went off.

"Come on,' I grumbled under my breath. Before standing up, I looked to the balcony door and thought about closing it, but we are on the top floor and it was likely that Tom, Contessa and Jared would need a place to shift back, so I left it before grabbing my bag, keys and scrambling off to the hospital. The night was balmy and as much as Tom hated it, it was much easier to take my bike through the busy roads.

"What have we got?" I demanded, throwing my stuff behind the nurses' station, grabbing a gown, and sliding on a pair of gloves.

"Mohammad Agoud. It appears to be an animal attack, and he's losing a lot of blood," Nurse Cora said.

"Did they say where they found him?"

"Carter Street, west of Donahugh."

"That's way too far into the city for an animal attack like this," I mused.

"That's what we thought," Cora said.

"What have we done?" I asked the resident.

"Pupils are uneven, ultrasound shows internal bleeding; we've hung two units of o-negative, pushed morphine, and packed the wounds as best we can," Dr. Schmidt explained.

"Okay, hang another unit. We're taking him to CT. I want to know exactly what we're dealing with before we get in there. Also, page neuro and have them meet me up there," I demanded. I pulled out my phone concerned.

"Hey, Francis. It's Astrid."

"How did you get my number?"

"I'm married to Tom, what do you think?" I said, conscious of the people around me, pulling Beta's Bride rank would've been too noticeable.

"Never mind, what's going on?"

I took a step into an empty room, carefully shutting the door behind me. "I just got paged in on a possible animal attack, but I don't think it is. However, you're the highest ranking one of you not out patrolling the city, can you please come to the hospital?" one of you — my oh so subtle way of referring to them being shifters.

"I'm on duty."

"Tell them it's police business."

"Astrid."

"Francis, I need your help to find out if it's one of ours or a vampire. You want to argue with me? Because this person needs surgery and we're just taking him for a CT first."

"I'm coming."

"Hey, Cora." I exited my hiding spot. "My cousin is a police officer and he's coming to look at this victim. When he gets here can you bring him to me?"

"Yes, Doctor."

"Thank you."

I was just finishing in CT when Francis arrived. "Great timing, I was about to have to take him up."

"No problem." Something about his tone told me the opposite, but I ignored it.

"No brain bleeds fortunately, but the transfusions are going too quickly, and there is one wound on his neck that looks particularly deep."

"I see it." He sniffed and looked, before simply nodding at me.

"What do you think?"

"I think your suspicions may be right, but I should really talk to Tom and Jared."

"Well, they're busy, you can either try to join them, or the balcony is open at ours, head over and wait for them," I directed him, trying with all my might to sound authoritative. "I need to go and try to save this man's life."

He nodded again before stepping away. Myself and others started maneuvering the gurney down the hall.

The surgery thankfully wasn't as bad as I was expecting. Once we got the internal bleeding stopped I moved to the thicker gash on his neck. There didn't appear to be anything major, but there were definitely two deeper sections of it. I closed it. "Okay, Dr. Schmidt, and Dr. Jenkins, you guys stitch up all the remaining wounds and treat them. Give him another transfusion when you get him into the ICU, monitor him closely. I'll be back in the morning."

"Yes Dr. Davis." They both nodded. I quickly scrubbed out and went to the nurses' station.

"You okay, Dr. Davis?" Cora asked.

"Yeah, just something seemed off about this one."

"Is that why you brought in that man?"

"Francis? Yeah," I said, putting on my coat.

"Well, have a good rest of your night," she told me. I looked up at the clock. Ten o'clock, it was officially dark. Tom was not going to be happy.

"Thanks, you too," I said.

I kept an eye out for anything odd or suspicious on my drive home, but nothing stood out. I parked my bike between mine and Tom's cars.

"What did you see?" Jared asked me as I stepped through my own doorway.

"Wow. Hi. Yes, the man is stable, and yes, I'd love a drink after a three-hour surgery, thanks."

Jared just looked at Tom. "Yeah, she's usually like this when she comes home from being called in," Tom smiled, grabbing me some cranberry juice. "Here," he said handing it to me and stroking my hair after pulling me against his side. "That'll help." He kissed between my eyes when I glared at him as he knew it was the low blood sugar that put me in that mood.

"I didn't know what I was looking at, at first. Too distracted by the larger injuries, but when they said where he was attacked, something seemed off."

"So, you called Francis."

"Present," he said, shifting back into a man, and slipping on his jeans. Charlie quickly appeared behind him. Earlier Francis had been on duty. Wonder how that changed.

"Yeah, so I called him, mostly because I didn't realize Charlie knew."

"Oh, he didn't. After Francis caught up with us and told us what was going on we called Charlie and clued him in, figured we could use the back up."

"Hey, little lady," Charlie called over, flopping down on the sofa.

"Who's still out there?"

"Contessa and Markus. Now keep going."

"Well, most of the cuts were deep, but there was one on his neck going over to his shoulder where the depth was inconsistent."

"He'd been bitten," Tom translated.

"Yeah, that's consistent with what Francis said. He said he could smell something acidic and wrong. Also, there was no evidence of anything below his waist, which would be inconsistent with an actual animal attack or even one of us," Jared said.

"However, what we're most concerned about is the age of the pyre, today's attack happened during sunset. It takes hundreds of years for a pyre to be able to start spending time in the sun just before sunset and after sunrise," Tom explained.

"Okay, so this pyre situation is worse than we imagined. What's the plan?" I let Tom pull me to the sofa and I sat between him and Charlie.

"We're going to have to tell the pack, encourage them to stay in groups, not engage and set up a rotation at sunrise and sunset," Tom told me.

"We'll use your place to come and go from," Jared told Tom and I, "it's better protected from view and people can come and go with nothing but a number in the keypad."

Tom nodded and I refrained from saying anything.

"What do you need me to do?" I asked.

"Keep your head down, let us know of anything unusual at the hospital, like tonight, and just be patient. Hopefully they'll pass through without incident."

"And no more biking," Tom told me.

"How did you know?"

"Francis told me. I'm not a fan of it on a good day, and although you aren't a shifter you still smell of us. A pyre could pick up the scent."

"Understood, I'll take Bluebell." I smiled and Charlie laughed, we all knew he hated my little rust bucket just as much, but I refused to get rid of her.

"Okay, Tom, you and I should get back out there."

"Charlie and Francis, fuel up, do what you gotta do and get back out there too."

"Be careful," I told my husband.

"Always." He disentangled himself from me.

"Charlie, how often does this kind of thing happen?" I asked.

"About once or twice a decade."

"Okay…"

"Last time Tom and Jared's uncle died from a run-in with them; they're just anxious to avoid another tragedy."

"Oh… I didn't know."

"Nah, you wouldn't. They don't talk about it, and you weren't here," Charlie explained. I just stared at the floor.

"Relax, Astrid, everything will work out fine." Francis nodded to me.

"You're on call tonight, right?" Charlie said.

"Yeah."

"Well why don't you go catch some sleep, we'll grab an energy bar and coffee."

"I don't know if I can."

"They've already fed tonight, chances are we won't find them and give up soon."

"Charlie."

"Tom will be angry with us and you if you don't take care of yourself and if we didn't encourage you to."

"Not us, just you," Francis told Charlie. "Tom swore you to protect and watch out for her, not me."

"Tom did what?" I asked, quite taken aback.

"It's fine, we're like brothers Tom and I. It's nothing weird, he just trusts me and wants to make sure you don't get hurt with all your reckless human tendencies."

"Okay... I can't take any more tonight. Help yourselves to whatever you want, I'm going to bed." I grabbed my pager and went to bed, folding my clothes next to me in case I needed them again in the middle of the night.

"Hey, I didn't mean to wake you," my husband said, crawling into bed beside me as I turned towards the rustling that had woken me.

"What time is it? Did you just get in?"

"It's three a.m. Charlie said you went to bed. I've been back and forth a couple times."

"Any sign of anything?"

"Unfortunately not," he said, pulling me against him and resting my head on his shoulder.

"That good or bad?"

"Neither, now go back to sleep." He gently kissed me before laying back himself.

"I don't understand why we're here," Terri said.

"Because the Alphas demanded that we convene here tonight," I told her. I was secretly cursing Tom and Jared for deciding to go on a quick patrol of the surrounding couple of blocks and leaving me at home as the pack filed into mine and Tom's home. This wasn't Sanctuary, forty-eight adult pack members in my living room was a lot.

"Spoken like a true Beta's Bride," Allain nodded to me. "Just keep them in check until Tom and Jared get here." He lowered his voice.

"Oh, that'll be easy, I'm the smallest one in the room and the only human. Plus, they don't have to listen to me." I pointed out.

"They're in your home and you speak for Tom and Jared in their absence."

"Allain, do you know what is going on? Why are we here?" Faelen demanded. The man in his fifties was graying at the side, the graying barely noticeable in his sandy hair. Tall, he was lanky like the others, but he was showing evidence of his age around the middle.

"I do not know, and it isn't my place to say even if I did."

"Well, you know." He turned on me. His face was stoic and intimidating.

The room was filling, Charlie was manning the door letting everyone in.

"Look," I raised my voice, sitting up on the counter, trying to gain some height and dominance over the room. "I understand all of you are anxious and confused, but we have to wait for Tom and Jared. Now, please just be patient." The room was predominantly made up of men, with only a small smattering of women here and there.

I was pleased when the room went quiet.

"Everyone is here." Charlie came up beside me, leaning on one elbow.

"Except..." I drawled out.

"They're making sure everyone is safe, they'll be here any minute."

Voices were starting to raise again when they finally decided to arrive. My husband gave me a knowing look and smiled. "Thank you all for coming," Tom said, walking over to stand on my other side.

"Why are we here?" Ragnor asked. "Your wife wouldn't tell us anything."

"And she was right not to," Jared answered for Tom, at the same time Charlie and Francis moved out the back window. I jumped down off the counter and moved to the other side of my husband, as Contessa finished slipping on her sundress and stood to Jared's side.

"We have disturbing news to share," Tom told his family.

"There appears to be a pyre in town," Jared told them, a murmur went through the pack. "So far there has been a civilian casualty and one near fatality, who was saved by our own Beta's Bride, because of her quick thinking, she was able to get Francis to look over the body before too much of the material we needed was destroyed."

"What do we do?" Landry wanted to know.

"Same things as always. I will be setting up pre-dawn and twilight patrols. There will be no pups under twenty-four on any patrols, and if you do see anything, you are not to engage, you are to get Tom or myself."

"How long?"

"Until we are sure they are done passing through and are gone. This is pack territory; we have protected rights by the council. I'm sure once we explain the situation they'll leave. In the meantime we do not want an interspecies war."

"If we see them attacking a human?" Ragnor said, and I could tell that he was itching to get his hands dirty.

"No! Absolutely not. We all know how feral a pyre is mid feed, you will not engage," Tom said picking up the same feeling I had.

"You can consider that an order," Jared punctuated. "There will also be a curfew for all shea and children, between sunset and rise, unless they're at Sanctuary."

"You cannot be serious," Terri said from the back of the room: Terri a bitch and a brunette, who fortunately makes me not the palest person in the pack.

"You all work in the firm, it will not be a hardship," Tom told her. "Plus, it's for your safety."

"I'm assuming the same is being expected of your wife," Stephan — Terri's husband — demanded.

"My wife is none of your concern," Tom growled.

"Precautions have already been put in place, given the nature of her employment. We require the information she can provide so, we cannot expect the same, but that doesn't mean she's not given restrictions," Jared said, attempting to diffuse the situation. However, I was suddenly very curious as to my new restrictions, but figured now was not the best time to voice my objections and confusion.

"Tomorrow you will all have your orders sent to your phones, tell your families, warn them, and be careful," Tom demanded of all of them.

"Now, I would like to give a quick prayer to the beasts," Jared said. Everyone bowed their heads except Contessa and I who each proceeded to kneel low beside our husbands, our hands held upwards to the sky. I was certainly getting better at knowing my duties as the Beta's Bride and didn't need so many hints. "We thank the great Phoenix and Wolf for protecting us thus far, and pray that they continue to have mercy on their children as we maneuver our way through this perilous and difficult time."

"Y ffenics a'r blaidd mawr," I said in Welsh, as everyone else sang 'the great Phoenix and Wolf.' Our husbands offered Contessa and I each their hand for us to get up.

"Go home, be with your families, and if you have any concerns, feel free to ask." Jared nodded. Many nodded back, and with a few short goodbyes left.

A few conversations looking for details we didn't have were struck, but I just remained silent.

"I know what you are thinking about," Tom said, as what's left of our meeting left. Contessa and Jared took their leave through the balcony window.

"Oh, do you now?" I asked.

"Astrid, you are wondering about those restrictions Jared mentioned."

"Well, you aren't wrong."

"It's not as bad as it sounds."

"Okay, prove it."

"Astrid," he warned, turning towards me.

"Yes."

"You knew what you were getting into when you joined the family. So when you're not working or on call the same curfew applies to you. If you are working at night, someone will escort you there and back, and we will have regular patrols at the hospital. You will also be required to check in with me."

"Tom, I'll be at work, I'll be safe."

"I will be the judge of that."

"Well, that's not good."

"And why is that?"

"You have a few overprotective tendencies," I told him.

"What can I say? I protect what is mine."

Chapter 11

"What's going on?" I asked the nurses at the station, who were huddled around whispering.

"You haven't heard?"

"Heard what?" I demanded.

"The blood bank here at the hospital was broken into last night. Apparently, something like fifty bags were stolen."

"But how? It's behind a locked door and then you need codes to get into the lockers."

"Door was kicked in and apparently the machine was ripped open."

"I'm assuming the police are involved."

"They are."

"Good. So we should continue our work, not worry about it. I'm sure between the hospital, their security cameras and the police they'll get it dealt with."

"I'm sure you're right," they nodded getting up. I walked down the hall, dialed the first number in my phone.

"Hey?"

"Hi, did you hear?"

"Hear what?"

"Blood bank was broken into last night. So I'm thinking it might be a good time to visit your wife at work."

"I'll bring lunch, it'll provide a good excuse for why I'm there."

"Perfect."

"Hey," he said as I met him at the hospital door a little later.

"Hi." I smiled. "How's your day going?"

"Well it was uneventful."

"Never a dull moment where we're involved." I smiled at my husband.

"Well, I have to admit, I am looking forward to it calming down anytime now." He followed me down the wide corridors.

"Patience," I told him.

"So what can you tell me about the robbery?"

"I can tell you that it shouldn't have happened," I told my husband.

"Meaning?"

"It's a heavy steel door with an intricate locking system, you need codes to get into the lockers."

"I'll have to take a look."

"I know, just be sneaky about it," I warned. "It is a crime scene, and there is restricted access to this part of the hospital."

"Understood — don't get my wife fired."

"That would be appreciated, it's just around the corner."

Even though the room was roped off, Tom was able to get a good look at it. "Let's go eat," Tom said when he was finished. His face was unreadable. But this wasn't the place for him to explain it to me. People were around. 'I think it was a pyre', probably wasn't the best thing to be said here. He took my hand and I guided him to a lounge where we would be alone.

"You going to clue me in?" I asked, sitting down.

"It's not just one," Tom said.

"One pyre?" I felt my body stiffen and a small bead of anxious perspiration formed on my forehead.

"Precisely… its two, there were two sets of hands used to prise the door open. How much was stolen?"

"From what I've heard, a rough estimate… fifty bags."

"They're not passing through," he declared, his lips pursed and brow furrowed.

"So these restrictions aren't going anywhere?" I observed.

"No, they're not."

I closed my eyes, taking a bite of the sandwich he had gotten me. Roasted vegetables and goat cheese from Vinny's around the corner from the firm.

"Look, I hate to do this, but I have to talk to Jared. Charlie will pick you up and drive you to Sanctuary after work."

"Tom, it will still be daylight."

"Please, Astrid. Do this for me."

"Okay," I conceded.

"Plus, I hear they have a surprise for you."

When Tom said there was a surprise for me waiting at Sanctuary he wasn't kidding. The clinic was now a finished building with wood paneling outside and large windows. My office resembled a gorgeous conservatory, with its couple feet of wall before wall-to-wall windows. It was beautiful, the gutters perfectly matched the paneling and the roof of darker wood shingles topped off the building. Tom and Jared met me at the path and insisted that I followed them.

"It's beautiful, I love how well it matches." I felt my eyes tear looking at it.

"It's sort of the theme, we're well practiced." Charlie smiled at me.

"Can I see inside?"

"Of course, it's your building." Jared's gaze didn't waiver from the clinic. "Plus, we've already got everything you had in storage set up inside."

"I have to say, I love the sound of that... it's mine."

We went through everything; it was immaculate and everything was laid out exactly as I had imagined it and planned it. I'm sure over time I would organize things as I figured out what works best for me. But for now, I was in awe of my rooms and technology.

"You had a say in the decorating of this, didn't you?" I said, squeezing Tom's hand in the doorway of my modern office, yet it reflected the outside amicably.

"They just asked for some advice on my wife's tastes."

"I'll have to thank everyone tonight."

"I think that would be a nice gesture," Tom agreed.

"I had a little input in it as well," Jared said, sitting down on my new sofa. "I had them build the built-in bookshelves, and added all of the books that I could find."

"Books?"

"We have a few more on old pack medicines and anatomy, but we haven't had anyone who knows what to do with the information before now."

"You know I'm not a veterinarian, right?" I joked.

"Just take a look and see what you can figure out from what you're reading," he smiled.

"Will do." I nodded.

"We'll let you enjoy it for a little bit, okay?" Tom kissed my head before they left me with the only thing I have ever been proud to call mine. Other than my husband — of course. I skimmed through the shelves of books, then opened a filing cabinet to find the records of every member of the pack. Okay, this was pretty cool. So I picked up Lorelai's — if there was anything to be found, or a clue, hopefully this would point me in the right direction.

"Think I could be your first patient?" Laura asked, knocking on my office door. "I know you're just getting settled." My head snapped up as she claimed my attention.

"Hey, come on in," I said, putting down and closing the file. "What's the problem?"

"So, I told you, Markus and I have been trying to conceive for a while," she said.

"Yes, I remember," I said.

"Well, I think maybe, but I don't want to get my hopes up."

"Come with me," I said, standing up.

I pulled the curtain around the bed after pulling up the ultrasound machine. "This will be a little chilly," I said, squirting the gel on her abdomen.

"Ah…" she gasped.

"I warned you," I smiled, using the wand to move the gel around.

"Is that what you call bedside manner?"

"Thought you'd appreciate the humour," I said, pushing a few buttons on the machine.

"Astrid," she smiled. I moved the wand re-adjusting the angle on her pelvis until we heard a little noise.

"Laura, I think you should probably call Markus," I smiled.

"Why?"

"Because… that is your baby's heartbeat."

"Oh my god," she breathed.

"Call him while I take a couple quick measurements."

"Markus," I heard her breathe. "Can you come to the clinic?" there was a short pause. "Because I said to." I don't know what he said but she hung up.

"Laura?" I heard Markus call a minute later.

"In here," she called.

"What's going on?" he asked, moving the curtain, taking in me and his wife.

Laura looked at me. "Don't look at me, you tell him," I said, moving to bring the heartbeat back up.

"We're pregnant," she told her husband.

"What?" he said and the heartbeat suddenly drove home the words.

"Yep."

"After so long?"

"Yeah."

"Do you know how far along?" Markus asked his wife, my presence all but forgotten. Laura looked at me.

"Because we found the heartbeat on the ultrasound, I'd say somewhere after nine weeks."

"Nine weeks?"

"Yeah, but I'll need to run a couple tests."

"Would you like to see your baby?"

"Please," Laura said.

I angled the screen towards them and pointed out the little person in her belly.

"Wow," Markus said, grabbing his wife's hand.

"Yeah."

"How was your first day in your clinic?" Tom asked when I finally made it home for dinner, after running a small armament of tests on Laura; I knew basically nothing about her medical history, and if I was going to be her OB, my word, I was going to need to know exactly what I was dealing with.

"Amazing," I smiled.

"Did you get much accomplished?"

"Well, I managed a bit of reading and I had my first patient."

"Well, that's both surprising and unsurprising. Is it anything I should know about?"

"First of all, doctor—patient confidentiality, second you'll find out tonight."

"What?"

"Just trust me." I leaned up, kissing his cheek, he had to bend to meet me.

"Okay," Tom shook his head directing his attention back to the stove.

"You really should allow me to cook for you more often," I said to my husband.

"Look, darling, I love you but you really should stick to what you're good at."

"Surgery."

"And chemistry."

"Isn't cooking chemistry?"

"Chemistry one doesn't have to eat," he clarified and I smirked at him dejectedly. Let's face it my husband could cook, and it was delicious every time. Where a compliment for my food would be that it was edible.

Tom made something called Jeera Chicken — his contained chicken mine was tofu — and rice for dinner; it was spicy but delicious. Apparently, he'd found a new cookbook with a bunch of new Middle Eastern and Indian dishes and was excited to try many of them.

"Tonight, we are again calling to the beasts of the sky to continue to watch over us. We have been fortunate that there haven't been any incidents over the last week. However, we received some disturbing news today, on what should have been a joyous occasion. It does not appear that this threat is merely passing through, which is why we will be encouraging the pack to spend as much time here at Sanctuary as they can. We have been reaching out to neighbouring packs. But before we get to our circle for tonight, Astrid has requested to say a few words."

Jared nodded to me and Tom put a supportive hand on my back as I stepped forward. "I'm going to keep this short and sweet," I promised. "I wanted to tell all of you how honoured and thankful I am for the support on the clinic, especially those who helped to build it during this uncertain time. Please, all of you feel free to come to me. One of you already has, with a fantastic outcome," I said, smiling at Laura, and everyone turned.

"We're pregnant," she announced for herself and Markus.

Every person in the circle smiled, a few clapped and those closest to them hugged them both. Markus and Laura were getting into their mid-thirties. So the happiness was genuine among the entire pack.

"That's what you weren't telling me?" Tom said only to me as I stepped back.

"She wanted to tell the pack all together."

"You did good." He kissed my temple, I melted into the praise watching the smiles on Laura and Markus's faces as they were congratulated by the pack.

"Now we have more to thank the gods for tonight. A child to two of our most deserving pack members and friends," Jared said, beaming at them. "We pray the gods watch over this woman and child, as they grow together."

The circle was so much slower tonight. It felt like Jared was really trying to draw out the power of the gods, to change what we couldn't and make this danger plaguing us disembark. But try as I could to believe that the gods would help us, I knew we'd have to help ourselves.

Chapter 12

With my clinic newly ready I was disappointed when I had to go back to work the next day. It was quiet for the majority of the week, nobody else was found drained or attacked. My guess, this was due to their little stockpile of blood bags. It was like everything had gone quiet. With few emergencies, I was able to perform a number of scheduled surgeries. But work was better than being home. Tom was never home any more, always out patrolling or taking point. This turned my job into my solace for the first time since before the trial.

With everything being so quiet, when something unusual finally did happen, it went right through the hospital grapevine. It's worse when it's a young woman. Today was worse again. At least it was for me. "A young woman was found unconscious in a car in the parking lot," Cora said to me as I wondered what had happened. I'd been paged and was rushing to the room.

"Do we know who she is?" I asked, throwing on a gown and gloves

"No idea, there was no I.D. and she was unconscious."

"Great, you're here already," Dr. Lewis said, peeking her head out of the door as I moved towards the room.

"Where do you…" I stopped.

"Dr. Davis, is everything okay?"

"Laura? Laura," I cried, grabbing her face. "Can you hear me?" I demanded.

"Do you know this woman?"

"Yes, her name is Laura Forestal, she's a family friend," I said. "Can I have a mobile ultrasound in here, now please," I called to the nurses' station.

"Dr. Davis?"

"She's pregnant," I said.

"How far?"

"About eleven weeks; I did an ultrasound a couple of weekends ago."

"Dr. Davis, are you too close to this? Do you need to step away?" Dr. Lewis asked.

"No, I'm in, this one. What are we looking at?"

"Well, as you know, she is unconscious but breathing on her own, pupils are even and equal. Her abdomen is rigid, I also suspect a number of fractures in her leg, but we won't know for sure."

"Here you go, Dr. Davis." A nurse wheeled in the cart.

I turned it on and waved it over her stomach. "There is definitely a fetal heartbeat," I proclaimed. "But I also see blood in the belly. Okay, that's it, we have to move," I said raising the rails.

"Call the OR and tell them we're on our way up," Dr. Lewis demanded. "Dr. Davis, do you have anyone you need to call? If you do, call them now and scrub in."

"I will be there in two minutes," I said. I rushed my phone out of my pocket.

"Hey, babe," he said.

"Look Tom, Laura has just been brought in unconscious, and severely beaten, we're rushing her into surgery right now,"

"Laura Forestal?" he asked, more in shock than anything else.

"Yeah, look I am sorry, I have to get in there, but I would recommend that you get her family here. I'll update you when I can."

"Astrid, save her, okay?"

"I'm going to do everything I can," I promised. The scrubbing in was the longest two minutes of my life. But by the time I was in the operating theatre she was hooked up to machines and tubes and the anesthesiologist had her well sedated. Her heart rate was clear on the screen, and I thanked my lucky stars she was a shea and her heart rate reflected that of a mortal. Blood was being prepared nearby.

"Ready?" Dr. Lewis asked me and the other doctor assisting on the surgery. We both nodded as betadine was rubbed along her torso. Opening her, it surprised no one that blood was welling in her stomach.

It was three hours before we had things under control and we had the bleeding repaired, the blood being in the way had made it more difficult, but once we figured out where it was coming from, it was a simple fix. The mobile X-ray looked at the leg and she had a minor ankle fracture, which we were going to set and deal with as soon as we had her settled.

"Her family is here and getting anxious. One man in particular is getting particularly difficult. I was wondering if we have an update yet," a nurse popped into the operating room.

"Is his name Jared?" I asked.

"Yeah, or something like that," she said.

"He's my brother-in-law, don't worry, his bark is worse than his bite." I laughed at my personal joke.

"Astrid, we're going to be closing up now, why don't you go update your family, I'll page you when she is in her room," Dr. Lewis said.

"Thanks," I said, stripping off my surgical gown, booties, mask and gloves, leaving the sterile zone. I scrubbed out and made my way to the waiting room.

"Is that really your family," Kelly an administrative assistant asked, just before I got into the waiting room's line of sight.

"Yes, they are. I'm sorry if they gave you a hard time."

"Don't worry about it, they're just scared, I am used to it."

"Thanks." I smiled. "I'll talk to them. They're my family. If anyone can calm them it's me with the news I have."

I walked around the back of the desk and through the door. When they spotted me they all stood up. "Astrid, what's happening?" her husband asked, Tom and Jared on either side of him.

"She's okay," I announced, my eyes skimming along the number of other members of the pack all waiting for good news. "Laura came in with quite a bad abdominal bleed but we have it completely under control. Myself, Dr. Lewis and Dr. Heinrick have insured that there aren't any other life threatening issues. She has a broken ankle but it's not bad. There aren't any signs of a brain injury, we will still be monitoring her just to be safe. She isn't out of the woods yet, but we're optimistic."

"Oh, thank you, Astrid." Markus grabbed my shoulders and pulled me into a big hug.

"Hey, I'm just thankful I was here."

"And the baby?" he asked, watching my eyes.

"She is still early in the pregnancy, and Laura has experienced severe abdominal trauma, so we will be monitoring the baby closely, right now he or she is okay, but the next twenty-four hours will be crucial."

"Can I see her?"

"Right now she is still being closed, once she is in the ICU I'll know, and as soon as you can see her I'll come get you." I promised squeezing his upper arm.

"I understand, thank you."

"Tom and Jared, can I talk to you a moment?" I motioned to the other side of the room.

They looked at each other, then they followed me.

"The police have already been called, it's out of my hands. We're legally required to call them in cases like these."

"It's not good, but we can probably handle it," Jared said.

"What do you know? Was it a pyre?" Tom asked me, lowering his voice.

"It doesn't appear that way, there were no cuts, or puncture wounds. Other than some internal bleeding there was no blood loss. So there isn't much to tell unfortunately. I know that she was left outside of the hospital, that is the way she was found. In my professional opinion, the ankle fracture looks like she twisted it in a high heel, and I know I don't know Laura as well as the rest of you do, but it doesn't sound like her, does it? Just falling like that?"

"No, it doesn't, even if she had, her advanced reflexes as a shea would have kept this from escalating this badly," Tom said.

"The abdominal damage was too severe; this wasn't an accident."

"But who would want to hurt Laura?"

"I don't know but I am going to have to talk to Markus and Francis." Jared just turned on his heels.

"Thanks," Tom said to me.

"I'm going to see what's happening, I'll let you know things as I hear them," I promised.

"Have I ever told you how amazing you are?" Tom said as I curled into his side at the end of the night.

"Yes, but I never get tired of hearing it." I smiled.

"You're amazing." He kissed the top of my head.

"I only did what I could," I promised.

"Jared will never admit it, but you did the right thing today, by calling me."

"Thanks, I debated calling her husband directly but figured you'd have more success."

"You were right, thank you. She is going to be okay, right?"

"We've done everything we can. The additional tests we ran today were all clear so that is always a good sign; we're keeping her sedated for a couple of days. Then she won't be allowed to leave the hospital until after she can walk by herself and her pain is managed. Even after that she won't be allowed to do anything for about five weeks. There's a greater risk of complications with the pregnancy, even with her being shea."

"Okay."

"Don't worry I am going to be watching her like a hawk. If I get the slightest inkling something is wrong, I'll be on top of it."

"Want to know something I noticed today, for the first time?"

"What's that?"

"You sounded like a member of the pack, like what happened mattered and they were your family and not just your in-laws."

"They are," I said.

"I am sure everyone was thankful for you today."

"I was doing my job."

"All the same."

"Jared's here," Tom said to me without looking up when I got home the next day. The sun had already gone down and I wondered who had been responsible for following me home, considering Tom and Jared's were current positions, reclined in my living room.

"I see that," I said, grabbing a glass of water and sitting down with them.

"I want to talk to you about moving Laura."

"Laura Forestal, the woman who was severely beaten yesterday, had surgery and whom I currently have in a medically induced coma," I asked, and noticed a slight smirk and a raised eyebrow from Tom. This is why he warned me Jared was here.

"Yes, that one."

"Do I need something other than water for this conversation?" I asked my husband, whose response was to hand me his drink. *Great,* I thought, taking a large mouthful. "So where exactly do you want to move her to?"

"We built you a clinic, use it."

"Jared, that clinic, though a great idea and something that we will be able to use, is not suitable in this situation. Laura is better off where she is. She isn't a shifter; her healing is only slightly quicker."

"But we have you."

"And when I'm not there, what if something happens? At least at the hospital if something happens and I am not there, there are others that can help her."

"She's safer at Sanctuary."

"If you're worried about the pyres, there are shifters and security at the hospital twenty-four seven."

"I want her moved," Jared said very slowly.

"With all due respect, she is my patient. She is in critical condition and a coma. I will not risk her life or the life of the baby to move her to appease your need to keep everyone under your thumb."

"I'll have Markus have her transferred."

"You can try," I said.

"Excuse me?" He stood up.

"Oh you heard me." I squared up to the Alpha who stood a foot and a half above me. "You have no authorization to do so. Markus would have to have a private facility to transfer her to, and as the owner of said facility, I say 'no'. In two days, I will take her off the sedation — if I think she is ready — and we can re-open this discussion. In the meantime, if you still plan on getting Markus to have her moved, I will put Markus on a psychiatric hold, for trauma, and you will have two pack members you can't move."

"What makes you think you can say this to me?"

"A medical degree. I understand you want your pack where you can keep them safe, but right now it's my job to keep Laura safe, and to insure she's getting the best medical attention available."

"We will be revisiting this when she wakes up."

"Understood," I said. He turned on his heels and moved to the balcony.

"I'm going to be in so much trouble for that later," I said, sitting back down, and taking another large mouthful of Tom's drink.

"Yeah, he's not used to being stood up to or not getting his own way."

"Fantastic."

"But…" he smiled. "It was incredibly attractive, watching you stand your ground like that. Not just because of your stature, but because he's the Alpha, and you still chose to do what is best for her not him." Tom's fingers traced my face and held my eyes with his.

"Was it? Because it was terrifying for me." I would have said more but Tom had apparently found another use for my lips; and just like that, my little confrontation was long forgotten.

"Hey, Charlie," I called, sitting on the deck at the pavilion drinking a cup of coffee, observing the comings and goings of the pack as they moved from place to place and the kids played a hilarious version of tag.

"Hey, Little Beta," he said from below the deck.

"Hey, Charlie, can you come here for a moment, I have a proposition for you," I said.

"Okay," he said, curious as he took the stairs two at a time.

"What's up, Astrid?" he asked.

"Can you build a dock?"

"A what…?"

"Well, not so much a dock, but a floating platform?"

"A what?"

"Charlie," I said, shaking my head.

"Okay, well no, but I mean I have built buildings and you know an entire medical clinic, so it probably won't be that difficult."

"Well, I have done some research, and I thought maybe it would be something that the kids would really enjoy?"

"Okay, and you know what we need?"

"Sure," I said, pulling out the instructions that I had printed off from online, "cement, buckets, chains, barrels, I was thinking maybe a slide, and we have so much wood left over, do you think there is enough for an eight by eight-foot platform, and a ladder?"

"I think some different wood would be better for the ladder and we might need some brackets, but it's doable."

"Feel like a Saturday afternoon project?"

"Seriously?"

"Oh yes. I'll help?" I clapped, enthusiastically.

"And how much help will you be exactly?"

"Okay, not a lot, but I am willing to take direction, and I'm a surgeon, how much harder can it be?"

"I am not answering that." Charlie made a mocking frown and shook his head at me.

"Come on, it'll be fun! The kiddos will love it and Uncle Charlie will be a hero."

"Okay, fine. Let's do it."

"Yes," I said, jumping up. "You own the big truck, right?"

"Yeah."

"Will it hold what we need?"

"Probably not, I'll hook up a trailer and well go."

"Fantastic," I said. "Just let me tell Tom where I am going and I'll be right there."

"Sounds good, I'll meet you in the parking lot."

"I'll be two minutes, I also need my purse."

"Sure thing, little lady, I'll be sure not to leave until you get there." He winked at me, jumping over the deck railing and casually walking to his cottage. Show off, I smiled to myself, rolling my eyes.

Tom was in the pavilion working on something for the pack this morning with Jared, so after I deposited the cup in the dishwasher, I turned to him and Jared sitting at the kitchen island, a pile of papers between them.

"Can we help you?" Jared asked, looking up from his papers to me, our argument from the other night clearly not forgotten. Even though Laura was now awake, I still wasn't moving her until the end of the weekend at the earliest, an opinion that wasn't making me very popular with my brother-in-law.

"Yeah, I'm just letting Tom know I am heading out but I shouldn't be long."

"Uh… where are you going?"

"To a hardware store… with Charlie."

"Okay." He smiled. "Let me know when you're back. Have fun."

"Will do, love you!" I cajoled.

"Love you too, baby girl." He turned back to his papers. I firmly shut the patio door behind me as I left. It took me no time at all as I retrieved my purse before taking the familiar path to the lot.

"Ready?" Charlie asked from the driver's side window, his truck already connected to the trailer.

"You know normal people have cars people can actually get into," I said, heaving myself into the truck.

"Normal people aren't five foot two," he said.

"Thanks, Charlie." I rolled my eyes.

"So, should I ask?"

"What?"

"Why do you want to build this?"

"Do I need a reason?"

"Sort of, no one has thought of it before, and if they have, they've never done anything about getting one built."

"It was something I used to do back home. There was this huge lake everyone used to swim in, we'd have dock wars, biggest splash and diving competitions. I thought there are so many kids here, maybe they'd love it too."

"You have a big heart."

"I don't, I'm just trying to thank everyone."

"Nah, your heart was waiting for a family."

"You're very observant, you know that?" I said to the burly man, who was not known for his intellectual fortitude.

"People don't always notice me, they know I am there, but they're never worried about me, they let their guard down. I don't know why, I'm just one of those presences."

"So?"

"It allows me to see; look at Tom for example, he gives this persona of being strong and confident, but he is dependent, he is careful. Believe me when I say he was lost before you."

"What about me?"

"You're harder, you're hiding something. I still don't know what but you are running from something. You also have this immense capacity to care. You see everyone as being deserving of respect and you are determined to see the good in everyone. I think it's something so deeply ingrained in you even you don't understand it."

"Jared?"

"Nah, you and I both know you already have Jared pinned."

"Charlie?"

"Yeah?"

"No one ever gives you enough credit you know that?"

"I am not looking for credit," he said, watching the tree lined road. "But it's still nice to hear. Thank you."

"Any time, Charlie."

"So, how are things going at the clinic?"

"Slow, but I am working on some things that might be useful eventually. Lots of tonic, salves and traditional remedies that Jared gave me."

"And Laura?"

"Well, we're not discharging her yet. We want to make sure that her and the baby are completely out of the woods and everything has healed."

"But?"

"With her having a doctor in the family, as soon as she is stable I'll probably push to get her discharged so she can come here and I'll handle everything from the clinic. Just don't tell Jared I said that."

"Why not?"

"We're sort of arguing."

"About?"

"My refusal to transfer Laura on Jared's command."

"Woah. Can't imagine that going down very well."

"It's not, but as soon as I think it's safe, I will."

"Well, that's good at least, I'm sure that she and Markus would prefer to be here than in the city."

"I know they would, you forget I am dealing with them every day. Neither of them are quiet about voicing their displeasure at having to be there."

"Well, as much as I don't blame them, I do encourage you keeping her there as long as required."

"Thanks, Charlie," I said, appreciative that someone was understanding I wasn't just keeping them there out of some sick, sadistic enjoyment, as he parked the truck.

The salesman was helpful with figuring out everything that we were going to need before helping us cart it out to the car and loading it; not that Charlie really required much help, but let's face it, beyond the couple of bags of smaller items I wasn't really of the greatest assistance. After much discussion with the salesman it was decided that we would use a number of cylinder blocks instead of barrels of concrete to anchor the platform.

"Have to say, I am looking forward to the kids' faces when we drag this through Sanctuary," Charlie said.

"Me too."

The drive was quieter on the way back, maybe Charlie was thinking, maybe we were all talked out.

"Charlie, what are you doing?" I asked as he drove right through the parking lot but stuck to the edge of the woods.

"How else did you think we were going to get the supplies to the lake?"

"I hadn't really thought about it actually," I said.

"Well, here we go."

"Okay, well this definitely works," I said, holding the handle above the window.

"I thought so." I heard Charlie's low throaty chuckle.

I was quite happy when we were stopped, the bouncy trip was getting to me. "Let's get her unloaded and we can get the wood."

"Okay," I said beginning the unloading process. As we were doing so, Colby came over.

"Hey, what's going on?" Colby asked.

"Beta's Bride's got me working on another project," Charlie said to the eighteen-year-old boy with shaggy, dirty-blond hair and green eyes.

He stood almost as tall as Charlie, but was lankier, though I had a feeling that when the time came, he would fill out.

"Would you like a hand?"

"Sure." Charlie nodded. "Astrid said she'd help, but I'm sure the extra hand from someone who knows the difference between a wrench and a hammer is going to be appreciated," he said for my benefit and no one else's.

"Thanks, Charlie," I scoffed pursing my lips.

"Help us unload the truck and trailer," Charlie ignored me and said to the boy, who like Charlie made too light work of unloading the heavy items from the truck bed and trailer.

"Is there anything I can do where I won't get in the way?" I asked.

"Depends on what you can lift?"

"I'll get the bags."

"Hey, Colby, why don't you jump in and we'll go get the wood and tools."

"Hey, I'm coming," I said, irritated that they were ignoring me from my own project.

"Then hop in," Colby said, offering me his hand which I took graciously.

"Look, Charlie, he's capable of being a gentleman."

"Colby, stop making me look bad," Charlie whined.

"You don't need any help with that," he said, stretching out along the back-bench seat of the truck.

I heard Charlie growl, "Okay, boys, play nice." I giggled. Colby mimicked me with his own laughter.

"Think you two can handle loading the trailer with wood while I gather the tools we're going to need?" Charlie asked, putting the truck in park.

"I think we'll manage," I said, disgruntledly getting out of the truck.

"Colby, make sure she doesn't hurt herself; Tom is not going to be happy if she does."

"Charlie," I said in a tone that told him to watch it.

I saw Colby purse his lips but say nothing. Colby uncovered the wood pile as Charlie went into the tool shed. Colby was much quicker than I was at loading the trailer, with armfuls at a time. I was slower with only a few boards at a time.

"I'm so used to being around our family all the time that I forget about the difference in ours and human strength," Colby said.

"Yeah, unfortunately us humans don't quite have the same abilities, but we manage all the same." I laughed.

"As far as I can tell you aren't one to shy away from a little hard work."

"Nah, never had a problem with that."

"So, I have a good idea about what we are about to make, care to clue me in?"

"We're building a floating dock for the kids to play on. From my first day here, I thought it was a shame the kids didn't have one already."

"Don't you have anything more important to do?"

"Nah, there's so much time to do things for the clinic. I can't spend all of my time holed up in the room, I need to do other things."

"What if something comes up?"

"They'll find me and if they can't, I have my phone, everyone has my number."

"Fair enough," he said, sitting on the tailgate of the truck beside me as we waited for Charlie to finish collecting the tools, having already loaded the wood into the trailer.

"So you're going to help?"

"Of course, it was my idea, I want to see it through, plus, I'm not just going to get someone else to do it for me."

"Isn't that what happened with the clinic?"

"That was different, Jared ordered that, and paid for the time, never mind the fact I've never built anything before."

"And you want to build a dock, ever think of maybe starting with a bird house?"

"Colby come give me a hand," we heard Charlie call from the shed saving Colby from my sarcastic response. Colby shrugged, getting up, but I stayed where I was, leaning back on my hands, facing the warm sun; it felt amazing on my face and shoulders.

"You get the feeling that this is going to be what to expect from her this afternoon?" Charlie asked.

"Nah, she wants to help," Colby said as I straightened up glaring at Charlie. They carried a saw between them; in their other hands were bags and an interesting case.

I moved as they deposited them in the bed of the truck. They ducked into the shed one more time and came out with a few more tools.

"This should be everything we need," Charlie said, getting in the truck, "coming, little lady?"

"I think I'll walk this time, I'll meet you down there," I said. It wasn't a long walk and they wouldn't need me right away. So I took my time walking along the treeline watching the sky and the sun, touching a few trees as I went. Why this seemed to relax me every time I don't know, but the woods felt calm and a quiet energy always gave me something to meld into.

"Connect the extension cord to the outlet on the outside of Francis's house," Charlie said, handing an end of the cord to Colby.

A lot of measuring and prep work were things I was allowed to help with. Basically, holding one end of the measuring tape, while Colby notched off where Charlie was going to cut the wood. Six eight-foot lengths of the thicker wood were cut. Then a number of the thinner wood. To be honest I understood almost nothing that was happening, it was probably better that all I was allowed to do was hold and pass things.

Until they gave up on me… I mean how am I supposed to know the difference between a spanner and a socket wrench. It actually went faster once I was out of the way, so I opted for moral support sitting on a rock. I watched, frequently mentioning that if they needed anything they need only ask. They never asked.

Charlie and Colby were just finishing up attaching the slide to the top of the platform they had built to house it, when Tom and Jared came down to the shore.

"What is going on?" Jared asked.

"We're building a dock for the kids to play on in the lake," I said, getting up and walking over to the two confused looking men.

"We're?" Tom asked.

"Okay, they are. I tried to help, but I was just in the way," I said.

"Little Beta, needs to stick to medicine," Charlie said, standing up and brushing sand off his knees.

"I say that every time she tries to cook," Tom said.

"Okay, stick to what I'm good at… got it." I raised my hands in surrender.

"Is this why you went to the hardware store?" Jared asked.

"Yeah."

"I assumed that you needed something for the clinic."

"Nope, had an idea for something way more fun. Plus, with everything going on, I thought it would be something nice to get our minds off it." I smiled.

"I was worried about you," Tom said, kissing my temple. "You were supposed to let me know when you got back."

"I'm sorry, I forgot, I got invested."

"I see that."

"What do you think?" I asked Tom and Jared, shifting my gaze between them.

"I think the kids will love it," Jared said. "Almost wish I had thought of it, now I can't take the credit, little sister," he winked at me. Oh, little touch of forgiveness there. I smiled.

"I'm sorry, you can if you want to."

"Oh no, I am teasing."

"So, Charlie, is it seaworthy yet?" Tom inquired from his best friend.

"I think so."

"Finally," Colby said, but I could tell he was joking.

"Why don't you go and get some kids together to help christen it," Tom said to me.

"What, you don't think they're going to need me to chaperone the launch?" I stared up at him.

"I'm going to say no."

I let go of my husband's hand. The first house was Carmellia and Francis's, the same house the extension cord was attached to.

"Astrid," Carmellia said surprised, answering my knock.

"Hi, Carmellia, I have a surprise at the lake for the kids, think you could get them changed and meet us down there?"

"Sure," she nodded. The woman still didn't like me, but she seemed to respect the fact that I like her daughters and they'd taken to me.

In the end I'd managed to track down almost all thirteen of the pack kids. Their faces seeing the raft for them made everything worth it. Tom was right, getting them over to see it was a great idea. It was so much fun to watch them. When I leaned into Tom, as we sat watching them, Tom whispered to me. "You did good." I smiled as a peal of laughter came from the water.

"Astrid, do you think we could borrow you for a few minutes," Jared asked, coming up beside Tom and I.

"It's actually why we came down here in the first place," Tom said.

"Sure," I said, as Tom began pulling me towards the pavilion.

"We need your opinion," Jared said sitting down at the table.

"Why mine?"

"Because you have better ties to the human communities."

"Jared, I don't know if you noticed, but I am not really linked too much."

"All the same, we're noticing that high risk victims are being targeted."

"By the pyres?"

"Exactly."

"And you want me to do what?"

"Talk to them, reach out, ask them to call you if they notice someone unusual hanging around or a fellow friend with any unusual wounds."

"Jared."

"This is only one of the steps that we are planning on taking," Tom said.

"We want to take more precautions and steps to make sure everyone remains safe," Jared clarified.

"Meaning?"

"We're going to start training all pups and sheas over the age of eighteen to protect themselves. All pups eighteen and over are going to begin patrolling next week."

"That's great, what do you want me to do?"

"Well, we've decided not to train Lesley, plus she carries a gun anyway."

"Oh, good we're about to start on me now." I crossed my arms.

"We will be training you."

"Jared?"

"You don't have a choice, they've been in town far too long, the men are getting tired. You will still have your protectors when you go to and from work at dark, but Tom needs you safe."

"Okay great, self-defence classes it is."

"Not exactly, I am going to be training you," Tom said. He leaned against the counter across from me.

"And I'm going to help."

"There is more isn't there."

"We need you stockpiling medications and things that we are going to need in the event something happens."

"Understood."

"We are making the announcement today, and a lot of parents are not going to be happy about their sons patrolling, we need you to back us up."

"Why me?"

"Because you are a woman, human, and I think they're starting to really respect you."

"Why me?"

"We don't know, but we think that it has something to do with your selflessness," Jared said.

"Okay."

"Jared wants us to lead the circle tonight."

"Why?"

"It's not unusual, it does happen from time to time," Jared said.

"I am going to be doing the majority anyway."

"Before Tom gets started with the circle, I have a few announcements," Jared began. "We have been taking this threat too lightly. For weeks we have been plagued with the possibility of a run in with these pyres. Tomorrow, anyone eighteen or over will begin training, wolf, shea or otherwise. Exceptions being for the pregnant and the elderly."

"You cannot expect children to be fighting battles and patrolling."

"We are not expecting them to fight the battles for us, we just need some fresher eyes."

"And what exactly are you expecting the sheas to do?"

145

"We will never put our women in danger, but we do expect them to be able to protect themselves. We are not willing to have another Laura situation," Tom said. "All we want is for you to be able to protect yourself."

"What about Astrid," Carmellia said lifting her chin towards me.

"I will be getting self-defense training from Jared and Tom. I am the Beta's Bride and human, which makes me an easy target."

"You'd allow her…"

"We're not allowing her to do this, we discussed it today and she will be doing it," Tom made it perfectly clear.

"The other thing I will be doing is personal fitness tests on everyone, as well as a stress test. The equipment should be in early next week, and it is mandatory," I told the circle.

"The last thing we are doing is a Sanctuary lockdown, every night you have to be here."

"Astrid being the exception again?"

"No," I announced. "I have spoken to my workplace and told them I am having some family issues and can't work nights for a while."

"And they accepted that?"

"They did."

"What about Laura?" Lesley asked.

"She is being transferred here to Sanctuary tomorrow, where I am going to need your help during the day."

"Of course," she nodded.

"Is everything understood?" Jared asked.

The group nodded.

Tom ran the circle, and I went through the motions but my heart wasn't in it. Pyres, really? Laura couldn't have been attacked by the pyre? Is there another threat out there? What if I called Penelope? Then dismissed the idea, she couldn't help me here, and it wouldn't have been fair to expect her to.

"Earth to Astrid, are you still with us?" Tom asked me after the circle closed and everyone broke up without the extra run today.

"Yeah, sorry."

"What is going on in that pretty little head of yours?"

"I'm just trying to think."

"And how is that going for you?"

"I'm trying to figure something out."

"Do I need to know?"

"Not yet," I said as we walked back to our little house.

Once we'd settled, I started sending emails to some of my friends from when I was in university. I gave them a vague description of what to look for.

"I'm stressed," I told Tom sitting up on the bed.

"We all are."

"Tom, what if something happens before we are able to talk to these people?"

"Listen we are not going to worry about that tonight. You have a busy day tomorrow."

"Oh, yes, moving Laura."

"You know it's for the best."

"I know that but I really didn't want to move her without having a choice in the matter."

"It's fine."

"I don't know… I have a weird feeling."

"For now, I think you should ignore it and get some sleep."

"All right."

"Please tell me that that isn't the front door," I said to Tom, listening to the pounding, covering my head with a pillow.

"It is," he said rolling over and getting up.

"It's six o'clock, what could they possibly want?"

"I'll go find out," Tom said.

I started to fall back to sleep when I heard one too many sets of footsteps in the room.

"Jared would like us to go get Laura now," Tom said.

I didn't move. "Tell Jared, that if he doesn't leave and allow me two more hours of sleep, I will leave her in the hospital for another week."

"She's kidding, right?" Jared asked Tom.

"Get out," I told them.

"I'm going to say that she isn't kidding, let's get you out of here."

"I'm telling you, Contessa, you need to get a better handle on your husband. Six this morning, really? The hospital wouldn't have let me take her even if we did show up then. He wants everyone safe. I understand that, but normal people sleep once in a while." I complained.

"Yeah, well he has been sleeping less and less lately."

"Do you think something I can make would help?"

"Nah, he wouldn't take it."

"I'll try and talk to him."

"I don't know if you'll be any more capable of getting through to him than I am."

"Medically I might, also, maybe you're too close to the situation."

"Yeah, but don't you have kind of a turbulent relationship with Jared."

"Yeah, but I think that's what he needs, someone who is going to challenge him."

"Wolf and Phoenix know that I don't and I certainly never get my way."

"I'll try after he's a little happier with the fact that his last two outstanding pack members are safe."

"Let's give it go." She gave me a hug. We took separate cars, Tom and I, and Contessa and Jared.

"What was that about?" Tom asked me once we hit the road.

"Contessa says that Jared isn't handling the whole situation very well."

"And what exactly do you think you two are going to be able to do about it?"

"First I am going to talk to him, then I am going to force him to let me help him."

"You think you can?"

"That depends on how much he lets me."

"Well, so far you're the only person I have ever met that is capable of challenging him and winning."

"He's a sore loser," I mused.

"And yet."

"Hey, he got his way, we are going to go and get Laura against my better judgement."

148

"You know we need to do this though."

"I know."

"What should I expect from this?"

"Not a whole lot. I have already spoken to hospital administrators, I have to sign something, so do Markus and Laura, then we put her in a car and drive her away."

"That's not helpful."

"Well, Tom, I don't know what to tell you, that's as easy as it is going to be."

"Give Contessa your keys," Jared told Tom as we got out of the car in the parking lot.

"Why?"

"When we're leaving, I'll text her and she'll bring the car to the front."

"Shannon will be in the room with Laura and Markus, we just have to meet them there," I told the two men following me.

"Okay."

"Hello, Dr. Davis," Shannon said to me.

"Thank you for helping us with this," I said to the lovely hospital administrator.

"Hey, no problem, I heard that you are still going to be her primary doctor," Shannon said.

"That is right, and don't worry it's strictly on a volunteer basis."

"I am not worried in the least, you wouldn't be the first doctor with privileges in other hospitals that come from us."

As I was signing and filling out the last of the paperwork, Cora came running up the corridor. "Oh, thank god, Dr. Davis."

"Cora?"

"I heard you were here, we need your help."

"I'm supposed to be transferring Mrs. Forestal," I told her.

"I know, but there was another animal attack victim, came in last night. Dr. Crowther operated, but something is wrong and she's not answering her pages. Dr Goulding is trying to handle it, but he is in way over his head, we need a general surgeon."

"What about Dr. Lively?"

"She's not answering her pages."

"Where is the victim now?"

"Goulding is taking her up to surgery."

"Goulding is an orthopedic surgeon,"

"My thoughts exactly."

I turned to my family. "Contact Lesley, she knows what to do to get her settled and tell her to put in an IV. Use the lorazepam to help her sleep. Tom I've told you what to do, you got this."

"What about you?"

"It's daytime, send Charlie to pick me up."

"I'll stay with her, brother." Jared put his hand on Tom's shoulder.

"Okay."

"Please, Dr. Davis," Cora said.

"Tom."

"Go," he said, and I nodded.

"Which OR?"

"Three."

"Thank you, show Jared where he can wait."

"I'll try not to be too long, I promised him."

"Don't worry about it, you're saving lives, take all the time you need."

"Thank you," I nodded before taking off down the stairs beside the nurses' station. I scrubbed quickly after changing into some scrubs that we keep in a cupboard above the sink in case of emergencies such as these.

"Dr Goulding, really?"

"I did the same first couple years as you did."

"Goulding really?"

"He's all yours."

"Thank you."

"Now what happened to this guy?"

"He was attacked by some animal."

"What was done last night?" I demanded.

"We had to amputate the left leg just below the knee, and he was already opened once, we removed the spleen but a few minutes ago he bottomed out and the ultrasound showed more blood," Dr Goulding explained.

150

"His leg was amputated?"

"Yeah, the damage was extensive, there was almost nothing left of the foot."

"Where was he located?"

"Pike Street."

"That's in the center of the city."

"I know."

"So it's an unusual area for an animal to be."

"I know."

"And you're sure it was an animal?"

"Between the claw marks and the roughness around the mostly missing foot."

"Okay, it was an animal."

In the end it wasn't a hard fix, it took about an hour to repair the small bit of perforated bowel before returning him to his room in the ICU.

"How did it go?" Jared asked me when I finally cleaned up and made it to the waiting room.

"It wasn't as bad as I expected it to be," I said, sitting down beside him.

"Astrid, I might not know you like Tom, but something is bothering you."

"The victim was found on Pike Street."

"One of the busiest streets in Seattle, not even a pyre would risk that."

"Jared, it didn't look like the one I patched up that night, and the injuries were too extensive from what I have been told for it to be a pyre."

"Any signs that he fought back."

"Anything like that was probably cleaned off the body. I'm thinking maybe you should take a look, and see what you think."

"Is that okay?"

"If anyone asks, I'll say you have experience hunting, and I was hoping you could give me a better idea of what is doing this."

"But?" he urged.

"As long as you're with me no one will bother."

"Okay, lead the way."

The waiting room was just outside of the ICU, so I didn't have to take him far. I slipped on a pair of gloves and lifted one of the dressings. Jared's face hardened. I set it back and lifted the one on his chest, then finally the leg. "Jared, are you going to tell me?"

"In the car."

"Okay."

"Are you done here?"

"I am."

"Okay let's get going, then."

I followed him to the car; he remained silent which was doing nothing but making me more anxious. "Jared, you're not helping my nerves here," I said as he pulled out of the parking lot.

"Those weren't from a pyre."

"Okay, how do you know that?"

"Pyres like to play with their food, but that was strictly about the kill, and there was no puncture wound, he wasn't fed on."

"Jared?"

"It was a shifter."

"How can you know that?"

"Two different kinds of wounds."

"But they'd have to shift in front of the victim."

"Still no name?"

"None."

"Did you catch any scents?"

"No."

"None?"

"Which is just as worrisome."

"Maybe it was washed off."

"It doesn't work like that. You could take ten showers and I would still be able to smell Tom on you."

"But he's not married to the shifter."

"No, but that's just how it works, supernatural scents are more potent."

"Jared, what are you doing? Where are we going?"

"Pike Street."

"Really?"

"Yeah, I need to see what I can find out."

"In the middle of the city in broad daylight?"

"Yes."

"Okay, what can I do?"

"Keep your eyes open."

"Totally, thought I was supposed to walk around with them closed… my bad?"

"What?"

"It was a joke, I was trying to lighten the mood. Apparently, it didn't work."

"Not really."

"I'm going to call Tom really quick and see how Laura is doing."

"Damn, I should be getting you back to her." Jared said, looking torn between the two situations, and what he should do.

"Jared, don't worry about it, this is important too."

"Hello?" came Tom's voice from the end of the phone.

"Hi, Tom, how's Laura?"

"She's fine, sleeping comfortably."

"Okay, good, we're just dealing with a little errand and we'll be home."

"You're running an errand with Jared?"

"Yeah, don't worry. Everything's okay, we'll be home soon."

"Okay, love you."

"I love you too."

"Laura is asleep."

"I heard."

"You didn't say anything about today's surgery being a shifter-related?"

"No need to worry him, besides, if I did, we both know that the next sentence out of my mouth would be we're headed to the scene of the crime, I'm fine."

"Good call, but still you are going to be with me."

"To the place where a shifter attempted to murder a man," I tacked on.

"I'm going to stop trying now," he smirked.

"Good plan. Now about you?" I began.

153

"What about me?"

"I was talking to Contessa, she says you're not sleeping, which is why I got a little visit at six this morning."

"Don't you think we have bigger things to be worrying about?"

"Not at all, we're stuck in traffic and can't do anything until we get there. You're going to talk to me, because having an overtired, overly stressed Alpha is good for no one. The pack is going through the ringer and we need you to have your head on straight."

"What do you want to know?"

"For now, your sleeping patterns. Are you having a hard time falling asleep?"

"Yes."

"Staying asleep?"

"Yes."

"What's waking you?"

"Anything, it doesn't take much."

"Do you feel like you are on guard all the time?"

"I'm the Alpha, that's my job."

"No, that's every male in Sanctuary's job. You just lead them."

"It's my job to protect the pack."

"And mine."

"Oh yeah, what are you going to do?"

"I'm going to make sure our Alpha doesn't give himself a mental breakdown or heart attack before he turns thirty-five."

"What are you going to do?" This time it was asked more kindly.

"I am going to handle it, but most importantly you are going to take what I give you tonight before going to bed."

"If something happens?"

"If something actually happens you will wake but I'm sure nothing is going to happen, but you have to sleep."

"Okay."

"Good." We parked a block from the street, getting parking in the city is so hard, that anything would have been considered good. "What am I looking for?"

"Anything that looks related or out of place." Jared instructed, we walked up and down the street a few times but we weren't finding anything.

"There's nothing."

"No scents?"

"None. Not shifter or otherwise." I could tell Jared was confused. "I don't understand it," I offered.

"Neither do I."

"I think we should just get home."

"I agree."

"What are we going to tell Tom?"

"While you are checking on Laura, I'll brief him."

"If you are sure, once I am sure Laura is good, I'll bring you that tonic and we'll head home."

"Astrid."

"Look, you may be the Alpha but I am a doctor, a title I have earned, and I say you need to sleep."

"Yes, ma'am," he mocked.

During the drive home my mind couldn't help but run away with me, everything seemed so odd. So now there was a shifter in the area that has gone rogue, what was I supposed to do with that information?

"Thanks for the ride and sticking around, Jared."

"Of course."

I headed up the path to the clinic and he went to the pavilion.

"Hey, how'd that go?"

"Surgery went well but you need to go and talk to Jared."

"Why?"

"He'll explain it to you."

"I'm just going to check on Laura, give her a couple things and I'll be right behind you."

"Okay." He kissed my head.

"How are things going in here?" I asked Markus who was beside a sleeping Laura.

"We're okay."

"That's what I like to hear. I'm going to put these in her IV. They're just a couple medicines that should make her heal a lot quicker."

"Why didn't you use them in the hospital?"

"Because they're not FDA approved and I rather like my medical licence."

"But you'll administer them now?"

"Because these are specially made, from old mage books and for her specific kind."

"Okay," He held his hands up in surrender.

"If she needs anything else you let me know, and feel free to catch some sleep on one of the other beds."

"Yes, ma'am."

The last thing I needed while I was here, was something for Jared.

"You took my wife to a crime scene." I could hear Tom loudly before I'd even entered the room.

"It's not really a crime scene any more."

"That doesn't make me feel any better."

"Tom, she sees worse than what she could have potentially seen on that street, every day."

"Does she know that this wasn't a pyre?"

"She knows that it was a shifter."

"Are you trying to scare her?"

"Something tells me, that girl of yours doesn't scare easily. Also she was the one that pointed out that this body, didn't look like the past vampyre kills."

"She's mortal and you want to take her to places we know that pyres and shifters that are not us have been?"

"Tom, please, relax. I am fine. We just went to take a look, and the guy lost a part of his leg, I knew there was no way this was pyre related."

"I'm still not happy about this."

"I know, and none of us are happy that this is happening, but there is nothing that we can do about it, so come take me home, make me dinner, and let's not worry about this tonight."

"Fine." I took his hand and I handed the purple vial to Jared. "You take that or you will be the first one on all of my fancy new machines next week."

"Yes, ma'am."

"What was that about?"

"It's nothing for you to worry about yet. Contessa voiced some concerns, so I spoke to him, that's just going to help him sleep."

"What did we do before we had you?"

"Honestly, I'm surprised the packs lasted this long."

"Come on, little lady, you're going a little loopy without food," he said, using one of Charlie's pet names for me.

"I'm fine."

"I'll be the judge of that…"

"Will you now?" I responded, giggling, before trying to escape from his hand and running away. I failed miserably at getting away and ended up being carried by my husband into our little house.

"Contessa and Jared are going to meet us so you can start your training."

"I thought we were going for a run?" I said.

"Well, you are, I'm going on a light jog." He smiled, grabbing two bottles of water from the fridge.

"Tom, is this really necessary?"

"Of course it is, we need to make sure that you can protect yourself."

"Tom, I'm five foot two and a hundred pounds soaking wet, I really hate to break it to you, but under no circumstances am I going to be a match for a pyre."

"I don't need you to be a match for a pyre, what I need is to know that you are capable of running away and handling much more mundane threats."

"Okay, let's do this," I said, pulling my hair back into a high ponytail. We ran first along the lake shore before heading onto a path, which we followed for about half a mile, which is where we ran into Jared and Contessa.

"I really shouldn't be too far from the clinic."

"Did you or did you not give her some of the tonics that you have been working on?"

"I did."

"And is she or is she not healing at twice the average shea rate?"

"You know she is, I came and reported that to you and Jared after I saw her this morning."

"Then stop worrying about her, it's time that we worried about you."

"Okay." I nodded.

"Just pay attention to what I do," Contessa said. "Now in terms of strength between male and female shifters it is about the same ratio, so what you need to be able to do is use his own strength against him."

"Are we not accounting for the foot and a half size difference between Tom and I here?"

"Watch. This is how you get out of a bear hug attack."

"Okay."

"Get low, use your elbows to hit low, when he loosens his grip, twist."

I practiced it a couple times, but I knew he was going really easy on me. Then came the getting out of a head lock, and a couple of jabs.

"Guys, can I be perfectly honest with you?"

"Go for it."

"This isn't working, I know you're letting go quickly, I think maybe going to self-defence classes may be a better idea for me."

"Why?"

"Because then they won't be so afraid of hurting me, and I will have a better idea of what I am going to be up against because an actual human will be my partner."

"That's acceptable," Jared nodded. "But during the day… okay?"

"I'll let Tom pick where I go," I promised my brother-in-law.

"I'm going to run back down."

"I'm coming with you," Tom said.

"That's fine."

"Where are the pups?"

"They're on a ten-mile run to the top of the mountain, then they'll fly down."

"Interesting."

"Are they going to be trained?"

"That's part of what they're doing."

"How so?"

"I think you're probably better off not knowing the specifics."

"Do I need to be prepared?"

"Nah, they'll be healed before they even get down here."

"It's part two of the training that you need to be worried about."

"Why is that?" I said, happy that for the time being we were just strolling down the path, instead of running down it.

"We get them to fight each other in their different forms."

"I'm going to be there."

"Yeah, especially with so many boys."

"When I get back and showered, I'll check on Laura and start making even more supplies."

"You need help?"

"No, I think I am going to be okay, you go do what you need to do."

I ran the length of the path. Why? I'm not really sure, I just felt like I needed to. "How are we doing in here?" I asked, peeking my head in from my lab.

"I feel like I could run a marathon," Laura said.

"Okay, well, as your doctor I am going to recommend that you refrain from such activities until after the baby is born."

"I think that's a reasonable recommendation." She laughed at me.

"I must say I am really happy you are feeling better."

"Me too."

"Can I check your incision?"

"You're the doctor." She smiled, lifting her pajama shirt.

"You are so lucky you're a shea."

"Why do you say that?"

"I think that will be completely healed soon. How does the ankle feel?"

"Like it was never broken."

"Tell you what, one more day and we can test the theory. And I'll let you go home and sleep in your own bed."

"That sounds amazing, but hey, Astrid."

"Yeah."

"Thank you."

"You don't have to thank me."

"You did more than you have to."

"You're family. I will always do everything that I can for my family. Now I am going to be in the next room working on a few things. You need anything, you let me know, okay?"

"Understood."

I opened the mages book and began on another batch of the sleeping draught followed by a couple of healing tonics and a few salves. It was very likely my most productive day in the lab yet. When I was done making what I needed, I pulled out a vial of Lorelai's blood. Putting a drop on a slide I went back to observing it. I'd added a protein to it and it was thriving.

"Come on, we're going to be late."

"Hello to you too."

"Remember we agreed to have dinner with Jared and Contessa tonight."

"Oh, right… okay."

"What were you working on?"

"Nothing important yet, when I have it figured out, I'll let you know."

"Well, I look forward to hearing all about it."

"Me too… Look, Tom, I need to go into the city for a couple of days."

"Okay."

"I need Jared to let us stay at the apartment."

"I'll talk to him."

"If you have to stay here I'll be fine."

"Absolutely not."

"Understood."

During the first course we all ate our appetizers with polite conversation. As the second course was served, it became a little more serious. "How is Laura?" Contessa asked.

"She is good, I should have her walking and discharged tomorrow."

"Really?"

"Well, that is excellent news," Jared said raising his glass.

"I agree, I don't have any worries about her any more, those remedies that you gave me are incredible."

"Well, that's good," Jared smiled. "They were just waiting for the right person to come along for those books."

"Hey, Jared, can I ask you a favour," I asked.

"What do you need?"

"I need to go to the city for a couple of days."

"You want to stay there," he said, already knowing where this was going.

"It would make it so much easier to do what I need to."

"And that would be?"

"I need to meet up with a couple of people."

"Astrid?"

"Please trust me."

"Okay."

"Tom will stay with you at night, mostly, because if I said otherwise, he might kill me."

The rest of dinner progressed slowly, but dessert was the best, not that I had a sweet tooth or anything?

"Are you going to tell me who you are meeting with?" Tom asked on our way home.

"I can't."

"Well, if I am going to be there."

"Here's the thing, you're not."

"Nope not an option."

"I'm sorry, Tom, but it kind of has to be, they won't talk to me otherwise."

"There are monsters running around Seattle."

"And if I believed that for one second, then I wouldn't be here right now."

"Astrid."

"Please, Tom, do you trust me?"

"You know I do but…"

"Then trust me now."

"If anything happens…"

"It won't, I have got this entirely under control."

"I don't like this," Tom said.

"I've agreed to let you drop me off but you stay in the car."

"Astrid."

I pulled my purse up on my shoulder, inside of which were two potions that were essentially undetectable bombs. "I mean it, Tom, don't follow me."

"I don't even know where we are?"

"That's because you never had to live on a low income and what little you could afford."

"That really isn't making me feel any better about this," he said, looking up at the dark concrete buildings.

"Relax, I know what I'm doing, stay here."

"Fine."

I got out of the car and did the last thing Tom would want me to do, I turned up the alley. The metal door had always been heavy but today, it might as well have weighed a hundred pounds. As I got the door open Reggie stood in his spot. Reggie is blond and broad and tall, everything that you'd expect a bouncer to be, but Reggie has a heart of pure gold.

"Hey, little pixie, way too long time no see." The bouncer gave me a hug.

"Hi, Reggie. The boss here?"

"Of course."

"I need to talk to him."

"He won't help you."

"Reggie, I started my own life, I'm not looking for his protection. Just his information. Penny is with him, yes?"

"Of course."

"Let me see them."

"Follow me." The Asylum never changed, dark, and underground, it operated a club at the front, but for those in the know, there was more to it. It was the perfect hideaway for anyone who knows enough.

"Boss, Astrid is here to see you," he said, opening the door.

"Ahhh. The doctor is in," Charmaine said.

"Hello, Charmaine," I said. "Penny." I nodded to Penelope sitting on the sofa next to him, her body pressed to his side, his hand moving up and down her leg.

"Needing protection? Well I hate to break it to you, you walked away from that."

"I don't need protection." I lifted my head. "What I need is information."

"Information about what?"

162

"A rogue shifter in the area," I said, sitting down on the other end of the sofa.

"And here I thought you'd be more interested in the pyre," Penny said.

"I wouldn't dare, I know you have half the pyre community in your pocket, but a rogue shifter is a threat to all of us."

"I haven't heard anything."

"Well, when you do, it will benefit you greatly if you send Penny with a message."

"Oh, don't worry, I heard of your little stunt at the hospital."

"Look at her, does it look like she needs our help?" Sylvester said, coming around the curtain, still gaunt and frail, but I knew he was dangerous.

"Hey, Syl," I said.

"Ahh... you remember us."

"Of course."

"You left five years ago, why come back? The wife of a shifter, you don't need us anymore."

"This community exists because it's hidden, don't make me change that."

"You're mortal, you may have married into a pack, but don't threaten us, little girl," Charmaine hissed.

"I'm not threatening anyone. I'm just reminding you that if word gets out to Wales that there's a rogue, I will be the last of your concerns."

"Astrid Alora Wren Davis, such a pretty name, don't push me so the only place that's mentioned is a tombstone."

"Don't push me," I said, pulling out a small bottle from my bag. Trading threats was staring to annoy me.

"Oh, little girl has learned some new tricks, by the look of it."

"I was a bigger fan of the old ones. Reggie you can see her out."

"Just remember, I have the means to make it worth your while if you decide to help me instead of fighting me."

"We made you, girl, don't forget that." Charmaine placed a gentle finger on the charm around my neck. His eyes glassed over briefly, before he let go.

"Goodbye, Charmaine."

Reggie escorted me from the building. "Little pixie is brave, but you need to remember your place," he said, closing the door. He had no idea of my place. I stood there for a moment staring at it, but was surprised when the steel door opened again to reveal Penelope standing there.

"Penny…"

"Look he can't know that I am telling you this."

"What?" She closed the door and stepped up to me. "There aren't any new shifters in town."

"You think it's the pack?"

"I think that you can't find a scent. The pyres, I can't help you, but you need to be careful, all the signs say there's danger coming."

"Thanks, Penelope."

"I mean it, Astrid, be careful."

"Aren't I always?"

"You married a shifter, so no, I'd say not."

"Penelope, I had no idea he was a shifter, I fell in love with the man."

"Love will make you weaker."

"Really? Because I am fairly certain you and I love each other."

"We did once, then you made your choice and I made mine."

"I didn't belong in Charmaine's world and you know that."

"Charmaine protects us."

"You keep telling yourself that, Penelope."

"I wouldn't come back here if I were you."

"Tell Charmaine to let me know what I need to know and I'll make it worth his while," I said, handing her a twenty-five-thousand-dollar check.

"You know that's not what he wants."

"Yes, well, we can't always have what we want… I wanted a quiet life."

"You're not built for a quiet life."

"Goodnight, Penelope," I said, backing out of the alley.

"So? Did you get what you needed?" Tom asked as I got into his car.

"No."

"And what were you trying to get."

"Nothing, just needed to see a friend."

164

"Down there?"

"An old friend. Please just take me home."

"Now that I'll do."

Chapter 13

Three days of peace after my meeting. Three days where Tom and I actually got life back to normal. I went to work, so did he, and we came home to peace and quiet, until Tom got a phone call. "Two of the pups are missing," Tom said, sitting down at one of the barstools after hanging up on Jared.

"Excuse me?" I said, placing the hand towel down on the counter.

"Brady and Colby went out on a run early this morning and haven't come back. A number of pack members have gone searching for them, but they just disappeared." Tom put his head in his hands.

"Did they take to the sky?"

"We're hoping so."

"Have we seen any signs that something bad could have happened."

"None."

"Okay," I said, grabbing my shoes, and my *Mages and Vampyre* book I'd been working my way through.

"What are you doing?"

"What do you think?"

"You're on call." He raised his head from the counter.

"Right…" I picked up my phone.

"Hello." Dr. Hendrick picked up first ring. Dr. Hendrick is a friend, she was upset by what happened to me and we've been more than happy to help each other out since the beginning of our residency days.

"Hello, Sierra, it's Astrid, I need a favour."

"Astrid?"

"My husband's cousins went out hiking today and didn't make it home, I'm going out to look for them. Do you think?"

"Astrid, don't say another word, I'll call the hospital. I hope you find them safe and sound."

"Thank you, I cannot tell you how much I appreciate this," I said.

"Good luck," she hung up.

"There, problem solved," I told him, sliding my phone into my back pocket.

"You're amazing," he kissed my forehead grabbing his keys.

"So what's the theory?"

"I don't know."

"The 'but' is implied, I got it."

"When we get to Sanctuary can you go to the clinic, make sure you are prepared for anything? Hopefully, we won't need you at all, and they just got lost, and ended up in Canada," he said, turning on the engine.

"If it comes down to it, I may need help."

"Hopefully it won't, but you'll have what and whoever you need."

"Okay, well, in order to help anyone, we need to make it there alive, so can you slow down," I demanded. Outside was a blur as he raced down the streets.

"Sorry," he said nervously. At Sanctuary Tom had a couple shea help me before turning to go into the woods. Between Rox, Lorelai and I we got everything set up from the surgical suite to two beds and all the machines I could possibly need, set up for the boys.

It was dark when we finished. I sent the women home and I walked down to the lake and knelt down in the rough rocky sand.

Please, beasts, help our men find the boys safe and alive. I prayed. This became my routine every night the boys were gone before heading home. Every night I watched the moon dance off the lake and felt the gentle wind between my shoulder blades as it ruffled my red hair, and I prayed to the beasts for the two boys, for their parents, for Tom and Jared.

"Three days," Tom screamed.

"I know," I told him, much more calmly, "but right now all we can do is keep looking and keep up hope." My hand ran between his shoulder blades.

"I need some sleep before I have to go back out there again."

"Okay, it's late, I'll join you," I said, hugging his side, praying it would help him calm down.

"I'd like that." He stroked my head, before we walked together to bed for us to get some sleep.

"Tom," I screamed, elbowing the man next to me, and sitting up from the most peculiar dream, with a feeling I've only had once before, a feeling that forced me into action. A bad feeling.

"Astrid," Tom said, sitting up.

"Is there a cabin… well it looks more like a shack about six miles north of here?"

"Yeah, it's on an old farm, but the farm hasn't been occupied for years."

"We need to go there now. Get Jared or do whatever it is that you have to do." I jumped out of the bed.

"What the hell?" He followed me as I threw on a sweater and an old pair of jeans.

"Astrid what is going on?"

"Brady doesn't have much time… I'm going to get my bag."

"Astrid, calm down, we've already cleared the shack."

"Tom, they're there."

"Astrid, how do you know that?"

"I don't know, it was a dream, but, Tom, I have a really strong feeling about this. Please I need to get there." I was reaching the point of hysterics.

"Astrid, you sound crazy."

"Tom, please. If you're so concerned, just get Charlie or Jared? I don't know where it is, I need you to get me there."

"Okay, I'll get Jared, fuel up the four-wheeler and come for you."

"Thank you."

"I'll meet you outside the clinic in ten minutes."

"Understood," I said, running down the stairs and out the backdoor.

I poured everything that I could think of into the bag, much of what I needed was already packed, but from what I'd seen and felt, I knew that I needed extra.

"Are you ready?"

"Yeah," I said, shouldering my bag.

"Jared's going to scope out ahead," Tom said. Jared was already in his eagle form, as I eyed the trailer attached to the back.

"If you're right, we'll need it to help bring them back." Tom helped me onto the back of the bike.

"Is it bad that I hope I'm right, but I also hope I'm wrong."

"No, it's understandable," he said, as we lunged forward.

We were speeding through the woods faster than I'd thought possible, especially with the trailer on the back. My arms were tightly fastened around my husband's waist as I fought the bumps and turns. Fifteen minutes after we'd left, the three of us were on the steps of a little shack. Jared had already transformed back. Tom threw him a pair of jeans. "I'm going in," Jared said. "Stay here with her."

It was barely a few breaths later when I heard, "Tom, get her in here."

"Holy crap," Tom cursed, taking in the scene as we rushed into the cold, damp and dark shack. In the middle of the small, cramped room were Colby and Brady, shackled and chained to the wall, beaten black and blue.

"Tom, check on Colby," I said, getting on my knees between the two boys, but focusing my attention on Brady.

"Colby, it's Tom can you hear me?" I heard Tom say to him, nudging him gently.

"Tom?"

"Yeah." I could hear the relief in Tom's voice as he realized Colby was okay.

"Damn, man, am I ever glad to see you."

"Oh, thank the gods," Tom said.

"Tom wrap this around his neck." I threw a neck brace to him.

"Dude, I'm fine," Colby said.

"Dude, you don't get to make that determination, she does." Tom motioned to me.

"Brady," I tried again. "Can you hear me? Can you open your eyes for me?"

Nothing. "Damn idiot didn't know when to quit," Colby said as some sort of explanation.

"His breathing is shallow. Do you know if he took any hard blows to the chest?"

"We both did, the problem is he is stupider and wouldn't concede."

"I'm going for back-up," Jared said, sliding out the doorway. Next thing we heard was a loud howl, then half a dozen more answering shortly behind, but from a distance.

"Tom, I need to get him back to Sanctuary."

"Astrid?"

"His heart rate is low, his belly rigid, he's black and blue and I'm worried about his breathing," I said, carefully wrapping a brace around his neck. "Tom hold this," I said, handing him an IV bag before attaching it to the back of Brady's hand.

"They're coming, what do you need?" Jared demanded of me.

"I'm going to need Lesley and Leonora."

"I'll have them at the clinic waiting."

"Thank you," I said. I was thankful Lesley was an operating room nurse before a palliative care one — a fact I had only learned on my wedding day — and Leonora has been doing this for years. The closest thing they had to a medic before I arrived. Which is why I'd been working with the two of them whenever I'm at Sanctuary so they knew their way around and how to help me.

"Okay, now, Colby," I said, turning around to him. "You're going to be honest with me, where are you hurt?" I flashed a light in his eyes.

"Astrid," he complained, turning his head from me as best he could with the brace around his neck.

"I can make you call her Dr. Sharpe if you think that will make you more compliant," Tom said to the boy.

"Just my left leg," he complied.

"Any headache, nausea or dizziness."

"All of the above."

"Okay, I'm just going to take a quick look at your leg." I pressed gently. "Good news, nothing feels broken or out of place, but I am going to splint it until we get you an X-ray." I made quick work of it, before checking Brady's pulse again.

"Tom, Jared," I called out. "It's going to be much more dangerous if I have to crack his chest here." Jared came and knelt down beside Brady. "No one wants me to have to do that," I said, before taking an IV bag from Tom, and handing it to Jared. Before giving Tom the one I was about to attach to Colby. "Small pinch," I warned, before sticking him with the needle. "Is this really necessary?"

"Let me ask you this? Have you had anything to eat or drink in the three days you've been missing?"

"No."

"Then the answer is yes, it is necessary."

Colby went to say something else. "Colby, it's not worth it, she's more stubborn than I am," Jared said over my shoulder.

"He's learned that from experience," Tom tacked on.

"Yes, sir," was all Colby said.

And just like that the small shack became very crowded. "Colby," Faelen said, falling to his knees beside his son.

"How did you find them?" Faelen looked to Tom, his face worn and covered in dirt, evidence of the last few days.

"Just a feeling," Tom said, making eye contact with his brother over my shoulder.

"But we checked here yesterday."

"We were moved frequently," Colby told his father.

"Who did this to you, son?"

"I don't know, there was no specific scent and we never saw them."

"I searched the perimeter and came up with nothing," Jared assured him.

"Brady," was the sudden scream over my shoulder. Lucas was here and rushing to his son.

"Careful, Lucas," I warned as Jared stopped him from pouncing on his son.

"What's wrong with him? What happened?"

"I won't know exactly until I get him back to Sanctuary," I told him. "But I am going to do everything I can for him." I made eye contact with the terrified father, then nodded.

"Thank you," Lucas said, gently taking his hand. "Please, son, I'm right here," he called to his unconscious boy.

"Okay, guys," I said to the men gathered around us. "There should be enough of you here to help me move them. But we need to do this gently, with as little jostling as possible."

171

"Brady, son," Lucas said. "You're going to be okay. Dr. Davis-Sharpe," I hated how that sounded, "is going to make sure of it, just hold on."

Slowly as a unit they moved Brady; Colby was more stubborn and insisted that as long as he had someone to lean on, he was perfectly fine to move under his own power. As long as he didn't put any weight on his left leg, I was inclined to let him. So his father brought him outside. Brady was laid out in the trailer as I crawled in beside him.

"Oh, no you don't," Tom said.

"It took us fifteen minutes to get here in the first place and that was without two passengers. We'll have to be more careful this time, I need to be able to monitor him."

"Then I'm coming with you."

"There's no way we'll all fit."

"I'll ride behind whoever's driving."

"Colby, I don't know. What if you feel dizzy or faint?"

"I'm fine."

"I'll be driving," Jared told us.

"Okay, Colby, you listen to me. If you feel even the slightest bit off balance, you tap Jared on the arm three times and he will stop, do you understand?"

"I understand," he nodded. I disconnected his IV, taking the bag from Tom and tucking it in my bag. Tom crawled in behind me, one knee resting on my back. I handed him Brady's IV. "Hold it between your chin and your shoulder and you'll have your hands free.

"Jared, whenever you're ready," I said, putting on my stethoscope. The only sounds were the engine, the sound of the trailer bouncing off the ground and the paws running along beside us. When I recognized where we were the worst happened. Brady's breathing just stopped. "Tom, there's a resuscitation kit in my bag, get it now." I followed up my statement speaking directly to Brady, "Don't you do this to me, Brady."

"Got it," he said, placing the face piece over Brady's mouth and nose and holding the bag.

"Great, every fifteen compressions you're going to squeeze the bag."

"What?" he said, alarmed, but I was already pumping Brady's chest. A howl came from one of the wolves.

"Lucas, that's enough," Tom barked at him.

I pushed down on his chest, hard and fast, making up for the increased heart rate of the shifters. "Come on, come on, come on," I muttered, then checked his pulse. "Dammit," I cursed, restarting compressions. "I mean it, Brady, don't you give up on me."

Leonora and Lesley were already in front of my clinic with a backboard and stretcher. We transferred him quickly. Tom kept one hand on the small of my back, the other on the bag as we wheeled him into the clinic. "Crash cart! Now!" I screamed, continuing. "Leonora, take over bagging, Jared, hang the IV bag." But Lesley's gaze never left her concerned looking stepson.

"Got it."

"Tom, take over compressions." He did as I grabbed the paddles. "Charge to two hundred," I told Lesley, snapping her back. "Clear. Damn, no change," I cursed as Leonora attached a bunch of wires to Brady's chest. I pushed epi. "Charge to three hundred. Clear."

"He's back," Leonora said.

"Okay, let's move." Once in the OR I got him intubated, hooked up to anesthesia and made sure all my monitors were set up. "I'm going to scrub," I announced. Tom followed. "I'm nervous," I admitted, grabbing the betadine soap.

"Why?"

"Because it's Brady, and I don't have spare hands that know exactly what they're doing."

"Do you want me in there?"

"I don't know. I do know I'll have Lesley and your mother."

"She said she isn't comfortable with this; she'll take care of Colby. Lesley says she understands that Brady needs her, and as long as you promise Colby will be fine."

"Okay, are you sure you don't mind?"

"Not at all."

"Okay, scrub too."

"You got this, you know that, right?" Tom told me. "This was your plan. You wanted this clinic, you're ready, I know you have this, and so do you."

Chapter 14

"I have to say hoarding the pack's blood was a great idea," I said, scrubbing out of the surgery.

"It's over?" Tom asked.

"It is, he should be okay. Now that I've got everything repaired, his shifter self should kick in."

"So, we should probably tell his parents," Tom said.

"Let's wheel him out there and I'll get him situated first."

"They'll be out there. As is half the pack." Tom warned me, probably hearing them now.

"Okay," I said. Tom, Lesley and I moved together, wheeling him into the ward.

"Brady," Chezzy said, moving towards the bed; she looked like she'd aged three years in the past three days. Her eyes were swollen her face blotchy, her long silver hair in a mess of tangles.

"Chezzy," I said quietly.

"Is he okay?" she demanded.

"He will be, I'll be closely monitoring him, particularly due to the shifter abilities. I have no idea how it will affect the healing process, in a case like this."

"The ventilator?"

"Necessary for surgery. As soon as I've determined it's safe and he is breathing on his own, I will remove it."

"So everything went well?"

"It did, all things considered. Go sit with him, I'll be over to check on you soon."

"Thank you, Astrid," Chezzy said.

"I'm just glad he's okay," I said.

Lucas squeezed my shoulder, before leading his wife back to his son. I watched them for a second, before rounding back to Colby.

"Hey, Doc. How is he?"

"Physically, he'll be okay — eventually."

"Good."

"How are you?"

"I feel fine."

"Uh huh." I didn't believe him. "Tom, can you run and get me a wheelchair?"

"Absolutely."

"Astrid, please."

"No, I gave you a break before but until I have a full idea of exactly what's going on, we're playing by my rules now."

"Colby, listen to Astrid," Faelen said.

"Yes, sir," he nodded.

"Okay, I'm really happy with everything," I told Faelen after I'd run my tests and brought him back his son. "Other than a minor concussion and a small ankle fracture which I reckon will be fine in a day."

"Okay, thank the gods."

"I'm going to give him something to help him sleep, and for the pain."

"If he's got a concussion, should he be sleeping?" Lesley asked, concerned for her stepson.

"It's my opinion that the sleep coupled with his abilities, will be better than forcing him to stay awake."

"And the ankle?"

"I can temporarily immobilize it. With a little luck he'll be up and running by the day after tomorrow," I told them, inserting the medications into his IV.

With both boys asleep and safe, I retreated to my office.

"Hey," I said, exhaustedly, to the two men. "Are you waiting for me?" I asked, flopping down on the sofa.

"Yeah," Jared said, sitting forward.

"Astrid, you know what we're going to ask." Tom moved beside me.

"You want to know how I knew where the boys were." I stated.

"In our defense, the way you found them raises a lot of questions."

"Well, I really wish I could answer a few of them, but I really don't know."

"You don't know?" Jared said, incredulously.

"How could I?"

"Walk us through it?" Tom suggested.

"Okay. Tom was upset before we went to bed, after he'd been out searching. I had this dream but it was just that —a dream. It had only happened once before, before I left home, each time it gave me a feeling and I knew it was what I needed to do. It hasn't led me wrong before. This time, though, it was a strong urge and dark feeling."

"That doesn't really explain it though, does it?" Jared said.

"Well, I really don't know what else to tell you."

"A dream led you to two missing pups?"

"Look, you don't have to believe it but it is all that I've got."

"Tom, I don't want the pack knowing how she found them." Jared instructed.

"We aren't going to say anything."

"No story is best, the searching paid off."

"Okay," I nodded, shrugging one shoulder.

"I think we need some sleep," Tom told me.

"I can't leave here yet; I need to be close to Brady."

"And Colby?" Jared asked.

"Once he's slept, I'll run a couple of tests, but his parents should have him in his own bed tonight."

"Okay, keep me informed, I'm going to speak to their parents. Sleep and we'll talk later."

"Understood," I nodded.

"Do you want me to stay here with you?" Tom asked.

"No, go home and get some sleep. I'll do the same thing here."

"Okay, I love you."

"I love you too."

"I'm proud of you." He wrapped me in his strong arms.

"Thank you." I hugged him back.

"I'll bring lunch by later."

"Go to bed." I leaned up to kiss him and he met me halfway.

"Yes, ma'am," he said, smiling. He left my little office as I laid down on my sofa to nap.

Now that the matter of the missing pups was over, we were going back to the other crisis: there were still pyres in shifter territory and a rogue on our hands. "Though our pack is larger than most in the region we have had to prioritize our own over that of the threat that still exists," Jared told us.

"While we have been here searching for ours, two new bodies drained of blood have shown up in our morgue," I said, recalling the frantic phone call I'd gotten from Penelope after examining the two men. 'Don't worry we're on it,' I'd assured her. 'You need to stay very far from this,' she warned. 'I'm fine, thanks for the information.' 'Be Careful,' was the last thing she said before hanging up on me. "My contacts at the hospital are worried."

"The police are ruling it a homicide," Francis tacked on.

"All it takes is one eccentric cop and our secret could be blown," Jared said. "I am going to be upping patrols, I want them gone, enough is enough."

"Remember though, do not initiate contact unless you have no choice," Tom added.

The small meeting was now being held in our apartment, anyone of consequence was having an opinion. Somehow, lately that had been including me. "Can I suggest something."

"Astrid?"

"We've been patrolling the wrong areas. The bodies have never strayed far from the city, why are we circling Sanctuary?"

"In case they follow us there?"

"But that's the thing, they probably don't want a fight with us as much as we don't want one with them, but more and more people are worried that this may be more than animal attacks. As I said, the last two were ruled homicides, but it won't take them too long to figure out that it is the same sadistic person that has attacked the others."

"I agree with Astrid, I think we need to be concentrating on finding them in the city," Jared said seeing my view on things.

"We can't be wolves in the city," Tom said.

"Be eagles, circle."

"What about our families?" Francis said.

"Keep the pups, women and children there, they'll be safe and we'll stay here and search." I offered.

"Honestly, she has a point," Jared said.

"You know that is going to have to include you." Tom leaned down to me.

"What part?"

"The part about staying at Sanctuary."

"You don't think I would be better off here?"

"Not at all."

"You'll be taking point at Sanctuary," Jared said. "Contessa is one of our best in eagle form, she'll be too much of an asset here."

"That's okay, I'll keep an eye on everyone," I nodded taking on my role with my while heart

"Is there anything else you think we should know?" Tom asked me.

"There's a little bit of a pattern as to the location of the victims when they were found. I was talking to detectives today afterwards I overheard them mention that almost all the bodies have been found northwest of the city."

"Great, Charlie will escort you to Sanctuary, you can handle the majority of what needs to be done there and we are going to go searching."

"Just be careful, okay?"

"Always."

Chapter 15

"You are going to tell me that this is going to work and we are not just sending our husbands out to slaughter."

"Really, Laura? I thought you had more faith in me and the beasts than that."

"It's not that."

"It's dangerous having this many threats in one place, and believe me, I am nervous too, but everything is going to be fine," I said, hugging my coffee cup to my chest.

"There's not a woman here who doesn't hate what is happening."

"We're safe here."

"There are children watching the perimeters at night."

"Why don't we have a bonfire tonight, we'll do a few prayers as a group, increase morale."

"I don't think that's going to work, some of these women haven't seen their husbands in a week."

"They're staying in their homes in the city, not in a hobble in the woods."

"Still."

"Still, they are out all night and sleeping all day, it's better for them to be there."

"Hey, Colby," I called and waved him over, all evidence of his injuries, as predicted, had faded after just a couple of days. He ran over to join Laura and I now like nothing had ever happened.

"What's up, Doc?" He skidded to a halt a foot in front of me.

"Colby," I warned.

"What do you need, Astrid?" he said more respectfully.

"I need a favour."

"Anything."

"Can you and a few of the guys build a bonfire for us?"

"You want to have a fire?"

"I do."

"Why?"

"Because I think the pack will benefit from it."

"Why?"

"Because we are all missing someone, and the women are going around with these long worried looks on their faces and the kids are starting to take notice."

"So you want to have a fire, in the middle of the night with vampyres somewhere in the near vicinity?"

"I do."

"Why?"

"Because we all need to pray."

"Pray?"

"Yes, and sing."

"Sing?"

"Oh, and don't worry, you are going to be singing too."

"Oh, I wouldn't bet on it." He smiled. "But hey don't worry about it I'll have this fire up and going before you know it."

Everything that I wanted from the fire I got. We sang, I even got Carly and Marlee to lead, then we said a couple of prayers and sat around the fire, while the kids made smores and we talked amongst ourselves. We were just starting to wind down the fire when my phone started vibrating. The name flashing on the screen read: Jared.

"Astrid, it's Jared," he said when I answered my phone.

"Yes, I got that, why are you calling me?"

"There has been an incident and we need you in the clinic. We are coming in hot."

"Jared, who?"

"Charlie and Tom," Jared said very slowly.

"How bad?" I asked breathless, tears coming to my eyes.

"They'll live, but they're in pretty bad shape and won't wake up."

"I'll be there."

"What's going on?" Lesley asked, standing up.

"Charlie and Tom are hurt," I said, "I don't know anything else. Leonora and Lesley, you come with me. Colby put out the fire and everyone else get inside."

They nodded and did exactly as I told them too. In the clinic I grabbed everything that I was going to need and pulled it next to the side-by-side beds, before putting a number of jars and bottles on the little cart.

"Astrid," Lesley called out, she was watching out the window.

The door crashed open and Charlie was hobbling between Faelen and Markus, but thankfully he was awake. "Put him on the first bed," I commanded.

"Hey, Doc," Charlie winked.

"I would not go there with me right now; flirting is not going to get you any brownie points today."

"Sorry."

"Where else are you hurt?" I asked, looking at the long scratches that dragged along his chest.

"It looks a lot worse than it is. If it wasn't for the fact that they are from a pyre, they would have healed by now."

I reached for a bottle behind me. "This will neutralize the effects of them being pyre."

"What?"

"Don't worry about it." I opened the bottle as the door slammed open again.

Jared and Landry carried Tom between them. The scratches on his face and chest were deeper than Charlie's, and I didn't like the bruising around his left eye and temple.

"Lesley, take this, put it along the scratches and cover them with gauze."

"Tom… my boy, wakeup," Leonora said, grabbing his face after they got him on the bed.

"Leonora, I need space to work," I said, looking at my husband and feeling a lump rising in my throat.

"Jared, what happened?" I demanded.

"They found the pyres, unfortunately one was feeding and took them as a threat."

"Help me wheel this bed to the CT scanner, please."

We moved together and, unfortunately, I was right to be worried, blood was welling on his brain.

"Something is wrong, Astrid, what's happening?"

"Jared, you should take Leonora to my office for a few minutes, you'll find a bottle of scotch in my bottom drawer, give her a glass," I said to him quietly.

"What's happening?" he demanded.

"There is bleeding on the brain. I need to remove it and release the pressure then I can help him start to heal, but I am not a brain surgeon, so it's going to require a lot of concentration."

"Are you going to be okay to do what you have to? That's your husband."

"Let's put it this way I am going to need one of those drinks afterwards," I said putting in the IV. I hooked up a small syringe to the valves. "Lesley, when I say, I need you to push that." I pointed to it.

"Will do," she nodded as I pulled the curtain around the bed so that no one could see what was going to happen.

"Jared, where are you taking me?" Leonora cried.

"We're going to go into Astrid's office for a minute."

"Jared." I said through clenched teeth, as Leonora fought Jared's effort to grant me some space. I really did not want to kill my husband today and a frantic mother, as I drilled into her son's head, was not going to alleviate any of the tension and stress I was feeling as I pressed the end of the drill to his head.

I turned on the drill and put it along where I had made the tiny incision. *Just remove the blood, just remove it,* I told myself. Once I was in and the pressure was off, I said, "Now, Lesley."

She nodded and pushed. I watched the brain of my husband, after the blood had drained, it was like I could see it healing and the swelling decrease.

I applied the same salve that I had used for Charlie on Tom's wounds and sealed the incision at his temple. I quickly made sure that Charlie was bandaged and healing properly, before administering a saline drip to both men to keep them hydrated while they slept off their injuries.

"How are they?" Jared asked me, coming up behind me from where I was watching them and holding steadfast to Tom's hand forcing myself to take some steadying breaths as I took in everything that had just happened.

"They'll be sore for a couple of days but they'll live."

"Tom?"

"He may want to avoid any serious knocks on the head for a while."

"Well, hopefully this experience will knock some sense into him, so I don't have to."

"You know I was out there tonight, telling all the wives that everything was going to be fine, now look at me. I'm holding my unconscious husband's hand after having to drill holes in his head."

"You're strong, I don't think there is a woman in the world who could have done what you did tonight."

"I don't feel strong. I don't think I realized how dangerous this was until now." I could feel the tears forming rivers down my cheeks.

"It never really gets easier." Jared knelt down in front of me, before wrapping his arms tightly around me and letting me cry.

"Am I supposed to be okay with him going headlong into danger?" I asked.

"You will, because you know that whatever happens, our lives are not ours, not mine, Contessa's, yours or Tom's. Our duty is first and foremost to the pack."

"I thought I understood that, but I don't know if I can any more," feeling as though I got what I needed from my release.

"Listen to me, the sacrifice we ask is not something that just happens, it takes work and effort."

"Jared," I said.

"Did you get the pyres?"

"Tom killed one."

"And the other?"

"It ran away."

"They know we're here now."

"We will be expecting some sort of retaliation in the coming days."

"Damn."

"Don't. We don't want to scare the pack yet."

"Listen, Jared, I've got them pretty well doped, they'll be better in the morning, but they're not going to wake up tonight, you might as well go home and sleep, I'll be here."

"Okay, good night, little sister." He stood up.

Just before he left the room I said, "I'll never be okay with him going headlong into danger, but I do understand why."

"I know," I heard, and the door clicked shut.

"I love you," I told my husband and kissed his hand.

"Hey, you should go home and get some real sleep," Allain said, gently waking me, his hand clutching Leonora's beside him.

"No way, I'm not leaving until he does."

"How bad?"

"They both received their injuries along their upper body and Tom had a pretty scary couple of minutes. But I did manage to neutralize the effects of the scratches from the pyre."

"That was definitely appreciated, those stung," Charlie said groggily.

"Hey, how are you feeling?" Allain asked him, his hand clamped down on an uninjured shoulder.

"Like I got into a fight with a pyre."

"Not funny, Charles," Leonora scolded him.

"He still not awake yet?"

"Not yet."

"He will, he's tough that one. Killed the pyre and probably saved my life in the process," Charlie said.

"He what?"

"He saved my life."

"Jared didn't mention that."

"The first pyre was dead by the time the rest of the pack caught up to us, and scared the other pyre away."

"I'll call Jared, he's going to want to hear this," Leonora said.

We sat quietly and waited until Jared and Contessa arrived.

"That was quick," I observed.

"Yes, well, we were on our way when we got the phone call from Mom," Jared said.

"Charlie was just telling us what happened before the rest of the pack caught up with them," Allain explained.

"Oh yes, I would so love to hear how you two almost got yourselves killed." Jared crossed his arms. His jaw went rigid.

185

"I assure you we didn't do it intentionally."

"Well, that's comforting," Contessa said, balancing herself on the armrest of the chair I was sitting in and placed a soft hand on my back.

"We were following a trail, and something seemed amiss, so we kept following the scent. We followed it to a patch of trees. One of the women was just standing there leaning against a tree, but the other one was full hunt, had herself a young man. Something must have alerted the feeding one, because the next thing I knew she was lunging at me, all claw-like nails. She got a good couple swipes at me and I'm sure she would have bested me if Tom hadn't pulled her off me; there was a struggle, that I couldn't give you a play by play of if I wanted to. Then the pyre was decapitated and Tom passed out."

"That's it?"

"Pretty much, by the time I heard you guys coming up the paralysis was starting to set in."

"Hmm…" Jared said, as though he wanted more.

"Can we see if I am healed yet?"

"Seriously?"

"Yeah."

"You're still staying here until I say otherwise."

"Hey, until that man wakes up we are staying right where we are together." Charlie smiled at me.

Begrudgingly I let go of Tom's hand. Carefully I lifted the bandages and there was nothing but a couple of pink lines. "Cool, looks like I'm all better. Nine hours." I rolled my eyes at his carefree optimism.

It was another hour before I felt a movement from Tom. "Hey, Tom, are you with us?" I asked, looking into my beautiful husband's face.

"Hey, yeah," he said, opening his eyes and the flood I had been holding back released into a single sob.

"Welcome back, son," Allain said.

"Thanks, Dad."

"How are you feeling?" Leonora asked.

"A little achy and my head hurts, but overall, I'm okay," he told his mother before turning back to me. "Hey, I'm okay," he said, pushing himself into a sitting position and placing a hand on my face.

"Don't you scare me like that again."

186

"I'm sorry."

"It's okay."

"Did I manage to get it at least?"

"You did, but it didn't get rid of the problem all together, she still has a friend."

"Now you listen to me, and you too, Charlie, neither of you are going to be leaving Sanctuary, to do anything that looks like patrolling or searching until I give you both a clean bill of health."

"So, we can go patrolling tomorrow — understood," Charlie said.

"I wouldn't push your luck there, Charlie," Tom said, watching my face. "How far away are we from that happening?"

"I'm not going to be answering that, because I know that one of you will hold me to whatever I say." I motioned to Charlie.

"And you two will be listening to her," Jared said, "especially you." He looked to Tom. "She performed brain surgery on you last night. I think you've shot your poor wife's nerves enough for a few days, besides, for the foreseeable future, I am putting everyone on lockdown. Tonight, we will be holding a circle and I'll be letting everyone know of the new arrangements. It won't take long, but I'm sure we will have a retaliation on our hands eventually. Think you can let them out for that at least?"

"Charlie can leave now, and I'm not too worried about Tom, but as long as he has a headache, I don't want him too far from me."

"So what you're saying is we don't have to stay?" Charlie said.

"Only because I am really good at what I do," I made it clear.

"You can say that again," Jared said. "I am pretty sure that you've made our healing twice as fast."

"I have."

"Can you do that for regular mortals too." Tom asked, clearly indicating the potential benefit for me the slow healing human.

"I'm sorry, I can't, the ingredients won't react well."

Charlie went home while I checked that there was absolutely nothing wrong with my husband.

"I would like to go home," Tom said.

"Me too, we should probably get some food into you." I smiled.

It didn't surprise me one little bit, when two days after I had finished treating Charlie and Tom we received an unwelcome visitor. There was a reason why all of us were promoting hyper vigilance. I'd even cleared Tom and Charlie for duty, but I wasn't happy about it. The woman stalked out of the woods as the sun was setting. Her blonde hair hung in long tangles, her thin arms and fingers splayed. I finally understood the marks on Tom and Charlie, her nails were long and pointy like knives. Her thin legs and torso were adorned in simple yoga wear. The shadows made her face look more angular, almost ancient looking.

"Tom," I said slowly backing up, but he was already moving his body in front of mine.

"Francis, get all the women and children inside," Jared ordered.

"Astrid, go with him," Tom said.

"No." I shook my head, remembering the talk that Jared and I had a couple of nights earlier.

Tom pursed his lips but said nothing.

"Him, I want him," the woman snarled, lifting a finger to my husband. Every man in the pack stood side by side. Contessa and I stood a foot behind our husbands.

"I am Jared Sharpe, I am the Alpha of this pack. Our territory is declared by the councils. We apologize for what happened to your friend, but we ask that you please leave peacefully."

"My mate. Shara was my mate for the past hundred and twenty-four years." Her eyes rested on me carefully tucked behind my husband.

"We were attacked," Tom pointed out.

"You've been hunting us for a month," she snarled.

"And again, I remind you that this is pack territory, what happened was not what we intended. But there has been a long-standing animosity between the species."

"One rightfully started."

"Not with us, leave here."

"Not without justice."

"Jared, this isn't going to work," I warned.

"Well, it's this or violence," he told me.

"Let me try something, let me talk to her."

"Astrid. No," Tom said.

"I have an idea. I'm human, I'm not a threat, maybe she'll listen."

"Astrid."

"She's angry, how many will die or get hurt? You know as well as I do, she's an older pyre."

"Tom, she's right."

"Please, trust me."

"I don't like it."

"Tom neither do I, but she is right, she's not a threat she might listen."

"Fine," he said.

"Go ahead."

"Hi, my name is Astrid." I stepped around my husband. "The man that you want to kill, he's my husband." I kept walking towards her, I felt Tom try and stop me but I moved out of his way. He wouldn't use shifter abilities against me, I knew that as well as he did.

"I haven't known him the time you knew Shara, but I do know what love is. Because someone here felt I was worth it. Now, I'm human so I can't stop you, but I can implore you to allow me a future and family with him." I stood directly in front of her now. Inches between us. I reached up, wrapping my arms around her shoulders, but her height meant I had to stand forward on my toes. I was really careful to keep my voice low so no one of supernatural hearing behind me could hear. "Just because I left Wales doesn't mean I am not of Llangollen. I am sorry for your loss. Now leave and don't come back." I broke away.

"You're…"

"Go," I motioned with my chin.

"I am sorry." She looked behind me before speeding off into the woods.

I took a few steps back, but before I knew it, I was being turned and my face was crushed into my husband's chest. His hand wrapped into my hair and the other tight against my shoulders. "It worked," I told him. I felt him widen his stance against me.

"I see, but I don't care, I think I just had a hundred heart attacks."

"Do I need to take you back to the clinic?" I looked up. He didn't feel the need to answer with words, choosing to trap my lips with his, breaking only due to a hard thump on my back making me cough, I looked to my husband apologetically.

"Hey, Charlie," I turned into a more respectable position, remaining in Toms arms.

"Way to go little Beta, gotta say of all the ways I saw that concluding, a peaceful interaction between the pyre and our little lady was not one of them."

"You guys think I am so soft, I can be tough," I smiled feigning a tough expression, making Charlie laugh, Tom did not.

"Walking over to her like that was brave and stupid," Tom growled down my ear.

"You know what they say, fortune favours the brave."

"And insane," Charlie added.

"I'm sure what they really mean is thank you," Contessa said, grabbing my shoulders and wrenching me from my husband.

"Oh no, don't do that. I didn't do anything, I just talked to her."

"How did you know it would work?"

"I didn't," I said.

"Right, now… I didn't need to hear that," Tom growled again behind me.

"Look I'm sorry, but I had a thought. When I looked down the line at our family, I knew if violence could be prevented it needed to be, so I did the one thing I thought might actually work."

I looked around, women and children were coming out of their homes, fathers embracing their families. Weeks of patrolling, stress, and curfews were over, I took a deep breath and smiled, before starting to tear up. Maybe somewhat from shock, but mostly from relief.

"Okay, I think you need to sit down and have a cup of tea," Tom said to me.

"I think you might be right," I nodded.

"Come on." He took my hand, taking me around to the front of the pavilion. "Sit, I'll go make it," he said, leaving me in my favourite spot where I could watch the pack spread out then come together going about their formerly all too dramatic lives.

Carly and Marlee were dancing down by the water.

Colby, Brady, Matteo and Tobias were coming back and forth from the woods carrying branches and logs. Some of the mothers chased their pups trying to persuade them into sweaters and jackets. Lorelai was sat next to the fire pit cradling William in her lap, while the older boys moved around them.

I stood up, leaning over the railing, just watching everyone else's happiness. "Here." Tom handed me a travel mug.

"Thanks."

"Don't mention it," he said as I took a sip. He just stood there, wrapping my free hand in his.

It was completely dark, night finally taking over, the moon shone bright above our heads and they had a roaring fire going by the time our silence was disturbed.

"Hey, think I could borrow your wife for a minute?" Jared said, coming up to my other side but looking over me at his brother. I hate when they do that.

"Sure, I'll be at the fire when you're finished." He kissed my hair a little longer than necessary, before walking away from us.

"What can I do for you?" I asked my brother-in-law.

"Well, first, for my own peace of mind, you know that if I'd known that your intention was to walk away from us and hug the vampyre who wanted to kill Tom, I would have said no, right?"

"I'm aware." I continued to stare out over Sanctuary.

"Okay."

"I also know that if Tom had known my plan, Charlie would have forcibly removed me from the situation."

"This is true and you probably should have been. When Tom got hurt you said you'd never be okay with him putting himself in danger."

"Jared."

"What do you think you just did?"

"This is different."

"No, it's not," he said gently.

"I know and I also know that as angry as he is with me right now, he's not about to let me out of his sight."

"Astrid, I thank you on behalf of the entire pack, but he may not. You are human, not a shifter. Even though your plan worked, it was still reckless. It's our job to protect the pack not yours." That's not what he was saying the other night, I thought to myself.

"I appreciate that, but if I knew a way to save the pack again, I'd do the same thing. And as far as I am concerned, as long as I am the Beta's Bride, shifter or not, the pack is my responsibility too."

"I see your point. As the Alpha, my first thought has to be the pack not myself."

"Just like Contessa, Tom and I do."

"Again, you are not a shifter, you won't heal."

"I'm fine."

"This time, but I have to know, how'd you know that would work?"

"Because I appealed to the woman not the pyre it's what I would have wanted but I also told her she needed to leave."

"You're peculiar, but not again okay?"

"No promises." I smiled.

"Come, let's go to the fire," he gave in, giving the same exasperated look his brother gives me. As we approached the bonfire, Tom stood up and came over to us.

"She's a wise, stubborn and brave woman," Jared said.

"Don't I know it," he rolled his eyes, "but I knew who she was when I married her."

I smiled, biting my lip. Jared smirked at me, then, "Tonight we had a close call. We all need to thank Astrid for her quick thinking and kindness, that has made us and our land safe again."

"Cheers," everyone called, lifting their drinks to me, the only person who didn't was Charlie, who was too busy screaming his cheers to do so.

I just smiled and nodded at them. "Come, let's sit down," Tom said.

"Yes please," I nodded, uncomfortable with the praise. He sat back down on the ground, leaning against a log, then pulled me down with him so that I was sitting between his legs, my back to his chest, one knee resting against his, my other leg running down his.

"Not drinking?" I looked up, motioning to his bottle of water.

"I think someone has shot my nerves enough for one night," he kissed my temple.

"Okay, I guess that is fair. Anyway, now you know how I felt."

I could tell he was teeing up to say something else, but we were both suddenly very distracted when a couple of the girls insisted on leading us in campfire songs, which did nothing but make me smile and happy that everything had worked out today.

I was laughing so hard Tom had to feed me his water when Jared decided to join in terribly followed by Charlie; the two of them with their arms around each others' shoulders swaying enthusiastically.

"I've never seen this side of him before."

"Oh, he can be quite lighthearted when he's not worried about a million other things."

"I like it."

"I'm sure the fact that he's on his third beer has nothing to do with it," Markus said, rolling his eyes and explaining to me. "He's not much of a drinker."

"You should have seen him at New Year's last year, it was the craziest I have ever seen him," Laura agreed.

"Too bad I wasn't around then."

"Well, you were, but I wasn't allowed to say anything yet," Tom said squeezing me gently and kissing my temple.

"Very true."

"Well, with a little luck I'll get to see it this year."

"And Christmas," Markus said. "That's always a good time around here too."

"Snow and Sanctuary." I cringed.

"Not a fan of snow?" Lesley asked.

"Definitely not."

"Can't really blame her though, can we? I can't imagine she saw much snow in the UK," Rox agreed.

"Not much, no."

"So, about what you did today," Rox said.

"What about it?"

"How did you know it would work?"

"I didn't, but I knew that if something happened to Tom, I'd need a hug."

"What she said to her today, was beautiful," Contessa said.

"I wish I'd seen it," Laura mused.

"I'm glad you didn't," Markus told her, touching her now-showing pregnant belly.

"Why did you do it?"

"Because what we were doing was getting us nowhere and I needed to protect everyone if I could."

Tom still hadn't said much, many had spoken to us and particularly to me, thanking me or congratulating me on my quick thinking, but I wished he'd say something.

"Hey, so a bunch of us are going to go for a run, you coming?" Jared asked.

"Not tonight, someone has to make sure this one doesn't come up with any more reckless ways of getting herself killed," Tom joked far too easily, holding me tighter. I leaned my head back onto his shoulder.

"You can go if you want, let off some steam," I told him. "I'll be here safe and sound waiting for you when you get back."

"I'm not going, I've had enough excitement for today," Leonora told her son. "I'll keep her safe."

I felt him growl.

"Tom, the pyre is gone. We're fine."

"I'm not leaving."

"I think he's staying," Charlie said. "Leave him."

"Suit yourself." Jared shrugged.

"I will."

"Sorry, guys," I told them. "Guess he's mine tonight."

"Enjoy him. We'll get him out for a run before the weekend's over."

"Only if someone keeps her from any more stupid and dangerous tendencies."

"Leonora just volunteered."

"No."

"Wait a second, I'm an adult, I don't need a babysitter. Also, I talked down a pyre, I didn't go ten rounds with her."

"Although at this rate my money would be on the little Beta," Charlie said.

A feral growl came from Tom.

"I think that's your cue to get you as far from them as possible," Jared told Charlie. "For the record, no getting into fights with supernatural beings." He turned on me.

"I didn't get into a fight today, did I?"

"No."

"Exactly," I said, leaning my head back against Tom's chest again.

"Still, you can consider that an order if you want."

"Does Tom count?"

"Nah, he needs to be challenged more often." Jared winked at me. "It'll probably do him good."

"Thanks, brother," Tom said, and I could tell he was glaring at him over my head.

"Well, see you probably tomorrow," Charlie smirked as they both jogged off into the woods. All that was left were women and a small smattering of men, most of the kids long gone to bed. I stared up at the moon and smiled.

Quietly I whispered under my breath.

"'Tis moonlight, summer moonlight,
All soft and still and fair;
The solemn hour of midnight
Breathes sweet thoughts everywhere,
But most where trees are sending
Their breezy boughs on high,
Or stooping low are lending
A shelter from the sky.
And there in those wild bowers
A lovely form is laid;
Green grass and dew-steeped flowers
Wave gently round her head."

"What was that?"

"Emily Bronte."

"What?"

"A poem I learned back home. I thought it was appropriate."

"It is, but I think we should get home, don't you?"

"I think that sounds like a marvelous plan," I said, letting him help me up before getting up himself.

"Goodnight everybody," I called to what was left of my family around the fire.

"Goodnight," they called back. Tom grabbed my hand and we worked our way back home.

"What am I going to do with you?" he said, closing the door, then pinning me against it, his face inches from mine.

"I'm sorry," I tried.

"I know, but I still don't know whether to worship at your feet or be angry."

"I know which one I'd prefer, I leaned up to him."

"Do you now?"

"Of course." I wrapped my arms around his neck.

"I was so scared watching you walk away from us."

"I'm sorry."

"Are you though?"

"For worrying you? Of course. But not for doing what I did."

"For the pack."

"You've drilled that into me for a long time."

"Since you married into danger."

"I don't regret it."

"I do, because I love you and I can't bear to see you in danger."

"Shh." I leaned up kissing him deeply. His hand gently lifted me.

"I love you," he whispered against my cheek, his lips tracing my jaw.

"I love you," I said, increasing my grip on his shoulders.

Chapter 16

"So let's take a look at baby boy, shall we?" I said to Laura, finishing measuring her protruding tummy. This was going to be the last thing I needed to do before heading in to work. Tom had tried to convince me to take the day off after all the excitement of the last couple of days, but I needed to work. Last thing we needed was me losing my job.

"Still no names?" I asked, looking between the baby's parents.

"No, but we promise you'll be the first to know," Markus said.

"I showed them the baby and his little heartbeat; he was playful today hiding behind his little hand. But it made his parents laugh and I saw their happiness and excitement which made me smile," I told Tom as he drove us back into the city.

"You aren't thinking?" he asked.

"Well, I mean, not yet, but we haven't really discussed it."

"I know, but you do want kids, right?"

"As long as we're better parents than my parents were," I told him.

"Says the teenage runaway, I think that's a given, plus, you know what they say, it takes a village."

"And we have a pack," I smiled.

"Exactly, they'll grow up wild and well and loved."

"So yes, to kids?"

"Yes, one day."

"But not yet."

"Exactly."

"Well, that was easier than I thought it would be. Do all couples have this easy of a time making that decision."

"I don't know and I don't care, we aren't most couples." He kissed my hand.

I wasn't in the building all the way after Tom dropping me off when my pager started going off, demanding I go to Human Resources.

"Come in," Caryn said after I'd knocked on the door reading Caryn Lane, HR Manager.

"Hey, Caryn, you wanted to see me?"

"Yeah, hi, Astrid." She barely lifted her head.

"Is something wrong?"

"Oh. What? No, of course not." She shook her head. "Just this came for you by courier." She handed me a hard FEDEX envelope.

"What is it?"

"I don't know."

"Okay, well, thank you," I said to her.

"No problem." She turned back to her work and I left, closing the door quietly behind me. I don't know what she was doing but I was sure that whatever the problem, it wasn't mine.

Curious, I looked at the envelope, but before I had chance to open it, I was paged down to the emergency room. I left the envelope on the nurses' station before pulling on a paper gown.

A three car pile up on the highway left us flooded with injuries. I had a middle-aged man with a head laceration, broken arm, three broken ribs and internal bleeding, likely caused by the steering wheel. It was lunchtime by the time we had everyone patched up and resting as comfortably as they could. Suddenly I was missing the nice, relaxed atmosphere of a vampyre at Sanctuary.

"Cora, I left an envelope here," I said, making it back to the nurses' station.

"Here," she said, grabbing it and handing it to me. "I put it aside out of the way."

"Thanks."

"No problem." She winked at me.

I went to the doctors' lounge and sat down and took a bite of my sandwich before opening the envelope. Inside was a single piece of paper. In the center of the page in a typed block script read:

GLAD TO HEAR YOU'RE STILL OF LLANGOLLEN.

Fruitlessly I turned my head from side to side looking for something or someone that I'd recognise. Of course, there was nothing. I took a deep breath, sliding the paper back into the envelope; there was no address, just a UK postmark. I slid it into my backpack and decided to ignore it until something came of it. I'd tell Tom when he came to pick me up after work.

Another surgery — this one scheduled — and some checking of charts, and Tom was outside waiting for me.

"Well that doesn't look good," I joked, noticing that he was on the disheveled side.

"Don't," he warned.

"Tom, what happened?"

"Let's just get home and have a drink."

"Okay, now I am worried."

"I promise I will tell you, just let me do it at home with a beer in my hand, okay?"

I sat there silently, one leg tucked up against my chest, watching him and wondering what on earth had gotten him into such a weird state. Pursing my lip, I opted for constantly staring out the window wondering what was going on. The pyres were gone, everyone was safe, why was he still in a mood? He remained quiet, as he parked the car in the garage, grabbed my backpack and walked across the lobby. I watched the tension in his shoulders desperate to know what was going on in his head. The elevator ride was unenjoyable. As soon as we made it to the apartment, I didn't bother taking off my shoes or removing my scrubs, I walked straight to the kitchen. I noticed him moving to the bedroom out of the corner of my eye.

"Don't even think about it." I stopped him without even turning my head. "Get over here." I grabbed a beer, opened it and placed it on the counter. He arrived over to the counter. "Drink." He looked at me, fighting back a smile, lifting the bottle. "Good," I said, "now talk."

"Astrid."

"Don't Astrid me, everything should be sunshine and roses, we had a great morning, the threat is gone, you're healing, and we are together."

"This is why I love you." He leaned across the counter and kissed me.

"I'm glad, now talk."

He smiled at me and led me to the sofa. "There was a break-in."

"The pyre?"

"No, and there was no scent."

"None?"

"None."

"Okay. Maybe it was just an ordinary break-in."

"That only broke into our offices, left claw marks inside and outside of the building, and managed to make it so that not a scent was left in the office, literally no one's, not mine, not Jared's, not Contessa, no one's."

"Is that even possible?"

"I don't know."

"So it's freaking you out?"

"We've spent the entire day with the police, combing the place. Trying to figure out if anything is missing."

"And is there?"

"No."

"Tom?"

"Jared and I can't believe this is still happening? I mean, was it the pyre before she left?"

"But you've been tracking their scent. If they were going to or could mask it, wouldn't they before now?"

"Exactly."

"So, you don't think that it's a pyre?"

"Nope."

"And you never got a scent at the shack the day we found…"

He stopped me. "Jared and I have talked about that at length."

"So you're worried that there is a secondary threat."

"We hope there isn't anything, but…"

"I understand. Too much is telling you to worry."

"Exactly, which is why you wouldn't talk to me?"

"Astrid."

"Hey, we both have long days, this doesn't work if you don't let me help." I told him. There was suddenly a rap at the balcony window. "You expecting someone?" I asked, surprising myself that someone knocking at our high-rise balcony door had somehow become normal.

"I wasn't."

"You get the thirty-second-floor balcony door, I'm getting out of my scrubs."

I couldn't hear what was being said but there was definitely more than one other person out there with Tom. I threw my hair up and put a flimsy comfortable dress on.

"I understand that," Jared said. "But she's…"

"Okay," I said, stopping whatever argument they were choosing to have, "what's going on."

"Don't worry about it," Tom said to me without taking his eyes off Francis and Jared standing in our living room.

"We're arguing about me." I figured out, pursing my lips.

"We were wondering if you'd help us out?" Jared said.

"But I told them that you have enough on your plate, we've asked you for enough already."

"Jared," I said.

"I know you have work and you're busy, but with everything that's happening we were hoping you would help us."

"With what?"

"We have some books, Francis reminded me that we had them."

"Okay, are they medical books or something?"

"A little different?"

"Stop playing, just tell me what you need, and I will do it."

"They want you to translate them," Tom said.

"We are hoping that there is information in them, the kind that will tell us there is a way that they can hide their scent, or all scents, or traces or something that none of us understood."

"You're hoping that old magic, or old folklore is the answer."

"Yes."

"Okay, so here is what I'll tell you. The way that I see it, the faster the pack gets some sort of an answer and we can figure out what is going on, the better."

"Exactly."

"I am willing to eventually translate the books, but for now, the best way for us to find an answer is for me to just read them and see what sense I can make of it."

"How do we know that you aren't going to lie and say there's nothing there when there is?" said Francis, and for the first time since I joined the pack, I was really annoyed.

"And how do you know I won't lie when I translate it for you," I said, stoic.

"Francis, go," Jared said, and fortunately he did as he was told.

"Ignore him," Tom told me.

"Here's the problem," Jared said to me. "The only person with any understanding of the ancestral tongue is Tom, and he can't read it."

"I haven't used my Welsh since I left, even then my speaking is better than my knowledge of the written."

"I know that, but whatever you can do."

"I'll give it a read and if I find anything, I'll let you know."

"Can you come to Sanctuary and get them?"

"I'll make it over tonight."

"You worked all day," Tom objected.

"I understand that, but I can make it over for them, then I can get started."

"We can't thank you enough."

"For the pack it's no big deal," I promised.

Chapter 17

"Astrid," the tall man said to me, questioningly. He'd grown so much since I had last seen him. He gained some muscle and cut his hair and looked every bit the Earl of Llangollen that he should. I saw my own green eyes in his and red hair, the two things that made it evident we were siblings, but in truth we are twins.

"Brandon," I said, tears forming in my eyes, I felt my lips quiver as I bent, giving him a quick curtsy. I'm not sure where it came from, I just knew that Mom would be reminding me with her eyes if she was here. "Lord isn't here, is he?" Suddenly I felt Tom behind me, keeping me from losing myself, protecting me.

"He's not here, I promise. Asie. Look at you, you've grown up so much."

"Astrid?" Tom pushed me behind him.

"Tom, it's okay, this is my twin brother," I told him. "Oh, this is Tom by the way. My husband."

"Husband?"

"Yeah," I smiled, nodding.

"Brandon Alfred Charles Davis, the Earl of Llangollen." He offered Tom his hand.

"Earl?" he asked, taking his hand. I flinched at how that was the word he picked up on looking quickly at me before returning his gaze to my brother.

"Yes," Brandon said, not taking his eyes off me.

"Bran," I cried, the shock finally lifting, surprising Tom and running headlong into the arms of the brother I hadn't seen in eleven years.

He held me, then picked me up and headed to the kitchen counter. We'd always been the same height, Bran and I, until we were about thirteen and he quickly overtook me. Not too much later I completely stopped growing, a solid five foot two, to his almost six feet. Tom closed the door behind us. He hadn't forgotten my penchant for sitting on counter tops. Got more than one slap for that one, you'd think I'd have learned.

"Astrid, I am so sorry, I couldn't protect you," he told me backing up again to get a better look at me.

"Don't," I told him, "we were both kids there was nothing that we could do."

"Still, I was the rightful head of the family."

"He wanted that power, he was never entitled to that title, but every day I feared the man that made us call him Lord. It's not your fault."

"The day I got your letter."

"I am so sorry," I said. The tears were a steady stream pouring their way down my face. At this point Tom was standing behind me situated on the counter with the twin brother I didn't think I would have the courage to ever see again in front of me. I could feel Tom's confusion regarding everything happening, but the circles he was rubbing on my back told me that he was understanding that above all I needed him right now.

"Look, I understand. But I wish you'd told me."

"If I had told you beforehand and he found out I'd never have gotten away."

"We don't know that, although he flexed his power over us, he never did me, and I'd never tell him."

"Do they know you're here; do they know you found me?"

"No, they don't, though I can't say that suing a hospital, becoming a doctor and being in a relationship with Mr. Thirty under Thirty is going to help keep the secret." Which reminded me that to others, we still weren't legally married.

"I'm not alone anymore, and I am not sixteen," I reminded him.

"You were never alone."

"Bran, you know I don't mean it that way, it's just it was different back then. We were kids. Anyway I have Tom and a massive family that will back me up now, so don't worry."

Bran's eyes widened at the large man that stood half a head above even him.

He pulled back and I jumped off the counter. "Can I get you a drink?" I asked him.

"Please," he said.

"What would you like?"

"Anything will do." So, I pulled out the kettle and began boiling the water for a brew. The two men watched, both clearly studying me making me feel self-conscious.

I set up out the cups, made the tea, handed them their cups and led our little trio to the living room. Tom and I on the couch and Brandon in a chair.

"So… what are you doing here?" I asked him.

"Do you really think that once I found my sister I was going to wait for her to disappear again?"

"No, but still, I thought you'd be mad."

"I couldn't, I think I knew you were going to leave eventually, long before you were even considering it. I have to say, I am really impressed though, you've built a great life for yourself."

"Thank you."

"I was a little surprised to hear how well you did in school though." Part of my wondered how he got his hands on my school records.

"She wasn't good in school back home?" Tom asked, before I had the opportunity to ask.

"Never, when she left and dropped out I figured that would be it for you."

"All I needed was a chance, once I got it, and I was away from everything, it was like it clicked."

"I'm glad to hear it. And to think my little sister is a doctor."

"Yeah, hard to believe," I agreed, but in truth it was all hard work, I earned where I was now.

"Especially with that lawsuit."

"Don't remind me."

"So how about you, what happened after I left?"

"Well, Lord freaked."

"Naturally."

"Mom?"

"Nothing."

"Really?"

"Yeah, I don't know if it was a not caring or a cancelling out of emotion, being grateful that you got away and upset you were gone."

"Sounds like Mom."

"Where are they now?"

"Cornwall."

"Really?"

"Yeah, I kicked them out when I inherited my birthright."

"Huh, can't imagine that went well."

"No, but it was oh so satisfying, plus they had it coming."

"I bet. You got into politics then?"

"Did I have a choice?"

"No. But I couldn't have done it."

"I know. Too free spirited."

"You said you were married, was it a civil ceremony?"

"It was sort of an alternative ceremony," Tom said.

"It goes more with his family beliefs and well, Lord has everything, the fact that I got my hands on my passport is a miracle in itself, it's the only thing that has allowed me to get my work and student visas."

"Well, if you ever do decide that you want to get legally married, maybe apply for that green card."

"No," I said, smiling.

"Yeah," he said. He handed me a large folder. Inside was my birth certificate, as well as a few mementos, and some photographs.

"How did you not tell me?" Tom asked, indicating my title.

"It never fit me to begin with. Not using a title made it less likely for Lord to find me." I smiled, grabbing a photograph from the pile. "Do you see this?" I said to Tom.

"I do, Lady Astrid Alora Wren Davis of Llangollen. That's quite the mouthful."

"Thanks. Hey darling, look at this," I said, handing him a photo of me when I was nine.

"You were gorgeous even then." He kissed my temple. It's the first childhood photo he'd ever seen of me.

We ordered take out for dinner, all of us quite content to sit and get to know each other again. My two favourite men finally getting to meet each other. It was incredible and uplifting and something I desperately needed. Before he left, he handed me two things, one was another manilla envelope the other a small card.

"What are these?" I asked.

"The big one was found with our father's files, the second is an invitation to my wedding. I know you might not be able to go, but Lord can't hurt you anymore, you're an adult now and we will all be there," he nodded at Tom. "I am trying to find a way to not let him come but so far it's not going well. It's Cynthia, Asie, and I think she'd like to see you too. Even if you don't, do you think you could invite me to yours, even if it is just a Justice of the Peace or Judge when you get legally married? I would love to be there."

"I'll think about yours okay. As for mine, you got it."

"That's all I can," he smiled.

"God, I missed you," I said, hugging him.

"I miss you too." He hugged me tighter. "Take care of her," he called to Tom behind us.

"With my life," he promised.

"So, you have a brother," Tom said, as I closed the door behind me.

"Yeah, I do."

"He seems nice, pity I had no idea he even existed until he showed up at our front door."

"I never thought he would see him again," I said, looking at the floor and moving past him, heading for the bedroom. Going to my side table, I threw the envelopes he handed me, in the drawer beside my bed.

"He is an earl in the United Kingdom, did you really think he wouldn't have the resources to find you?" I just looked at him as he said this. "I'm sorry, that was disrespectful, I should have ended that with, my lady."

"I am no lady. Do you have any idea what that cost me? Because if you did you wouldn't be throwing that back in my face."

"How could I? I didn't even know about any of it until a few hours ago."

Quickly I changed without saying anything.

"Trust," he said to me. I know he knew I was still reeling from everything that had just happened, so he was trying to be calm, but I could tell he wanted answers and was upset. I could tell by the curve of his shoulders and the vein in his neck. "I have trusted you. Yet everything about you up until you were sixteen you just kept from me. Do you not trust me?"

"It wasn't just like that." I defended myself, sitting in the center of the blue king size bed with the gold curtains that made me feel like I was swathed in stars. I wore my shorts — the little ones — that kept me cool while pressed against his warm body at night — and a tank top.

"What was it like then?" he asked me gently.

"It's hard to explain. I've left that all behind me."

"I'm your husband."

"I know, and I love you."

"But even though I told you my biggest secret, a secret that literally threatened the life of the entire pack, you still chose not to tell me. I've held back nothing."

"I'm sorry." I looked down at my feet.

"Not that you did it, you're sorry you were caught."

"It wasn't like that. I've left it. It wasn't easy for me back in Wales. It's too hard even to mentally go back there."

"Nothing is so hard that I can't help you get through it."

"You remember when you told me that I was strong and courageous when I should have been broken, and that you liked that."

"Yeah."

"I was strong then, because when I came to America I wasn't just broken, I was shattered. I spent years before I met you building myself up with steel. But this one thing turns me back to a broken pile of glass again."

"I'm supposed to be the one you lean on when you need to be the glass," he said, continuing the metaphor.

"Okay, do you really want to know this?"

"I feel like I need to now."

"Well, then, you have to promise me that you won't think any less of me for it."

"I don't think I could."

"Hold onto that thought. Do you remember that day when you told me that you never want me to feel unsafe in my own home?" I asked.

"Yes," Tom said, he was a cautious distance away.

"Well, I was. Do you remember when you asked me why I left Wales when I dislike it here so much?"

"Yes," he said.

"Do you remember the day you asked me what happened to my thigh?"

"Yes, I also know that when Brandon asked to see it you were happy to show him it and your shoulder and he ran his hand directly over the scars," he said, glancing down at the scars that were camouflaged by the tattoo. But with Tom's sight he could see the mess underneath perfectly and gently ran his hand over it, willing it away every time he saw it. Knowing it was worse than I was letting on, and that looking at it brought back memories. He never would have expected what I was about to tell him. Well, that reaction was about to get stronger, if he didn't shift altogether.

"Look I think you need to sit down for this," I said, offering him my hand, which he took as he sat down across from me. I took both his hands in mine even with his being so much larger. "I need you to be calm when I tell you this, because I am going to tell you the truth of my past and it's not easy or good."

"Go on," he encouraged.

"As you probably guessed, the answer to all three questions is Lord. Well that is what he made us call him, after he married my mother following my father's death. My brother and I were six. He wanted one thing, control. It is why he was so adamant that he be called by a title that doesn't belong to him. It belongs to one person only. My brother, Brandon.

"Lord wanted to take everything, he knew that Brandon's birthright was going to make him Earl one day, and though I was called Lady, I held no power, had no right to any lands, and had a rebellious nature. He took up the mantel to try to control me. His belt, his hand, slipper. And when he was drunk, so much worse. Whatever he could find. He never raised a hand to my brother and to my knowledge, he never did my mother. It's like he thought he could control all of us through me. So, when I was sixteen I ran, grabbed everything I could, started applying for student visas — while dancing to make ends meet — stopped using my title and for all intents and purposes became an American.

209

"The thigh?" His hand grazed my leg multiple times.

"When I was fourteen…" A sob escaped from my chest.

"You can trust me, that's what we built everything on," he promised. I know it was probably the last thing he wanted. But this was going to be hard, so I crawled into his lap, hoping to ground him and me.

"When I was fourteen, I came home late one night; it wasn't my fault, my friend's parents' car broke down, but he wouldn't listen," I said, watching his eyes as he did mine. "As you know I have a slight tendency to be hot headed and he wouldn't allow me to explain. I was in my school uniform, a kilt, knee-high socks and blouse. He was drinking. He got so angry and kept grabbing me, and I kept pushing him away. The bottle on the table fell and smashed." Tom's arms constricted tighter around me. "He picked up the broken bottle, he brandished it at me until it cut down my leg. The glass dug and stuck into my thigh."

"You were a child."

"I should have known better. I knew I should have given in, and been apologetic, but I didn't, it had been eight years. Eight years of living in fear. Eight years of threats and eight years of his tyranny. I was tired of giving in, tired of not fighting back, honestly I was just tired."

"Didn't the police wonder what happened?"

"My family isn't like that. Mom didn't want the scandal."

"You never went to the hospital?"

"No, I didn't."

"What happened?"

"I sat leaning against the wall and waited for him to pass out. I put pressure on it, sitting quietly. The wound was deep but didn't really affect anything major underneath. My brother found me, but I motioned for him not to say a word. He picked me up and brought me to the bathroom, placing me in the tub. He got Mom against my wishes."

"You never went to a hospital?"

"No."

"You cleaned it up?"

"We did."

"But your mom stayed with him."

"She did."

"And the burns?"

"Cauterizing."

"Please tell me you're kidding," tears welled in his eyes matching my own.

"We couldn't get a couple spots to stop bleeding after removing the glass."

"With what?" I just shook my head. "Why didn't you tell me that before?" I could feel him shaking, so I gently stroked his cheek to calm him, his arms tightened around me and I pressed myself into his body.

"It's all in the past, I am moving forward. It's why I have been doing everything in my power to never be the victim. It's why I try not to think about home. It's why I love it at the Sanctuary so much, the area is beautiful, like Wales but I am not tortured by memories of my past, and for once in my life I feel like I belong somewhere."

"Listen to me, you know how they say wolves mate for life? It is the same for us, I am yours as you are mine. All I want is to protect you, help you, and bring you comfort and solace. I can't do that if you aren't going to let me in."

"Is now a bad time to say that I have known what a shifter is, since before you told me?" I pressed back looking into his perfect blue eyes.

"Considering the Earl of Llangollen just walked into our apartment, I'd say yes I have already figured that out."

"I'm really sorry."

"Are you going to be okay?" he asked me, angling my chin up and kissing me gently between my eyes.

"I can't believe I just saw Brandon again. So, many memories of my life before coming here."

"Yeah, and that's another thing, I get that you didn't want to tell me about some things, but we are going to have to tell Jared. The Earl of Llangollen is your brother, if he or your stepfather know what we are it could be potentially dangerous. We survive due to secrecy." I understood what he meant and nodded.

Chapter 18

"There are things you need to know about my wife, things I didn't learn until yesterday," Tom said to his brother, as I did as I was told by him, kneel repentant to the Alpha, our personification of the gods. Yeah, apparently my background was that important.

"Tom, what happened?"

Tom explained everything that happened the day before, that I was from sect aristocracy, and that I had fled for personal reasons believing that if I cut myself off, it couldn't come back to haunt me. "You entered our family with sect related baggage?"

"It's family baggage, its personal baggage."

"Your brother is Earl of Llangollen, your stepfather is infamous for being a brute among the sects," Jared spat. "Your being here is a threat to the pack."

"I assure you, I'm not a threat," I swore.

"Clearly you're not a reasonable enough judge on the matter."

"Jared," Contessa said coming to kneel beside me. "There's too much to this, we have to understand where she is coming from. We cannot imagine what Astrid has been though, we are fortunate to have a loving family."

"You are still a threat," he growled.

"How exactly am I a threat?"

"What if you were recognized, to have the Lady of Llangollen as hostage, that's one hell of a leverage, imagine what they could extort."

"So far my being who I am has been nothing but an asset to the pack."

"How so?" Contessa asked me.

"First of all, the medical examiner I have been getting information from, she's a mage, I've known her since medical school, she's the only person who did better than I did in my undergrad. She taught me about mage practices, you have her to thank for what I have been able to do for you medically and for the fact that your brother is still alive. If it hadn't been for what I was able to do, doctor or not he would not be standing there." I did not mention Charmaine or the others, they weren't going to come out in my favour.

"Second?" Jared pushed.

"Remember the vampyre who came to Sanctuary after Tom killed her mate?"

"Of course."

"She recognized me, I knew she had based on the way she watched me. So... I used my social standing to get her to leave."

"What did you tell her when you hugged her?" Tom demanded, realizing I didn't tell him that certain truth.

"I told her, 'Just because I left Wales, doesn't mean I'm not of Llangollen.'"

"That's all?"

"It was enough, there are only five people that govern all five sects and one of them is me brother, kill any member of my family and that was going to end very badly for her."

"That's why you wanted to try; you knew exactly what you were doing."

"In so many ways I want to thank you because your resources have assisted the pack, but in other ways your holding things back and lying has put us in a precarious position, our lack of knowledge is a liability. Others know who you are still out there. And as I mentioned earlier imagine the benefit of having Lady Llangollen as a hostage. Tonight, you will apologize to the entire pack for your insolence, and undergo the dance of the claws, as penance and sacrifice to the gods." Tonight, was a full moon and the entire pack would be at the ritual and spending time at Sanctuary.

"Absolutely not," Tom declared, indignantly.

"I have passed a sentence, don't push me, brother. You are to blame as she is. You brought her into the pack, she's your responsibility."

"Jared, please, he didn't know. This is all on me."

"Jared, she's human. You can't do this," Contessa pleaded with her husband.

"Jared, don't make her do this," Tom begged for me, even Contessa who had her reservations about me was sat beside me looking at her husband, begging for him to reconsider. One hand was rubbing my back the other clutched my hand tightly, as we knelt before the pack Alpha. And I was suddenly happy that Jared had allowed me to open a small medical clinic at Sanctuary.

"She knows how we operate here, she agreed to our rules and laws. She failed to divulge who she is in the strictest of senses to all of us. She will explain herself to the pack and she will apologize for deceiving us."

"She didn't lie maliciously, she lied by omission out of fear. She didn't even tell me, and I am her husband."

"And though that speaks to her not committing treason, it doesn't make it right or grant her automatic forgiveness. Her stepfather is married to the Dowager Countess of Llangollen. You were so worried about telling her about being a shifter, it never occurred to you that when she didn't freak that she might know more than she is letting on. Can you imagine what he might do, if he figures us out and where she is?"

"She's human, not a shifter, or shea," Tom said. "She knew of shifters, by her birthright, but didn't know I was one."

"She's Lady Llangollen, the only family of mortals, who know inherently that we exist," Jared reiterated. "Her failure to disclose her past even to you speaks more to your marriage than anything else brother."

"My family was tasked with assisting the sects to protect their secrecy. Outing any of you would have gone against the entire mandate of my family."

"This man probably knows."

"He knows. I knew of them, but was never allowed around them, plus they sort of cut off ties with my family. I don't think they trusted Lord."

"Why do you call him Lord?"

"Because he demanded it."

"How are we supposed to trust you now?"

"I walked away from my title and position years ago."

"Jared, this is madness, she didn't do anything."

"She has lied to the pack, she has put all of us in danger, not informed us of something pertinent to pack survival. If it wasn't for the fact that I don't think she did it maliciously, I would call this treason. Do you think her brother knew you are a shifter?"

"No, I don't."

"There is a reason sect heads are in one place. To keep the rest of our lives secret from each other."

"My brother—" I was cut off.

"I have heard enough out of you," Jared barked, I lowered my head further.

"Jared, there is no need for that; she is still my wife, your sister-in-law and a member of the pack."

"She is irres—"

"Let me stop you here, you tell me you have never made a mistake as pack leader."

"She is not pack leader and she swore an oath," Jared declared. Tom's hand balled into fists and were shaking.

"Tom, stop," I said. He looked down at me, fury in his eyes. "Jared is right. I should have said something. I swore my oath, not just to you, but the pack. I am going to do it. I have to apologize to the pack and take the claws as penance. I knew the laws and the familial bond when I joined. They have taken me in as family, which is more than I have ever had or deserved. I owe them this and so much more."

"NO," Tom said, kneeling in front of me and placing his hands on either side of my face.

"It's was my responsibility," I told him. "And you will do your duty as Beta of the pack and my husband." I could see the darkness in his eyes, but they were starting to soften. My hands moved to hold his face.

"It won't heal for you like it does for us."

"I have taken a lot worse," I promised him.

"You say that now," Contessa told me.

"It's okay," I promised. "I'm strong."

"You survived your stepfather, not the dance of claws," Contessa said, having listened to the entire story.

"Look, the purpose is sacrifice and to apologise to the gods, not to kill me. I'll live and be stronger for it."

"I don't know if your wife is brave, stupid or both, brother," Jared said to Tom before he left dragging his wife with him.

"He's gone, get up," Tom said gently. "You know when I said you were the woman of steel, I didn't mean it seriously."

"Tom, stop it, if I knew this was a possibility the moment you told me that we had to tell Jared, you certainly did."

"Still you are mortal."

"I am strong, I will leave instructions for what to do."

"No."

"Yes, Lesley has been working with me, she can handle it, with a little help."

Chapter 19

"I was born Lady Astrid Alora Wren Davis of Llangollen," I said on my knees with my head dipped towards the circle containing the entire pack. "I have known of the sects my entire life, and kept my knowledge from all of you, I sincerely apologize," I told the watching eyes of the pack around me.

"Keep going," Jared told me.

"My stepfather is a terrible man and he does know of the existence of the sects. He is ruthless and an evil man. My brother is the Earl of Llangollen; he was born to be the voice of the sects and the human representative, like my father before that. But my father died when I was a child. My mother remarried a man who insisted I call him Lord. He was violent towards me, ultimately leading to severe injuries to my shoulder and thigh." The gaze of every man around me dropped to the tattoo that apparently didn't conceal my scars well. "My dishonesty will and does put the pack in danger and for that I willingly submit myself to the gods."

"Astrid has been sentenced to the dance of the claws. Through which she will give herself to the gods and seek forgiveness from the pack."

From the majority of the pack came outrage. It was reassuring I still held their support.

"It is done, the sentence has been laid and the gods demand penance," Jared boomed.

"Stop," I called out, and the pack went silent, my posture straightened, and I held up my chin, feeling their outrage at what was going to happen. "I knew the consequences; I am the wife of your Beta. I knew what I was keeping from you and what it meant. I will take my punishment." I silenced the pack. Once settled I retook my repentant posture.

"Tom, grab a log, from the side," Jared demanded. It would be Tom's own punishment, forced to aid in preparation of his wife's punishment.

"Jared, you don't have to do this," Tom tried one last time.

"Go and get it," Jared said, no nonsense. I watched Tom head to the outside of the circle and bring a large round trunk in front of me. "Bare her back," Jared told him.

"Jared, he is the one who brought me to you. He made me tell you the truth, stop making it harder than it has to be for him."

"When he brought you into the pack, he took ownership of you and spoke for you. He will assist and watch what he brought upon you," Jared said, but I noticed the inflection in his voice told me that he was pained by what he was going to do.

Tom didn't say a word, helped me out of my sweater, grabbed the neckline of my shirt and pulled. With his strength it was too easy. Unhooking my bra, he rubbed my back quickly, bringing goosebumps to the surface before guiding me forward, placing my hands on the stump.

"You have studied the words?" Jared said, it was a question, but it wasn't.

"I have," I told him.

"Tom, you will not interfere," Jared demanded.

"Yes," he said, watching my back exposed to the cool air.

"Start," he told me.

"I give myself as penance to the Phoenix, whose great fire burns through all of us. I repent my transgressions," I said in fluent Welsh, I was told that if I could, I should. I knew by the ruffling of wings that Jared had turned to his eagle and readied myself.

The talons dug into my back and I locked my jaw, willing myself not to utter a sound, unwilling to hurt Tom. I felt my skin open as my blood began to flow. It would be shallow, but it didn't diminish the pain.

"I give myself as penance to the great Wolf, whose wisdom and intellect guides us, I repent my transgressions," I said again through shallow strained breaths, again in my own Welsh mother tongue. I knew he was now a wolf, based on the heavier breath of his great black wolf. This time I couldn't stop myself as his claws ripped my skin.

When the screaming settled, I said, "I, Lady Astrid Alora Wren Davis — Sharpe of the Seattle pack and Llangollen — do give myself to the great beasts of the sky," I panted, collapsing, resting my chest onto the stump.

"Astrid," Tom whispered fervently.

"No don't touch her," his father said quickly.

"But, have you—?"

"No, wait for it to stop, they're taking their sacrifice."

I breathed deeply through my mouth, as the burning pain continued through my back. It was painful but expected, I knew what was coming, but never imagined the ripping of my back would be that intense. Now it was a tingling burn as I slumped forward onto the hard stump.

It wasn't long and the pain jumped in intensity, and I was screaming, then whimpering. *Please go into shock, please go into shock,* I chanted internally as I knelt in pain, I needed the pain to go more for Tom's benefit than my own.

"Now," I heard Tom's father say, and Tom got on his knees before me.

"Hey, hey," he lifted my face. "You did so well."

Contessa joined him. "Is she okay?" she asked Tom, as I heard footsteps urgently moving from us.

"Contessa, go after him. Tell him I am okay and I am sorry," I forced myself to say, sending her after her husband.

"He did this," she said.

"No, I did this. He did his job, tell him this, help him." I sent her. "He isn't going to be okay right now." She got up and nodded.

"Tom, her back is still weeping, we need to get it cleaned and closed before it gets worse," Leonora said.

"Are you kidding? Did you see what just happened? She's human, she should be bleeding profusely," Lesley argued.

"Not now," Tom said. "Let's get her to the medical center." My back was stinging and painful, but shock was closing in and my head was resting on Tom's hand. "Okay, baby, I need to lift you."

Vaguely I noticed everyone was gathering closer, concerned.

"Carefully," Leonora said to her son.

"I know," he nodded to her. "Dad," he pleaded.

I felt hands on my sides, careful not to get too close to my new wounds, they moved me as Tom moved around and my body rested against his.

"We have to move you," he said, kissing the top of my head.

"No, let's just stay here," I said feeling sleepy, my head against him.

I felt Tom look up. "I am sorry, beautiful, but you can't stay here," Leonora said to me. Then to Tom, "The bleeding is starting to get worse, you need to go." She was right, through the shock I felt the blood start trickling down.

"I am so sorry, baby," he said to me. He picked me up and any reprieve that the shock had given me disappeared, as I screamed from the pain in my back.

I felt him tense and whisper, "I'm sorry, I'm sorry, I'm sorry," before I passed out.

I woke up far too quickly. "Anyone who doesn't have to be here, really should go," Leonora said.

"I can't get it in," Lesley cried. I opened my eyes and Tom's eyes were watching my back, as I opened my eyes. Lesley was freaking, trying to get the needle in my hand. It was probably the poking and re-poking that woke me. "I do know but I haven't done this in a long time," she cried.

"Get it in," Tom said, putting the weight of his being the Beta behind his voice.

"Tom," I said reaching for him.

"Give her a break," Leonora said to Tom. "She isn't a doctor." But Tom wasn't listening.

"Tom," I demanded. "Help me up."

"No," he said.

"Honey, with what you just went through it isn't advisable," Leonora tried a little more gently.

"We're going to need an ambulance," Lesley declared. I can't get a vein. It's like she's dehydrated, and they've collapsed."

"I can get it in with some help. Do you want to explain to me what just happened?" I asked them.

"She shouldn't," Tom said.

"Son, do it," Allain said behind him.

"Clench your teeth," Tom advised me. I did as instructed as he lifted me and the blanket under me. It hadn't occurred to me that they'd stripped me.

I breathed deeply a couple times before speaking. "Leonora, tie the blue band around my bicep and hand me the needle." They both did as they were told. "Tom, keep me still," I insisted. I found the vein and stuck in the IV. Lesley was correct, my veins were collapsing but I got it in anyway. "Okay, and the tape." I taped it down. "Bring over the IV." Lesley set up the bag so the IV was flowing.

"Tom, lay me back down." He did, and a few moments later I passed back out while holding his hand.

When I woke up the next day, Tom was exactly where he had been the night before. His hand still held in mine. "Hey," I said, squeezing his hand.

"Oh, my gorgeous girl." He kissed the back of my hand.

"You should go lie down."

"I'm not leaving you."

"Thomas," I tried.

"Astrid," he said.

"Is it sealed?"

"Yeah."

"Help me up," I told him.

"No."

"I need to check it, and I'm not going to be able to do so lying here on my stomach."

"It's fine."

"Did you flush it?"

"We did."

"Okay, good," I said sleepily.

He looked at my back. I knew my back was bare but a sheet was pulled around my hips. "I wish we had someone other than you with real medical experience."

"I am fine, if it was anywhere other than behind me I probably could do it." He refrained from saying anything. "Tell me what happened."

"I don't know what you are talking about."

"Tom, I love you, and I know you way better than that. What happened?"

"Your blood flowed the wrong way."

"Excuse me?"

"Jared cut into you, and your blood flowed upwards towards the sky and dissipated. It lasted for an anguishing couple of minutes before the moon flashed red and I could go to you. When it ended the majority of the bleeding stopped."

"It's a ritual, I am sure that this happens all the time."

"Astrid, the dance of the claws may be unusual and ritualistic, but that doesn't happen."

"Oh."

"Exactly."

"Why?"

"We have no idea."

"We?"

"My mother and father came to talk to me while you were asleep."

"Jared?"

"No, but Contessa came."

"Tom, go get Jared."

"He won't listen to me."

"Tell him I want to talk to him, he'll listen."

"He is the Alpha, he doesn't have to, and he makes sure everyone knows that in case the present situation was not enough evidence of that."

"Tom, he has a lot more of a gentle soul than you know."

"Seriously, Astrid, look at what he has done to you."

"I hope you never have to experience what he does. He is our Alpha. Go get him for me, please."

"I am not leaving you."

"Where do you think I am going to go? I can't sit up on my own, not that you'll let me find out."

"I will be back in a minute."

"Okay, and bring me back my book."

"The Welsh one that you are reading as a favour to the pack?"

I knew where he was going with the statement. However, "Yes please," and a smile was my response.

After removing the tube from my IV, and sealing the end, I closed my eyes, not to sleep, just to relax. But I was drifting when I felt a gentle hand on my shoulder. "You still with us, my love."

"Did you get him here."

"He's here." He sounded surprised.

"Leave us."

"No."

"Tom, I need to talk to Jared, he'll get you when we're done." I kissed the hand that had moved to my face.

"You come get me," Tom said to Jared, placing the book I had asked for on the bed beside me.

"I will, brother, I promise." Jared clapped a hand on his shoulder. Tom kissed my temple, I didn't say anything, and I heard footsteps. "He's gone."

"Help me up, I can't do this like this," I told him. He moved and twisted me gently so I was sitting properly. He was careful to avert his eyes as I lifted the blanket over my chest.

"Here," he said, unbuttoning his shirt leaving him in his T-shirt.

"Thanks," I said as my brother-in-law helped me into the shirt. I buttoned it quickly.

"Tom said you wanted to see me."

"He didn't think you'd come."

"I—" He never made it past that letter.

"Jared, I don't blame you, I don't hate you, I don't resent you," I told him.

"Astrid you're—"

"I'm not the one I am worried about."

"Tom."

"No not even him. You."

"I'm fine," he said.

"Go ahead, fool everyone else. Tell everyone that you are okay, I know better."

"Astrid."

"Sit down," I instructed softly and he did, sitting gently next to my knees. "Last night I sent Contessa to you, if I thought he'd go I would have sent Tom. Now listen, I am going to be fine. You did what you had to do. I can't fault you for that, and I can only hope that Tom never gets to understand it. But listen to me."

"It's only the second time I've ever done that," he said.

223

"It can't be an easy decision," I said.

"As the Alpha I am required to oversee the survival of the pack. If one person gets away with something that could endanger the pack or the sect as a whole, it sets a bad precedent and eventually we have chaos," he said to me.

"As such I am going to tell you something, something that won't endanger the pack, but that I think you deserve to know. When I fled I had help from a friend, a caster friend, and some of the medications that I have made in the clinic are old mage salves, that not even your books contain or that my mage friend knows."

"You have a caster friend?"

"Yeah," I said.

"Look, I'm not worried about that or the mage stuff, we have been using their remedies for generations, the fact that we have someone who is able to use and make their remedies is beneficial to the pack."

"I am sorry," I said.

"I know."

"It was never done maliciously. My life just wasn't like this, its harder for me to be open."

"I know."

"And I didn't know you guys were shifters until Tom told me before he asked me to marry him."

"I know that even if I didn't think that yesterday. Just try and trust us okay? So that we can trust you, because I do."

"Thanks."

"Jared, what do you think happened last night?"

"They told you?"

"I knew something weird happened, but I wasn't sure what until I asked."

"That's not surprising, but I don't know what happened. I am going to be telling the pack that it isn't to leave the pack, and that goes for you as well."

"I won't be telling anyone."

"I know your family is connected, but this could make us more vulnerable."

"Don't worry, I'm not connected anymore. My brother found me, that doesn't mean that I am going anywhere or going to tell him what is going on with me and my life. As for my stepfather, the sects ceased connections with my family as long as he spoke for my family."

"And your caster friend?"

"She has been an amazing friend to me, has helped me out of a situation I never would have gotten out of myself. But we parted and have only spoken a couple of times since, I trust her, but I won't tell her."

"Look I know it hasn't always seemed like it, but I do trust you and you are my sister-in-law," he said.

"I know you wanted better for your brother, someone with true shifter bloodlines."

"It never mattered to me who he married as long as he was happy. Did I have a preference? For sure, but the first day when he came to me to tell me about this new client he had, I knew there was going to be something different, there was something different about him."

"Really?"

"Yeah, I think I knew before he did." My body shifted and my breath caught in my throat. "I'm—"

"Don't stop being sorry, it aches, but I am fine."

"We're having a meeting tonight; I should probably go prepare."

"I'll be there," I told him.

"You don't need to be there."

"I am the wife of the pack Beta, I will be there in my rightful place."

"I'll send Contessa to help you get ready beforehand," he said standing up. "Thank you."

"For what?"

"For being you." He kissed my forehead. "I'll send Tom back in. He won't leave you."

"I remember the feeling," I nodded at him.

While he was gone, I shifted slowly, throwing my feet slowly over the side of the bed. With a little luck Tom had gone to change and maybe have a shower so he'd be a few minutes. I placed my feet gently on the floor. Okay, I thought, I'm still strong enough. I kept a hand on the bedrail getting up.

"What are you doing?" Tom said, rushing to my side.

"What do you think?"

"I told you this is a bad idea." Both his hands held my hips.

"Well, I have been just full of those lately, haven't I?" I pointed out.

"Astrid?"

"Help me and I promise to get back into bed."

"Then we will discuss this crazy idea of joining tonight's meeting." I moved to unbutton the shirt. "Here let me help." He swiftly and deftly helped me out. I held onto the bed as he removed the bandages from my back. In a few places they stuck and pulled but were otherwise fine. He grabbed a hand mirror so I'd be able to see without turning.

"I can't see."

"Stay still," he said, placing the mirror back on the table beside the bed. I held onto the bed exposing my back. "Here," he said, putting his phone in front of me. Two sets of lines crossed my back, and they were well stitched, which I wasn't expecting.

"Stitches?" I asked, confused. I'd left a ton of steri-strips for them.

"Yeah, Mom and Lesley know how to stitch, a useful trick around a pack of wolves. Her mother was a nurse in the war, so she taught her."

"I'll have to thank them," I said.

"I don't think she's looking for thanks." He went to find some bandages, tape and the salve. "Stay still," he told me."

"I will." I smiled as I watched him put on a pair of latex gloves and open the bottle, applying the liquid to a piece of gauze. Moving behind me he dabbed the clear liquid on my back. "Damn," I squealed.

"Seriously? Razor sharp talons open your back without so much as a groan, apply a healing salve on those same wounds and we get a reaction."

"First of all, that stings," I said.

"Jared is going to love to know that this is more effective than the dance," he said.

"You're not funny, finish and dress it." I rolled my eyes then closed them and concentrated on my breathing and the gentle movements of his hands on my back.

"Did Jared lend you this," he said, helping me back into my borrowed shirt.

"Yeah, it was better than the alternative of having the blanket pulled under my armpits."

"True, now we can get you back into the bed."

"Fine, but leave me sitting up."

"Okay, but only until you're tired, then you're resting."

"Okay," I agreed, knowing arguing was futile.

"Now what's this about you insisting on being there tonight?"

"I am going."

"No you're not."

"My back is my punishment and my penance, it is over, now it is my duty to be your mate as I am first and foremost."

"I'm not going to risk anything else happening to you."

"Contessa will be coming to help me get ready," I said. "Because above all else our duty is to each other and the pack." I reiterated.

"Nothing is going to change your mind, is it?"

"No."

"Okay."

"Why don't you come up here and hold me until that time?" I said, moving over slightly. He did, gently. I knew he was tired as well; he lay his head back and I cuddled into his side.

"Go get ready," Contessa told my husband.

"I'll help," Tom insisted.

"No, your mother is on her way here, she'll check the stitches and we'll have her ready and deliver her on time."

"Go, do your job." I smiled at my man.

"I love you," he told me.

"I love you too."

She put down two bags at the foot of the bed as I watched her. "I don't imagine you have eaten much, so I brought some food." She smiled.

"I'm not hungry."

"Yes, Tom told me of your penchant for not eating when you're not feeling well, but you have to keep your strength up, if not for you then for the pack," she said, pulling out a salad and handing me the utensils.

I opened the lid and looked at her. "This is my favorite." I smiled at my sister-in-law.

"I know," she said as I stabbed the spinach, raspberries, goat cheese and almonds with my fork. "I have to thank you and apologize."

"For what?"

"It's no secret that I haven't been the most welcoming, I am sorry."

"It's okay, I was an outsider, I'm also different and pig-headed and I am used to people not warming up to me. And so much is on your head. I have had to learn a lot, and even then it's less than you. The Alpha's Queen."

"There's something else I have to say. When Jared passed sentence, I was against it for a number of reasons, one I have grown to love you like the sister you are. Two, you aren't a shea and I knew it was going to be worse for you."

"I'm fine," I said as I watched her purse her lip. "There's another reason, isn't there?"

"The last reason is a little more selfish. Jared is the love of my life, and though he seems strong and controls the pack and our secrecy and our livelihoods, he is sensitive, gentle and kind, even though he doesn't show it."

"I know, I see it."

"Most don't because he doesn't allow them too. But you do see it, you're wise and see things in people. You see a gentleness and kindness in people that most don't see in themselves. Yesterday, you had every reason to hate him, but there was never defiance in you, always sincerity, and submission. When the dance was over, you told me to go to him because you knew he'd need me."

"I would have sent Tom, but he wouldn't go."

"Not sure Tom would have been the best to console him at that moment; he was ready to kill him last night." When Jared was doing what he had to do, I was watching Tom. I've known him a long time, I've never seen him so angry or pained. If he had gone, we could've been having a very different conversation.

"But if he saw Jared, I'd hoped he'd see the pain he felt doing it. The pain worse than the physical."

"Then today you sent for him."

"I did."

"How did you know he'd come?"

"Because Jared needed to."

"When he came back, he was different, lighter. I don't know what you said, I don't need to, but thank you."

"You're my family," I told her. "We are sisters after all." I smiled.

"Come now, let's get you washed and cleaned up."

Between Contessa and Leonora they had my hair washed, me cleaned up, hair done and dressed in loose fitting clothing, in no time. "Thanks, guys," I said.

"No problem, we're family remember," Leonora said, and Contessa nodded beside her.

"So, Lady, huh?" Charlie said, standing next to me after Leonora and Contessa deposited me outside the circle. "Got to say I didn't see that one coming."

"What you don't think I could be a lady?" I looked up at him.

"Well maybe if you got rid of the motorcycle, steel toe boots and quick wit that is always getting you into trouble," he smiled.

"Really?"

"No not even then, you're just so Astrid, I can't picture it."

"In your defence, I was never much of a lady," I smiled.

"You seem like you were supposed to be part of a pack, not an aristocracy," he laughed.

"Really, do I really act like I was raised by wolves?" I kept my face straight.

"Hey, I didn't mean it like that." He got all defensive and I burst out laughing. The movement of the laughter caused a ripple down my back and I dropped.

"Woah there, little lady, you okay?" Charlie asked, catching me under my hip.

"I will be," I promised.

"Charlie, you're supposed to be watching out for her." Tom rushed over suddenly beside me on the ground.

"I was," he said.

"Tom, it's my fault I was cracking a joke, the laughing caused a pain."

"This is why I wanted you to stay in your medical centre. Usually you can't get enough of it."

"Not when I am the patient." I looked at him.

"Well, no more laughing, okay? And Charlie, that goes for you too, no more making her laugh," Tom ordered.

"You got it, boss." He saluted, causing Tom to roll his eyes before helping me back up.

The circle went on as normal. I kneeled next to my husband as he and his brother worked through the circle mostly because I struggled with standing for a long period of time.

The night was about to close when everything went foggy. My body began to buzz. It was like someone had taken over my every motion. I pulled a scalpel from my jean pocket, but I didn't remember putting it there. A symbol lit up behind my eyelids. Using the scalpel, I cut down my palm. It was the first time others noticed something weird was going on. I noticed the heads turn to me, but still my body made controlled movements not initiated by me. Squeezing the blood from my palm on the cement dais, I used the blood to create a circle with a moon and sun symbol inside, and a number of symbols I didn't recognize right away, around it.

Holding my cut hand above it, I heard myself say. "Blood of the Innocent. Scent of the ancestral air. I bring thee to protect my home, my land and my family." The blood burst into flame as my hand held above it. I could smell a scent I'd only experienced once before: the scent of burning flesh, but it didn't hurt this time.

My mind cleared and I lifted my face, first to the sky, then to Tom, my first conscious movement. Before passing out, staring into the blackness, I felt a small darkness around me. *Daughter,"* a voice gently called out to me.

"Is someone there?"

"Daughter, be careful, there is darkness around you. Pray to us, in the old language we hear best."

"We?"

"You know us as the beasts," a much more gruff voice said.

"What danger?"

"We can't tell you, it's up to you."

"Go back to your husband, Daughter, and remember what we said."

I blinked a couple times before my eyes focused and I noticed I was being cradled in my husband's lap. "Welcome back," he smiled at me, gently drawing his fingers along my cheek.

"What just happened?"

"We were hoping you could tell us," he said softly.

"I think I just…" but something in my gut told me I shouldn't say. "I don't know." I lifted my left hand and looked at the palm; the flesh should have been cut and burned but it looked like nothing had happened. "Great."

"And the little bit of redecorating, do you know what it means?" Jared asked, motioning to the symbol he knelt on the other side of me across from Tom.

"Yeah, it's the ancestral symbol for protection." Then, "Tom, I don't feel well," I looked at my husband as my stomach rolled.

"Charlie, take her home, I need to talk to Tom," Jared demanded.

Tom looked like he was going to complain but decided better of it. Carefully I was passed between them. Excitement over the crowd disappeared, and Charlie carefully carried me home and upstairs to bed.

"Are you okay, little lady?"

"I think so."

"What happened?"

"If I could tell you, I would, but everything feels wrong."

"Astrid?"

I didn't say anything.

"I'm going to go get you a glass of water." He stood up carefully and went to the bathroom.

"Amddiffyniad," — 'protection' — I started to say over and over again.

Charlie put the glass down next to me before giving me a look I ignored and left the room.

Looking around the room I kept looking for an answer, and explanation. The room was bare. Nothing gave me an answer to the questions I had swirling around my head. I closed my eyes. Saying the same word, it never losing its meaning to me. My legs tucked underneath me, I tried to will the beast back. "What danger? It couldn't be Lord?"

Chapter 20

Much to Tom's chagrin, I made the decision that I was going back to work a week after I had gone through the ordeal. We managed to talk to the hospital and they understood that I had been injured and I was put on a leave of absence, but today I was going back. I even managed to get Tom to let me drive myself. I love him but he's overprotective.

On my way through the lobby to get to the parkade I noticed that there were a number of people standing around the front doors. I looked at my phone and decided that I had enough time to take a quick look, and with my luck there was going to be something going on.

Tremain, the door man, with a confused look on his face, was standing with everyone crowded around the door with his hand on his head. "Tremain, what is going on?"

"Someone vandalized the front doors last night," Tremain told me.

"Do we know who?" I asked Tremain, the elderly doorman.

"No idea, ma'am," he wiped his brow.

"May I?" I asked, wanting to see what there was happening in the doorway.

"Of course." He opened the door and surprisingly there were claw marks in the wall, sidewalk and front of the building. If I didn't know that they were gone, I would have assumed pyres.

"Thanks, Tremain," I told him.

"Wait, Dr. Davis." He stopped me. "This came for you yesterday."

"Oh?" I asked.

"Yeah, you were late coming in last night."

"No problem," I said, but then I saw what he was holding in his hand. A FEDEX envelope with another British postmark.

Heading to my car, I called Tom.

"Hey, babe, did you forget something?"

"No... I was just at the front doors with Tremain, it's been vandalized."

"Astrid, it's a big city, vandalism happens."

"Tom, they look like claw marks."

"Like a pyre?"

"No, Tom, not like a pyre."

"You think it's a shifter?"

"I do."

"Okay, I'll go see if I can pick something up."

"Tom, be careful."

"Always, baby girl. Are you okay?"

"Yeah, of course, why?"

"You sound weird."

"I'm just worried, that's all."

"Thanks."

Hanging up on him, I got into Bluebell and quickly tore open the envelope. Again, another single sheet of paper with typed script, identical to the first.

PITY NO AMOUNT OF EDUCATION AND UPWARDS MOBILITY WILL CHANGE THE FACTS

I took a deep breath, realizing that it wasn't my brother. I'd seen him now and he certainly wouldn't have sent me a message with such a negative meaning.

Beep, beep, beep. *ER.* My pager alerted me. My back was smarting but it didn't stop me from running to the emergency room. "Cora, what's going on?" I said to the head nurse on duty.

"A man was just brought in, he won't let anyone else look at him or touch him."

"Okay," I said.

"Name?"

"We don't know, and he won't tell us."

"Room?"

"Thirteen."

I hurried into the room with her on my heels. "Crap, Charlie, what the hell happened?" I said moving to the tall man who was Tom's best friend. He was slumped over slightly and his hair was matted with the blood coming from his temple.

"Damn, Astrid, I don't even know, I think someone attacked me. But I can't remember."

"How would someone get the jump on you?" I asked, putting my stethoscope to his chest. His heart was a little fast, but from my observation of the pack, that was normal. "Other than the cut on your head does anything else feel off? A headache? Do you feel cold?"

"My shoulder and arm." His eyes darted to the nurse behind me.

"Cora, this is my cousin-in-law Charlie. I got this, can you take my phone and call Tom for me and tell him to come here and what's going on?"

"You got it," she said, taking my outstretched phone.

"Charlie, a mortal shouldn't have gotten this close to you," I said.

"You're telling me."

"You don't think it was, do you?"

"Not even for a second. I still have my backpack, so it definitely wasn't a robbery.

"Charlie, I am going to need to reset your shoulder, but I don't know if I am going to be able to do it myself."

"No."

"Charlie, I have some great colleagues."

"No, we'll wait for Tom."

"I'll stitch you until then and we'll hope he hurries." I numbed the area on his face, quickly swabbed it with betadine and after checking it was clean stitched it up. It took about four stitches and it was done.

"Am I going to have a cool scar?" Charlie asked me with a wink.

"Not as cool as mine," I joked, as I usually did with Charlie. It was one thing I loved about this man, he was in the hospital and I still felt at ease with him.

"Charlie, I am worried about your shoulder, please let me get someone to help reset it?" With how fast they heal I wanted it in before nerve damage set in.

"No, they don't know about us, or our physicality."

"What did you do before I came around?"

"Escaped the hospital before anyone noticed."

"How did you get in here today?"

"I woke up in an ambulance."

"Oh, Charlie."

"Don't oh Charlie me, I was attacked remember, we should be happy I didn't show up in the form of a giant dog or bird."

"Okay, I'll try," I said, knowing that the longer that it waited, the more likely it was to have nerve damage, especially with his quicker healing. I grabbed a local anesthesia, measured it out and injected it into the shoulder. "Stay still," I told him, kneeling up on the bed beside him. I grabbed the arm in my right. "Okay, straighten it for me," he did with some assistance from me. "This is going to hurt."

"I know." He closed his eyes. I pushed on his arm and pulled his shoulder at the same time, he let out a little grunt as I heard it click back into place.

"Crap," I said, letting go of his arm but unable to move yet my eyes shut.

"Hey, you okay there, little lady," he said, shifting towards me.

"I will be, I just need a second," I said and he went to put a comforting hand on my back. "No, don't," I told him.

"Oh, Astrid, I'm sorry. Your back, I completely forgot."

"Don't worry about it," I said, lowering my feet to the ground. As I did Cora came in with Tom and Jared in tow.

"Thanks, Cora," I said, taking my phone back.

"Ah, Dr. Davis. Are you aware your back is bleeding?" she said.

"No, I wasn't, I must have pulled a stitch, I'll come find you in a few minutes to stitch it for me, okay?"

"Yeah, no problem," she said.

"In the meantime, will you bring me a large men's left arm shoulder brace and another for his wrist."

"No problem." She nodded, closing the door.

Tom and Jared both looked at me. "So, Charlie has a cut on his temple, which I have stitched, and we just popped his shoulder back into place. I am going to recommend the braces until I say otherwise, I also think he should stay with us for tonight, just so I can check him over in the morning, but I don't really see any reason for alarm."

"His head, I heard reports he was unconscious?" Jared said.

"He doesn't have a headache and his pupils are responsive and equal, so I'm not worried about a brain injury; it was probably minor if there was anything and it's healing itself by now, anyway."

"Want to explain to me how he was attacked and you're the one bleeding?" Jared asked me.

"I am sure that it's just a stitch from when I popped Charlie's arm back in."

"You did what?" Jared demanded.

"In your condition?" Tom said.

"Seriously, Charlie was just attacked, by someone who was not a mortal and you want to give me the third degree about this?" I looked at the two heads of the family.

"She has a point," Jared said.

"Fine, you ask questions and talk, I'll look at her back," Tom said, looking at them and sitting down in a chair indicating I should stand in front of him.

"I was walking home from the office, I was staying late because Ragnor and Barty needed a few things copied and filed for their court appearance tomorrow, so I was walking home and I heard screaming. I was about to double back to see what was going on if someone needed help, and the next thing I knew I was in an ambulance being brought here. Fortunately, I remembered little lady works here and demanded to see her," Charlie said, keeping his eyes on the Alpha.

"You popped three stitches," Tom whispered, gently lowering the back of my scrubs.

"Cora is a friend, she'll fix it without too many questions," I said, lowering myself to his lap and filling out the chart in my hand.

"Charlie, are you going to give me your medical card, or are you going to make me look it up?" I asked the member of my pack. As the Beta's wife I had access to the entire pack's personal information, and it was easy enough to access on my phone.

"It's in my backpack," he motioned to the table near the bed.

Jared retrieved it, who in turn threw it to Tom before handing it to me. "So, when Cora gets back, I am going to help you into the braces. Then you are going home with Tom, if I thought you would, I'd make you stay here tonight. Try to get some sleep, and if anything changes, you get your feathery ass back here, or you'll have me to deal with, understand?"

"Goodness, and I thought the Alpha and Beta's orders were scary," Charlie joked.

"Charlie," Tom warned.

"Yes, Astrid, if anything changes, I will come right back here."

"Thank you."

Jared insisted he would be the one to get Charlie into the brace, with my instruction. So I got Charlie's signature and told them they could leave. "You won't get painkillers at this time of night, but there is some in the safe at home," I told Tom, "give him two Tylenol threes and I'll be home after work." I kissed my husband.

"Thank you, Astrid," Charlie said.

"And thank you for calling us so quickly, you did well tonight, little sister," Jared winked at me helping Charlie out of bed.

"Any time, get him home and I'll check on him soon," I motioned with my chin.

"Thanks again, little lady," Charlie smiled.

"Get those dealt with," Jared said. "If it helps, you can consider that an order."

"Get going the lot of you." I smiled.

I quickly moved things out of the way, grabbed a fresh suture kit and needle and poked my head out of the door. "Cora, can you join me in here please."

"No problem, Dr. Davis," she said to me. "You still need a stitch?"

"Yeah, apparently it's three," I said.

"Okay, up you go," she said.

I pulled off my top and laid face down on the bed.

"My god, Astrid, what the hell happened?" she asked.

"I had a little accident the other weekend. Don't worry about it," I said. I felt a gentle pinch in a few places.

"Should you even be working like this?"

"It's not as bad as it looks," I promised.

"Stay still," she encouraged. "So? How did you pop these stitches?"

"I was popping Charlie's shoulder back in," I smiled.

237

"You're nuts," I could tell she wanted to say something very different but restrained herself.

"My husband and brother-in-law agree."

It didn't take long to get the stitches fixed up and me dressed. I changed into a clean top. The rest of my shift was fairly uneventful. I pretty much stayed in the ER and checked on a few patients until the night ended.

"Hey, little lady, how is my favorite doctor?" Charlie said from the sofa, his hand in what appeared to be a half-eaten bag of crisps.

"Didn't I say you were supposed to be resting?"

"I was but then Tommy gave me those pills," Charlie started. I heard a low growl come from our bedroom; Tom hated when Charlie called him that. "And I got the munchies," he continued, ignoring Tom.

"See, on a normal person they would knock you out."

"Life of a shifter, baby." He smiled really big, around another mouthful of crisps.

"So, after I gave him the medication, he decided to eat us out of house and home," Tom said, appearing in the doorway in a pair of sweats. "Welcome home, baby," he said, giving me a big kiss, purposely to annoy Charlie.

"Oh, would you two get a room?"

"Sure, does the kitchen sound good to you?" He winked at me trying to get a rise out of Charlie.

"Okay, you two, that is enough, I am going to check out Charlie, then he and I are going to sleep, and you are going to hold me as I do so." I kissed my husband.

"Sounds like a job I was born for."

"But first you're going to go into the safe and get a needle and a vile called lorazepam and an alcoholic wipe."

"Yes, ma'am," he saluted me.

"Come on," Charlie objected.

"You and I both know your shifter abilities work better when you sleep, so unless you want to be medically sidelined next weekend."

"Fine," he said, putting down the crisps.

"Now take a deep breath for me," I said, placing my stethoscope to his chest. He did. "And again." He did. "And again. Very good. Now watch my finger," I said flashing my light into his eyes. "Now follow my finger," I said, placing the light in my pocket. "Perfect. Last thing grip my hand with your left hand." He did and, man, did it ever hurt. "But remember I am mortal," I reminded him, earning me a throaty laugh.

"Do I pass, Doc?"

"Yes, but you still have to sleep and rest, understood?"

"Yes, ma'am."

"Good."

"Here." Tom handed me what I asked for. I swabbed his right shoulder, measured what I needed and injected the sleeping medication into his shoulder. I got up, took the crisps and placed a blanket over him, because that was not going to take long to work. It suddenly occurred to me that I shouldn't be bringing my work home with me. Who was I kidding it was way too late for that.

"You know I love that man," Tom said, closing the door, "but, man, can he ever be trying."

"I'd say the same," I joked. "But he is just like every other uncooperative patient."

"Speaking of uncooperative patients, how is your back?"

"All fixed." I smiled. "But you wouldn't want to help me out of this shirt, would you?"

He said nothing, just closed the gap and carefully peeled off my shirt. "Should I put some more salve on it?" he asked, running his fingers ever so lightly over it.

"That would be nice," I said, stripping off my scrub pants and replacing them with a pair of shorts before laying down on the bed. The salve was cooling on my back and felt amazing. "Thank you," I said as he finished and wrapped the quilt around me before sliding in himself.

"Come sleep."

After two days I sent Charlie home with a clean bill of health. After him driving Tom nuts, I'd just got used to tuning them out, choosing to read the book Jared had asked me to work on; it required a lot of concentration so ignoring them was easy.

"Astrid, this arrived at the firm today," Tom said, holding an envelope out to me, identical to the ones that I received in the past. "Since when do you get your mail sent to the firm?"

"Who brought that?"

"It was given to a secretary, she recognised your name and gave it to me."

I pursed my lips and took a deep breath.

"Astrid, you've gone pale," Tom sat up straighter.

"Stay there," I said, running to the bedroom and grabbing the other two envelopes.

"What's that?"

"The other two."

"The other two what?"

"At first it was the one and I thought it was Brandon, but then he came here." I handed him the second one as well.

"Why didn't you tell me?"

"You didn't know I had a brother when I got the first, which was sent to the hospital, plus, we were just getting over the whole pyre incident. When the second one came we had more important things to worry about, because our apartment was vandalized, then Charlie was attacked."

"I never asked about that pyre, did you know her?"

"I did."

"Her name?"

"Agatha."

"You knew?"

"I was safe. There was no risk, but if I hadn't been there, mark my words, it would have been a massacre. Namely the packs, Agatha is over eight hundred and fifty years old."

"Shit, but Shara I managed to…"

"Shara was maybe two hundred, they were both accomplices of my stepfather."

"Astrid, I need you to back up. People are sending you what could be construed as menacing letters. I need to know. The pack needs to know. You haven't even healed yet and we're here again."

"This is the first one," I said, handing it to him.

"What is this supposed to mean?" he asked, opening the first then the second envelope.

"That's the problem, I don't know."

"Open the third one," Tom demanded of me.

I did and for the third time the same block script was on a single piece of paper.

YOU'RE ALWAYS GOING TO BE A DISAPPOINTMENT TO THE NAME — LORD.

The three pages were now aligned on the table.

GLAD TO HEAR YOU'RE STILL OF LLANGOLLEN
PITY NO AMOUNT OF EDUCATION AND UPWARDS
MOBILITY WILL CHANGE THE FACTS
YOU'RE ALWAYS GOING TO BE A DISAPPOINTMENT TO
THE NAME — LORD.

"That's not from your brother, is it?" Tom said. My legs were now bundled against my chest.

"No, it's not," I choked out.

"That's the man who…" Tom couldn't even say it.

"I guess I'm not so hidden anymore," I said, a lump rising in my throat. Out of nowhere I felt like I couldn't breathe, I reached out for him. "Tom."

"Hey… hey, hey, you're going to be okay," Tom said, gathering me against him.

"Tom, I can't. What if he comes here? I …"

"Then it will be different." Tom stopped me.

"How?"

"You have family this time, you're safe. He has to go through the entire pack in order to get to their little Beta."

"You know Jared was right."

"I know."

"We have to tell him."

"We do, we should go tomorrow."

"I can't, I am working tomorrow night."

"The night after then, when we're going to Sanctuary anyway."

"Okay, we can probably go early and talk to him then."

"You're nervous."

"I am."

"Why?"

"Because I have a second piece of bad news for him."

"Which is?"

"The book Jared gave me."

"Keep going."

"There's a number of chemicals that can be combined together with wolfbane to mask all scents in an area to shifters."

"Oh."

"And I might have gotten some information from a source that you're not going to like."

Chapter 21

"I don't understand why you aren't seeing it. I know when it comes to your own family you don't want to see the worst."

"Really? Because you were so close with your family, weren't you?"

"Tom, please."

"Don't 'Tom please' us, you are bringing up some extreme accusations." Jared shut me down.

"Both of you are blinded by loyalty. Who else would have had access to everything they need? Everything they'd need is in my lab. One person equipped with this information and they'd be able to do everything that has happened, before, during and after the pyre episode, and we wouldn't know."

"Astrid," Tom warned me to be quiet.

"Do you realize how many of our own people I've had to patch up, and we are the only ones who know how we operate and our routines."

"You opened a clinic."

"And how many people did you patch up before I was here?" I didn't wait for an answer. Anyway, none of the men and women I've patched up have been able to remember how they got into that state, and their attackers' scents were always masked."

"So, that is not indicative that it is necessarily one of us."

"Scratches, claw marks outside of mine and Tom's apartment building. The kidnapping of the pups, and getting the jump on Charlie in particular. My sources say that there aren't any new shifters in the area."

"Your source?"

"His name is Charmaine and that's all you need to know."

"Who have you told this theory to?"

"Really, who do you take me for?"

"Well, considering you have the audacity to say these things to me, after the letters that you have been getting and all the lies that you have told, you could be deflecting."

"You know what, forget I mentioned anything." I got up from my seat in Jared's office and headed to my clinic. For the rest of the weekend, I worked solely on my research trying to figure out what was going on with Lorelai, or trying to get a better stock of medications and tonics for the pack. No matter how angry I was with Jared and with Tom for agreeing with him, my loyalty would remain with the pack, and to my family.

"Hello, Lady Astrid." Landry stalked towards me, his arms held far from his side.

"Landry, can I help you with something?"

"Our Lady Beta's Bitch," he spat, but not the nicer way that we refer to the female shifters in the pack.

"Landry is everything okay?"

"As long as you do exactly what you are told it will be."

"Excuse me?"

"You heard me."

"First of all, I don't have to listen to you, and second this is my lab," I said pushing my microscope back, "I need you to leave."

"Awe and how do you propose that you're going to make me, little lady," he said, and I really didn't like the way he was using Charlie's nickname for me, which he'd been using, well before finding out the truth.

"Landry, I really need you to leave or I am going to get Tom and Jared."

"Tom and Jared aren't going to be able to help you soon."

"Landry, what is going on?"

"You'll know soon enough," he leered at me.

"Landry, where is Tom?"

"Have a seat and don't worry about it." He moved a chair to the center of the room and forced me into it. As I was forced down, my worst fear was realized as I heard barking, squawking and howling loudly from outside.

"What is happening out there?" I screamed, jumping up.

"Sit down," Landry demanded. "It's not for you to worry about yet."

"Landy, I am the Beta's Bride and I demand to know everything you know about what is happening out there."

"This is what is meant to happen, the strongest of the pack will survive." Landry turned to the door. "As it always has been, as it should be, as it would be." Quickly I took the opportunity, while his back was to me, to reach for a scalpel in an open drawer a few feet away.

"Landry, please stop," I said as I heard whelping outside.

"Shut up," he spat at me.

"Landry, this isn't you. You're my friend. Shiloh is my friend."

"You have no idea what you are talking about."

"You forget I have been a part of this world my entire life, not just upon my marriage to Tom," I said, making sure that the scalpel was hidden. "No council will recognise a coup, if someone wanted to vie for leadership you needed to make a formal plea to them."

"You know nothing. The strongest earn the right to lead."

"That's what it was like hundreds of years ago, people have evolved since then. Things have changed by agreements, to ensure the survival of the species."

"We aren't humans, this is how it is done." He turned, coming towards me and hitting me hard across my right cheek, ringing my bell. "Now be quiet."

"No council will recognise this."

"You know nothing." He grabbed both my shoulders and pulled me up. "They told me I couldn't kill you, but what is one less Beta's Bride." I felt his claws extend into my shoulders. His eyes were dark and angry. I knew he meant it. Stealing a hard breath, in one quick movement I grabbed the scalpel from my belt loop and drew it across his throat.

He spluttered and I pushed him away from me, causing me to go backwards over the chair behind me. The wound was deep and lethal as I had intended it to be. Thirty seconds was all I needed to stay away from him before he passed out. I quickly got up and ran to the bathroom, locking the door behind me and leaning against it. I slid down into a heap on the floor.

What is happening? Why? Are they really staging a coup? Tom? Is this what the beasts meant when they warned me about danger being all around me. "Please, beasts of the sky, make everyone I love be okay." I calmed my breathing and moved. Carefully and slowly I opened the door. Landry's head sat in a pool of his own blood just inside my lab.

Still clutching my crude blood covered weapon, I ran out the door only to run into Francis mere feet outside of it.

"Francis, what is going on?" I said, fearfully scanning the area. "You need to help me; I have to find Tom."

"Landry is supposed to be watching you," he growled, and for the first time I noticed three angry-looking gashes weeping slightly down the side of his face and I knew, once again, I should be afraid and needed to get away.

"What?" I started to back away, but it was too late, he grabbed both of my arms forcing my crude weapon from my hand.

"Matteo, get over here," Francis called to his son.

"Why are you doing this?" Matteo looked just like his father, round faced, with bushy dark hair, neither of them however, looked like Carly or Marlee.

"Once we get everyone who would oppose us out of the way, everyone will understand."

"Tom will oppose this. I will not understand if you hurt him." I began to struggle to get away.

"Be quiet." Francis demanded.

"Why not me?"

"What about you?"

"Why not eliminate me?"

"Dad?!" Matteo suddenly said to his father, his voice shook seeing his uncle.

"I guess now we know how she got past Landry," Francis said to Matteo, before turning back to me, "have to say I am impressed. I never thought you'd have it in you. Tie her up."

"Help," I started to scream, repeatedly.

"Gag her," Francis said emotionless.

After they had my arms behind my back attached to a chair and removed my ability to scream for help, Matteo asked. "What now?"

"I am going back out there to help which is where I should be, you watch her here," Francis commanded his son.

"Oh, please, a shifter would be lucky to get out of those," Matteo said while I fought fruitlessly in my bonds, while watching the body of Landry lying on the floor beside me. I'd seen plenty of dead bodies in the past, but none that I had killed myself. Matteo flexed unnecessarily; veins popped in his biceps.

"She's important and your responsibility now, do not fail us as Landry did," Francis told his son, leaving.

I was stuck in my lab, just Matteo, myself and a body. But Matteo was young, maybe if I pleaded with him with my eyes, hoping I could get through to him. But he just ignored me pacing around the room. I felt tears trickle down my cheeks with each howl, whimper, bark, scream, and pop from a gun.

But I couldn't know who was screaming each time. One scream in particular tore through my soul. High pitched and agonized, I was sure it was Leonora. It was one of us. But who? And the tears flowed.

Eventually I heard noises getting closer to us. "Don't make a sound," Matteo said, testing my now damp binds. I fought against his hands and they moved around my head and face. He quickly stilled my movements. "Stop fighting me," he warned, brandishing his claws along my face.

"Ughh…" I screamed into my gag as he clamped his claws down on my left arm, digging into my skin causing me to scream louder, he smiled as if enjoying it.

"Don't go anywhere, I'll be right back," Matteo laughed at himself. Unfortunately I was stuck here completely at the mercy of Matteo and whoever else was working against us. Matteo left through the lab door. Somehow being alone was worse than being with him. At least then I had someone to watch and observe, now I was just alone in the dark, stuck, wondering what was happening in the new quiet. Clearly whatever was happening was over, but what of Tom? What was left of my pack? Who was a mutineer and who was loyal?

I felt my heart quicken as I continued to panic. I tried to force myself to calm, but it was hard to steal the required deep breaths through the makeshift gag courtesy of Francis. Around the gag saliva was dripping down my chin. You need to relax I told myself, you're going to put yourself into shock.

Closing my eyes, I decided to try and forget where I was and what was happening, focusing instead on my laboured breathing and remembering peaceful green rolling fields and the soft rolling rivers instead of the blood dripping from my upper arms, smalls drops puddling on the floor.

My only sense of time was every time I opened my eyes and saw nothing but the quickly darkening sky. But the quiet was enough to drive anyone crazy. All hell had broken loose. I was left with nothing now, but the loudness of complete silence. All I could do was wait and with a little luck Tom would find me. Closing my eyes again, I must have lost consciousness because the next thing I knew I was being awoken by a loud racket. But it wasn't Tom who was entering the clinic.

"Astrid," Christopher the stocky older shifter said, his gray hair reflecting what little light there was.

"Someone wants to see you," Stephen added.

"Mmm… mmm," I shook my head as they came closer. Wide eyed I watched them as they untied the bindings around my torso, then the ones around my legs before attempting to remove the gag. When Stephen moved too slowly I was able to lurch my head forward and sink my teeth into his hand.

"Damn," he spat, quickly moving his hand out of the way.

"Get away from me!" I screamed.

"Astrid. Stop, we have orders."

"No!" I screamed again. Stephen and Christopher exchanged glances as I tried to hit them with my shoulders and kick them fruitlessly. They shrugged to one another before re-inserting my makeshift gag, grabbing an upper arm each. I tried to fight them as they dragged me from the room, but they were so much bigger and stronger than I was.

"No, you heard me, you find my wife and you find her now." I heard my husband's booming voice and gave up my fight against the shifters that were pulling me down the path of the compound.

"Did you hear that, Astrid?" Christopher whispered to me kindly, as though I hadn't just tried to fight them off.

"She's here, sir," Stephen called on my other side.

"Astrid," came Tom's much hoarser cry. He was standing on the dais steps, as I was escorted still bound down the aisle of the remaining pack members.

Seeing my husband, it hit me these men weren't here to hurt me, they came to help me and my knees gave out. Unable to support myself I dropped at the edge of the dais.

"Why is she tied up?" Tom demanded, accusingly.

"We found her like this."

"She's quite feisty, she bit us when we tried to remove the gag. We couldn't get her to trust us," Stephen explained.

"Well, can you blame her? Look at what just happened? She's a tiny little human and you're two shifters, are you telling me you couldn't handle her without restraining her?" he said, accusingly.

"I'm sorry, Tom, but I don't think we should underestimate her. It would appear that she killed Landry," Christopher said, bowing his head as my cheeks grew warm, knowing a large part of the pack was watching me knelt on the ground, gagged and bound.

"Really?" Tom said, then to me as he knelt down in front of me, "I've got you," he promised, his hand turned into a talon and he carefully tore off all my binds.

"Tom," I breathed, throwing myself forward, thankful that he was okay and safe, and as far as I could tell, unhurt.

"You're okay now," he promised me, hugging me tightly to him.

"What happened?" I asked, confused and overwhelmed.

"I'll explain everything later. Did you really kill Landry?"

"He didn't leave me a choice, it was me or him."

"Are you okay otherwise?"

"I'm a little sore and I have a headache, but I will be okay," I promised, both of us oblivious to the pack around us as we held each other tightly. I heard him sniff.

"You're bleeding," he said handing me a rag for my forearm. I'd forgotten about Matteo's little parting gift.

"Thanks."

"We have things to do then you can lay down." He kissed my temple. Keeping one hand on my back, he waited until I sat down on the dais steps.

"Tonight, has been a bad night for the pack, members of our own family have divided us, but we have risen up. Some family we lost, others betrayed us, but it is important that we remember who we are and that we support each other."

"What are you planning to do?" Lesley asked.

"I will call the sect leaders and work with them."

"They're our family," Shiloh said. "Shouldn't we keep this in the pack." And I suddenly realized she hadn't been part of the coup. My heart broke realizing what I had just done.

"No, they gave up that right when they murdered their own brothers and sisters, the sect leaders have facilities to deal with these kinds of matters."

"What kind of facilities?"

"Jails and things of the sort, but I am not sure where. It's privileged information for those of the Welsh colonies."

"Do you know?" Colby asked, glaring at me.

"I do, but all I can tell you is that they are humane facilities. And well managed. The information on their locations is privileged. Just be happy this isn't a hundred years ago."

"For now we need to get a hold of the Welsh sects, but only pack leaders have the number to contact the sect leader. Would anyone have an idea how to contact them?" I saw Tom's eyes lower and his Adam's apple bob. What is going on? Where is Jared?

"Um… I can help." I raised my hand, sitting on the dais steps before replacing the quickly reddening rag to my forearm.

Tom looked down at me. "How?" he asked.

"So, as we all know, I have mentioned a few times I have a friend that helped me flee Wales. But no one ever asked me who or what that person was. She's an old caster friend, she or her parents should be able to help, if not I'll call my brother, but I don't think any of us want that."

"Who?"

"Her name is Aeryn, last time I saw her, her parents were the sect leaders, but I was sixteen when I left, either way she should be able to help or at least talk to her parents for us."

"Aeryn Fitch?" he asked.

"Yeah, that's her."

"Oh, for the sake of the gods, call her," he said. "As for the rest of you, stay here, and if any of them get out of line, do what you have to do, but only if necessary. We do not condone violence for violence's sake. Charlie, you are in charge until I get back. And in the meantime, find someone to remove Landry from Astrid's floor." I looked at Shiloh as he said this, her face a mix of emotions. My heart sank. Her tears were unmistakeable and solidified the guilt I felt.

"Yes, sir," Charlie nodded.

"Here, come with me," Tom said, offering me his hand to help me to my feet. I took it appreciatively. He walked me into his office and sat down on the sofa.

"Tom, where's Jared?" I questioned, closing the door behind us. He didn't say anything, just held his hand out towards me sitting on the sofa that spanned the left wall. "Tom," I said, kneeling down on the floor in front of him and taking his extended hand.

"He didn't make it," he said, and I saw a single tear roll down his face.

"Contessa?" I asked. He shook his head. "And your parents?"

"My father didn't, Mom did, she's with them now."

"Oh, Tom, I am so sorry," I said, leaning up to hug him. He wrapped his arm around my waist and sobbed into my neck. It was a different dynamic, since meeting him I had been constantly reliant on him, needing guidance and reassurance, the tables were turning. He needed me now, and I was damn well going to help him.

"Should we go to Leonora?"

"No, we have things we have to do. Mom understands I am the Alpha now, my loyalties are to the pack. We have things to do. Are you sure you're okay?" he asked, searching my eyes.

"I am sure that by the end of tonight we are both going to need another good cry, but first we have things to do."

"Spoken like a true Alpha's Queen," he said.

"Or Beta's Bride," I said.

"I love you so much, when I thought I could have lost you as well, it just about killed me."

"I was the same way. I was going out of my mind."

"We should probably get to work," he said, kissing my forehead.

"I'll call Aeryn," I said.

"Oh, and we will be talking about that later." He kissed my forehead. "But first we handle this. One catastrophe at a time"

"Yes, sir," I said, kissing my husband, before getting up, going to his desk and picking up his phone. Aeryn's number was one of three that I had memorized, everything else was in my phone.

"Aeryn Fitch," was her slightly groggy greeting.

"Hi, Aeryn, I know it's been a long time and that it's the middle of the night there, but it's Astrid."

"Hey, I'd say it's been a while, how've you been?"

"Well, actually, that's the thing. I need your help."

"Your stepfather hasn't…?" she said, worried.

"It's not that," I said quickly. "I married a shifter and the pack — well a number of pack members — just staged a failed coup."

"You married a shifter?" she said, missing the important part of the statement.

"I did."

"Wasn't your goal to have a normal life?"

"Yeah, well, apparently I'm not meant for that."

"I'd say Lady Llangollen and shifter's wife," she yawned.

"Actually, I married Tom when he was the Beta," I said, watching my husband and how he looked slumped over and defeated, very different from what he was on the pavilion dais steps. I guess the adrenaline rush was over.

"You're the Beta's Bride."

"I was, I am now the Alpha's Queen."

"What happened to the other Alpha?"

"My brother-in-law didn't make it, which is why I am calling. We don't have the number of the shifter sect leader and we need it. I was wondering if your parents had it, I know that they headed the sects if they don't still."

"Here, I can give it to you," she said, then recited the Welsh phone number.

"Thanks, Aeryn."

"Before you go," Aeryn said. "You still have that book I gave you, right?"

"Yeah, why?"

"The last page is written in invisible ink, put it under black light and make it, it should suppress their shifting, you may also want to have some sleeping draught on hand, but the stronger one."

"I'll do it. Thank you."

"Hey, girl, anytime, you know I am here to help, but I do want to hear all about how the Lady Llangollen I knew has turned into an Alpha's Queen."

"I will, when this is over," I promised. We hung up and I handed the number to Tom. "Here you go," I said, handing him the sticky note with the number written on it..

"Thank you," he said.

"Tom, she gave me a draught that should suppress their shifting," I said.

"And you want to make it?"

"I think it is a good idea, as long as you agree. It's not a salve or medication."

"Go make it, but take Brady and Colby with you."

"I will."

"I'll find you when I'm done here."

"Tom, where are they?"

"The former members of the pack are in the cellar."

"Okay," I said taking a breath and heading to the dais.

"How are you doing, little lady," Charlie asked as I made it to him and the rest of the pack still congregated under his watchful eye.

"As expected," I told him not really sure what that was supposed to mean, but it was all I had at the moment. "I have to go to the clinic. Tom says I am to take Brady and Colby with me."

Charlie called on them and they agreed to go with me, not that they really have a choice. The Alpha gave them an order.

"What are we doing?" Brady asked, escorting me to my lab.

"I have to make a couple of things," I said.

"Do we want to know?"

"Probably not, but if one of you could go get me a couple of steri-strips from the top drawer, I would like to close this," I said, lifting my shirt, brandishing my shoulders to them and thankful I had worn a tank top under my sweater.

"It's like you're a magnet for cuts and scars," Colby said.

"Seems like it."

I flushed it with saline, added peroxide and Brady sealed it for me.

I grabbed a backlight and lit up the page. The steps were complicated and long. "This is going to take a while," I warned them.

"We don't have anywhere else to be," Colby said, pulling out a chair.

"Put these on." I threw them each a pair of protective glasses which they caught deftly. "I'm not in the mood to treat eye injuries today." They didn't say anything only did what they were told.

I set up two stations back-to-back. The first steps of the suppressant had to boil for two hours and started out a deep sapphire blue, the instructions said it would be lighter when it's ready to continue.

"Is this really what you do?" Brady asked.

"No," I said. "I'm a surgeon." I figured they knew that by now. I only saved their lives.

"Then how do you know what you are doing?" Colby wondered.

"My undergrad is in Biomedical Chemistry."

"I thought you did music?"

"I did, but the music was more for me."

"Oh."

"Can you show me?" Brady asked.

"Sure." I smiled. "Come here."

Together we made the sleeping draught. He seemed really interested in how the different chemicals changed the colour, scent and composition.

"So, what did we just make?"

"We made a sleep draught a lot stronger than your run-of-the-mill sleeping aid."

"Okay."

"Do you want to help with the other one? It's a lot more delicate, but between the two of us I'm sure we can handle it." I was excited to potentially coach someone into doing what I do.

"Sure," he said, staring at the light blue liquid, as I turned down the heat under the beaker. This time, instead of letting him just measure and be in awe, I explained everything, told him what things were called and helped him learn, how and why we did things.

Once it was cooled he helped me put both draughts in vials. "You know," I said, "if I could purify it, we could probably make it injectable," I said out loud, but inside I was thinking about making it into an aerosol, potentially weaponizing it.

We got the vials together and returned to the pavilion. "Can you go on ahead?" I asked.

"I don't think we're supposed to," Colby said.

"Please, I'll only be a couple of minutes."

"Okay, but hurry back." Their tones were serious. It was clear they were hesitant to get into trouble with the new Alpha.

I just nodded. Though I knew I wasn't out of their sight, when they were out of mine, I knelt down on the ground breathing in the cool night air. I looked at the moon and cried. The moon stared down at me and I pictured the faces of my small family, Jared, Contessa, and Allain. Those three hearts. It felt like they were with me. I reached up and fisted my hands in the sky.

"Astrid," I heard behind me.

"Oh, Leonora," I said moving to stand up.

"No don't," she said, kneeling down beside me grabbing my hand.

"What are you doing out here?" I asked.

"I don't know. I just felt that I needed to be here. Turns out you're why. Just like the first night you spent at Sanctuary, I find you with the night."

"I'm so sorry, Leonora," I said squeezing her hand.

"Thank you, as am I."

"I wish I could have been there to help."

"I'm glad you weren't."

"Leonora?"

"You were away from the scrap, so you were safe. Tom is going to go through something unimaginably difficult and the only thing that will get him through is you."

"Leonora, he's going to need both of us."

"I was the former queen, he'd need his father or his brother not me."

"He has neither." I pursed my lips, looking down in sadness.

"He has you."

"A human outsider," I said, sitting back on my heels.

"I think we both know you are more than that. We've experienced that already."

"Leonora, I can't be an Alpha Queen, I'm not Contessa, I'm not strong enough. I'm not enough for him now."

"Contessa once said the exact same thing, she couldn't do it, she wasn't me."

"What did you tell her?"

"Your husband is going to go to you, he worships the ground you walk on. You lean on him and he will lean on you, and you will navigate our family together. You know what you have that she didn't?"

"No what?"

"You have prior sect knowledge, you already know more, you're so much more capable, so stop worrying. Help Tom carry the weight, love, support, and trust each other."

"I have a hard time with that."

"You paid for that, push through it, move together as one."

"Leonora, how do I help him through losing his brother and father?"

"You lost your father, you survived, and you know he will. Help him, push him, listen to him."

"And you?"

"I have my gods, my son and daughter-in-law."

"I am so sorry, Leonora."

"I know, my daughter. For now, will you allow me to pray for my family's souls?"

"With peace," I told Leonora, standing up.

"With love," she nodded, raising her face to the sky.

As with most evenings I followed the sky and the trees to the pavilion. I moved through the groupings of people to Charlie. It occurred to me that it was late, everyone should be in their homes, but everyone was still there holding one another, remaining one, and being a support for each other.

"Are you okay?" Charlie asked me.

"As I'll ever be," I told him.

"Brady and Colby got here before you."

"That's on me, Charlie, the Moon and I needed a moment, then Leonora and I needed one."

"No one has seen her since…"

"Keep it that way, Charlie, give her the time and space, she needs it."

"To be fair, we all do."

"Charlie, then send them home, we all need sleep and time to come to terms with this night."

"You're the Alpha's Queen." He nodded towards the crowd, for me to proceed.

I stole a deep breath. "Christopher, Faelen and Stephen please stay here, everyone else go home, sleep, pray for our family. Hold those you love the most, tomorrow is going to be another day, we all need our rest. If any of you need medical attention, please come find me."

"If you need her, find her tomorrow," Tom said over my head.

"I can help them."

"No, go," he told everyone except those I had named.

"For tonight I need us to be wary. We have family in the basement, ones who have proven dangerous. I will need us to take turns watching them."

"Sir, you are injured, the rest of us are not, go rest tonight, we will watch the prisoners," Faelen encouraged Tom, and I have to say I agreed.

"Family," Tom said. "They made a terrible decision and they will have to pay the consequences, but they are still our brothers and sisters."

"All the same, we will take the rotation tonight," Charlie said.

"Thank you," Tom said.

"No problem, sir," Stephen said, and the others nodded.

"Come on." Tom grabbed my hand. "We need to get some sleep."

He led me to our little home next door to the pavilion.

"How are you feeling?" he asked me, sitting down on the sofa and pulling me down beside him.

"I am sore, and a little worse for wear, but I am more concerned about you." I palmed his cheek, forcing him to look at me.

"I feel like if I start to feel, I'll start to cry and I'll never stop."

"You're with me, don't hide."

"She was our sister. She conspired against my brother, my parents, our family and pack. My brother, Astrid, he and my father are dead, and our own pack did it." Tears flowed from him, and his face turned red.

"Tom." I leaned forward, wrapping my arms around his shoulders.

"I don't know how to do this without them."

"I know it seems that way, but you're strong, we're strong. I'm not saying everything is going to be easy, but you're not alone," I clarified, pulling his face towards me and wiping the tears away with my thumb.

"How?" he asked, grabbing my hand.

"By doing it one step at a time. Don't push or force things to work a certain way. Believe in that the pack is strong like they believe in you."

"Since when are you the voice of reason?"

"Because I have done this before, remember? Difference is I didn't have the support system that we have now."

"You chose to completely uproot your life, we didn't." The emphasis on chose was telling.

"This is true when I was sixteen, I did choose that. But I didn't choose to have my father die when I was still a child, I didn't choose for afterwards to have my life go from bad to worse. I survived it and we will now, remember we have a support system here."

"Astrid," came his agonized cry as he buried his head in my neck. I didn't say anything, just held my husband as he came to terms with everything. Tears welled in my own eyes as my heart broke for him. I gently placed a hand on the back of his head.

"Thank you," he said when he'd composed himself, lifting his head from my shoulder.

"Come," I said, offering him my hand, "we have a busy day tomorrow, we need to get some rest."

When we were getting ready for bed, I saw what Faelen had meant when he'd said that Tom was injured, across his chest were three jagged lines, now puckered angry red lines. "Tom," I said, cautiously moving towards him.

"It's not as bad as it looks," he said, noticing where my gaze lay.

"It looks pretty bad."

"It will be healed by morning."

"What happened while I was being held, for lack of a better word, hostage?" I reached out for his hand, getting into bed.

"So much we didn't see coming," he told me. "It started with a howl like the ones an Alpha uses for attention, and in a line were Jeremiah, Lorelai, Francis, Carmellia, Ragnor, Bartholomew and Raphael. Lorelai spoke and demanded that Jared hand the pack to Jeremiah. We pointed out that if he wanted leadership he needed to go through the right channels." Tom lay down facing me, before he continued to tell me what happened.

"'We're not interested in your channels, we have our own way to be recognised,' Lorelai told us. Jared looked at me, then told Contessa to go inside, which she refused, because her place was beside her husband. My mother and father moved beside my brother and I as a large number of the other men worked their way over.

"But Jared wouldn't let them. He told them that they weren't to get involved, he didn't want anyone getting hurt who didn't have to, and the three of us agreed.

"'Tell me something,' I demanded of them. 'Everything that has been happening to our family, was that you?' I needed to know of the cohort. "'You're going to have to define everything?' Lorelai responded, she looked quite pleased with herself. 'Colby and Brady's attack, Charlie, Laura, Faelen, the claw marks outside of the apartment and law firm?' Jared questioned. 'We'd hoped that they would turn from you, realize that you couldn't protect them,' Francis said. Then Carmellia said some very not nice things about you and how every time you fixed another member it was like the belief in the leadership strengthened, finishing her statement with 'The pyres passing through at the same time was a happy coincidence.'"

"You almost died that time..." I said in disbelief.

"Exactly, and then you fixed the problem peacefully."

"Reinstalling belief in pack leadership." I said, following the pattern.

"Funny how the human is what has been holding the pack together, when Dad and Jared were worried that you were going to be our undoing." Tom's face turned up in a hard smile, he looked proud.

"That makes sense as to why Allain never got close to me. Last time I spoke to Jared we fought over the origins of this threat."

"He mentioned that to me, under his breath post-confession from those who really betrayed the pack, he said to Dad and I, 'I guess I owe Astrid an apology.' 'We both do son,' was all my father had to say." I felt the tears well in my eyes and the lump in my throat. "Hey, hey, hey," he said, gathering me in his arms.

"I'm so sorry," I sobbed. "I never wanted to be right, and the last thing he will think of me is that I hate the pack and that I somehow knew the pack better and that I didn't respect him or his leadership," the emotions made me babble uncontrollably.

"Trust me, he would never think that."

"I still don't understand why did they do it?"

"We still don't understand, those that we have downstairs won't tell us. But after hearing what they had done, a few members of the pack moved to flank us."

"Who?" I asked curious.

"Markus, Charlie, Lucas and Faelen."

"What did Jared have to say about that?"

"He told them to go."

"'No, this isn't just your fight, this is ours,' Charlie told Jared. 'They almost caused Laura to lose the baby, they brought me into this the minute they touched my pregnant wife,' Markus added. 'They kidnapped, beat and almost killed our sons,' Faelen had said for himself and Lucas.

"'No one will follow you,' Jared said to them. 'They won't have a choice,' came Lorelai's reply."

"I thought she wanted Jeremiah to be the Alpha?"

"You and I both know that Jeremiah didn't come up with that plan, it was all Lorelai; he'd be Alpha in title but she would have his tail between her teeth, every decision and movement that man would make would come from her."

"What happened next?"

"Lor backed away, and the men and Carmellia shifted into different shifts."

"I'm assuming she was the prospective, new Beta's Bride?"

"You're probably right, but we have no idea. After they shifted, we looked at each other and did the same. I shifted to a wolf and Jared his eagle as they are our preferred forms, everyone flanking us did the same. We stalked forward, every time we moved, I was searching for you hoping that you were nowhere near the mess. What happened to you anyway?"

"Finish your story and I'll tell you mine."

"Off the bat Jared went for Jeremiah, and I, Francis, Mom and Dad were after Carmellia, and I am not sure how the others paired off. I was too busy in the middle of the fight trying to deal with my own.

"Francis like me had taken on his wolf form, our fight was a mix of claws and teeth pulling at our fur. I got an opening and slipped down his left flank and managed to dig my teeth into his hind leg, he jumped back, I went for his throat and missed. The fight went that way until I heard my mother's agonized howl, Carmellia had gotten her teeth around my father's throat, a blow that was meant for my mother but he jumped in the way. The moment of distraction resulted in a well-landed blow from Francis along my underbelly. I jumped back as Charlie stepped in front of me.

"Charlie's talons dug into the side of his face, sliding down to his shoulder from his ear. Charlie tossed him away, lifting him with his talons into a tree. A second later Francis had disappeared, and Charlie turned to get my mother as far from the scrap as he could. Carmellia began circling looking for him. Out of the side of my eyes I noticed that Jeremiah and Jared were still going at it, a whirlwind of fur and feathers.

"I stalked Carmellia slowly. She had killed my father, I was seeing red but I was trying so hard not to let too much anger get the better of me. She may have been a match for my mother and father at their more advanced age, but it went by so fast and before I knew it she was slumped back in human form with her husband. It got bad then, when I turned around, Lorelai was standing at the edge of the fighting with a gun in her hand. Before I knew it, it went off and hit Jared directly in the chest. She and Jeremiah were the only ones left. Jeremiah finished off Jared before I could get to him, but while he was focusing on Jared, I changed form, and dug my claws into his throat. He fell onto the ground beside the shifted human form of my brother.

"I wanted to stop, cry for my brother but my own sister, the person who killed our brother was still armed. Fortunately, Faelen was beside

261

her in human form, he turned one hand into talons and placed it at her throat, because none of us carry weapons it's the easiest kill.

"I demanded she put the gun down, and feeling the pressure of the talons on her neck, she complied. At this point Francis tried for a sneak attack on me, surprising us by coming from tree cover. Markus and Lucas got to him before he did me. He quickly turned to human form, surrendering, realizing that it was him versus three of us.

"Charlie had done everything he could to protect my mother and keep her away from the scrap, but just as Lorelai was being escorted to the basement by Faelen with Markus and Lucas each with their own unconscious mutineer, she came back. I shifted back and knelt beside my brother. I will never forget the sound as she took in the lifeless bodies of her husband and son laid out beside one another."

"What happened to Contessa?"

"We don't know for sure, but I have a feeling it had something to do with Lorelai. We didn't know anything had happened to her until Charlie came over to me and said he needed to talk. The last of our losses for the evening."

"No."

"She was the Alpha's Queen and from a strong bloodline so she would be considered a threat, whoever got to her must've had one hell of a fight. At this point, realizing that the worst of it was over, people started emerging from their houses. I had some men move the bodies, Leonora went with them and I realized that you were still nowhere to be found. My heart dropped and I started freaking, I sent people out to find you."

"Yeah, well, I was being held, tied and gagged in my clinic."

"Tell me what happened."

I told him my entire story, how Landry didn't give me a choice, he was going to kill me. Tom was as confused as I was as to why they wanted to keep me alive.

"Why wasn't he supposed to kill you?"

"Your guess is as good as mine, but after he was gone, I tried to escape but I ran directly into Francis, who had Matteo help him in tying me up. Next thing I knew he left and I was alone until Christopher and Stephen found me."

"Matteo was involved?" he said, suddenly sitting up.

"Yeah… wait, are you telling me he's not one of the people in the basement?"

"No, he's not."

"He's a puppy, maybe he ran off scared."

"I don't care if he's a puppy or not, he was involved in the death of three pack members and hurt my wife."

"What are you going to do?"

"Right now?"

"Yeah."

"I'm going to send a few people out to find him, he's a pup he shouldn't be much of a match." Tom called Charlie.

"Charlie." There was a silence as Charlie spoke from the other end of the phone.

"Matteo was involved in what happened tonight. Send Lucas, Brady, Rox and Colby out on patrol. I want him with his parents where he belongs."

"He's a pup, he was probably just being influenced by his parents."

"Influenced or not, he needs to come back here and answer for what he did."

"Okay."

"I'd say, now that we're both caught up, I think we should sleep, you look about ready to pass out."

"Did I mention I was pushed backwards onto my back?"

"You didn't."

"It's been sore since."

"You only endured that about two weeks ago… you really need to be more careful."

"Oh yes, next time I get held hostage by homicidal mutineers, I'll ask them to be more gentle with me." I said sarcastically and incredulously, to Tom.

"You're mocking me."

"I am."

"You know with your luck it could happen."

"I'll trade you. I'll put salve on you, if you do my back and shoulders." I tagged on for good measure.

"Mine's already mostly healed," Tom pointed out.

"Does that mean you won't help me?"

"No, I'll do it then we'll both sleep."

"Deal."

He put the salve along my back and on the places where Landry had dug his claws into me, before we both curled up and though a million things should have been going through our heads, we both fell asleep quickly, exhausted.

Chapter 22

Aeryn had given me a call when their plane arrived in Seattle. Now we were expecting them any second and were waiting at the dais in front of the pavilion, the entire pack ready and waiting respectfully. But the atmosphere of Sanctuary was somber and so different from the Sanctuary that I was used to. I held tightly to Tom's hand as we waited.

"Here we go," Tom said, a moment later two black cars pulled up driving directly through the center of Sanctuary and stopping just in front of the dais. From the first car came a large man who held himself with an eerie power, a smaller woman and two men dressed entirely in black. The second car produced Aeryn, and three more men.

Aeryn approached us first. "Hello, Aeryn," I said greeting an old friend.

"Hello, Astrid, how have you been?" she asked, innocently hugging me chastely.

"Maybe a question for another time," I pursed my lips.

"Quite right," she agreed. "This is Carlos," she said, introducing the large intimidating man that had come up behind her.

"Carlos de la Cruz," the intimidating, tall, dark-haired and olive-toned man clarified.

"Thomas Sharpe," Tom reached a hand out to the man who was the High Council's Alpha, making him the highest-ranking shifter in the world. "It's an honour to meet you, but I truly wish it was under different circumstances."

"Where are they?" he said, very matter of fact, his dark eyes darting from side to side.

"They're locked up in a facility that fortunately hasn't been needed before now. However, one member of their cohort has gotten away. We've had people out searching for him but he has yet to turn up, he's only a pup, so we figure he is scared and hiding out somewhere."

"We will help with the search, a few of my men will look for him. Do you have anything that they can use for scent?"

"Absolutely," Tom nodded. "Charlie," he called over.

"Sir," Charlie said, bowing his head respectfully, clearly for our foreign dignitaries' benefit.

"Help these men with anything they need to help find Matteo."

"Absolutely," he turned, motioning for the men to follow him.

"What exactly happened?"

"I really don't understand it myself," my husband admitted, and I could tell that it emotionally pained him to have to admit that this happened under his nose and we have no idea why. "Why don't we go inside and we can discuss everything."

I nodded to show my support of my husband's suggestion. We led them to a small seating area and closed the doors firmly behind us. "Please have a seat," I said to them, then realizing I hadn't been formally introduced to Carlos, I held out my hand to him. "I'm Astrid Davis-Sharpe," I introduced myself to him.

"Charmed," he said, taking my hand and kissing the back of it. I felt my cheeks flush before bowing my head gently and taking a seat beside my husband. Taking a seat, I noticed a slight flash of recognition on Carlos de la Cruzes face. "You aren't Astrid the sister of the Earl of Llangollen by any chance?"

"The one and the same," I nodded.

"Rumour is she's disappeared leaving no trace, and the sects behind," he told me.

"I did but then I accidently fell in love with a shifter."

"Well, it's an honour to meet you, my lady, I am a big supporter of your brother."

"It's lovely to hear that, thank you," I nodded again gently.

"So what do we need to know? What happened?" Carlos turned to Tom.

"I wish I had a better idea," Tom said. "My entire family is either dead or has worked against me and the pack. From what I can gather it started with a few members before building into more. They worked together, attacking our bond and our own people. The only one who saw it coming was Astrid."

"On many occasions it takes someone from the outside to see what is happening directly under your nose," Aeryn said, sounding very wise for someone who was only my age.

"The members of the coup have been planning this for a while, but we aren't sure exactly how long. My sister and her husband appear to be the ring leaders. They and a number of members worked to overthrow my brother as the Alpha." Tom stopped, taking a steadying breath. I reached over placing a steadying hand on his thigh. "My father, brother and sister-in-law, were all killed."

"Were there any other casualties?"

"One, of theirs," he said. My eyes welled with tears. I swallowed, forcing them back. "The rest we managed to incapacitate without resorting to lethal methods. Unfortunately, they didn't have the same sense of family. They were all in for the kill from the beginning."

"Shifters are known to have a problem after they kill, the get the taste for blood," Carlos said with concern.

"It wasn't a shifter who killed the man," Tom said, placing a supportive hand on top of mine.

"You?" Aeryn demanded of me, leaning forward. I suddenly became acutely aware that of the people in the room, I was the weakest, smallest and least experienced. Instinctively I leaned back behind my husband's shoulder.

"It was in self-defence," I said. "He made it perfectly clear that it was either him or me."

"We know." Tom kissed the top of my head, calming me. "They sent the man — Landry — to watch her."

"Why would they send one of their members to watch her?"

"We aren't sure, maybe because she's human," Carlos offered.

"I doubt that." Aeryn shook her head. "They wouldn't be afraid of her."

"Maybe they thought that when all was said and done, they'd need you." Tom looked at me.

"What would they need her for?"

"Maybe to encourage everyone else to follow their new chosen leader?" Carlos tried.

"I was thinking more to patch people up, they had to assume that they wouldn't get out of it unscathed," Tom said. Then clarified for Aeryn and Carlos. "My wife is a surgeon, she runs a medical clinic here at Sanctuary. Maybe they figured they could force her to patch everyone up."

"I'd sooner have them kill me."

"You almost got your wish."

"What can you tell me about the Shifters?" Carlos asked me. "We have five shifters, a shea and a bitch in the basement." Tom told him.

"That many?"

"Should we be concerned about them escaping?"

"Not at all."

Tom looked at me. "They aren't going anywhere, I made a tonic to suppress their abilities, we've slipped it into their water." I smiled.

"Excuse me?"

"I'm a doctor, but my undergrad is in biomedical chemistry."

"So, you just whipped up an extremely complicated and dangerous mage tonic," Carlos said.

"I'm sorry? Should I not have done that?" I looked to Aeryn confused.

"I just don't understand how you could?"

"I have a lab with medical and supernatural ingredients for making all sorts of things. I've made salves, draughts and tonics. I'm also looking into a number of other shifter and human remedies."

"Smart woman that wife of yours," Carlos said to Tom. "However, the use of such draughts is only to be used under the express permission of a member of the High Council."

"She had permission," Aeryn assured him.

"Okay." He nodded at her. "My plan is this, we are going to be here for a couple days. I'm going to talk to the people downstairs, my men will continue the search, and with a little luck, we'll have him here in time to transport."

"We haven't been able to get anything out of them."

"Well, with a little luck we should be able to get some information for you."

"And when are you expecting to get them out of here?"

"Two days' time."

"Great." Tom nodded.

"We've got some accommodation prepared for you," I said.

"Thank you." They nodded.

"Other than that, if you need anything, you can ask anyone here and if they don't have an answer for you, they will send you in the direction of someone who does."

I showed them to their rooms and over the next two days they came and went. It was requested that we not talk to what, according to Tom, they disrespectfully referred to as the prisoners. As far as he was concerned, they were family, and anyone else who said otherwise was wrong. Leonora had taken in William. She'd moved into Jeremiah and Lorelai's little cottage, and although William didn't understand what was happening, he was happier in his own home with Nana rather than staying with Markus and Laura, who was getting closer to her due date. Tom and I decided that I wouldn't go with Tom to aid in moving the family tomorrow, because I needed to be here in case she did go into labour.

Tom was being forced into many more decisions that he didn't want to make. Although he trusted my judgement and ability to run the pack in his absence, he needed to leave a shifter behind.

"Who do you think would be a good candidate?" Tom asked.

"I'm going to support whatever decision you make."

"It's like I have to rearrange the entire pack."

"I know but you need to figure it out. Then we can get the arrangements made for while you're gone, and yes the pack is going to need rearranging, but that's no different from any other Alpha," I said, staring at him over the book I was reading as he agonized over paperwork. In my defense, it was a book on laws and customs of shifters and packs. "The only advice I am going to give you, is to do what Jared did, and choose the person you trust the most."

"Well, that's you."

"Okay, the shifter you trust most," I giggled, shaking my head at him.

"Charlie," he said matter of factly.

"I know."

"You know."

"There's only one man that you trust to keep their eyes on me when you're not around. He's the first person that you introduced me to that wasn't your immediate family. And on the night of the coup, he was who you left in charge of the pack when we needed to handle other things."

"Why didn't you tell me?"

"Because it wasn't for me to decide."

"I want to honour Markus, Faelen and Lucas too."

"I think you should," I nodded. "While you're gone, I'll get everything organized and ready to go." There was plenty to do, with the change of leadership came the change in offices, housing, and pacl organization.

"Mom wants to stay in the smaller cabin that belonged to Lorelai, I'm having Markus and Laura move into Mom and Dad's house."

"What are we doing about Marlee and Carly?"

"Mom is still watching them."

"Your mom can't take in three kids."

"I don't know. I think we may have to talk to her. Their sister is in the Welsh pack and the last thing I think they need is to lose their home as well as their parents."

"What about Shiloh, she is their aunt?"

"Don't you think she is going through enough?"

"All the same I'm going to talk to her about it while you're away."

"You?"

"She's my friend."

"You killed her husband."

"We'll figure it out, I promise," I told him. Tom worked through the pack and managed to get the sub packs together. Tonight, we are going to be having a pack meeting where he would announce them, followed by the funeral rights for our family.

"The inauguration is going to be hard on you physically and mentally," he warned me again. Over the last two days I think he may have warned me half a dozen times.

"Having something be physically and mentally difficult I wonder what that's like?" I rolled my eyes over the book.

"That reminds me, this Aeryn how well do you know her?"

"She's a friend. We were never close because her family discouraged interaction between us because of Lord. But I'd call her a friend, all the same." "But you trust her, right?"

"Are you kidding? That woman helped me out of a terrible situation when we were both teenagers. I couldn't have done it myself and she has held my confidence since. I would trust her with my life."

"Good, because we are going to talk to her," he grabbed my hand pulling me off the sofa.

"About what?"

"Your dance."

"My dance? What about my dance? Do you really think she needs to be bothered by this of all things?"

"My wife, who is human, underwent a terrible ordeal during which her blood flowed in the wrong direction, and the moon, which is an inanimate celestial rock, glowed red. Do I really want to bother her with your episode?"

"Now you're grasping at straws as to what to call it."

"It's never happened before, remember?"

"That you know of."

"Are you trying to make my point for me?"

"Fine, knock," I said, leaning against the wall across from the door.

"Hey, Astrid, Thomas. What can I do for you?"

"We were wondering if we could talk to you about something?" Tom said.

"But if you're busy, we don't want to disturb you," I said.

"Don't be silly, I was just doing some paperwork, any distraction is appreciated.

"Let's go down here then, shall we?" Tom said, leading us back to the small living room we were in the day she and Carlos arrived.

"What did you want to talk about?" she said, taking a seat. "The look on Tom's face tells me that this isn't purely a social call."

"We have some questions regarding the dance of claws?" Tom mentioned.

"What about it?"

"Astrid underwent the dance a little over two weeks ago?"

"Wait a second, you underwent the dance of claws?"

271

"I did."

"Why?"

"I may have lied on multiple occasions," I pursed my lips.

"About?"

"Me and who I am in relation to the sects as a whole, and my reason for leaving Wales in the first place."

"Oh."

"It's a breach, our pack survives because of a closely guarded secret. My past happens to include a certain man and the title Lady Llangollen."

"Wouldn't the title Lady Llangollen grant more security?"

"But she doesn't have the protection of the Welsh clans behind her here. And if people knew she was here…"

"I get it, she'd be a target and you'd have no idea why."

"Precisely. Plus, at the time, we were going through a time when members of our pack were being targeted. So when my brother found out…"

"Okay, this all explains why your former Alpha chose to perform the dance, it doesn't explain why you wanted to talk to me about it," Aeryn said, perplexed.

"So something happened when she underwent it."

"Okay."

"When she'd finished her ritual words, her blood started to flow upwards instead of down. For a couple of minutes her blood streamed upwards towards the sky, then the moon glowed red."

"I remember that day. It became a topic of debate as to the meaning in the council. Now that I know why it happened, how did it happen?"

"What do you mean how?" I asked.

"What happened during the ritual, don't leave anything out."

"Well, there really isn't that much to explain. I knelt, gave myself to the beast of the sky. Two lines of claws cut down my back. At first it hurt like hell, then it became merely a dull ache and a tingling sensation. For a few minutes I knelt by myself, barely aware of what was happening around me. Then the pain increased again and I was aware that Tom was beside me."

"When you invoked the beasts of the sky, what language did you use?"

"Welsh. According to Tom and Jared it is our ancestral language and best used if you can."

"Can I see your back?"

"Really?"

"Why?" Tom asked.

"I just want to see it?"

I shrugged before standing up and lifting the back of my shirt. "Revelox," she said, and I felt a warmth spread along my back.

"It's healed faster than it should have?"

"Meaning?"

"Meaning there are a few things you should know."

"Like?"

"Your family history."

"I'm sure it was just the creams I have been using."

"It wasn't, though your talent for chemistry doesn't surprise me."

"Why?"

"The Earldom of Llangollen isn't strictly human."

"Excuse me?" Tom said, putting his arm around my shoulders.

"We created them over centuries, the sects were combined to create the Llangollens, starting with the shifters. We married a shifter woman to a high ranked human. After a few generations of them marrying humans only a slight trace of shifter blood ran through their veins. Next we married them to the casters. We did the same thing, waited a few generations and again there was only a slight trace.

"The next step was something a little less mundane or what could be called ethical. The goal was always to create something that encompassed all of the different sects in order to create someone who would hopefully innately be able to identify with all of us on the whole."

"What's not so mundane?"

"Vampyrism. The only way for it to potentially work was to make them genetically one of the seven, but once you're vampyric there was no going back."

"What did you do?"

"We fed vampyre blood to a pregnant woman."

"You what?"

273

"Just remember that it wasn't me it was the past council. I just happen to represent the current council. They fed it to her and it didn't create a pyre, but it did give the baby a few vampyric skills such as speed, strength and healing, much like it did with the shifters, except without the shifting. Our final conflation was them and the mages. Due to them being so much more recent, it doesn't surprise me that your chemistry prowess is so strong.

"It's also why you heal so much faster than a regular human."

"My dream," I said to Tom, shocked and trying to get my head around everything.

"You think the mage blood is still prevalent?" Tom asked me.

"And the caster," Aeryn said, "otherwise she wouldn't have been able to invoke the gods the way she did. I'd say that whatever happened was the outcome of a caster invoking the shifter gods, through a shifter ritual."

"There's something else, the day after the dance, I sort of went into a trance during which I sliced my palm. I spilt my blood onto the dais, drew a protection symbol, and said something no one seems to be able to remember before it caught fire and embossed itself on to the cement platform."

"Her hand healed immediately afterward," Tom tacked on.

"That's caster spells, by no means should her blood be strong enough to do anything like that."

"Look, I'm sorry, I need to back up for one second. My brother and I are the embodiment of the five species."

"Mostly human, but yes."

"And who knows about this?"

"The High Council members of the sects."

"So not Brandon?"

"No, only the chosen members of your family."

"And you're telling me now?"

"Because you are being forced to deal with the consequences of our past actions."

"So this hasn't happened before."

"Every sects ability should be completely dormant by now."

"But I'm suddenly manifesting all of them?"

"Maybe… can you tell me about this dream?"

"There isn't a lot to tell. A couple of our pups went missing, they were gone three days. One night we went to bed, when she woke up," Tom started, "she knew exactly where they were, and that Brady — one of the boys — wasn't going to last much longer without medical intervention."

"Most mages can't do that, at least not without channeling something."

"Maybe it's the combination of different bloods making it work differently," Tom put out there.

"I can't make it work either, it just happens," I explained to her.

"It's happened before," Aeryn told me. "It's why I helped you. When I told my parents about the dreams you were having regarding your stepfather, they said I needed to take you seriously. They knew something I didn't at the time."

"This is too much," I said, grabbing my head.

"So, I noticed that along with the back injuries, you have a few others including a bit of a black eye," Aeryn said.

"Yeah, Landry wasn't exactly gentle."

"I can heal you."

"What?"

"You're mostly healed and I know a spell that transfers and augments the healing abilities of shifters and pyres into another. When I'm done you'll still have scars, but that will be all it is."

"Um…" I looked at Tom.

"Do it," Tom told Aeryn. I knew it bothered him when I was sore, so it didn't surprise me that he was so excited by the idea.

"It will hurt a little bit," Aeryn warned.

"How is that different from anything else that I have had the honour of experiencing lately?"

"Okay," Aeryn shrugged. "Here's what I need you to do, I need you to remove your top and lean against Tom. I'm going to need to draw his energy into you, and I need to see where I have to direct it to."

Tom smoothly lifted me onto his lap after I'd lifted off my T-shirt, so that my back was bare to Aeryn.

"Hold her still," Aeryn told him. He clasped one arm around my hips and the other around my shoulders. Aeryn was not wrong, there was pain. As I had a couple of weeks ago, I locked my jaw. But this time it was better because, although there was pain, I had someone to help me through it. I buried my head into him.

I sighed as the pain eased, and I relaxed against Tom for another second. "You did well, baby." Tom kissed my shoulder.

"How does it look?"

"Healed and healthy," he told me, lightly running his hand down my back.

"Ready for a new addition to my tattoo?"

"You crazy little minx, put this on," he said, handing me my T-shift.

I did as I was told. "Thank you, Aeryn." I nodded to her.

"Hey, I'm more than happy to help, especially a friend."

"You're helping more than anyone could have asked of you, and it is really appreciated," said Tom.

"It's what I do."

"This is true, but it is still appreciated all the same," I told her.

"So, can I ask about your life these last few years? I've always been interested in what became of you and your life."

"Girl talk is my cue to leave." Tom stood up. "Come and find me before tonight," he said before kissing me and taking his leave.

"He's fine," she promised me.

"He's not but he will be," I said.

"Okay, so spill."

And I did, I told her about my life over here. What it is like to be anonymous, about the few people who did learn my secret. I told her how school went. She wanted to know if I still played my flute to which I answered, 'whenever I get the opportunity'. She was amazed that the shy, quiet girl who barely made it through school, got through not only university but med school.

I told her about my dancing, my working at the hospital and most important the fortune I had in finding the most amazing man. She was surprised though, for someone who had left the sects behind I had managed to immerse myself into one that became a family. She promised to have some genetic material sent to me so I could see to what extent I was more other sects than mortal.

She told me about the life she's had since becoming a member of the council. She regrets never having normal opportunities, but like her parents before her, it was her responsibility and she was thankful to all the sects. Her and Brandon are allies in the council and apparently good friends.

"I told him, you know."

"Told him what?"

"That you were safe, but never where you were. He was just happy to know that you had me looking out for you."

"He showed up here a few weeks ago, you know. It was the first time I had seen or spoken to him since leaving," I told her.

"I know. I also know that he misses you."

"I miss him too."

"You shouldn't cut him out of your life. I understand why you had to before, but you aren't a kid anymore and you have so many people looking out for you."

"I don't know, it just seems like an invitation for more pain, for some reason."

"He's not just your brother, Astrid, he's your twin and he wasn't the one who hurt you, but you are hurting both of you by cutting him out of your life."

"I don't know, how do I go back with how I left?"

"He understands, just remember he was a kid back then too, he couldn't have helped you any more than he did then."

"I know."

"I think he just wants his sister back. Go home."

"This is home."

"Who said you can't have a home here and a home in Wales? Think about what I said." She got up, squeezing my shoulder as she walked out of the room, leaving me to stare at the emptiness around me. So long running from Wales, could I go back there? Did I want to?

But I couldn't stay there long, the night was closing in. I needed to go and find Tom. He was going to need me. Tonight, would be his final goodbye to his family. We were also thankful that the High Council was going to ensure that there is no human interest in the missing members of the pack and the deaths were ruled a freak car accident.

I found him in our little house, sitting staring at his red shirt laid out on the bed. "Hey," I said, leaning in the doorway.

"Hey." His mouth turned up on one side.

"I'd ask if you're okay, but I think we both know the answer to that."

"I can't do it, Astrid." He shook his head back and forth.

"You can. I know it's hard."

"Hard? It's impossible. It hurts from missing them too much."

"I wish I could say I understand, I don't. But I have lost my father. It's never going to stop being sad and will hurt, but you get through one day at a time. Lean on those who love you, and eventually the sting gets better."

"Seems hard to believe that right now."

"I know," I told him softly. He stepped forward and picked up his red shirt. I went to the closet and grabbed mine as well. "You're going to make a great Queen." He pulled me against him once we were both changed.

"Not as good as you are going to be as Alpha."

"Any good I do will come from you."

We just stayed quiet for a moment, holding each other, seeming to take comfort and strength in the contact. "Ready?" he asked, pulling back and looking at me.

"Let's do this." I nodded quietly.

He took my hand and together we walked out of our little home and to the dais. Already there was our pack, well, those who were left. Too many faces were missing.

"Tonight, we are going to be honouring those whom we have lost. It's a night for respect, remembering and thankfulness for what they've been to our pack. But first there are a few things that need to be dealt with. As many of you know tomorrow, I am going to be going to Wales with the contingent moving those who acted against us. Which calls for the need for a new Beta to work with our new Queen in maintaining the pack, someone we all trust, love and respect. After much deliberation, Astrid and I have chosen Charlie to be our new pack Beta. He contains all the qualities we are looking for and his love and protectiveness for the pack makes him the best candidate."

Charlie stood staring at Tom for a second, before howling started and those who couldn't howl began to clap. The noise overcame the shock and he mounted the dais steps. "Really?" he said to Tom over my head before walking to stand on the other side where the Beta belongs.

"Yes, really."

"But I'm not smart enough."

"It's not always a matter of intelligence, sometimes it's bravery, kindness, and strength of character. During the mutiny you got my mother away so she was safe, and as Astrid pointed out, there is no one else I would trust with her wellbeing, and the same goes for the pack. Plus, you won't be alone, you'll have Astrid here and when she can't be here the pack will look to you." He stopped then raised his voice again to get through the crowd.

"As everyone knows, we have a tradition of the subpacks here, in that we each have our Betas. I'll understand if Charlie is unsure of who he wants yet, but I have chosen Markus to be mine. As my mother has decided to move into a smaller cottage with William, we will be moving him into one of the bigger houses." Markus nodded his appreciation to Tom. Laura was standing beside him with the biggest smile of pride for her husband.

"I am going to think about my decision and discuss it with the Alpha before I make any commitments," Charlie said, carrying his voice and sounding like a Beta. I could tell by the look on Tom's face that he was happy and appreciative of his response.

"Now, tonight, is for remembering those we've loved and lost," Tom said, which is when Aeryn and Carlos mounted the step and three shifters came out of the shadows, each carrying an urn with the cremated remains of Contessa, Allain and Jared. Landry's service had been held yesterday as we didn't feel it was respectful to have him with those he'd conspired against. They were each placed at the foot of the dais. As each man carrying an urn put it down, they swiftly turned into eagles and flew high into the night sky, acting as sentries to the protection of the souls.

"Before us lay two Alphas and a Queen. Contessa, Jared and Allain Sharpe all portrayed the absolute best of what it means to be leaders.

Strong, capable, magnanimous, intelligent, and courageous. They showed us what it meant to love their pack with every ounce of their being. Allain led us with his strength and wisdom, before handing the mantle to his oldest son, passing on his knowledge and wisdom to mould the leader that was Jared. Unrelenting and just, Jared was intelligent and capable and he was ready when he became Alpha. He led us these past years, bringing us into a better financial position. Contessa seemed to balance out her husband, and my brother perfectly. Where he was harsh, she was kind. When she disagreed, he'd agree. They were the two sides of the coin. She worked in perfect harmony with her husband as any good Queen should.

"Together we say farewell to our brothers and sister in the hope that they will find peace with the great beasts. That they will be proud to know that their legacy and sacrifice will not be forgotten in the minds and hearts of each and everyone of us."

"Our love will not fade. Their memory will not fade. May their souls be taken to the sky, spreading their wings one last time," I said in Welsh. At the same time the lids lifted on each urn and the ashes lifted into the sky spiralling together. I looked at Aeryn and she shook her head, indicating it was me again. I was going to have to stop speaking Welsh at night.

"Goodbye, until we meet again," the pack and guests said together.

"Tonight, go home, pray and think happy memories of those we lost. They are home, we can rejoice in the knowledge that they are at peace with their gods," Tom said. The circle remained as Tom dismounted the dais and ran into the forest.

Charlie looked at me shocked. "Should I follow him?" he asked me.

"No, leave him. He just needs to clear his head," I told him. "With Peace," I announced to the pack.

"And with love," they all repeated back.

The three eagles landed and turned back into men, their eyes were watching me with confusion. They each picked up an urn and departed. In typical pack fashion though, no one went home, choosing instead to start a bonfire. Some collected firewood, others got coolers together, and more got coats and chairs. It was starting to cool down at night as it got closer to the winter, and fall came to a slow close. I just sat down on the dais and watched a smaller discouraged pack work together.

"You okay, little lady?" Charlie asked, sitting down beside me.

"Is anyone?"

"He's not." Charlie nudged his chin, towards the woods.

"He's grieving. He just needs time and space," I explained.

"He won't always have the luxury of time and space." Carlos de la Cruz sat down beside Charlie as Aeryn joined me on my other side.

"Don't worry, he understands that," I told him, "but he just performed his father and brother's funeral and watched them float off in peace."

"Yeah, how did that happen?" Charlie said.

"We're not really sure," Aeryn told him.

"Okay," he nodded, seeming to accept the High Caster's explanation.

"Will he be back by tomorrow?" Carlos asked.

"He will be," I said. "Of that I am sure. He knows his duty; he won't neglect it. But he is no good to anyone tonight."

"Then I will turn in. I'll let your family have your time."

"Carlos, you should join them," I told him, motioning with my head to the now roaring fire, and the orange-lit faces of my family.

"I can't intrude."

"You won't be," Charlie said. "We're all family here, everyone is welcome. Invite the men and women you brought with you, get to know everyone." Carlos seemed to think about it for a second before waving all his people over to him. "Just one rule, everyone has to relax." Charlie stood up patting my head and leading them over to our family.

I watched them enter the circle and spread out. Moments later they were all talking and carrying on like they were old friends.

"I think Charlie was a good choice of your Tom's," Aeryn told me.

"Yeah, he was. The thing with Charlie is that he doesn't care who you are or how old you are, he will always treat you as an equal and with respect."

"Your family all seems like that."

"They are?"

"How are you taking your promotion?"

"It's no different than where I was before."

"What do you mean?"

"I was the Beta's Bride and now I am the Alpha's Queen, but you want to know the truth, the only real job that comes with either of those roles?"

"Sure."

"Our only job is to support our husbands."

"You're worried about him."

"I am, but he'll be back, and I'll hold him. For now we wait, would you like to come join us?"

"I'm not a shifter," she said.

"Yeah, well, neither am I so join the club," I said, reaching out for her hand. Shaking her head she took my outstretched hand and let me pull her to the fire, where just as predicted everyone made her feel at home. We all had toasts to our fallen comrades, our new Beta, and prosperity to myself and Tom. He never showed up during the fire and too soon Leonora decided it was time for her, William, Marlee and Carly to go home; I think it was just getting to be too much for her.

Six Months Later

Tom didn't come home the night of the bonfire, but he did come home in time to lay down next to me for a few hours' sleep. Well, attempted sleep. He seemed to want to talk, so we laid there staring at the ceiling, just holding hands and letting him get what he needed to off his chest. When dawn came far too quickly, we got up and started a brand-new day. Tom and the Welsh cohort took those who were under arrest to Wales where they were irrevocably found guilty. Each were sentenced and taken to our hidden prison. Tom was given what I asked for when he came back so I could get an idea what was going on in mine and Brandon's blood.

But the most important thing that had happened while he was there was Laura and Markus's son was born, mere days after we had finished moving everyone around. We were right to leave me back at Sanctuary. At eight pounds four ounces, Sebastian David Forestal was born and he was a beautiful, chubby-cheeked little man and exactly what the pack needed to lift their spirits.

When I wasn't working on my own blood, I was even more drastically working on finding out if I could figure out what had been stopping Lorelai from shifting. It was like I was trying to find something to prevent what happened, but unless time moved backwards, all I'd be able to do is add to my guilt.

"What are you working on today?" Tom asked, coming into my little lab.

"When I figure it out, I'll tell you, I promise."

"Why won't you tell me now?" He wrapped his arms around my shoulders.

"Because unless I figure this out, there is no point bothering you with it."

"Okay, well, if you think you can peel yourself away it's time to get ready." He kissed my neck.

Today was the sixth full moon marking the death of the previous Alpha, thus the night of the official inauguration for Tom to become the Alpha. "Yeah, let's go," I said, pushing away from my work and hopping down from my high stool. He took my hand and we moved towards the pavilion where the top floor was now our home.

He wasn't allowed to go any further than the bottom of the stairs, only the elder women were allowed to be there to prepare me for my husband's inauguration. The dress I had picked out for tonight was on the bed, laid flat. The thin black material had a low back with a cowl neck just above the curve of my lower back. The front was a high neck that tied behind my neck. A ceremonial knife was then attached by a gold sheath to my hip. My feet remained bare and although it was cool out, I was glad that it had begun to warm up. A chain of five conjoined rings was placed on each finger. Finally, the gold veil was then attached to my head and fell to my feet on all sides. "You're ready," said Leonora.

"Thanks," I said, scared to death.

"Don't worry, you're going to be fine," she promised me, grabbing my hands through the veil.

"I know. We'll see you down there."

I knew I was to go down to the dais at eight o'clock. I knelt in my dress and prayed for a minute. The beasts would be here, waiting for another of their sons' spirits to be lifted to them. After a couple of minutes I descended the staircase. I kept my eyes down going up the dais' steps from the back. Only one other person was standing in front of a makeshift altar.

"I present myself to you as a servant of the Alpha, a servant of the Phoenix, a servant of the Wolf."

"The beasts accept you as their servant, their subject, their daughter and a representative of their people," Tom said. His hands both pressed down on the top of my head.

"This daughter asks the beasts to hear her." I knelt down and raised my head and for the first time thoroughly taking in my husband. He stood tall and shirtless in a pair of black slacks with a black band around his bicep.

Kneeling for a second he lifted the front of my veil and placed it gently behind me.

"The beasts agree to hear her," Tom stood again.

I bent down and kissed the tops of each of his naked feet. A bowl of water was already sitting beside me. I picked up the cloth inside of it and washed each of his feet, before leaning up on my knees, I washed each of his hands, moving the cloth upwards on his arms, and his chest. Moving in meticulous circles I flushed, the act of worshiping and subjugating myself publicly to my husband was hard, but I had to remember he was just that my husband. At the same time my body became a flood of sensations, like thousands of pin pricks on my body. My mind felt light and fuzzy.

"Their subject, their daughter and their servant offers one man to be anointed. Thomas Neil Sharpe." I unsheathed my blade. I was about to hand it to him when I heard a scream and a hand pulled me back, the other pulling the knife from me and holding it to my throat.

I could tell my eyes were like saucers, and for the first time since the ceremony started, I looked into my husband's eyes and saw outrage and fear staring back. This wasn't part of what I have been told to expect from the ceremony. But when out of the corner of my eye I saw Brady,

Charlie, Leonora and Markus shift, I knew something was wrong. "I wouldn't," he said, pushing it harder against my throat."

"Matteo?" I gasped.

"Shh…" he said down my ear, punctuating his statement by cutting me slightly along my upper arm. Tom growled as a small trickle of blood ran down my arm and I felt it tickle my palm.

"Matteo, what are you doing?"

"No less than you did to my family."

"We didn't do anything to your family."

"That's right, it was up here that you cut my father." Matteo lifted the knife to the left side of my face, placing it firmly against my cheek, I scrunched my eyes together and flinched.

"Oh, don't flinch." He moved his free hand to hold my chin.

"We have been looking for you for months, where have you been?" Tom said. I noticed Charlie move closer, but if I saw it, Matteo definitely did.

"I wouldn't, Charlie, unless you want to see what the little lady looks like with a new set of scars."

"Charlie, back up," Tom told him, his voice housing a small bite that he meant business.

"What do you want?"

"I want my parents to be released from prison."

"Matteo, that is out of our hands, the High Council now controls…"

The knife was running across my shoulder, cutting through the thin strap and the skin just under my collarbone. Air seeped through my teeth from the sting of the blade. "Matteo, that is enough," Tom said, feeling my own humiliation. Nudity was common for the pack but I hadn't gotten used to it yet. Why should I? I am not a shifter.

"No, I have the control here."

"So, you plan on standing there with a knife to my wife's neck for days while we contact the High Council. So they can deliberate your ultimatum, then not allow them to be released. They're criminals."

"They're not you know, you are, you and your whore of a queen. You forget we all know what she was before she started prostrating around, pretending she was worthy."

"She was a lady," Tom said.

"No, she was a stripper. A whore."

"She wasn't for a long time before I met her, you know her story, she did what she had to do to survive. What have you done to support yourself while you were on your own without your pack?"

"Never stooped as low as your slut wife. We're going to go, I'll contact you." He stepped backwards, forcing me behind him. "If she plays her cards right, I'll let her go back in time, get back to her old roots, to save that pretty little face of hers."

"Matteo…" Tom stepped forward, the growl low and hard.

I held up a hand signal to him to stop, as the knife pressed closer to my artery. It would be too easy for him to kill me, just as I had Landry. Poetic justice. My past come back, two-fold. He kept pulling me backwards, until I was no longer on the dais, instead being pulled towards the woods.

"You know the second that knife is no longer pushed against my throat they will kill you."

"They'll have to find what's left of you first," he said, cutting along my other collar bone deeper.

"You mean with the trail of blood you're leaving?"

"I'm not."

"No, but I am. You cut me." Suddenly I was turned around, my back pressed against a tree. "A human," he said to me, "a weak, worthless, whore human. No shifter leader should be married to a human. The moment he chose you, he lost the right."

"What, you thought one of you should be the Alpha?"

"Better me or my father than your fool of a husband and his weak brother. That's right, I was there, a bullet was all it took to put him down, for Lorelai to end him. I can only imagine what would have happened if we hadn't been told to keep you out of the way. Tom would have died too protecting your useless human ass."

"Not so human," I smirked, lifting my hand to my collarbone, putting my fingers in the blood. "The beasts of the sky, protect my family," I said in Welsh, speaking the language for the first time since the funeral, and drawing the protection symbol that is still burnt into the dais onto his naked chest. It glowed before turning red and he stopped. "Matteo?" I said, pursing my lips and smiling. The only part of his body

286

that moved was his eyes. I made a move, and he stayed still. I bent down and crouched out of the way. He was completely paralyzed to the spot.

We hadn't made it far, so I began to move towards where we came. Leaving a trail of blood on the trees for Charlie and his second Colby to find.

"Tom," I called as I broke through the trees. Tom's face dropped when he saw me, then he started running.

"Astrid." He closed the gap quickly. He wrapped me in his arms, before pulling me back. Are you okay?"

"I'm fine, I'm okay."

"He cut you."

"I was about to cut myself anyway."

"Not from shoulder to shoulder."

"Semantics"

"Where is he?"

"He's not too far back there, I left a trail for Charlie to follow."

"Charlie, Markus, Colby, you heard her, go get him."

"Yes, sir," Charlie said, speeding into the wood.

"They're going to be in for a little surprise."

"How so?"

"You'll see," I promised.

Leonora suddenly showed up at my side. "Let's go get you fixed up, then we can continue." She wrapped a jacket around my shoulders.

"Yes, please."

"Come on," she said. Rox and a few elders followed. It took Rox no time whatsoever to get my dress sewn back together.

"Rox will come get you when we're ready."

"Okay," I nodded, excited this time. Let's face it, everything that could go wrong did go wrong the first time, so picking up from where we left off was going to be a walk in the park. Before Rox came in Tom did, with a smirk on his face that resembled him really trying not to die of laughter.

"What did your research tell you?"

"That I shouldn't speak in the ancestral tongue while invoking the gods." I smiled, amused.

"What do we tell people this time?"

"For now, the gods intervened."

"Aeryn and Carlos have been asking about you. I think when we call them for help with our Matteo-sicle we should ask for a meeting."

"You are probably right."

"For now, though, I think we should go get you anointed." I nodded for him to go.

"No, we go together, we weren't meant to have the traditional ceremony so we aren't."

"Okay," I said, taking his outstretched hand.

We made it to the dais and everyone was there waiting. "To the beasts of the sky, I ask you to anoint this man with the power of yourselves, your servant marks the one." I looked to Charlie hoping he would have the knife.

"We can't get it out of his hand, it won't move."

"That's okay," I said. Doing the same as I did before, I dipped my fingers into the wound of my collarbone reopening it.

"Astrid."

"I got this," I whispered to him.

I drew the Alpha symbol above his heart. "Your servant requests you take Thomas Neil Sharpe into your favour as the Alpha of your worshipers here," I finished off in Welsh. The mark lit up as did the wounds left by Matteo on my skin. My wounds itched then healed. My mark on his chest dissipated, leaving a faint scared remnant.

Every shifter below us turned into one form or another and made the correct sounds. He stayed standing tall and every shea and human knelt, including myself. I wasn't down long and he joined me on his knees and he kissed me deeply. As the night went on everyone started partying.

"Usually, we go for a run now."

"Go," I told him. "Lead your pack."

"Are you going to be okay?"

"I'm fine, Charlie locked away Matteo."

"When is he going to um... thaw out?"

"I'm not really sure."

"Okay, well either way he's not going anywhere. Thank you, my beautiful Queen."

"I love you." I wrapped my arms around his shoulders and he lifted me.

"I love you too." He kissed me.

"Come on, man." Charlie slapped Tom on the shoulder. "If you keep that going, you'll never make it out for a run."

"Go," I said. "I'll call Aeryn about Matteo." I encouraged him.

Chapter 23

"Do you remember when you asked me what I was working on yesterday?" I said, sitting across from Tom on the plane that Carlos and Aeryn had sent for us.

"Yeah?"

"Well, before everything happened six months ago, Jared asked me to look into why Lorelai couldn't shift."

"Well, I really wouldn't worry about that now," he told me.

"That's the thing though, Tom, I figured it out."

"You didn't," he said, putting down the legal file he had been looking over. His case load had doubled with the loss of his brother. However, after much deliberation we'd begun the process of looking for some new staff.

"I did, last night after calling Aeryn the results came in."

"And?" He looked at me curiously.

"She has sickle cell anemia."

"But she never showed any symptoms."

"From what I can tell, her shifter healing overcompensated for it, but the deficiency prevented…"

"Her from shifting."

"Exactly."

"Could you have prevented what happened?"

"I don't know but, Tom, I want to talk to her."

"Only if I can be there."

"By no means did I want you left out, just let me lead this, okay? You've been touchy when it comes to her. Not that I blame you, I'm just hoping for answers."

"She's all yours."

"Thanks, Tom."

The moment we arrived in Wales, Aeryn, Carlos, and two other people were standing waiting for us. Matteo begged us not to, but he hadn't left us any choice. He would be seeing his parents, shortly.

"Aeryn," Tom said when we arrived at the prison "Astrid was hoping she and I could have a word with my sister."

"It won't do you any good, she won't talk."

"I think she might talk to me," I told her.

"I hope she does. Anything from her would be helpful."

Aeryn led us to a small room where they'd brought Lorelai. Her nostrils flared and her mouth turned up in a smirk when she saw us.

"To what do I owe the honour, little brother?" she scoffed.

"Good luck," Aeryn said, leaving the room, closing the door firmly behind her.

"This is her request," Tom said, nodding to me, and she sat down across from me at the table. He chose to stand leaning against the wall behind me.

"Ahh… the Beta's Bitch, what can I do for you, my lady?" I ignored the attempt at a wind up, and lifted a hand to keep him from reacting, it's what she wanted.

"Here's what I want to know, how much of what happened could I have prevented?" I knew Tom would object to my self-flagellation, so I turned to make sure he knew not to say anything.

"How could you prevent anything? Our leadership was going soft, we needed to change the direction the pack was taking."

"No, I know that you brainwashed them into believing that. I was the weak whore, Jared was going soft, allowing weaker members into the pack. But it was all a lie," I said, calmly. "Wasn't it?"

"You have no idea what you are talking about."

"Jealousy."

"You have no idea what you are talking about," she repeated.

"I get it. Lady Llangollen, the daughter of an Earl, with no rights to the fortune or lands. The object of fearmongering in her own home, by a man who should never have been within a hundred miles of her. The least loved and unwanted. I ran away when I was still a kid. You think I don't know what it means to be lesser than you are."

"Every day I watched my mother, father and younger brothers be what I should have been but wasn't. In every right I should have been a shifter. In every right I, not Tom, should have been the Beta."

"I could have."

"You could have what?" She cut me off.

"You're anemic, Lorelai, because of your pack's previous aversion to going to a doctor, you never would have known."

"I'm sick, how come no one could tell?"

"Because you never went to a doctor, it was hard for me even to figure out. Your shifter traits made it harder to discover."

"Can you fix me? Can you make me shift?"

"I could have."

"Well give it to me."

"You and I both know I can't do that."

"Tom," she cried.

"You killed our brother, Matteo and Landry tried to kill my wife; you think I'm going to pick up for you?"

"What are you talking about? I protected Astrid. No one was supposed to hurt her."

"What are you talking about?"

"You weren't hurt, little sister. Yet a human like you can be snuffed out in the blink of an eye."

"Landry tried."

"Landry was pissed that he wasn't allowed to be part of the action, it doesn't surprise me that he went off book. What surprises me is that you won. We knew Shiloh would never approve. We also knew if she got close to him, he'd change his loyalties."

"Why would you want to save me?"

"I told you under a full moon that it was our job to look out for one another, an oath under a full moon is sacred."

"Try that again." I said, disbelievingly.

"The coup was primarily mine, Jeremiah's and Francis's."

"Okay. Why me?"

"Why save Lady Llangollen? Once I learned the truth every detail fell into place. We organize a coup when we aren't offered recognition by the High Shifter and the Council. We trade, they leave us to run the pack as we see fit and we'll give them back the little lady," Lorelai said.

"I was a pawn."

"Earl Llangollen wouldn't allow his twin sister harmed, would he? Especially after he failed you for so long."

"My twin brother watched me harmed for years, he knows I can take it."

"All the same, you were our bargaining chip. If you had been dead, you wouldn't have been any use to us."

"Meanwhile, Landry and Matteo tried."

"Ah, our youngest member. Haven't seen him anywhere, have you?"

"After interrupting my Alpha Inauguration by threatening to kill my wife, he's where he belongs, with you."

"Well, I guess that, it, for us, huh."

"Lorelai, I'm going to leave the treatments with the High Council, maybe one day they will give you the opportunity to have what you have always wanted."

"You understand what it's like to be the odd one, don't do this to me."

"I was a pawn to you."

"Astrid, please."

"Tom, do you have anything to say to her?"

"No," he shook his head.

"Can you tell me one thing, please, how is William?"

"He's coping, Mom's taken him in and is doing well. Goodbye, sister."

We met with Aeryn outside the prison in a small pub down the street as we had agreed before she'd left. Our walk to the pub was silent, I just held his hand and let him have what he needed. "Aeryn, there is something you need to know," I told her, after we had sat down with our respective drinks.

"Is it regarding the information I sent you?"

"Yes," I said.

"Okay?" She encouraged me to continue.

"The good news for you is that in Brandon all the genes are dormant."

"Okay, and yourself?"

"So… this is a little more complicated."

"Why?"

"The 'X' gene is carrying caster and mage genes in me. But they aren't working the way that magic and mage abilities are supposed to. From what I can tell it would have remained mostly dormant if I hadn't joined a sect that is so reliant on their gods."

"I'm not so sure, you had a dream while you were still here and the chemistry."

"But that isn't the gods granting me favour to cast."

"This is true." She seemed at a loss.

"However, we are having a problem, and we would like you to bring this up with the High Council," Tom said. "The pack is not believing when we tell them it's the gods intervention any more."

"We want to be able to tell them the truth with the promise that it stays within the pack."

"I'll talk to the Council," she promised.

"Thank you, Aeryn."

Aeryn had a car to take us to our hotel. After a very long night and day, we ordered room service and fell asleep early. Tomorrow we'd head home and hopefully have an answer from Aeryn as to what we could do regarding my little abilities.

"Astrid, wake up!" I felt a rough shaking me gently as I was forced awake.

"Ahh…" I screamed, sitting up quickly.

"Hey, you okay, baby girl?"

"Mmm mmm," I shook my head grabbing my husband.

"Shh…" he tried soothing me, but my uncontrolled sobs only got louder. "Okay, you're okay," but it wouldn't stop. "It was only a dream," he tried. The problem was it wasn't, it was a memory. He stopped trying with words then and just let me sob into him. I felt his hands move in small anxious circles on my back. When the movements increased in urgency, my sobs got louder and he tensed against me. Eventually I fell into exhaustion and slept dreamlessly.

The next morning it was daylight, and the sun appeared high in the sky when he gently woke me. "You want to tell me what happened last night?" he asked, helping me to sit up and offering me a cup of coffee. I thought we were supposed to be leaving early, I couldn't imagine they were allowing us to keep their plane waiting.

"I had a bad dream."

"Yes, I got that." He nodded, watching me and moving a stray hair from my face. "Problem is you've had bad dreams before and none have ever caused that."

"Maybe it was more a memory than a dream." I stared into my coffee.

"Astrid, look at me, what memory?"

"Killing Landry," I said ashamedly, but Tom wouldn't let me look away from him.

"Oh," he said. "Come here." He put my coffee on the table and pulled me against him again. "What happened that day was not your fault. He made his decision, they attacked us, not the other way around."

"He was our friend, Shiloh still isn't getting over it, and sometimes it's all I see when I close my eyes."

"You weren't given a choice, it was him or you. From now on you come to me when you are having a hard time."

"You're my rock," I told him.

"Good thing I am so solid, I can handle it," he kissed my temple. "So, would you like something a little happier?"

"Happier?"

"I have a little present for you." He got up and opened a dresser drawer, pulling out a large box. He sat down next to me, setting it down on the bed between us.

"What is it?" I asked curiously.

"Open it."

What laid inside the box was an absolutely gorgeous satin dress. "It's beautiful," I said. "But why?"

"I think it would be beautiful on you today," he said. "Especially paired with this." He held out a small, green, velvet, oval-shaped box with copper hinges. I knew what it was, recognising the box without needing to open it.

"It? This? Did Brandon?" I asked, stunned and completely incapable of completing sentences.

"Brandon said you always loved it, and your Gran would have wanted you to have it."

Gently I removed the velvet lid. Nestled in the box was Granma's geometric bandeau tiara. The dainty tiara was understated and simple yet beautiful. The highest point in the center was less then an inch high, where a circle housed a larger diamond. Two ridges of diamonds sandwiched more diamonds as it tapered to the ends.

"I can't take this," I said.

"Your brother wants you to have it."

"It belongs to the Earlship of Llangollen."

"That's your family."

"Not for a while," I said, gently lifting the delicate tiara.

"It's time you reclaimed that."

"What do you mean?"

"Put on the dress and curl your hair the way I like it," Tom commanded me.

"Okay," I said, confused but weirdly excited. I moved to the bathroom. Tom leaned back against the bed frame. He sat there and watched as I carefully curled my hair and applied a small amount of makeup, but still dark and true to myself. "Enjoying the show?" I asked.

"Always." He smiled at me. I lifted the dress out of the box. It was navy with large red roses scattered over the lenth. Tea length, and with a low back, its straps criss-crossed my back, but the high boatneck maintained its modesty.

"Want to give me a hand?" I asked Tom, turning my back to him. He zipped the dress to the small of my back, his hands lingered for a moment.

"I was right," Tom whispered.

"What about?"

"The dress perfectly accentuates your new back tattoo."

I turned my back to the mirror. The tattoo had taken a number of days to complete, but it was everything I wanted. A wolf and a phoenix surrounded by flowers, Welsh and Celtic knots and symbols of protection, power and strength. I managed to get them to merge with my shoulder and thigh tattoo that had already been there. He was also right, the dress perfectly framed them.

"One more thing." Tom smiled behind me. I noticed out of the corner of my eye that he picked up the tiara, and surprisingly expertly he pinned it to my head. A low whistle escaped his lips, making me laugh. "You look like a lady." He kissed my temple.

I noticed a cellphone in his hand. "What are you doing with that?"

"You look gorgeous, also, Charlie will never believe this without evidence."

"Tom." I rolled my eyes.

"Smile, beautiful girl," he commanded and for some reason I was all too happy to comply. We had a little photoshoot in our little hotel room, before Tom announced that he was going to get ready and I was to take a seat. I waited anxiously. What did Tom have up his sleeve?

"Very Suave, Mr. Sharpe," I cajoled when he came out in a gorgeous dark navy suit, white shirt and a red tie, coordinating my dress perfectly.

"Come on, the taxi should be waiting." He smiled, handing me a beaded clutch and stuffing his wallet and room key in his pocket. Clearly, he was uncomfortable with the compliment.

"Where are we going?" When he refused to answer I tried again. "This is my home, shouldn't I be taking you places not the other way around?"

"It's a surprise, so just trust me."

"Okay." I nodded. The taxi wasn't your typical cab, it was a sleek black town car. I noticed the driver's eyes widen slightly, taking in me.

"My lady," he nodded to me.

"Hello," I said back gently.

The drive was mostly quiet. I'd always felt awkward around people driving me, so this was expected. At least until I figured out where we were going.

"Oh no." I shook my head looking at Tom.

"Oh yes," Tom said.

"You can turn the car around and take me back to the hotel," I demanded of the driver.

"I was warned you'd say that, ma'am, I've been instructed not to."

"Tom, I can't go there, please don't make me."

"Your brother is getting married today, you owe it to him and yourself to be there. I owe it to you to make sure you are."

"You owe it to me to make sure I am there? Do you realize how many people will be there?"

"At the Earl of Llangollen's wedding? I think I could wager a guess. Also, yes I do, ever since you met me you've made sacrifice after sacrifice for me and my family."

"Tom, he and my mother are going to be there."

"So what? You undertook the dance, took on Matteo and Landry, put yourself through med school, and have taken on my entire family. Plus, you have me now. So if that isn't enough, you're not a child any more, he can't hurt you."

"Tom."

"He doesn't control you ." Absentmindedly I ran my hand down my thigh. "Stop, you're fine." He took my hand and kissed it, before placing his own hand on my leg.

"I really wish you would have spoken to me about this first."

"You wouldn't have considered it, so I took it upon myself and spoke to your brother."

"I don't think I can do this."

"Of course you can, I'm right here. Just breathe."

"Okay, well, let's just keep our heads down."

He didn't say anything, and I watched outside as it sped by. Eleven years hadn't changed a thing, the winding roads, high hedges, rock walls, rolling farms full of sheep and cattle. It was how I remembered it.

"I lived here," I said as we drove up to the centuries-old mansion, regularly renovated but almost entirely original from the outside.

"Seriously?"

"Yeah."

"It's bigger than all of the buildings in Sanctuary put together."

"It seemed so small and claustrophobic when I was younger."

"It's hard to imagine that this is where you are from, it seems so unlike you."

"That's because it never was, or rather it wasn't allowed to be," I said as the car stopped outside the stone porch bordered by stone pillars. A man moved to open the door for us. He offered me his hand, Tom got out the other side and paid the driver.

"Oh, Lady Astrid," the man said with a quick bow.

"Hello, Carlton," I said to the butler, surprised I hadn't recognised him at first.

"You've grown so much, Miss."

"Thank you."

"I must say, I never thought we'd see you again."

"I never thought I'd come back," I admitted.

"Well, a happy occasion then, Miss."

"Carlton, this is my husband," I said, feeling Tom behind me. "Thomas Sharpe."

"It's an honour to meet you, Mr. Sharpe." Carlton extended his hand.

"And you." Tom took the outstretched appendage.

"The wedding will be held in the back garden, miss," Carlton told me.

"Thank you," I told him, grabbing Tom's hand and leading him through the foyer, past the rotunda and into the back garden, the place I loved to spend the most time. It was always quiet and I could be alone. Brandon often came out to join me, and we'd spend the afternoon talking and laughing. It surprised me that after all this time I had found a happy memory of this place. The back gardens were every bit as beautiful as ever, lush, green and floral; the healthy smell of the fauna and flora wafting around us.

The gazebo appeared to be the focal point for the wedding, decorated in flowers the chairs emanated from there. Two hundred of them at least, all covered in linen, straddled by grand floral arrangements.

"Come on, let's go grab some seats," Tom said, pulling me out of my observational reprieve. Many others were already sitting. We chose a pair of seats about halfway back, hoping to avoid intrusion. "Cynthia, do you know her?"

"She was one of my friends when we were growing up. She's smart and kind."

"So, you know nothing about her."

"Not anymore. I haven't seen or spoken to her, since I left Wales"

"Pity, she is about to become your sister-in-law, after all," Tom said, which made my heart hurt, after everything, the idea of another new sister seemed daunting, like an invitation for more hurt. I reached over and placed my hand on his leg as he wrapped an arm around my shoulders, our mutual leaning posts.

The seats were starting to fill when I heard "… you did come," followed by my being wrenched out of my aisle seat.

"Uh…" I groaned at the ferocity of his hug. "Hi, Brandon," I said, hugging him back as he returned me to solid ground. "How are you feeling?"

"So happy and excited," he admitted to me.

"You should be, Cynthia is great."

"Thank you." Brandon turned to Tom. "How did you get her here?"

"I didn't tell her where we were going," he admitted, chuffed with himself.

"Oh, smart man," he looked at me, asking so much more in that look.

"Don't worry," I calmed his worries, "I want to be here."

"Then come on."

"Where?"

"You don't belong here," he pulled me down the aisle with him.

"Brandon, this is your day, I can't impose."

"You're right, it is my day and you are my twin sister, you only have one place you belong."

"Brandon?"

"Directly beside me."

"Brandon."

"You're my best wo-man."

"Brandon." I looked at him petrified.

"Hey, don't worry, Tom will be right there," he said, motioning to a chair directly in front of me. Tom took a seat pointedly, and nodded to me, as Brandon waved a man over.

"Michael, this is my sister Astrid," Brandon said.

"Hi," I lifted my hand.

"So, you're the elusive sister."

"Yeah, that would be me." I nodded as he handed me a boutonniere and I made quick work of securing it to my dress.

"I met Michael in university," Brandon explained to me. "We were on the same football team."

"Well, it's a pleasure to meet you," I told him.

"Oh my god, Asie? As I live and breathe, it can't be you, girl?"

"Hey, Gareth." I smiled at one of mine and Brandon's childhood friends.

"How have you been?"

"Pretty good." I genuinely smiled.

"There's also a rumor that you're a doctor now."

"Not a rumour, I'm a general surgeon back in Seattle."

"I never thought I would see the day that Asie would do well enough in school to become a doctor."

"Top of my class," I bragged, nudging him with my shoulder.

"Really?"

"Really."

"Dr. Lady. Astrid…"

"Davis-Sharpe."

"I like it."

"You forgot one part," Brandon said.

"What's that?"

"Of Llangollen."

And I smiled, but by then the bridal march began to play. Tom nodded at me as I took my spot beside my brother. Gently I placed a hand on my brother's arm, he placed a hand over mine and I could feel the nerves and excitement running through him.

I felt him take a deep breath. As my mother and stepfather led the procession, my mother's eyes settled on me, they narrowed as though convinced she was seeing things. When she realized I wasn't an illusion, her jaw dropped as she moved her gaze back to my brother. Lord on her arm locked his gaze on me as he proceeded to stand next to Tom. I took a couple of settling breaths. Lord had changed, slimmer, his face was gaunt, his hair now gray, his eyes were steady, his fat nose still took up too much of his face, but the expression on his face was still dark and menacing.

Following my parents were a number of bridesmaids dressed in a deep navy. After Cynthia was being walked down the aisle by her mother and her mother alone. It dawned on me, life didn't stop just because I left. I watched as her and Brandon's eyes met and they both began to cry happy tears, watching each other as she made her way down the long aisle.

Cynthia, the little girl with chronically scuffed knees and short hair and an inquisitive nature, was now grown with long hair, a lean and tall build. Her hair curled and to the side. Her dress a pure white satin gown, hung elegantly off her shoulders, she smiled at me, reaching a hand out towards me. I squeezed the offered greeting; I nodded my happiness for her and my brother.

The wedding was gorgeous as they offered traditional vows. You could see the light in the couple, when I wasn't watching them, I kept my gaze locked on my rock, even though I could feel Lord's eyes burning a hole in me, I could tell Tom knew exactly who he was beside and was doing everything in his power to maintain control.

Though the ceremony had religious notes, it was still short and sweet. It was over quickly.

"I now pronounce you husband and wife," rang out. We all waited as Brandon and Cynthia stared at one another, until the priest announced, "You may kiss the bride." Everyone cheered, Tom caught my eye and winked. They turned to their guests and we continued, everyone stood up and they worked their way back down the aisle.

Tom offered me his arm and we followed directly behind the bride and groom. "Thank you," I said increasing my grip on his arm.

"For what?"

"Making sure I was here for this." Tears of joy welled at the corners of my eyes.

"You don't regret coming?"

"No, I don't, you were right, I owed it to them and myself to be here."

"That's my girl." He patted my hand.

Figuring it was our turn, we went over to Cynthia and Brandon, who were standing off to one side waiting to greet their many well wishers. As we approached, Cynthia let go of Brandon and ran headlong towards me, that was the Cynthia I knew. Tom followed suit, and I could tell he was smiling. "Thank you, thank you, thank you," she chimed. "It means so much to us, and especially Brandon, that you came." Over her shoulder I saw Tom offer his hand to Brandon.

"I'm grateful that you were willing to have me, after all this time," I expressed my gratitude.

She stepped back but didn't relinquish her vicelike grip on me. "Don't think anything like that, Brandon has explained everything to me. There aren't any hard feelings from either of us. I'm just glad you came anyway."

"We have Tom to thank for that," I said, nodding at my husband, who was talking to Brandon quietly, and with certainly less enthusiasm than Cynthia.

"I heard you're married as well."

"I am," I said as we moved to our husbands, one arm still around each other. "Hey, Brandon, congratulations." I hugged the grown man that I now wished I knew better.

"Well, seeing as we're family now I should probably introduce myself," Tom said to Cynthia. "Tom Sharpe."

"Cynthia Davis," Cynthia beamed.

"Congratulations," Tom said.

"Thank you."

"Look, we'll let you get to your other guests, we'll catch up again later," I said, feeling bad for monopolizing the newly married couple.

"Let's go for a little walk," I said, taking Tom's hand, trying to get out of there.

"Head held high," Tom whispered to me. "Where's the confidence of my Queen." He flirted knowing exactly what he was doing.

"Back in Seattle where she belongs."

"What's the Welsh word for confidence?" he asked.

"You're not funny, there are leaders of all the sects here, the last thing we need is for them to be invoked and me casting accidently," I said, pointing out Carlos in conversation with Aeryn and a man whose arm surrounded her almost protectively.

"Then look like you're enjoying yourself like I know you are, understood?"

"Understood," I smiled.

"Astrid!" came a sudden high-pitched call from a tall redhead at a high cocktail table.

"Want to meet some more of my family?"

"Yes, please." He smiled, as I led him over to the table.

"Astrid," Carmen cried out again, this time throwing her arms around me.

"Hey, Carmen," I greeted her, returning the hug.

"I wasn't expecting to see you here, I almost had a heart attack when I saw you standing beside Brandon."

"Carmen is my cousin," I told Tom.

"It's a pleasure to meet you." Tom grinned.

"This is Tom," I told her. "My husband."

"Husband?"

"Yep," Tom smiled as, in typical Carmen manner, she pulled him into a hug. Happily, I didn't miss the shocked expression on Tom's face. I smirked, forcing back a small giggle.

"Where are you living now?" Kai, another redheaded cousin asked. He had only been a kid last time I'd seen him.

"Hey, Kai," I said, hugging him and suddenly it became a conveyor belt of cousins coming to hug me.

Ewen, Ara, Gavin, Jakson, and Ina. Both my parents were from the area and even though some were from my mother's side and others my father's we grew up all together, playing in the manor's gardens. "It's great to see all of you." I declared, then introduced again. "This is my husband, Tom."

"You're married?" Jakson, the youngest of us, a not-so-short blonde, with blue, grey eyes and an athletic build, was so very different from the chubby, freckle-faced eight-year-old I had known before. I was almost surprised he remembered me, he being so much younger than the rest of us.

Brandon and I had always been the middle cousins with Carmen, Ewen and Gavin, older, and Ara, Kai and Ina and Jakson younger. All of us not too far apart. "I am," I told Jakson.

"It's really nice to meet you all." Tom nodded and smiled to them warmly.

"So… spill, where are you living now?" Ewen pushed me, moving his too-long red hair out of his eyes. Like Brandon and I, Ewen and Carmen were redheads. Gavin, Ara and Ina brunettes. But the most shocking was Jakson and Kai who though there was a decent age gap, were almost identical, with their hair and blue, grey eyes.

"I'm living in Seattle, in the States," I told them.

"Really? You always spoke so poorly of the Americas," Carmen said, taking a sip of her Champagne, her nude lipstick leaving a rim on the glass.

"Exactly, so no one would go there looking for me."

"Did Brandon find you?" Ewen inquired.

"He did."

"Figures," Gavin explained. "Bloke never gave up on finding you."

"I'm glad he didn't." I took in the sight of my brother looking on top of the world with an arm around his bride.

"You were both inseparable once," remarked Carmen. "I wish you hadn't left." Carmen hadn't changed a bit, she still said exactly what popped into her head.

"What do you do?" Ara asked Tom, her eyes curious and framed by thick eyelashes on her poreless face, her burgundy lipstick brought out the dark auburn specks in her hair.

"I'm a lawyer," he answered her question. "Mainly dealing in criminal law."

"Do you work for a firm?" Jakson asked.

"I do," he nodded.

"He's being modest," I told them, looking for any excuse to talk about someone else, and bragging about my husband was one of my favourite pastimes. "Tom runs the top law firm in Seattle." They all looked at him impressed.

"How did you two meet?"

"I had the fortune of having her stumble into my office one day," Tom clarified, then said, "She was my client," Tom wrapped an arm around me and kissed my temple.

"Why did you need a lawyer?" Carmen asked.

"I was trying to sue my workplace?"

"And a top law firm was required?" Carmen pondered.

But before I could answer, Kai asked, "What do you do?"

"I'm a surgeon," I declared. A statement that was met with all blank stares. I smiled. I felt Tom chuckle.

"You're a doctor?"

"They gave you a medical licence?" Ewan looked disbelieving.

"I graduated at the top of my class, thank you. Also, it turns out as long as you do well in your undergrad they'll accept you even if you weren't such a great student in secondary school."

"And your undergrad was?"

Before I could answer, Tom said, "I am going to get Astrid and I something to drink." Then only to me he whispered, "you'll be fine with them, I will be right back."

"I like him," Carmen told me.

"Me too." I smiled, watching him walk away.

"It's like you're whole again, Asie," Kai said.

"Kai?"

"It wasn't a surprise to anyone when you disappeared. You hadn't been happy for a long time, you started shutting down," Ara said. "But now look at you, you look happy."

"Tom is such a huge part of that,". I admitted. "I didn't think I deserved happiness until I met him. Now along with my work at the hospital, Tom and I run a free clinic. I have friends and family. I even work on contract for the law firm, from time to time."

"You've made a life for yourself," Ara said, beaming at me.

"I have," I nodded. Then there was a hand on my shoulder. It was big and beefy, and so unlike my husband's.

"Your mother and I would like a word with you," came Lord's baritone command.

"I'll be happy to." I smiled. "But I am in the middle of a conversation with my cousins. I'll be sure to find you after." I forced every bit of Alpha Queen's confidence I had been acquiring into my voice. The faces of each of my cousins, however, had paled scared and intimidated.

"Now," he said, pulling me with him. I was no match for him, so I went.

"I'll catch up with you later," I promised my cousins.

Lord's grip hadn't gotten any weaker with the weight loss. Being unceremoniously dragged by my upper arm into the manor was both embarrassing and it hurt, I was certain I would have bruises on my upper when he let go.

I'd known there was no way, as we drove to the manor, that I'd get away with not being a spectacle at some point. I was dragged all the way to the main office off the main foyer. As Lord went to slam the door behind us a foot wedged itself in the door jam.

Tom, thank the beasts, I thought. "I recommend you take your hand off my wife this instant." Tom squared up to Lord. Standing a head taller than him, I could tell it was taking everything in my husband not to lose control.

"Excuse me?" A woman's voice behind me sounded confused. Mum.

Lord dropped my arm and Tom claimed me. During the ceremony I had avoided looking at this woman. She brought this man into my life, she'd stopped being a mother that day. "Astrid, I've missed you," the woman said, moving to hug me, but I recoiled into my husband. "Astrid?"

"No."

"Young lady, you will hug your mother and show her some respect." Lord told me.

"Respect for what?"

"She's your mother."

"She lost that right when she stopped protecting me from you."

"I was trying to tame you. You were so wild, your inner beasts."

"My inner beasts," I repeated, shocked.

"Tell me, how do you tame a young woman with a wild side," Tom spat. "Do you cut them out of her? Slap her, keep her scared?"

"Whatever she has told you is slander," my mother said. "My daughter is trouble; she didn't like that we had to teach her to behave like a proper lady."

"I've seen the scars, the fear in her eyes, the result of years of being terrorized. Your way of taming her, I've seen the effect, she didn't have to tell me anything."

The door opened then. "What's going on?" Brandon asked.

"Nothing, honey, go out there and enjoy your day."

"Try that again, Mother, because I know Astrid would never be in the same room with the two of you if she had a choice."

"We were just trying to make her understand, we were trying to help her," Lord said with a smile.

"With what?"

"She was wild growing up. She needed to be taught." My mother defended her husband's actions.

"She's still wild," Lord said, glaring at my husband.

"You know," Tom said, his eyes narrowing.

"Of course, I do."

"Agatha told you," I said.

"What does Lord know?" Brandon demanded.

"Your little sister is still as wild as she always was, her husband is a shifter."

"You're what?" Brandon looked at him.

"I'm a shifter," Tom shrugged. "A pack Alpha actually."

"She's married to disgusting filth. He's wilder than she is…" I could tell Lord was about to go on a rant as tears filled my eyes.

"Stop, I've heard enough, I don't care about that. I'm the Earl of Llangollen for goodness sake, you think that's a problem? What I do know is, I am done with this. Astrid is my sister. You're not my family. I want both of you gone."

"Imagine the scandal," my mother implored.

"The scandal is what kept so much from happening before. Like us not pressing charges when you cut her. She was ashamed of those for years, but she's turned them into something beautiful, show them," Brandon said to me. I lifted my hem slightly.

"What are those?"

"Tattoos," I told her.

"No lady would do that, you'll never get a good job looking like that."

"I have a job, I'm a doctor. And my patients don't care what I look like as long as I help them."

"You don't have it in you," Lord spat, "you're weak."

"Now you know that is untrue, don't you?" Tom said to him, pulling three pieces of paper from his inside pocket. My letters. One of which had been sent to my hospital.

"I've never seen those before."

"What are those?" Brandon asked and Tom handed them to him. "You can leave, go back to Cornwall and not come back," he said coldly, not looking up from the three pieces of paper in his hand.

"Brandon," my mother tried.

"No, you are going to leave, you are going to stop being a disappointment to our family, and if I ever hear of you contacting Astrid again, in any way, I'll let Tom protect his Queen however he sees fit."

"Brandon, please, I'm your Mum."

"No that's where you are wrong, you stopped being our mum the first time he tried to train Asie and you let him. Now leave quietly or I will have the casters, shifters, pyres and mages, all of whom are my honoured guests, show you out."

They said nothing as Lord grabbed my mother's hand and pulled her out of the room.

"Astrid, I am sorry," Brandon said.

"Brandon, you don't have to."

"I am sorry, I never protected you, I am sorry they were such terrible people and I never did anything about it until now. I am sorry that you had to leave in order to find a home and a safe place.

"However, I am happy that you did find a safe place. A place where you are protected and a place where you are happy and accepted, though I never would have picked a shifter for my sister, I would have picked Tom."

"Thanks, Brandon."

"Do me a favour, I know you have a job and responsibilities as the Alpha's Queen, but can we please be a family again. We're all we have."

"Of course, I want nothing more," I cried.

"So, now that they are gone, and, unless they are really stupid, not going to show their faces again. Can we have fun and enjoy the rest of the wedding?"

I couldn't speak, so I just nodded. "Brandon, you are a good man. Thank you." Tom offered his hand.

"I can see when I look at you that you will never allow anyone to hurt her. Protect her better than I did."

"I will and do protect this woman with my life."

"Thank you."

They shook hands and we joined the party. With Lord and my mother gone, they had to fill two seats at the head table, two seats that were appreciatively and with honour given to Tom and I. That night we danced, celebrated and were happy. Tomorrow we'd meet with Aeryn and the High Council one more time before we finally returned home, and with a little luck everything would go back to normal.

Who am I kidding? I don't know what normal was anymore. I haven't known normal since I, discouraged and humiliated, stumbled into the office of the most beautiful, strong, passionate, perfect and protective man on the planet. But hey, I couldn't have known that the most beautiful shifter inside and out, worked in that office? Right?

Ingram Content Group UK Ltd.
Milton Keynes UK
UKHW010838190423
420422UK00002B/195

9 781784 658601